NINJA BASEBALL
Kyuma!

STORY & ART BY
SHUNSHIN MAEDA

HOW TO READ MANGA!

Hello there! My name is **Kyuma,** and this is my very own book - **Ninja Baseball Kyuma**! It is a comic book originally created in my home country of **Japan,** where comics are called **manga.**

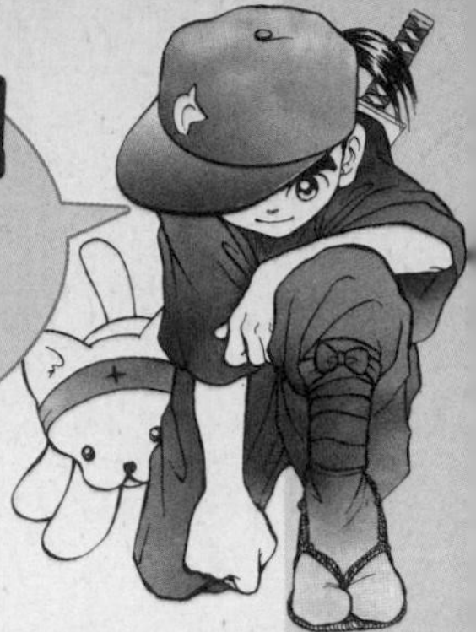

A manga book is read from **right-to-left,** which is **backwards** from the normal books you know. This means that you will find the first page where you expect to find the last page! It also means that each page begins in the top right corner.

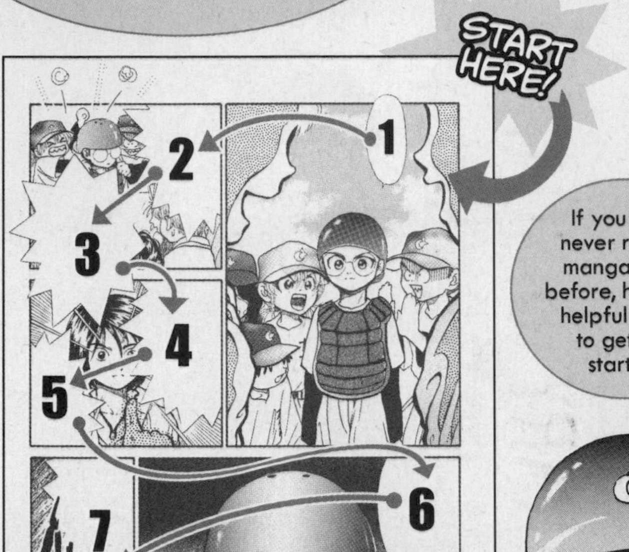

START HERE!
1
2
3
4
5
6
7

If you have never read a manga book before, here is a helpful guide to get you started!

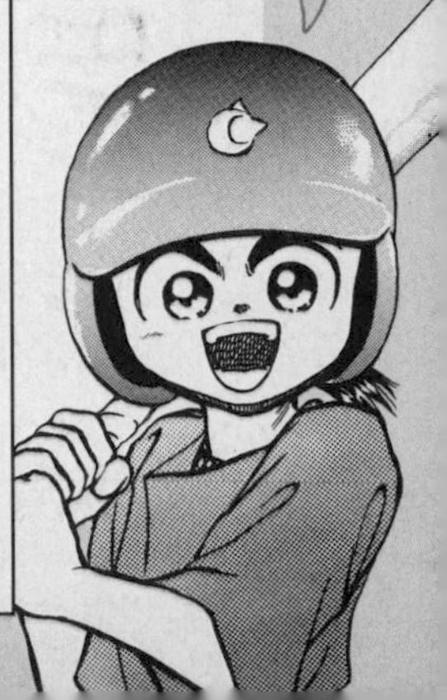

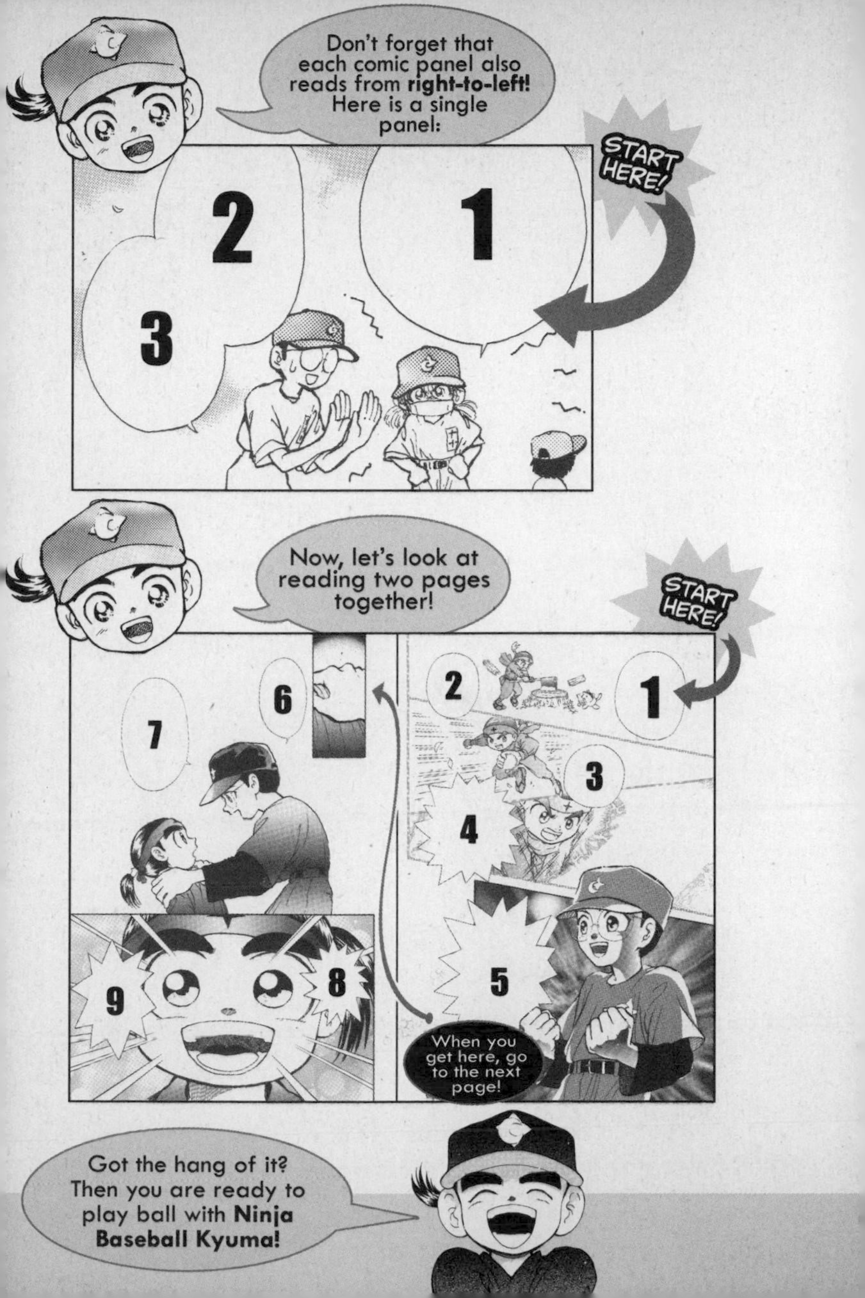
Don't forget that each comic panel also reads from **right-to-left!** Here is a single panel:
START HERE!
1
2
3
Now, let's look at reading two pages together!
START HERE!
1
2
3
4
5
6
7
8
9
When you get here, go to the next page!
Got the hang of it? Then you are ready to play ball with **Ninja Baseball Kyuma!**

NINJA BASEBALL Kyuma!

2ND BASE

✦ **MICHI** ✦

Assistant Captain,
always cool and calm.

RIGHT FIELD

✦ **KYUMA** ✦

A ninja who has been living
in the mountains since birth.

PITCHER

✦ **LUO** ✦

The slightly timid Ace.

SECOND BASE

✦ **KUNOSUKE** ✦

Moves in strange,
flexible ways.

COACH

✦ **TAMORI** ✦

A funny coach,
always cheerful.

BENCH

✦ **YOHKO** ✦

100% accurate
with her divinations.

BENCH

✦ **INUI** ✦

A ninja dog,
Kyuma's best friend.

MOONSTAR BASEBALL TEAM ROSTER

LEFT FIELD
NANA

A strong-willed girl.

CENTER FIELD
IWATA

Has a large build, but is quite quick on his feet.

THIRD BASE
TETSU

Full of energy, keeps team morale up.

SHORTSTOP
LINKI

A kind-hearted boy who loves plants and animals.

STORY SO FAR

Kyuma, the ninja, has join the Moonstar baseball team! After confusing Kaoru with a liege lord of ancient times, Kyuma has taken up this unfamiliar activity called baseball in order to aid Moonstar.

CATCHER
KAORU

The Captain of the team, very responsible.

CONTENTS

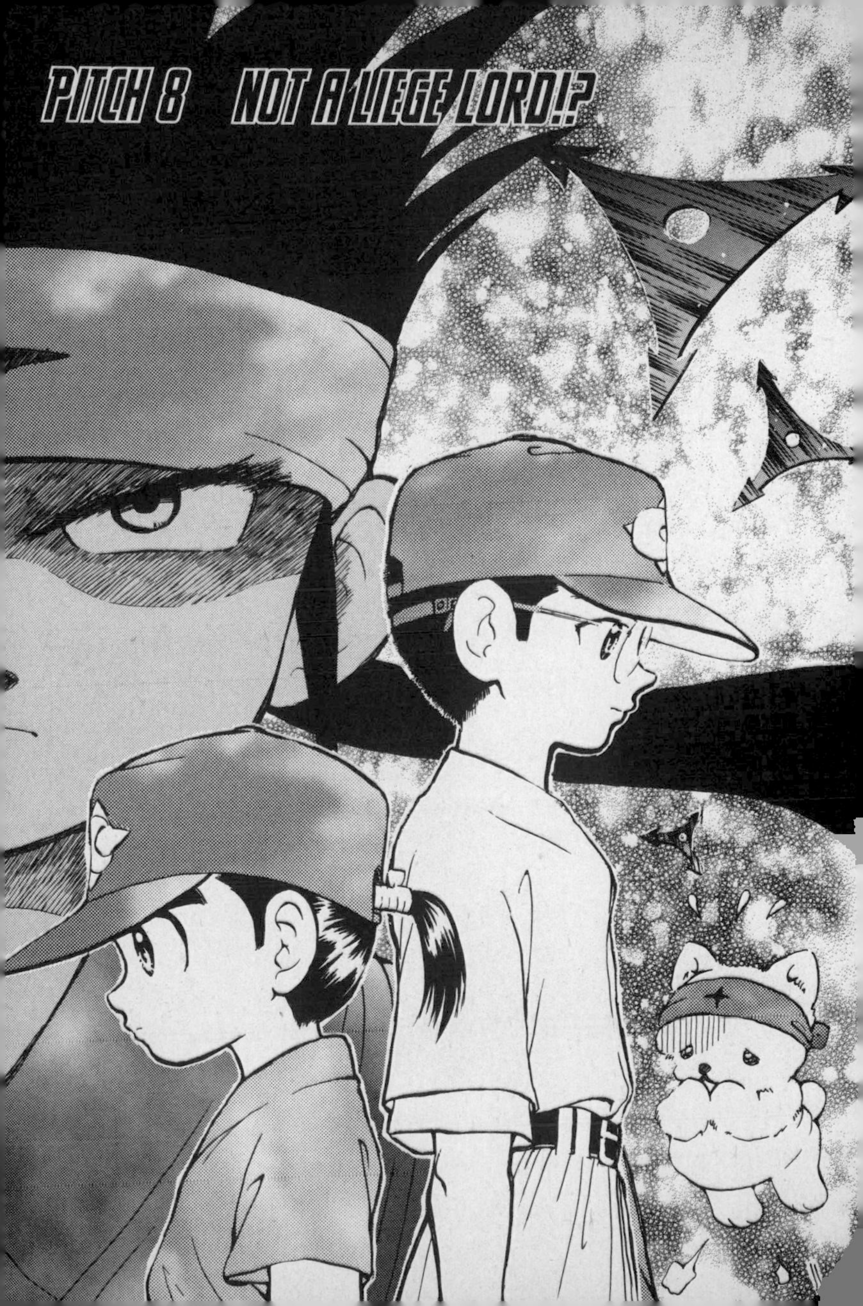
PITCH 8 NOT A LIEGE LORD!?

Read this way

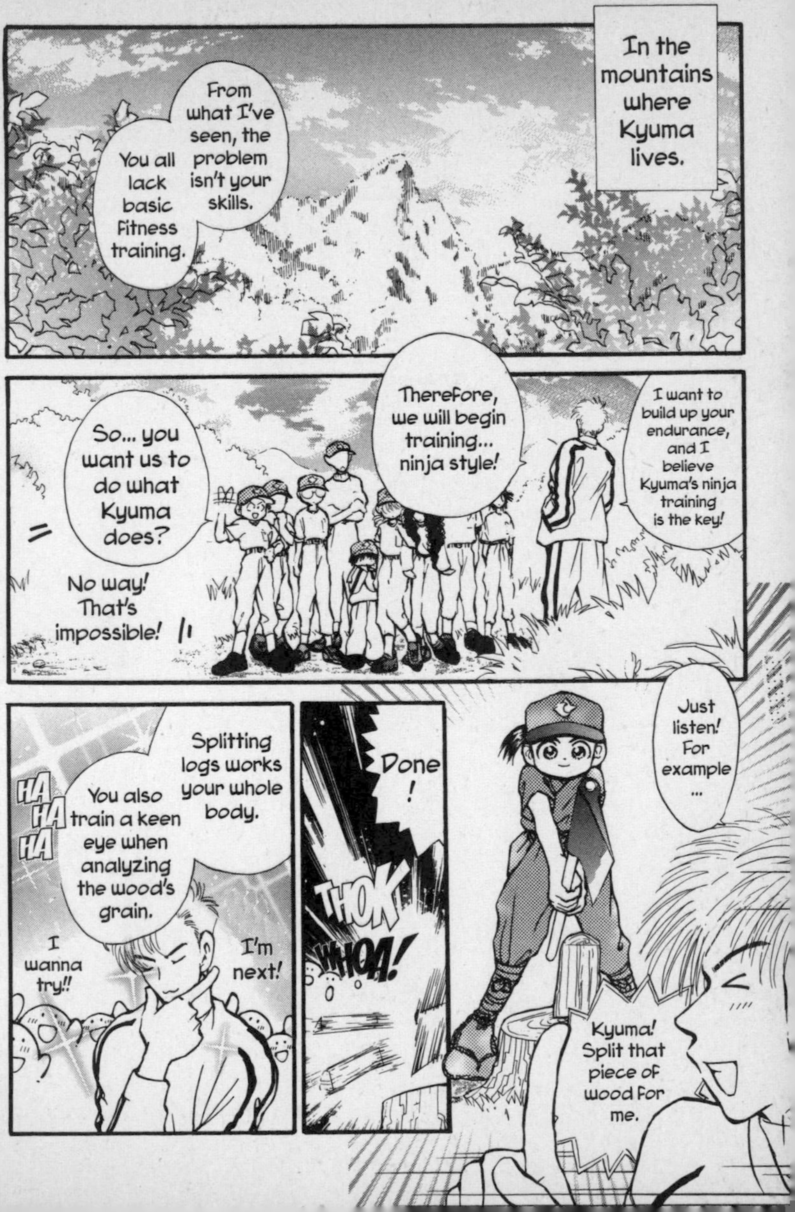
In the mountains where Kyuma lives.
From what I've seen, the problem isn't your skills.
You all lack basic fitness training.
I want to build up your endurance, and I believe Kyuma's ninja training is the key!
Therefore, we will begin training... ninja style!
So... you want us to do what Kyuma does?
No way! That's impossible!
Just listen! For example ...
Kyuma! Split that piece of wood for me.
Done!
THOK
WHOA!
Splitting logs works your whole body.
You also train a keen eye when analyzing the wood's grain.
HA HA HA
I'm next!
I wanna try!!

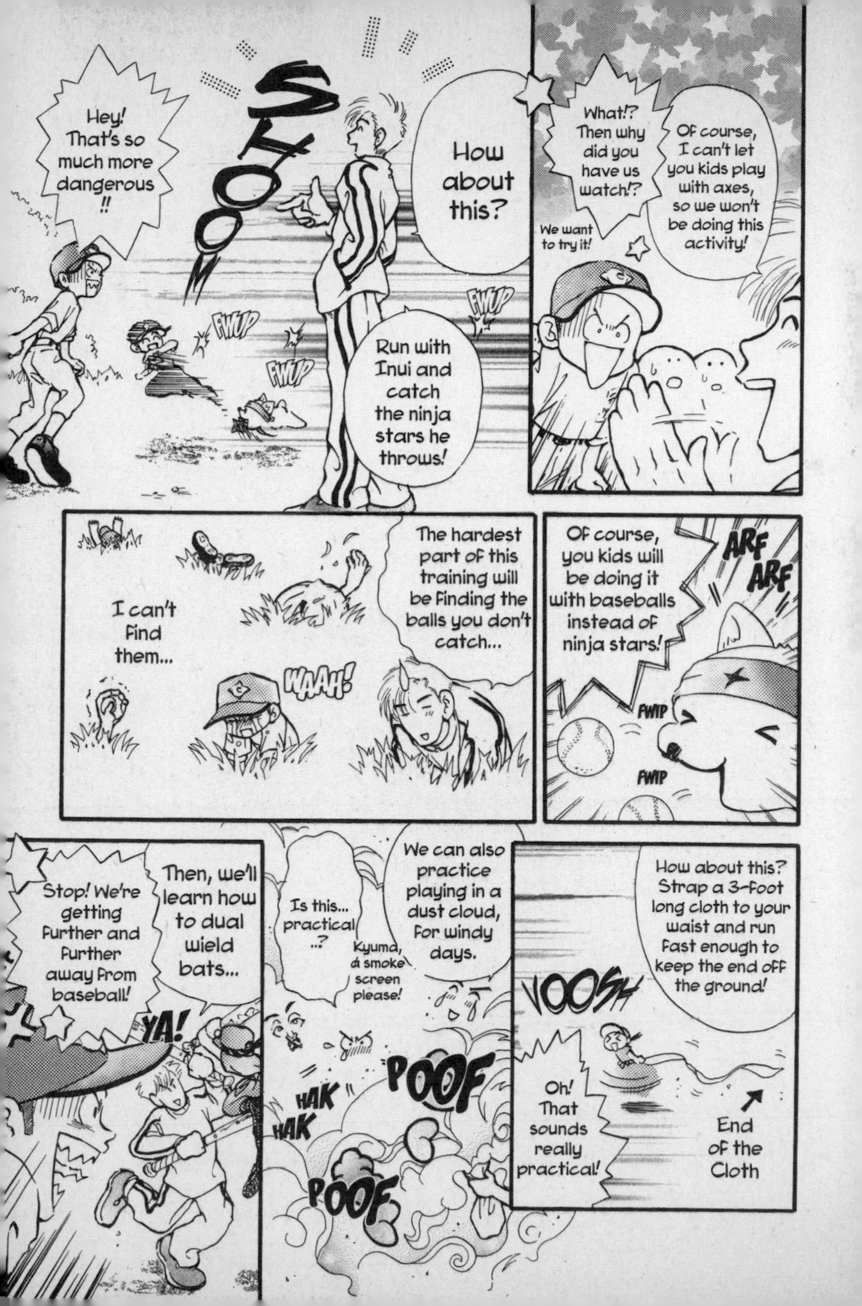
Of course, I can't let you kids play with axes, so we won't be doing this activity!
What!? Then why did you have us watch!?
We want to try it!
How about this?
SHOOO
Run with Inui and catch the ninja stars he throws!
FWUP
FWUP
FWUP
Hey! That's so much more dangerous !!
ARF ARF
Of course, you kids will be doing it with baseballs instead of ninja stars!
FWIP
FWIP
The hardest part of this training will be finding the balls you don't catch...
WAAH!
I can't find them...
How about this? Strap a 3-foot long cloth to your waist and run fast enough to keep the end off the ground!
VOOSH
End of the Cloth
Oh! That sounds really practical!
We can also practice playing in a dust cloud, for windy days.
Is this... practical ...?
Kyuma, a smoke screen please!
POOF
HAK HAK
POOF
Then, we'll learn how to dual wield bats...
Stop! We're getting further and further away from baseball!
YA!

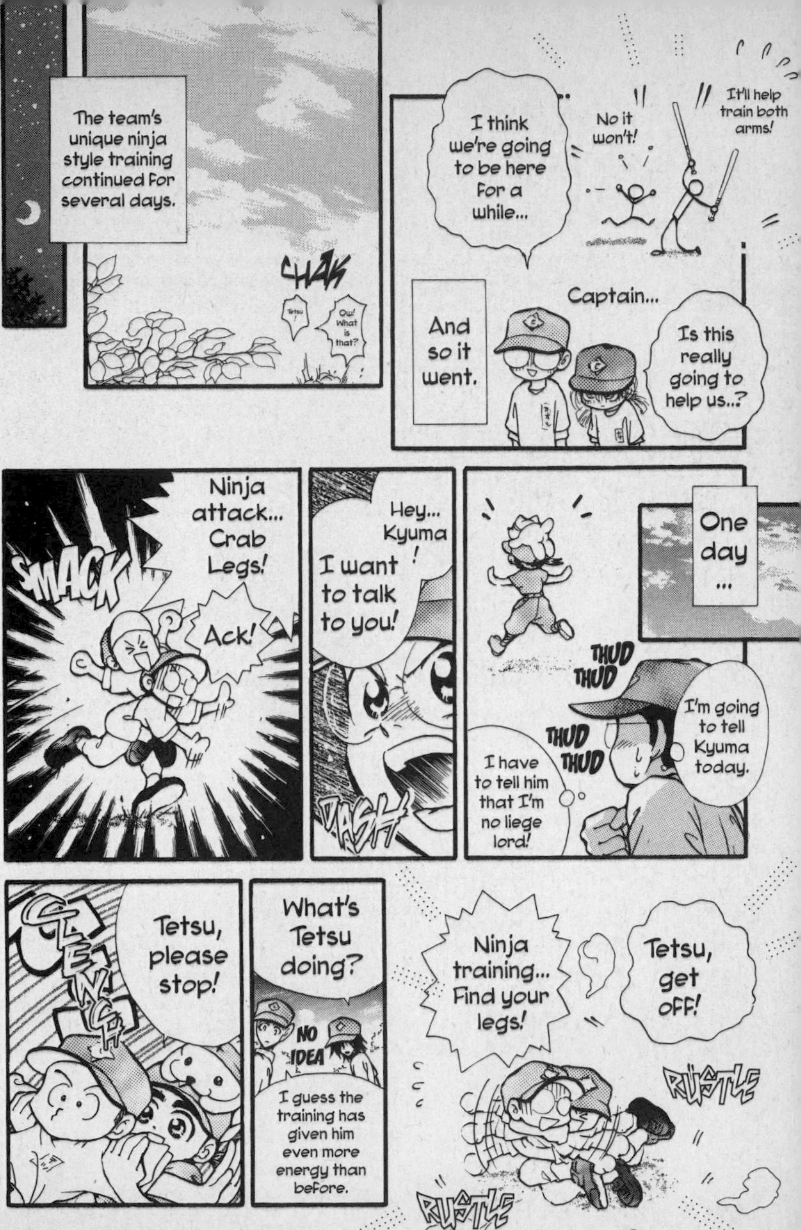
I think we're going to be here for a while...
No it won't!
It'll help train both arms!
Captain...
Is this really going to help us..?
And so it went.
The team's unique ninja style training continued for several days.
CHAK
Tetsu!
Ow! What is that?
One day ...
I'm going to tell Kyuma today.
THUD THUD
THUD THUD
I have to tell him that I'm no liege lord!
Hey... Kyuma!
I want to talk to you!
DASH
Ninja attack... Crab Legs!
SMACK
Ack!
Tetsu, get off!
Ninja training... Find your legs!
RUSTLE
RUSTLE
What's Tetsu doing?
NO IDEA
I guess the training has given him even more energy than before.
Tetsu, please stop!
CLENCH

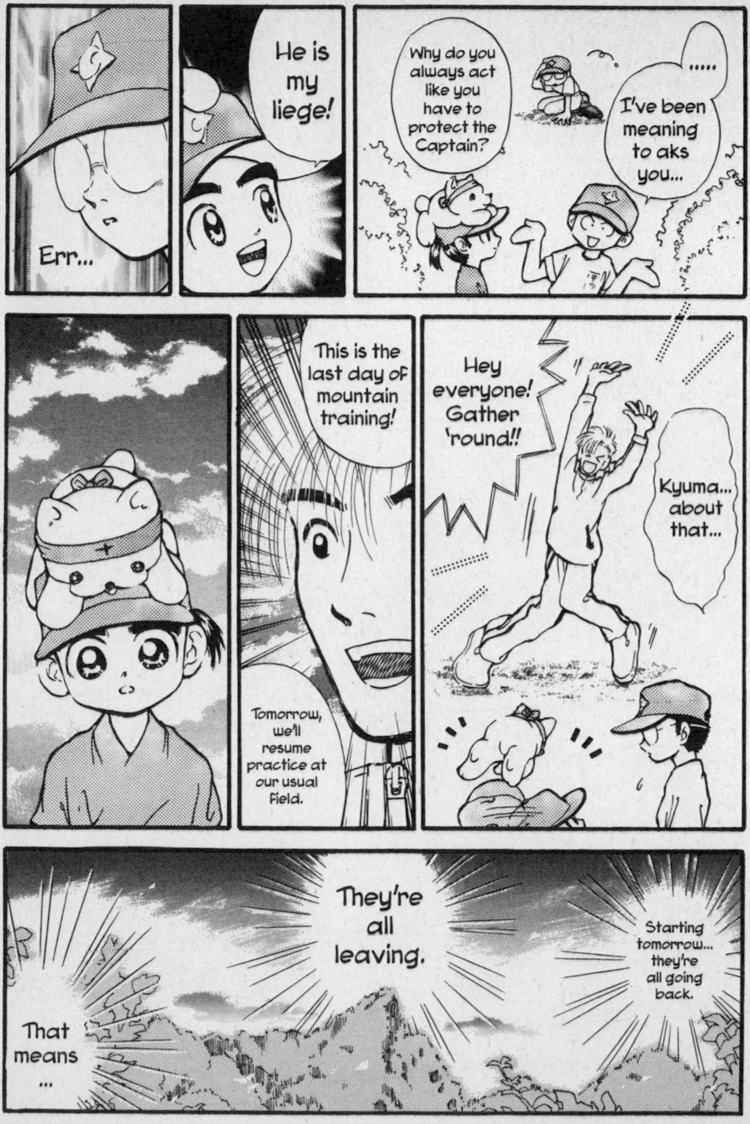

.....
I've been meaning to aks you...
Why do you always act like you have to protect the Captain?
He is my liege!
Err...
Kyuma... about that...
Hey everyone! Gather 'round!!
This is the last day of mountain training!
Tomorrow, we'll resume practice at our usual field.
Starting tomorrow... they're all going back.
They're all leaving.
That means ...

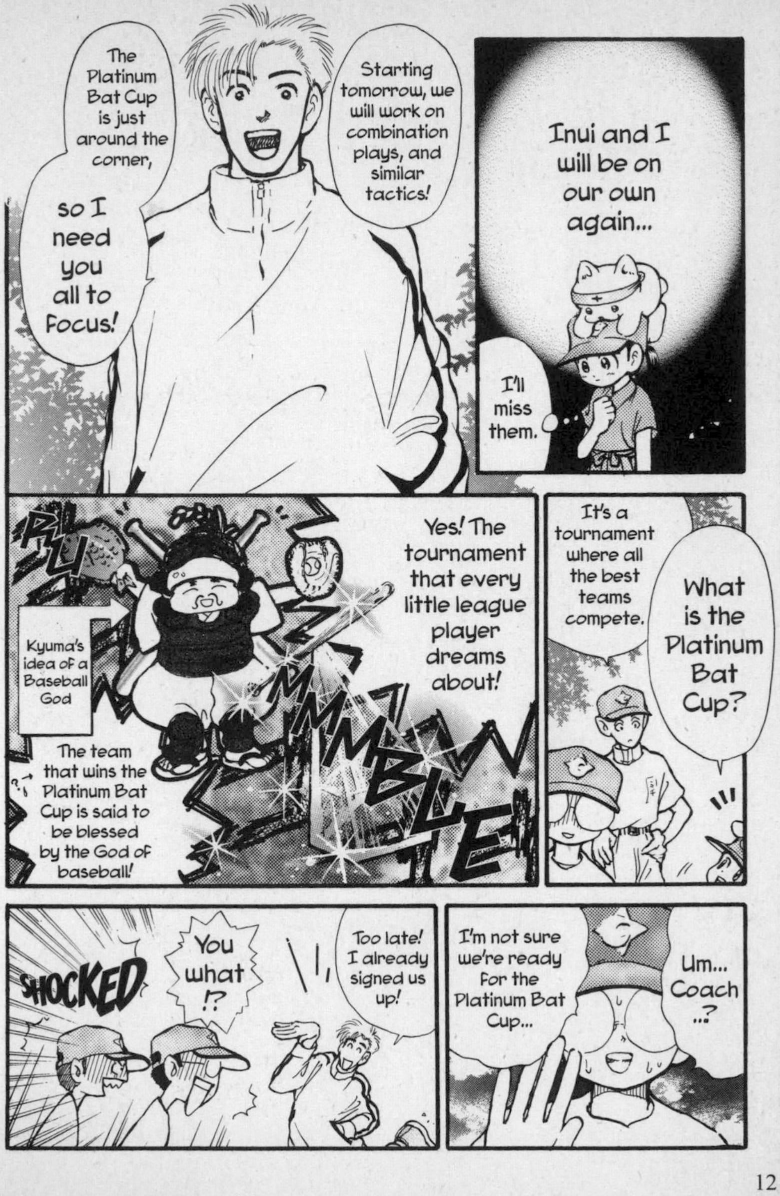
Inui and I will be on our own again...
I'll miss them.
The Platinum Bat Cup is just around the corner,
so I need you all to focus!
Starting tomorrow, we will work on combination plays, and similar tactics!
What is the Platinum Bat Cup?
It's a tournament where all the best teams compete.
Yes! The tournament that every little league player dreams about!
RU
MMMBLE
Kyuma's idea of a Baseball God
The team that wins the Platinum Bat Cup is said to be blessed by the God of baseball!
Um... Coach ..?
I'm not sure we're ready for the Platinum Bat Cup...
Too late! I already signed us up!
You what !?
SHOCKED

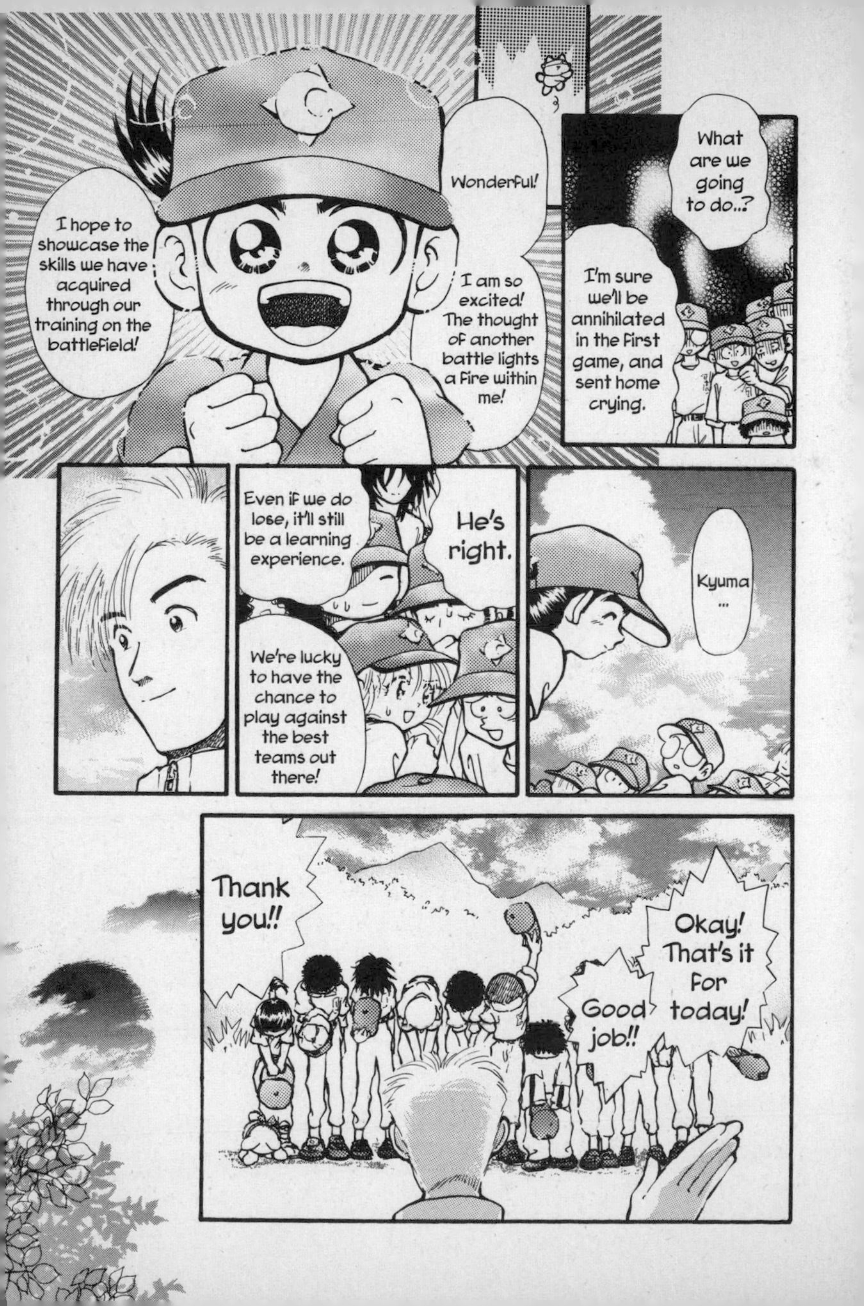
What are we going to do..?
I'm sure we'll be annihilated in the first game, and sent home crying.
Wonderful!
I am so excited! The thought of another battle lights a fire within me!
I hope to showcase the skills we have acquired through our training on the battlefield!
Kyuma ...
He's right.
Even if we do lose, it'll still be a learning experience.
We're lucky to have the chance to play against the best teams out there!
Okay! That's it for today!
Good job!!
Thank you!!

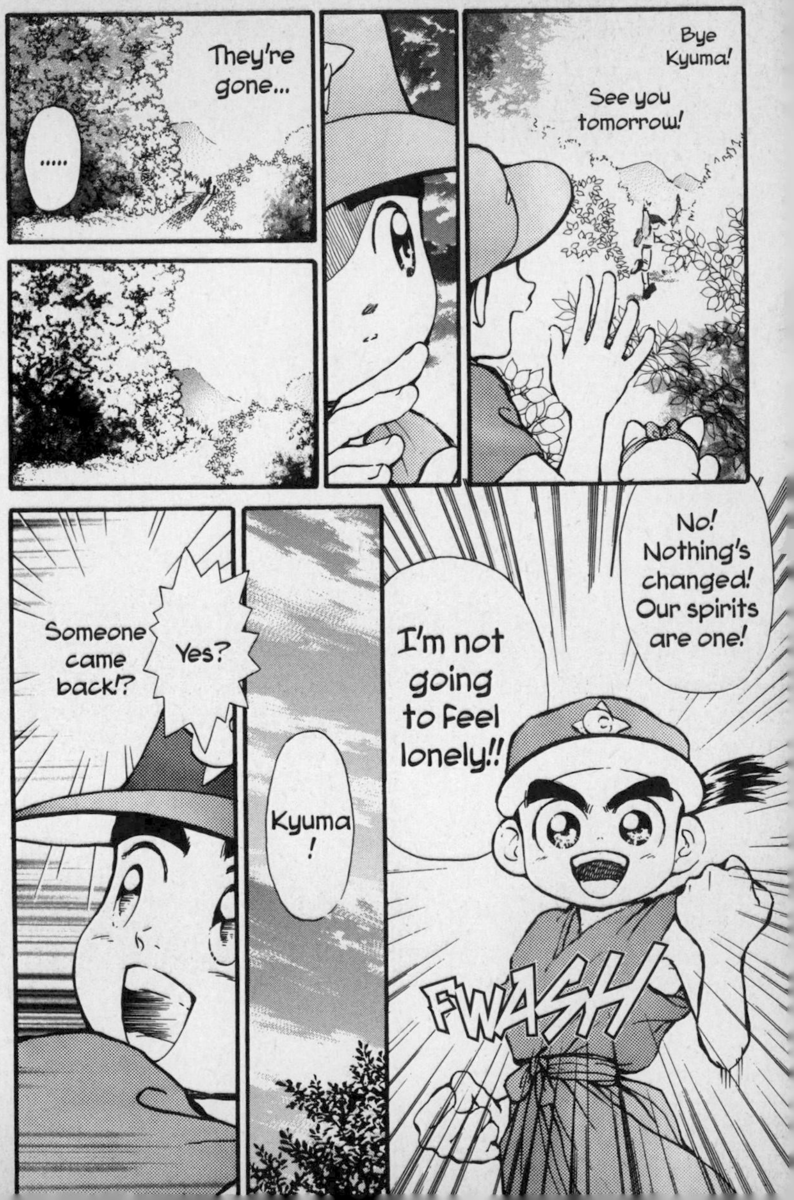
Bye Kyuma!
See you tomorrow!
They're gone...
......
No! Nothing's changed! Our spirits are one!
I'm not going to feel lonely!!
FWASH
Kyuma!
Yes?
Someone came back!?

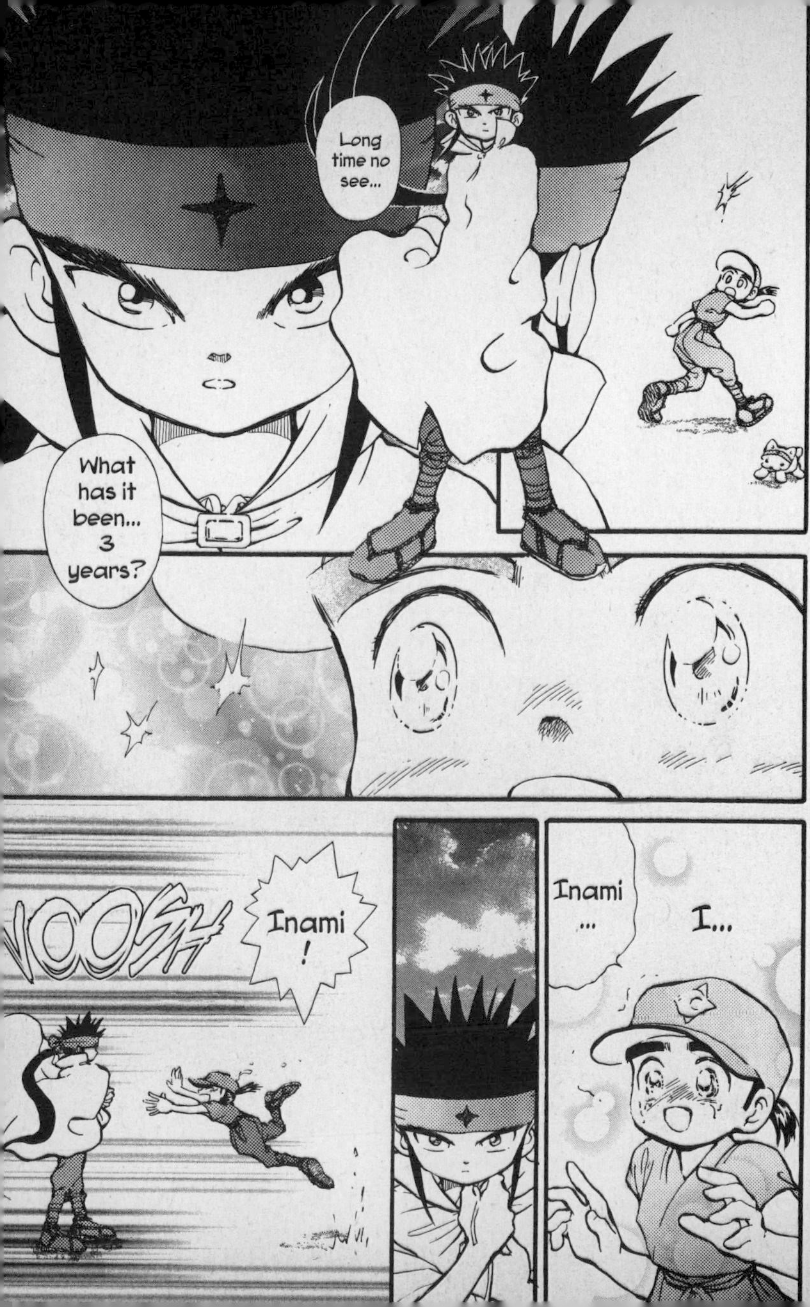
Long time no see...
What has it been... 3 years?
Inami ...
I...
WOOSH
Inami !

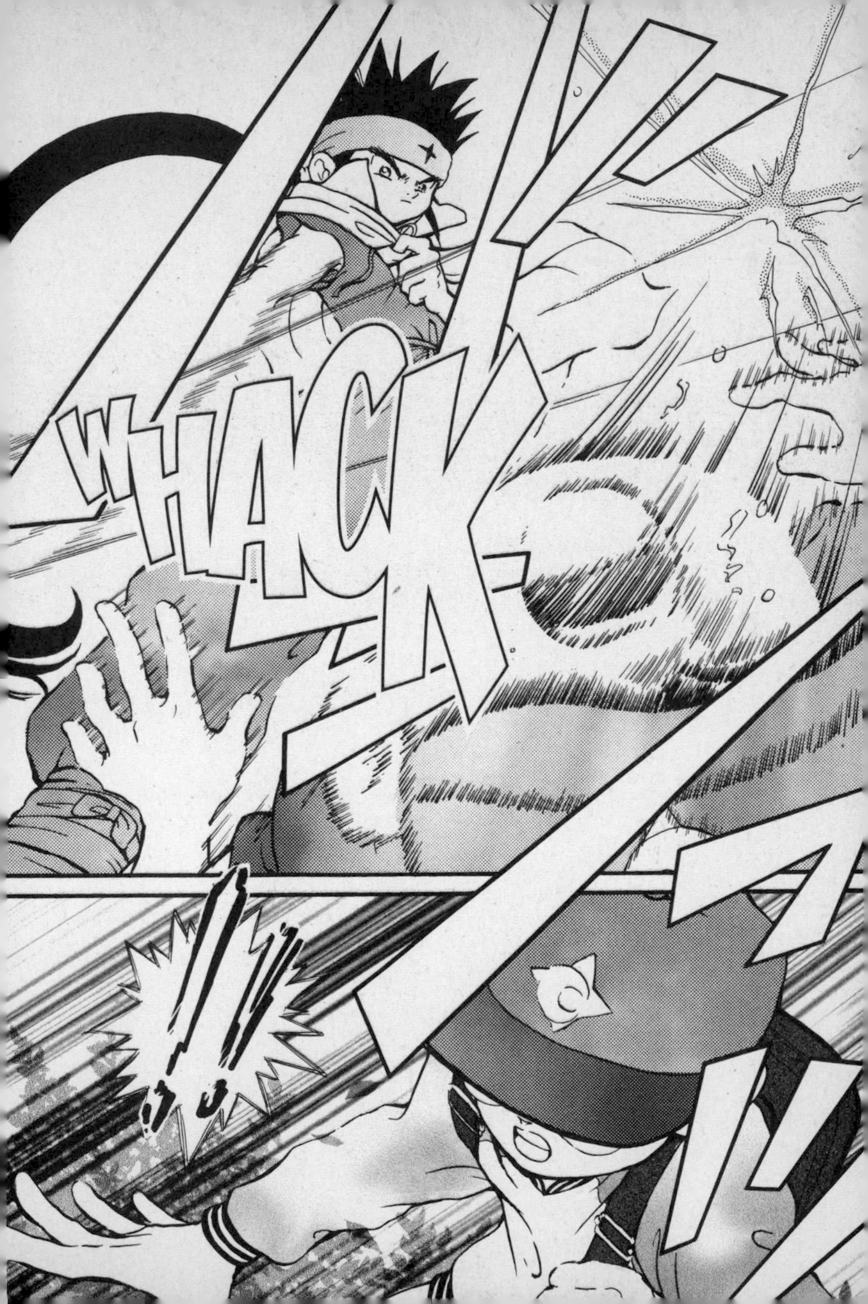
WHACK

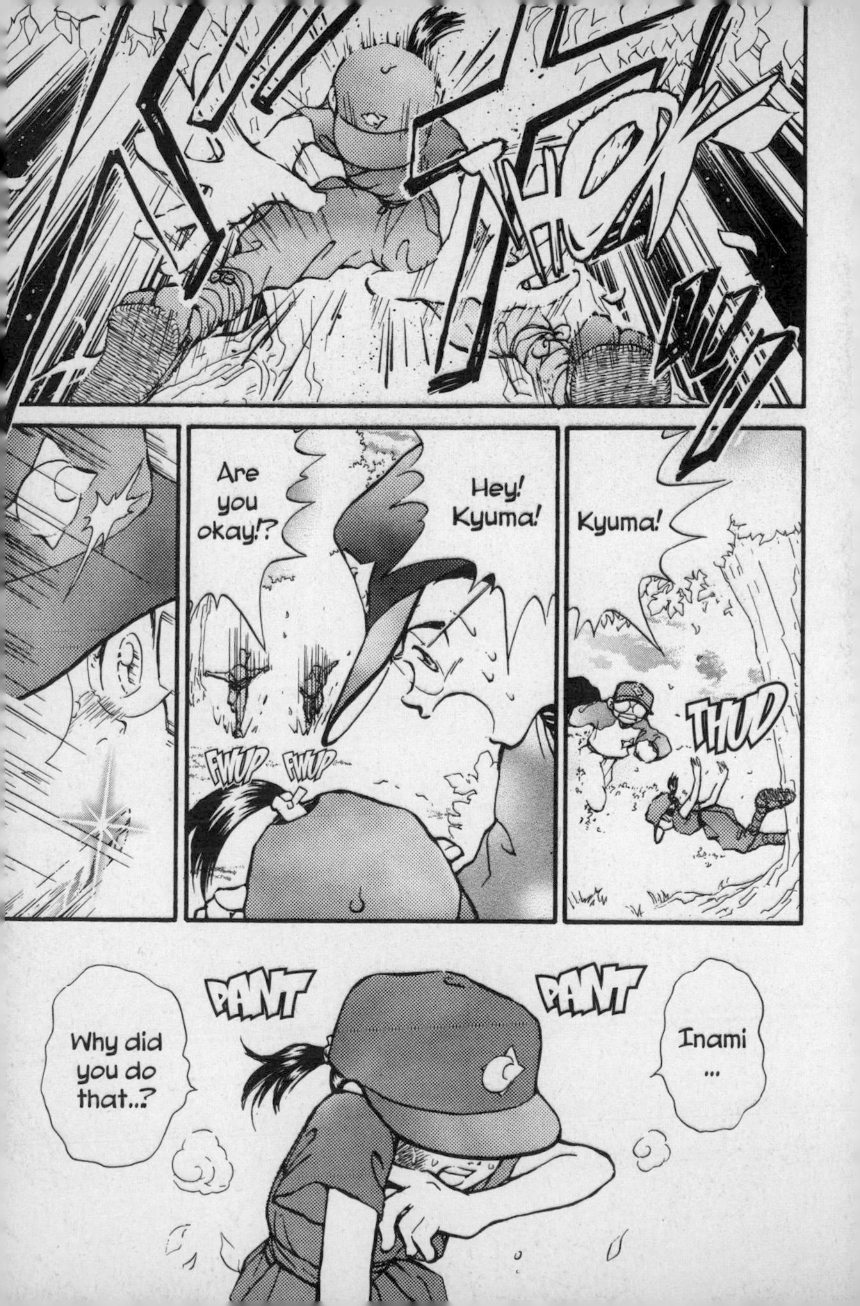
Kyuma!
THUD
Hey! Kyuma!
Are you okay!?
FWUP
FWUP
Inami ...
PANT
PANT
Why did you do that..?

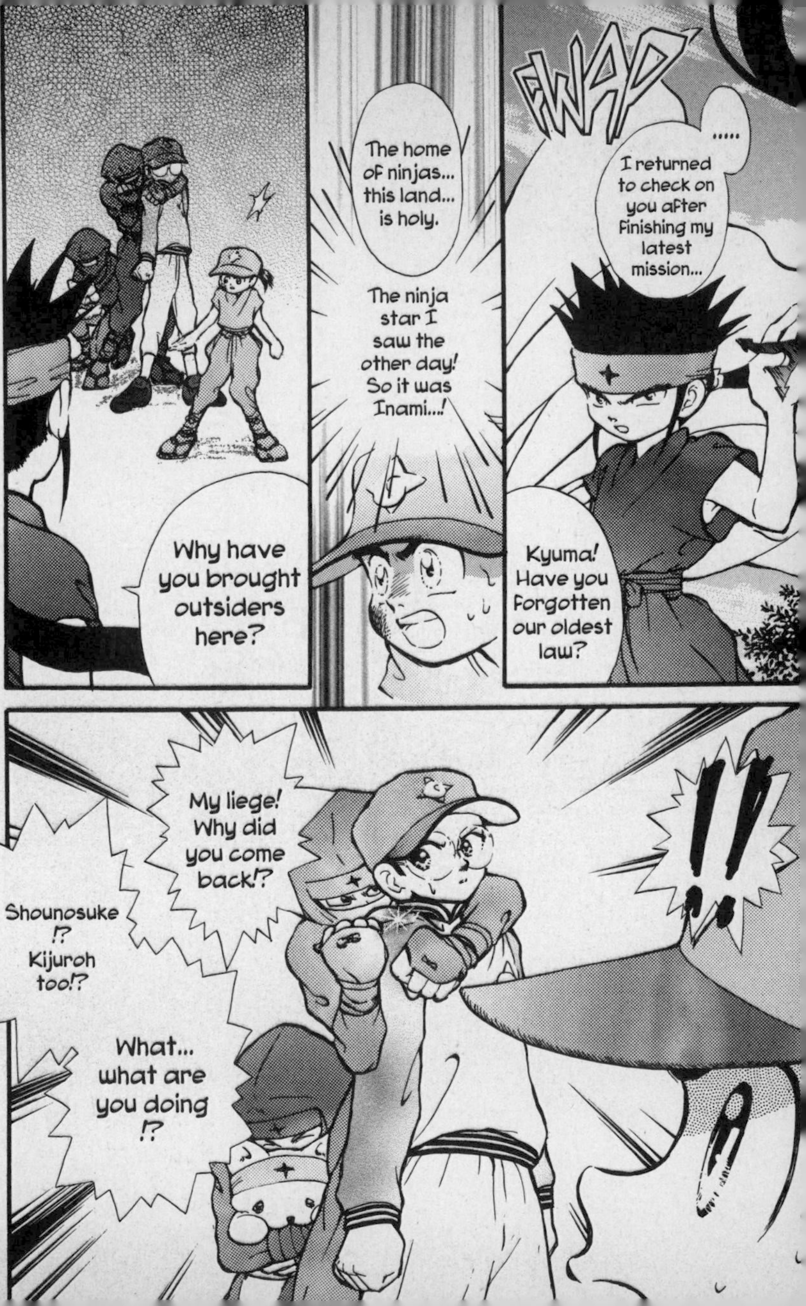
.....
FWAP
I returned to check on you after finishing my latest mission...
Kyuma! Have you forgotten our oldest law?
The home of ninjas... this land... is holy.
The ninja star I saw the other day! So it was Inami...!
Why have you brought outsiders here?
!!
My liege! Why did you come back!?
Shounosuke !? Kijuroh too!?
What... what are you doing !?

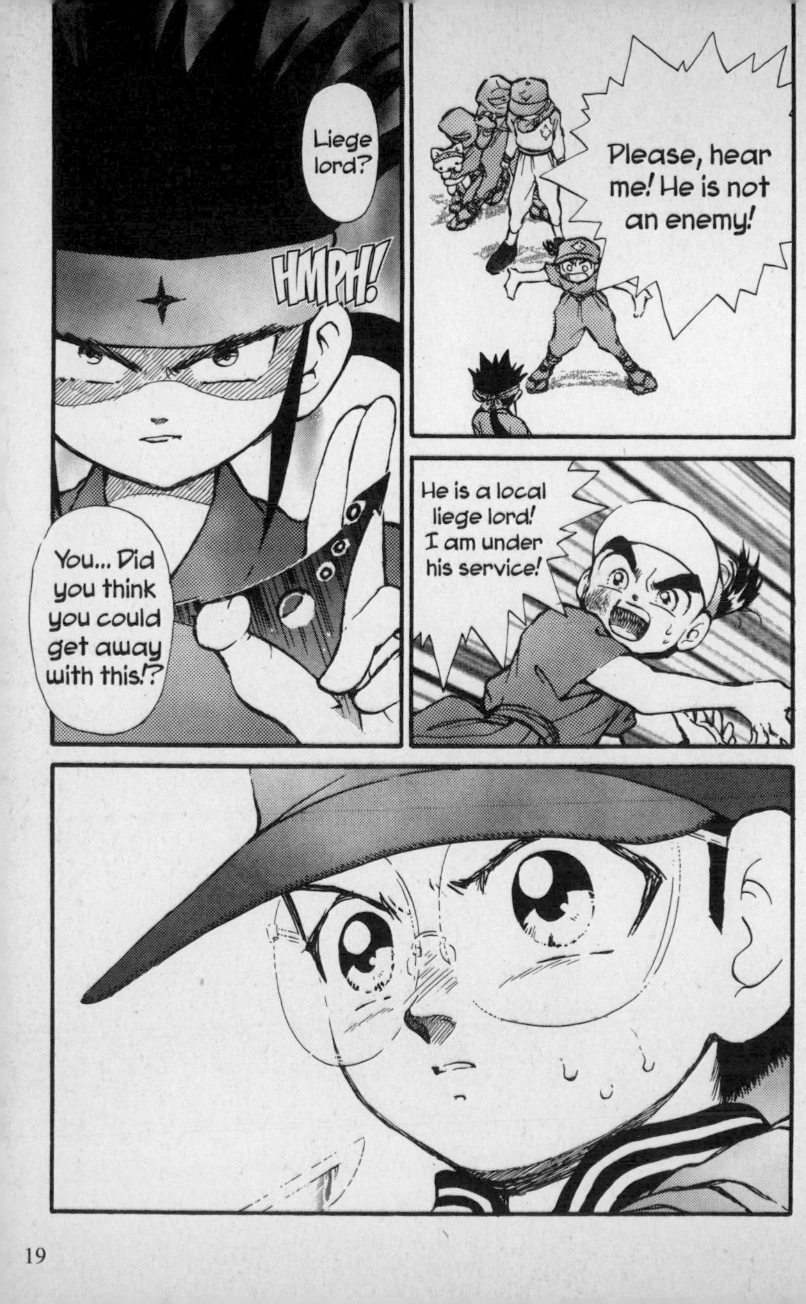
Please, hear me! He is not an enemy!
He is a local liege lord! I am under his service!
Liege lord?
HMPH!
You... Did you think you could get away with this!?

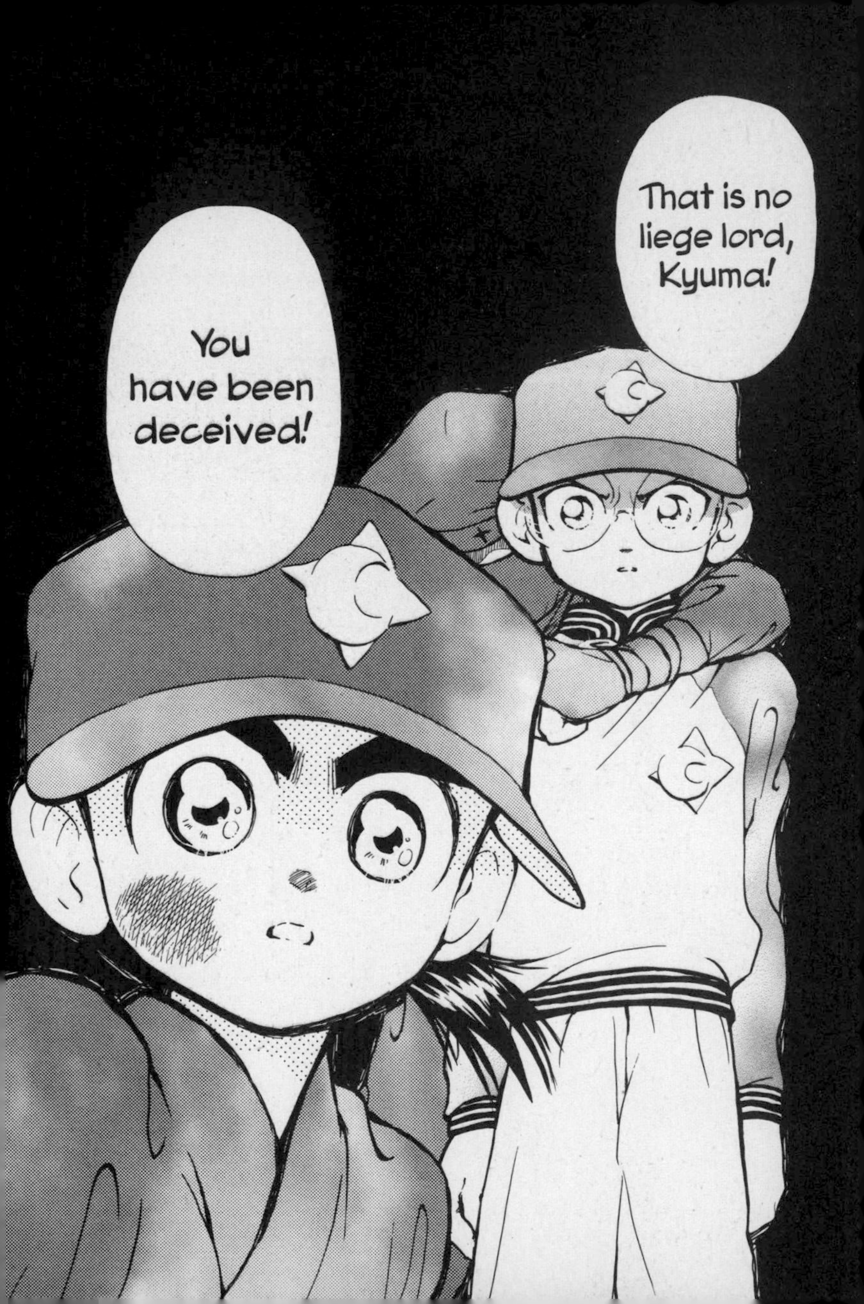
That is no liege lord, Kyuma!
You have been deceived!

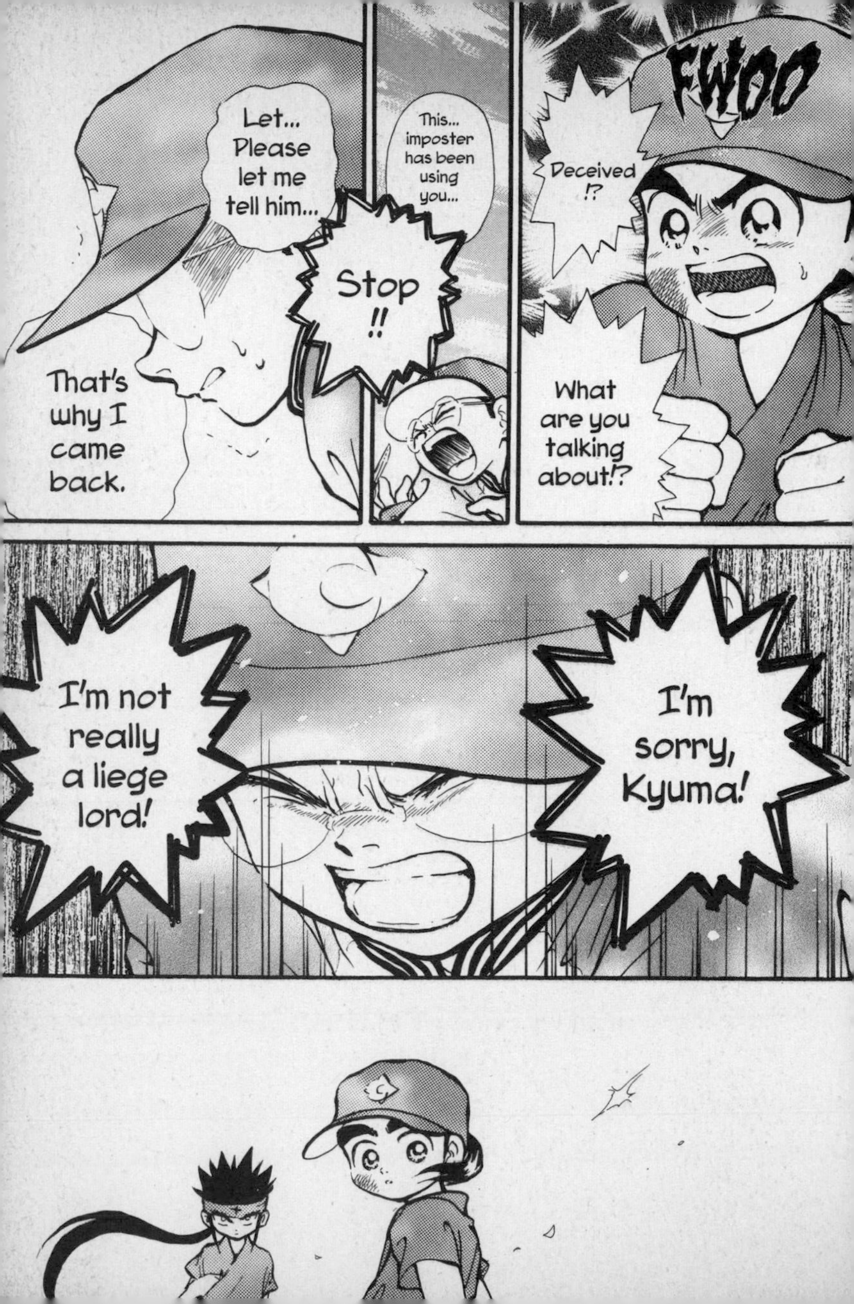

FWOO
Deceived !?
What are you talking about!?
This... imposter has been using you...
Stop !!
Let... Please let me tell him...
That's why I came back.
I'm sorry, Kyuma!
I'm not really a liege lord!

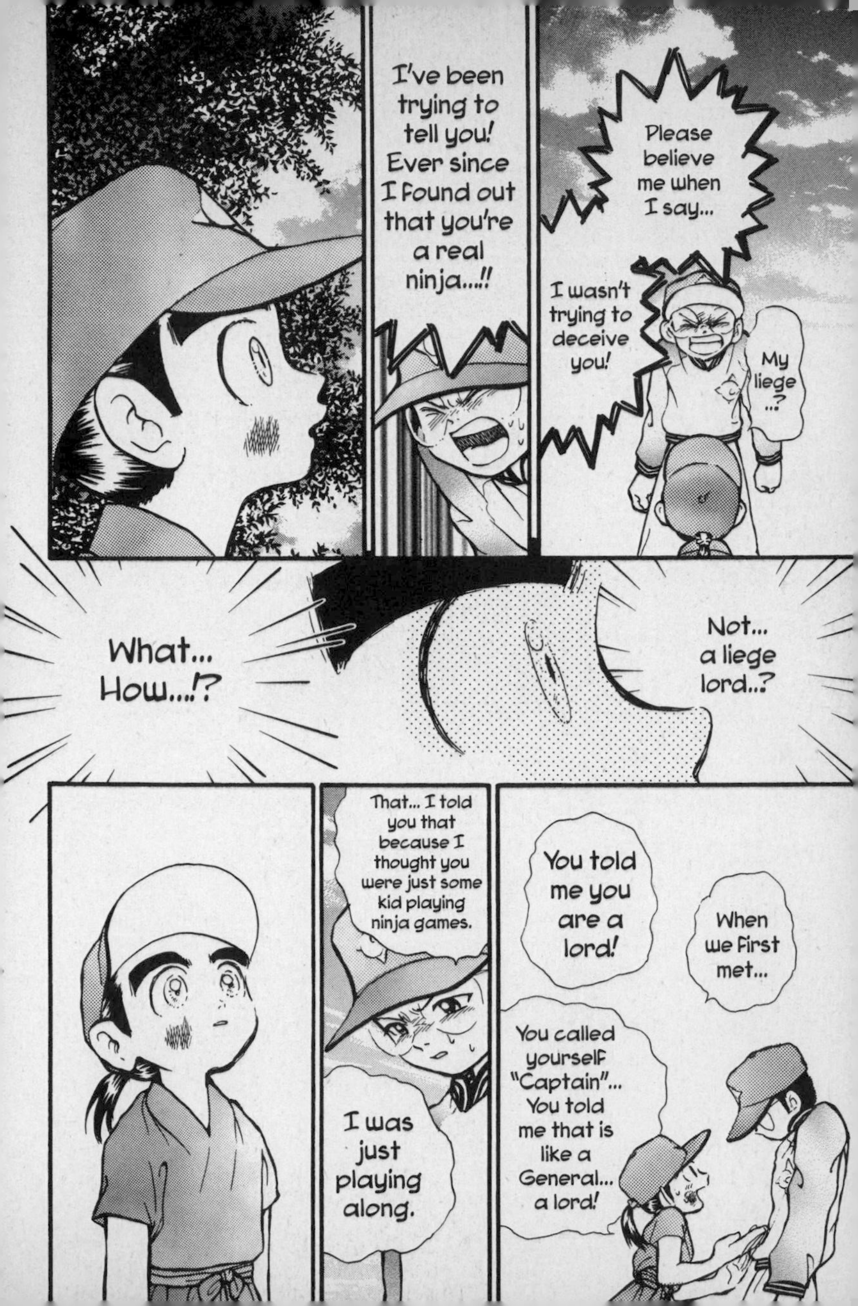
Please believe me when I say...
I wasn't trying to deceive you!
My liege ...?
I've been trying to tell you! Ever since I found out that you're a real ninja...!!
Not... a liege lord..?
What... How...!?
When we first met...
You told me you are a lord!
You called yourself "Captain"... You told me that is like a General... a lord!
That... I told you that because I thought you were just some kid playing ninja games.
I was just playing along.

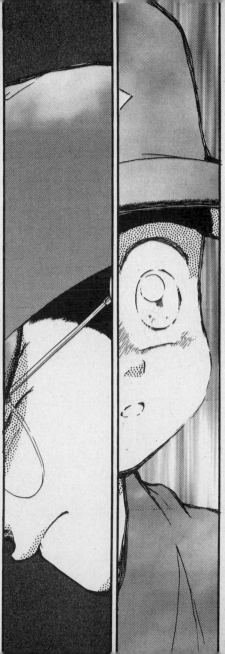

A lord!?

He isn't...

.....

Then...

What have I been doing this whole time..?

I followed him... believed in him...

I gave everything that I had in service to "my liege"...

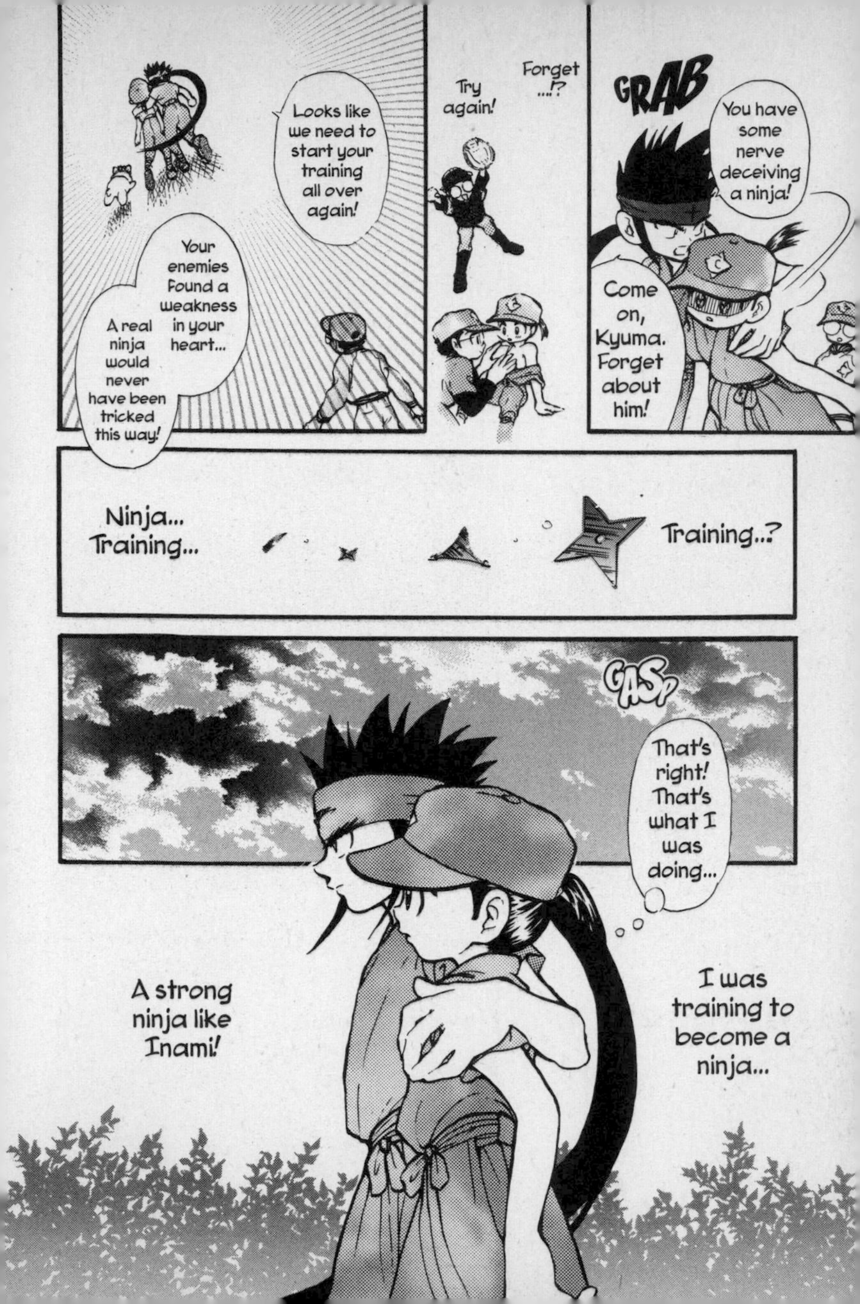
GRAB
You have some nerve deceiving a ninja!
Come on, Kyuma. Forget about him!
Forget ...!?
Try again!
Looks like we need to start your training all over again!
Your enemies found a weakness in your heart...
A real ninja would never have been tricked this way!
Training..?
Ninja... Training...
GASP
That's right! That's what I was doing...
I was training to become a ninja...
A strong ninja like Inami!

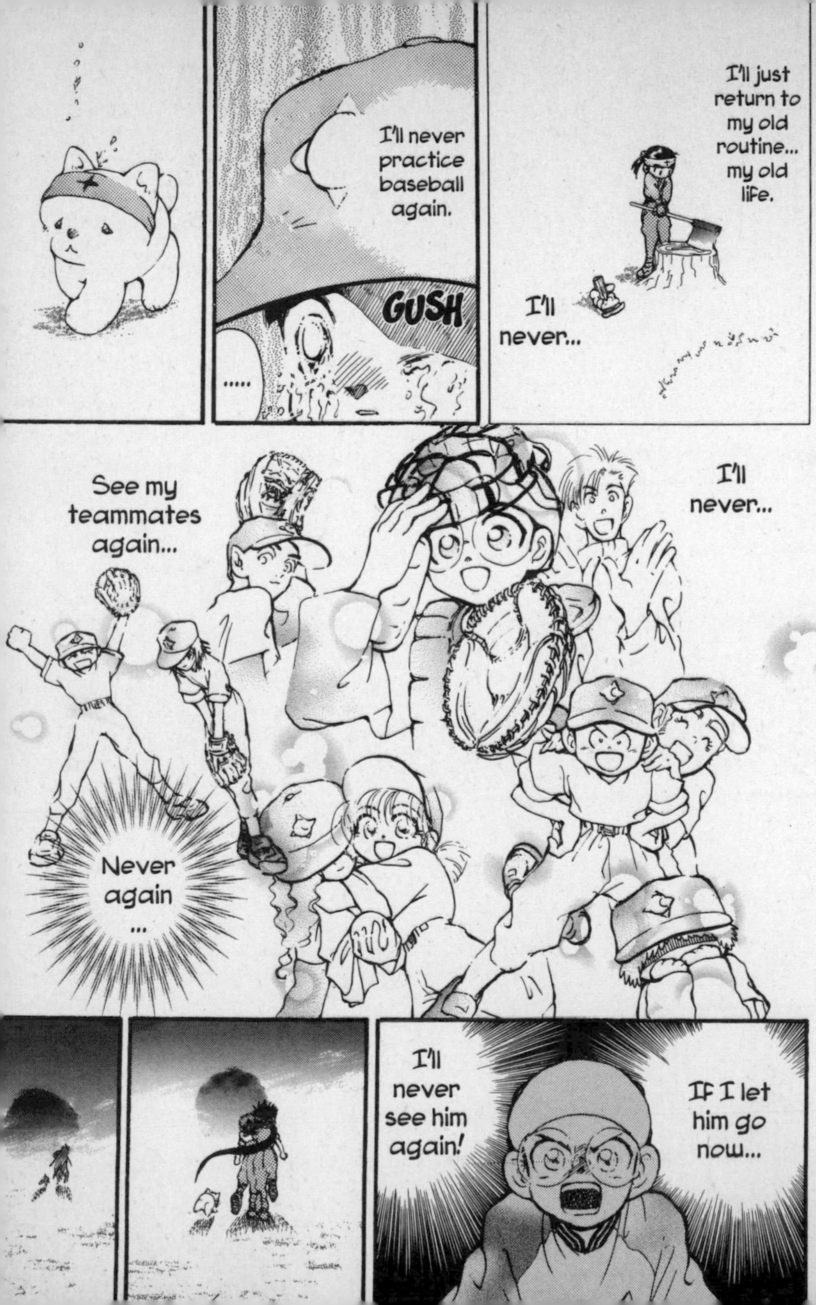
I'll just return to my old routine... my old life.
I'll never...
I'll never practice baseball again.
GUSH
.....
I'll never...
See my teammates again...
Never again ...
If I let him go now...
I'll never see him again!

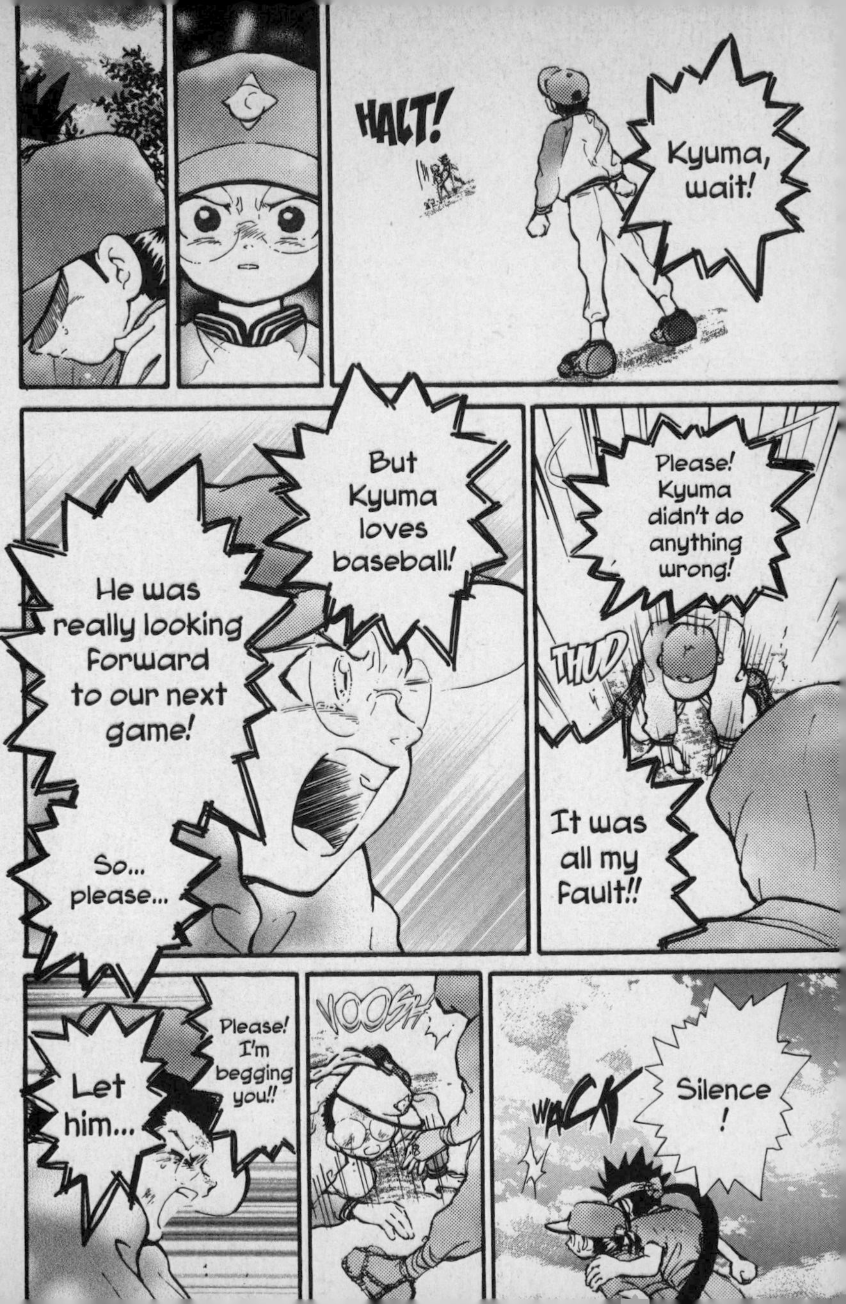
Kyuma, wait!
HALT!
Please! Kyuma didn't do anything wrong!
THUD
It was all my fault!!
But Kyuma loves baseball!
He was really looking forward to our next game!
So... please...
Silence!
WACK
VOOSH
Please! I'm begging you!!
Let him...

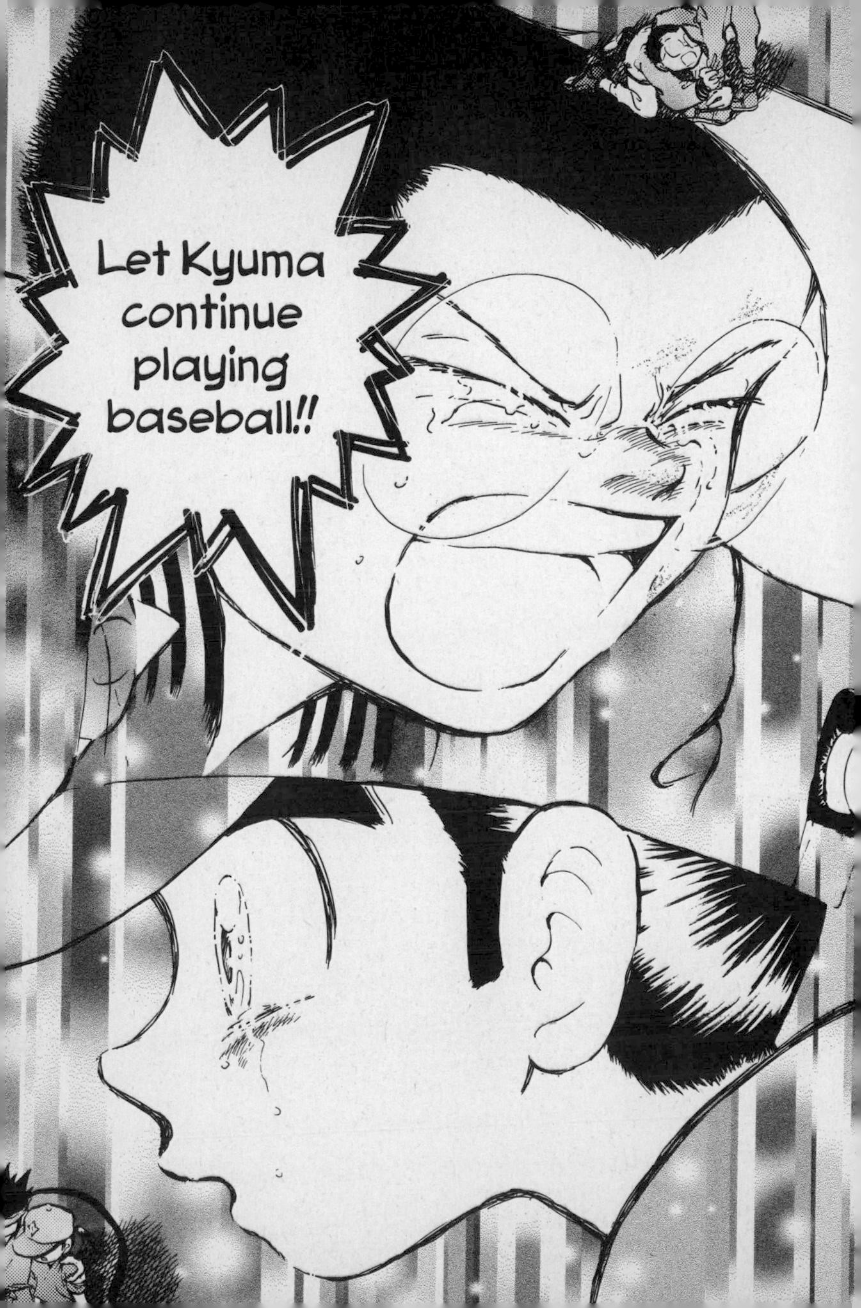
Let Kyuma continue playing baseball!!

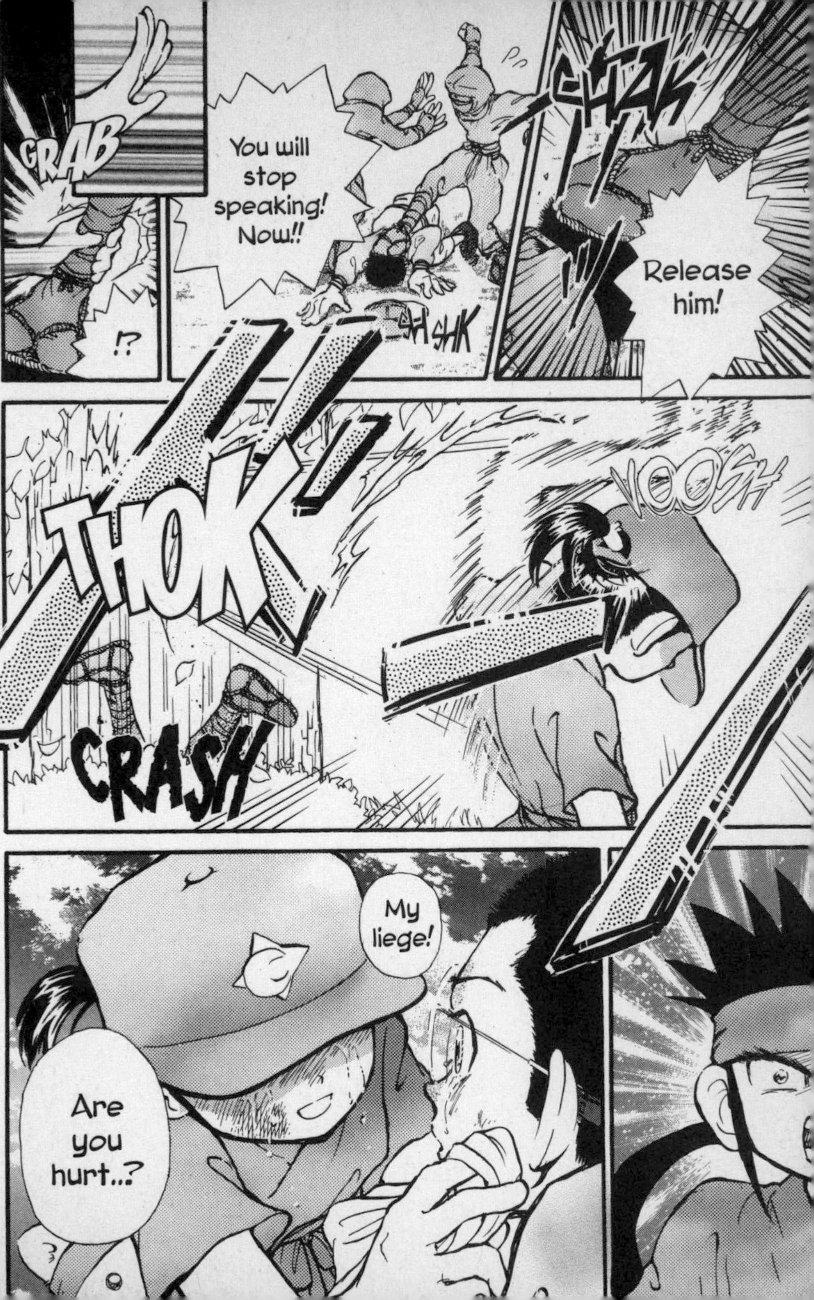
CHAK
Release him!
You will stop speaking! Now!!
SHK SHK
GRAB
!?
VOOSH
THOK
CRASH
My liege!
Are you hurt...?

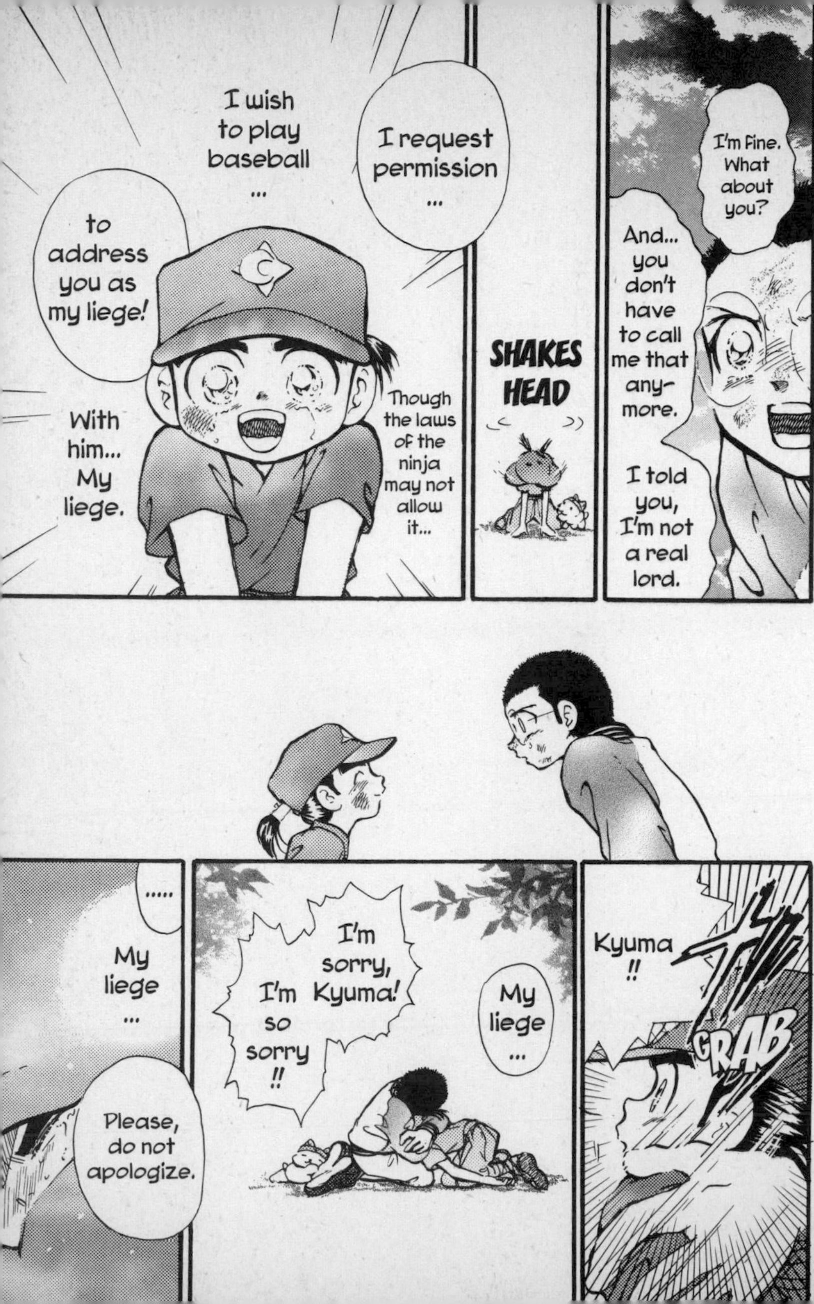

I'm fine. What about you?
And... you don't have to call me that any-more.
I told you, I'm not a real lord.
SHAKES HEAD
I request permission ...
I wish to play baseball ...
to address you as my liege!
Though the laws of the ninja may not allow it...
With him... My liege.
Kyuma !!
GRAB
My liege ...
I'm sorry, Kyuma! I'm so sorry !!
.....
My liege ...
Please, do not apologize.

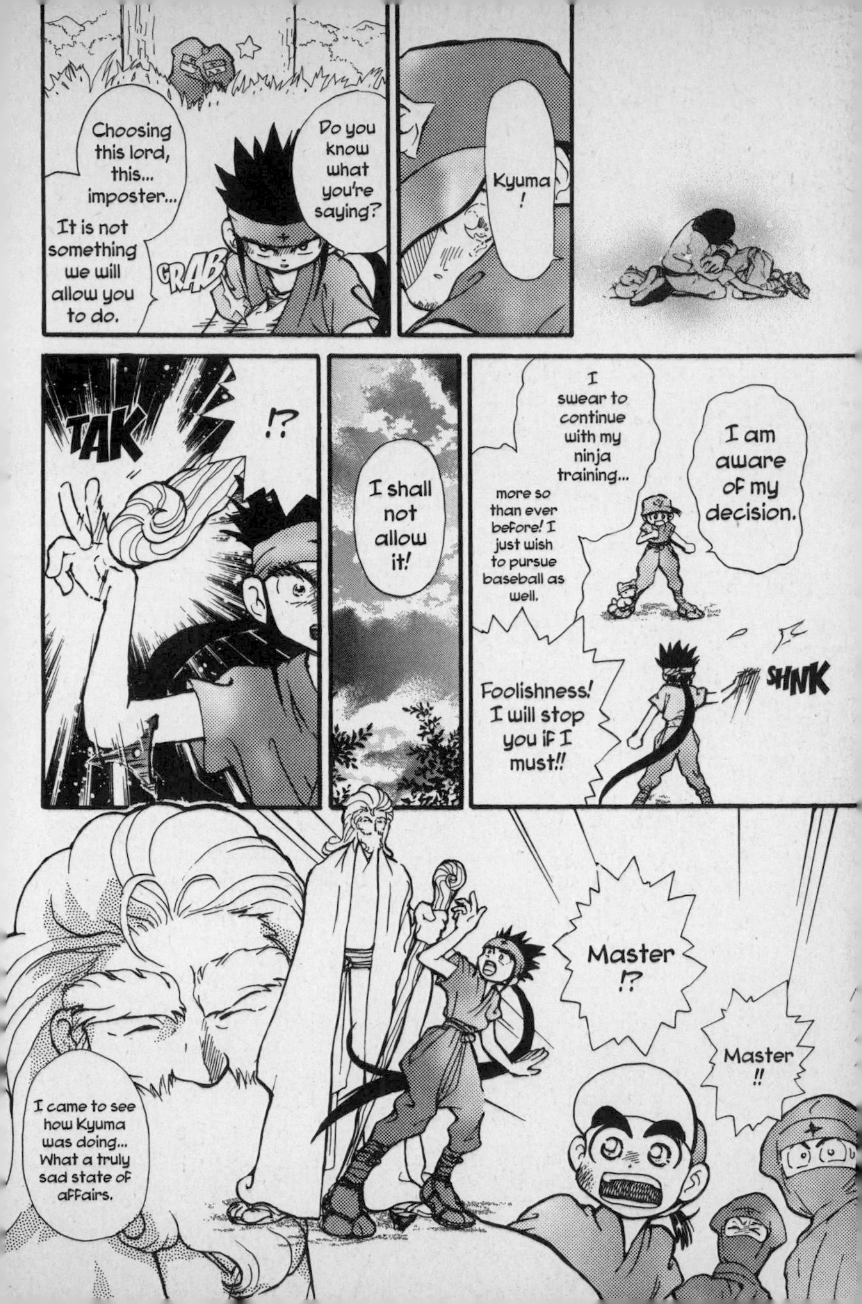

Kyuma!
Do you know what you're saying?
Choosing this lord, this... imposter...
It is not something we will allow you to do.
GRAB
I am aware of my decision.
I swear to continue with my ninja training...
more so than ever before! I just wish to pursue baseball as well.
Foolishness! I will stop you if I must!!
SHNK
I shall not allow it!
!?
TAK
Master!!
Master!?
I came to see how Kyuma was doing... What a truly sad state of affairs.

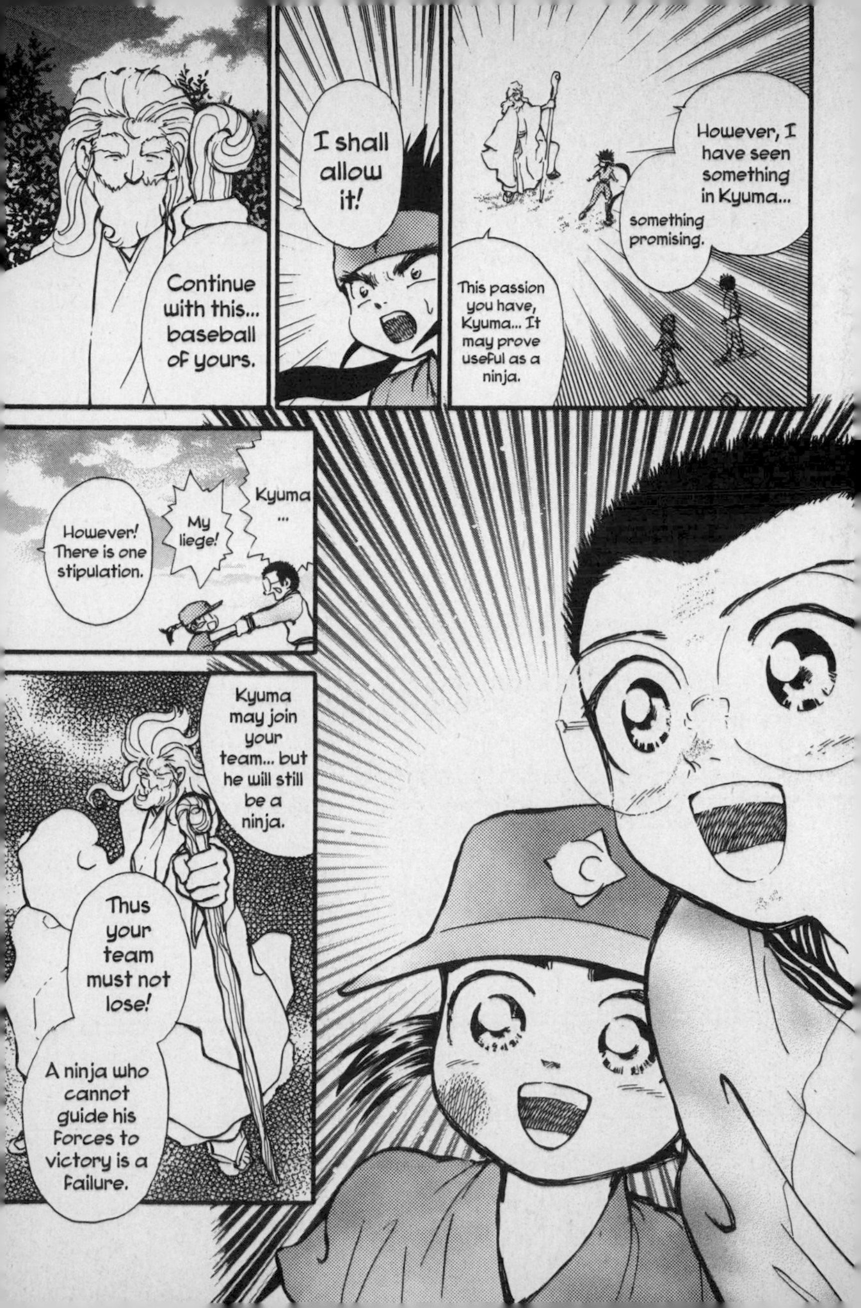

However, I have seen something in Kyuma...
something promising.
This passion you have, Kyuma... It may prove useful as a ninja.
I shall allow it!
Continue with this... baseball of yours.
Kyuma ...
My liege!
However! There is one stipulation.
Kyuma may join your team... but he will still be a ninja.
Thus your team must not lose!
A ninja who cannot guide his forces to victory is a failure.

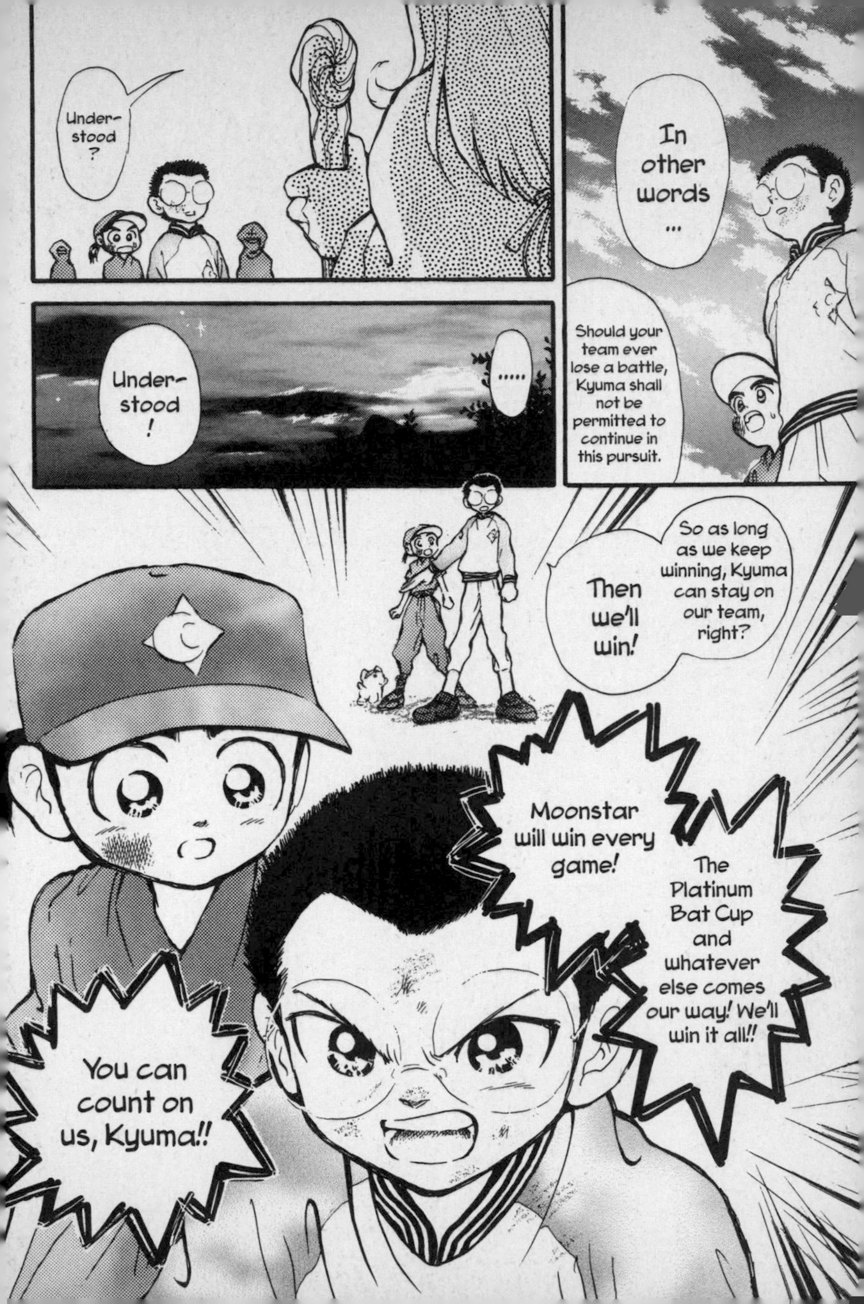
In other words ...
Should your team ever lose a battle, Kyuma shall not be permitted to continue in this pursuit.
Under-stood ?
......
Under-stood !
So as long as we keep winning, Kyuma can stay on our team, right?
Then we'll win!
Moonstar will win every game!
The Platinum Bat Cup and whatever else comes our way! We'll win it all!!
You can count on us, Kyuma!!

PITCH 9
THE PLATINUM BAT CUP BEGINS!

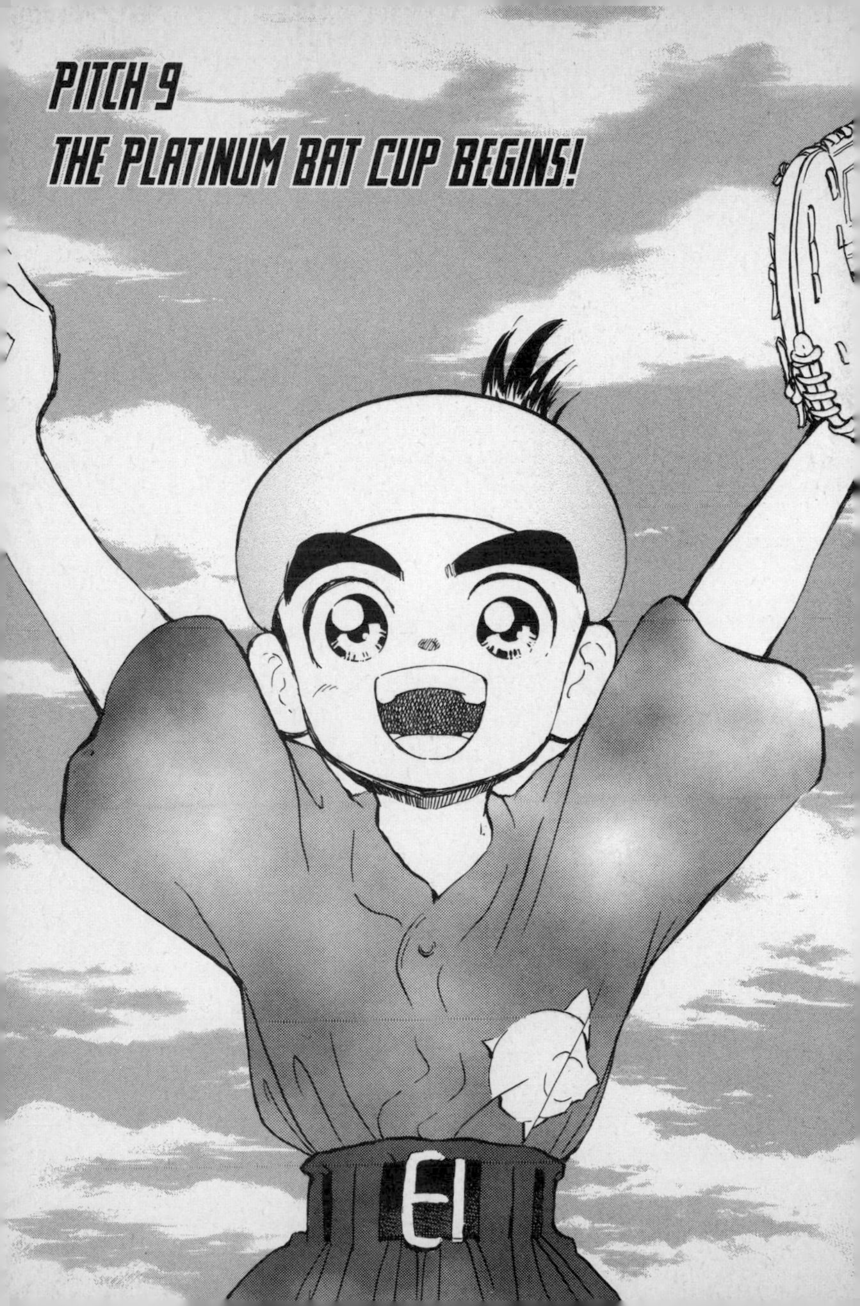
EI

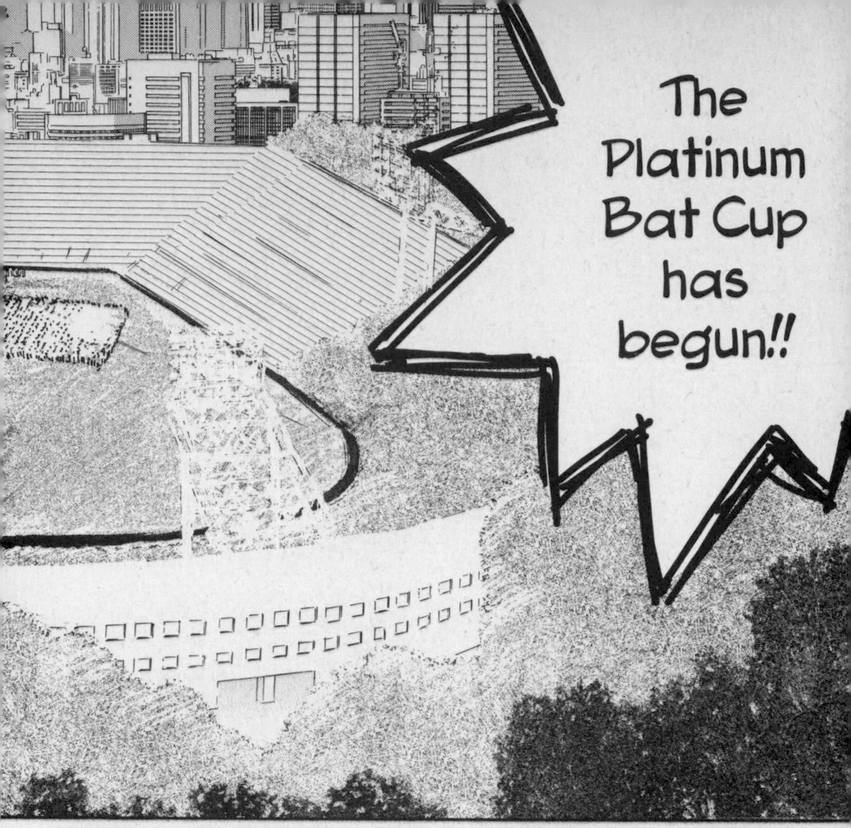
The Platinum Bat Cup has begun!!
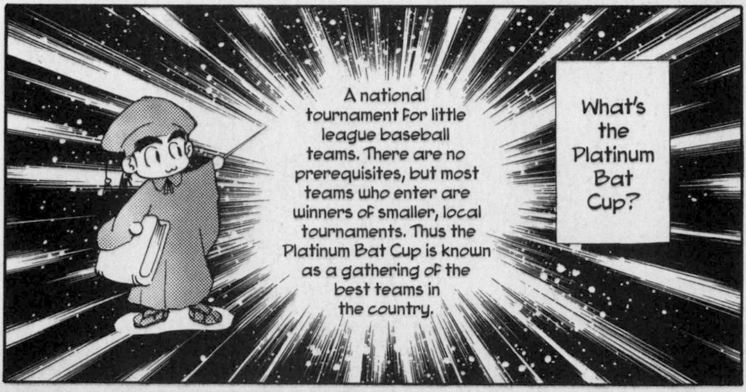
What's the Platinum Bat Cup?
A national tournament for little league baseball teams. There are no prerequisites, but most teams who enter are winners of smaller, local tournaments. Thus the Platinum Bat Cup is known as a gathering of the best teams in the country.

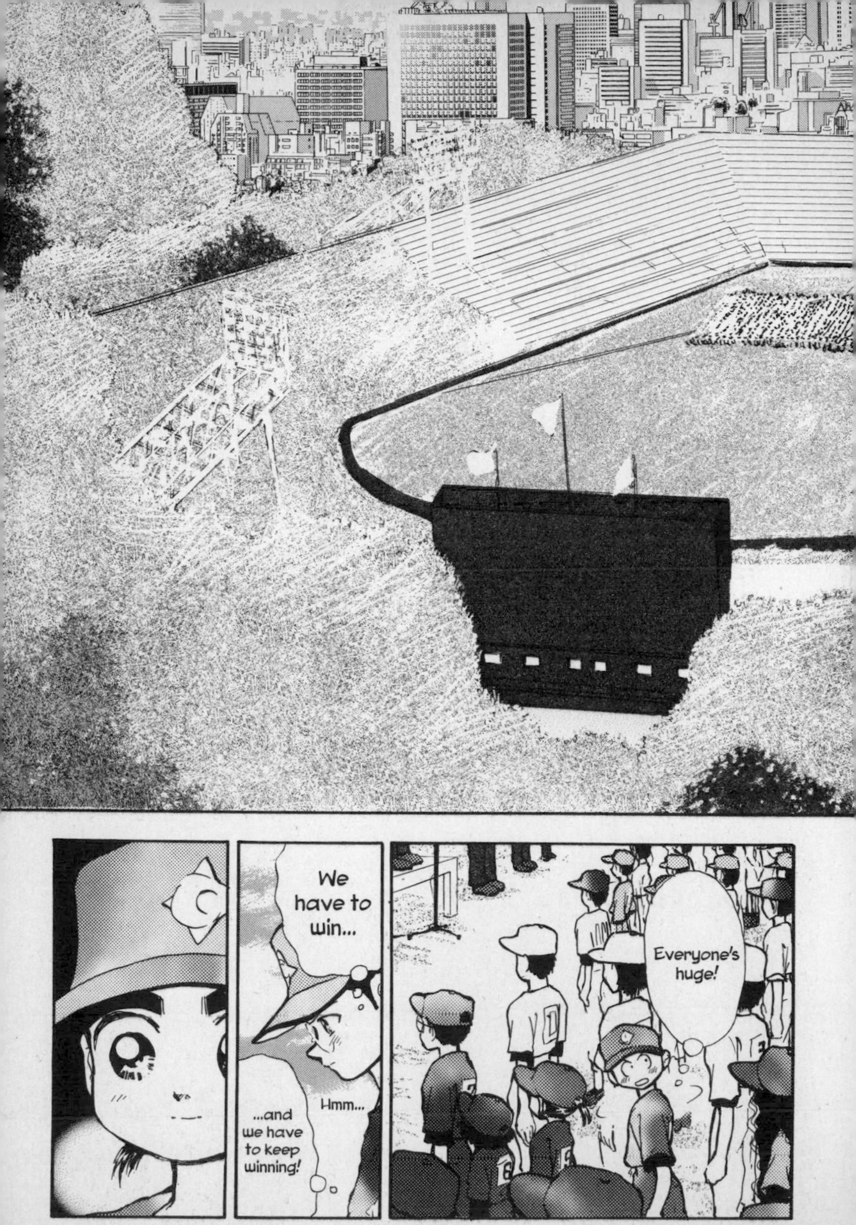
Everyone's huge!
We have to win...
Hmm...
...and we have to keep winning!

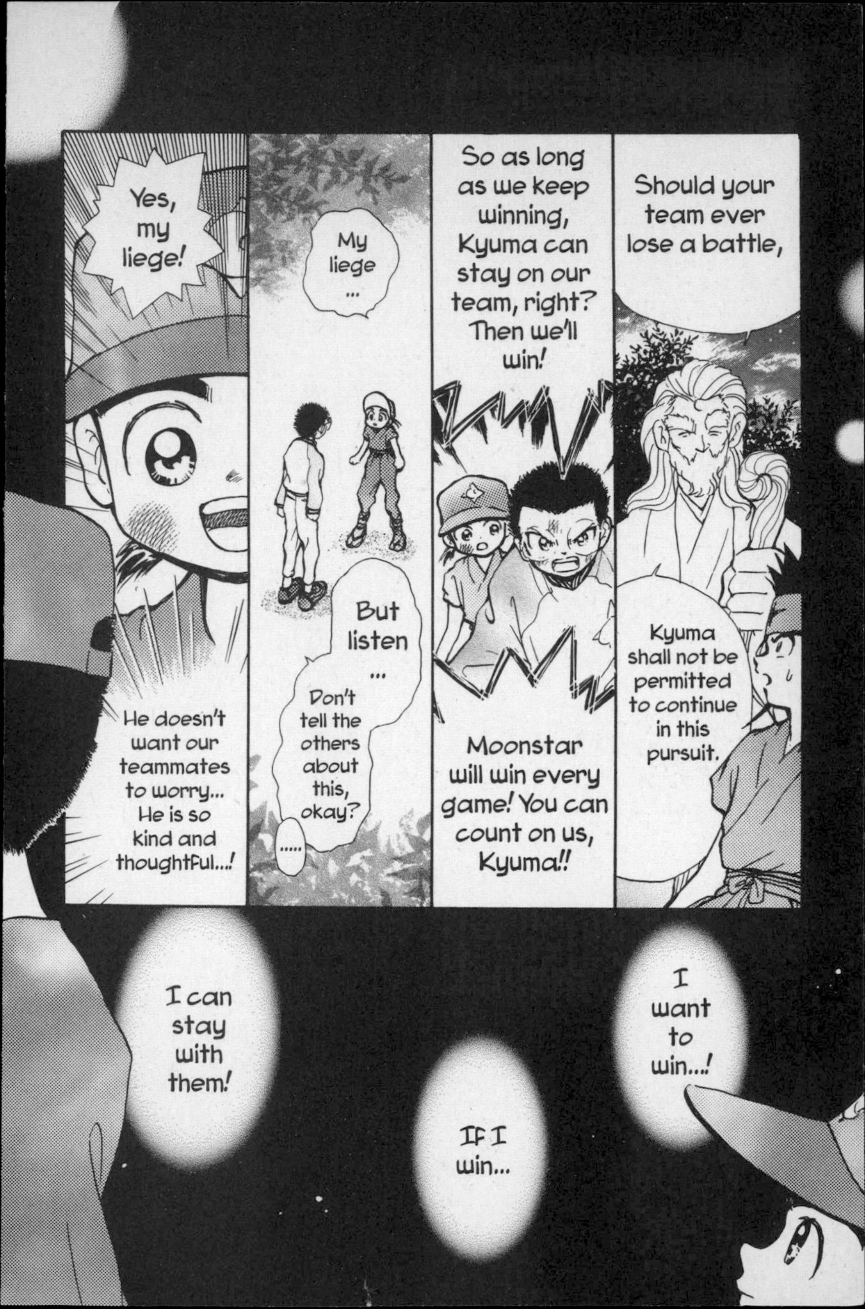
Should your team ever lose a battle,
Kyuma shall not be permitted to continue in this pursuit.
So as long as we keep winning, Kyuma can stay on our team, right? Then we'll win!
Moonstar will win every game! You can count on us, Kyuma!!
My liege ...
But listen ...
Don't tell the others about this, okay?
.....
Yes, my liege!
He doesn't want our teammates to worry... He is so kind and thoughtful...!
I want to win...!
If I win...
I can stay with them!

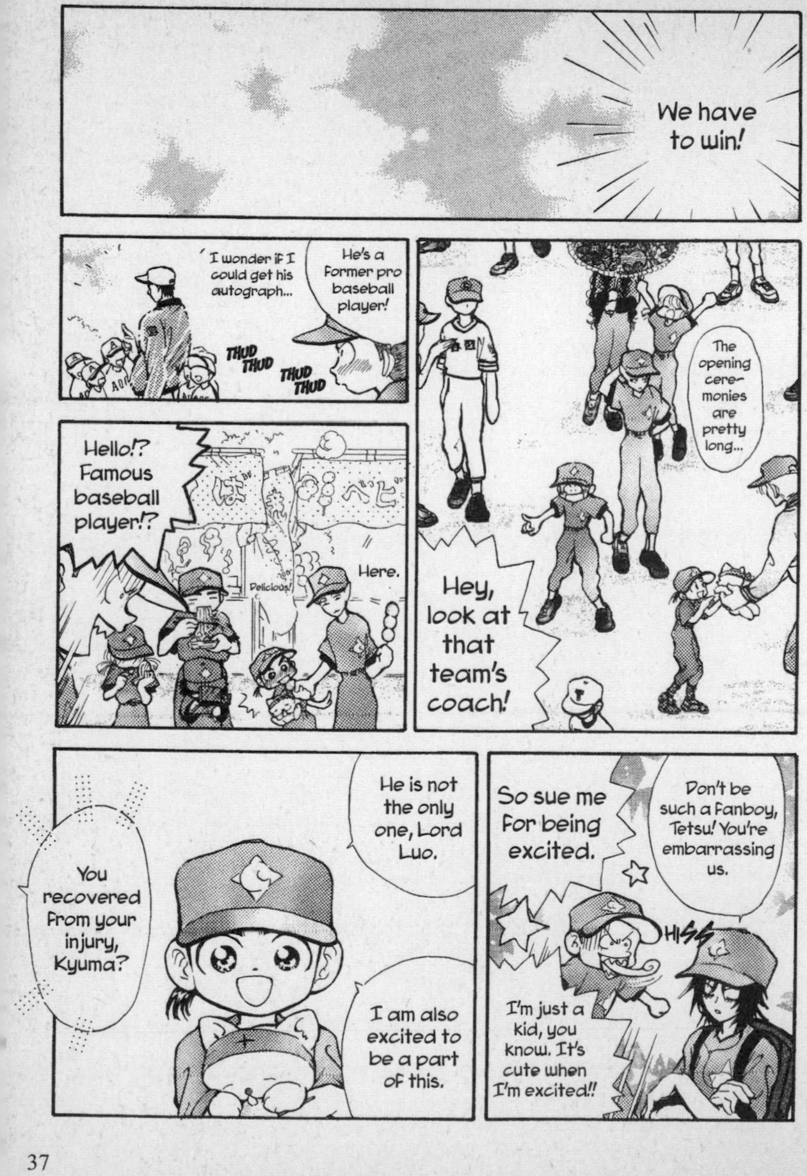
We have to win!
The opening ceremonies are pretty long...
Hey, look at that team's coach!
He's a former pro baseball player!
I wonder if I could get his autograph...
THUD THUD THUD THUD
Hello!? Famous baseball player!?
Here.
Delicious!
Don't be such a fanboy, Tetsu! You're embarrassing us.
So sue me for being excited.
HISS
I'm just a kid, you know. It's cute when I'm excited!!
He is not the only one, Lord Luo.
You recovered from your injury, Kyuma?
I am also excited to be a part of this.

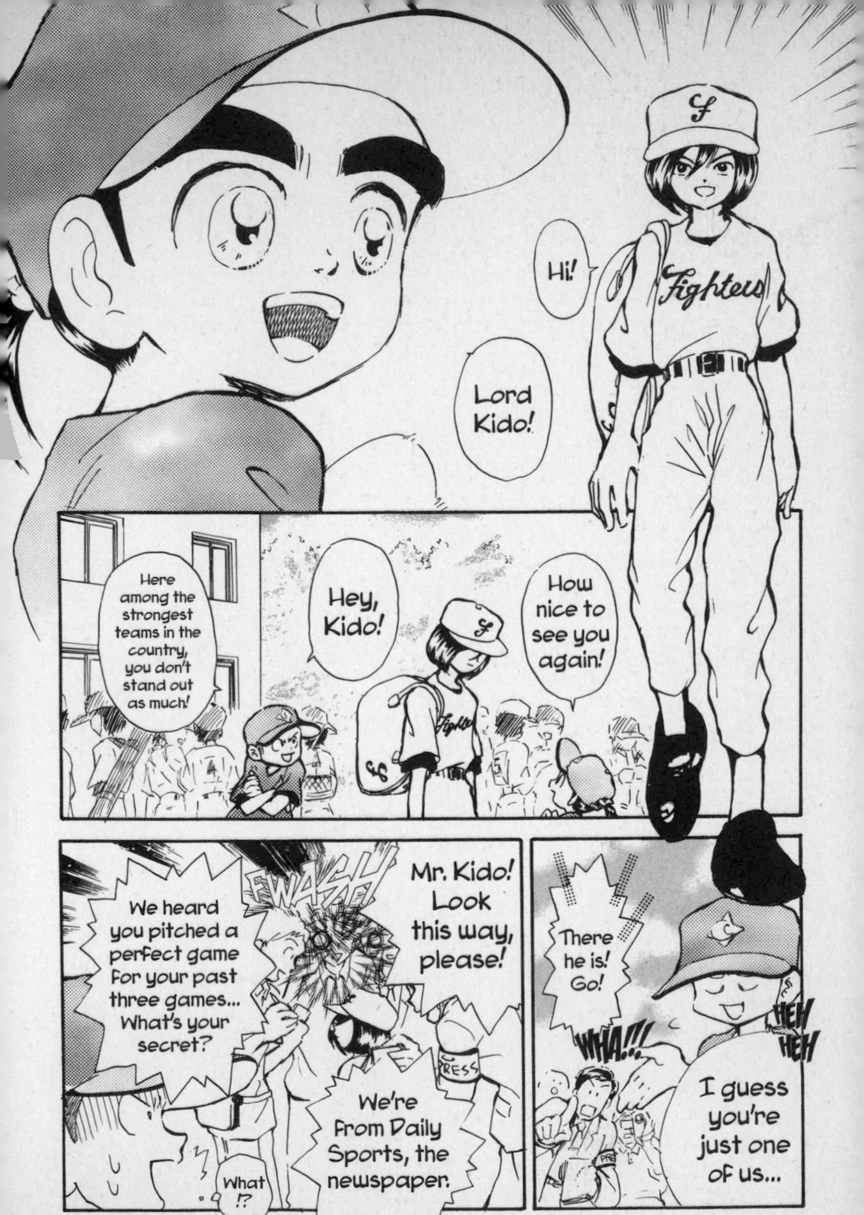
Hi!
Lord Kido!
How nice to see you again!
Hey, Kido!
Here among the strongest teams in the country, you don't stand out as much!
There he is! Go!
HEH HEH
I guess you're just one of us...
WHA!!!
Mr. Kido! Look this way, please!
FWASH
We heard you pitched a perfect game for your past three games... What's your secret?
PRESS
We're from Daily Sports, the newspaper.
What!?

Pitched perfect games...!?

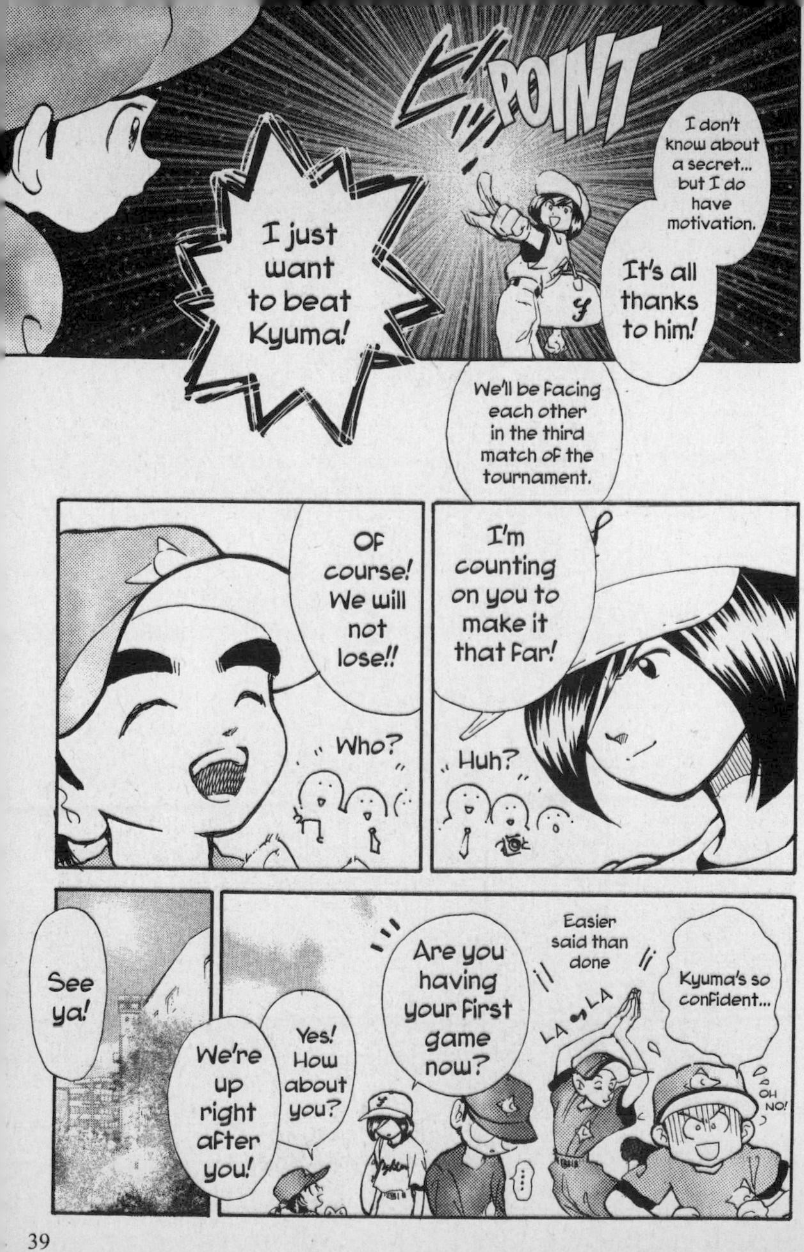
I don't know about a secret... but I do have motivation.
It's all thanks to him!
POINT
I just want to beat Kyuma!
We'll be facing each other in the third match of the tournament.
I'm counting on you to make it that far!
Huh?
Of course! We will not lose!!
Who?
Kyuma's so confident...
OH NO!
Easier said than done
LA LA
Are you having your first game now?
Yes! How about you?
We're up right after you!
See ya!

Read this way

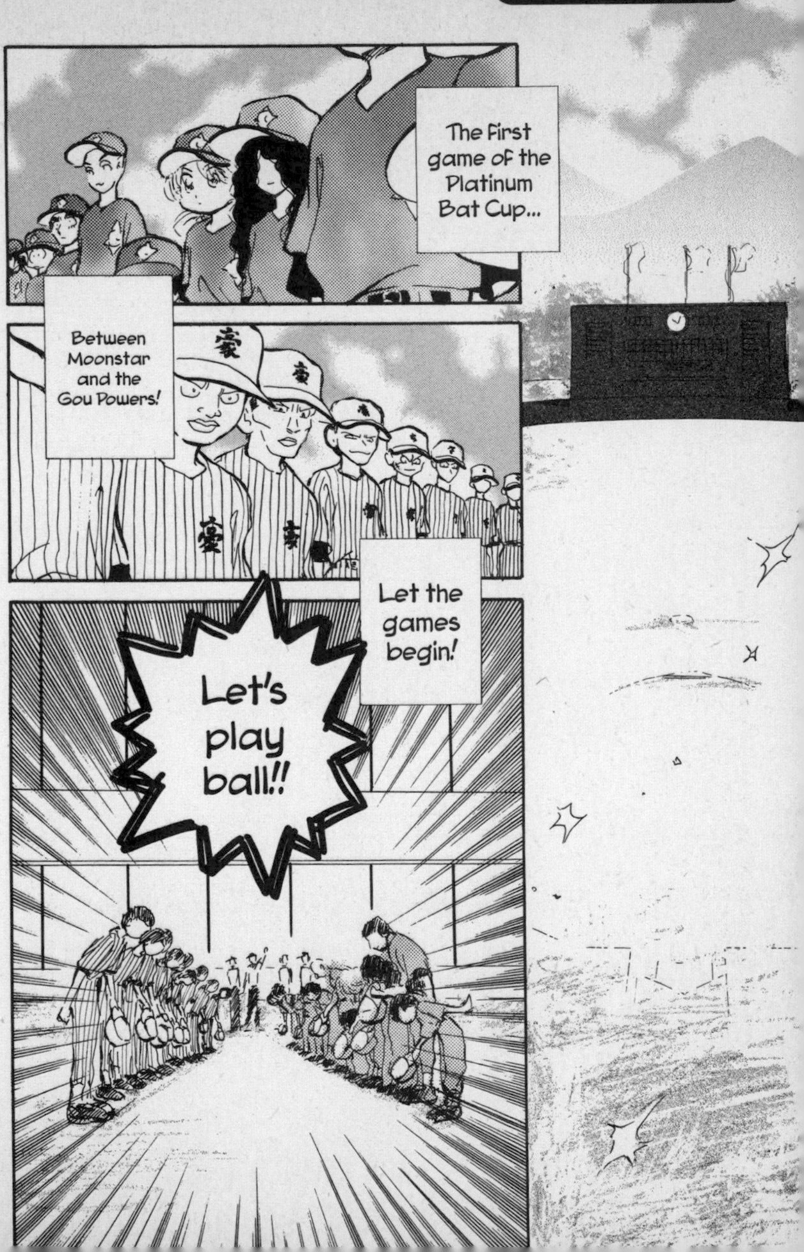
The first game of the Platinum Bat Cup...
Between Moonstar and the Gou Powers!
Let the games begin!
Let's play ball!!

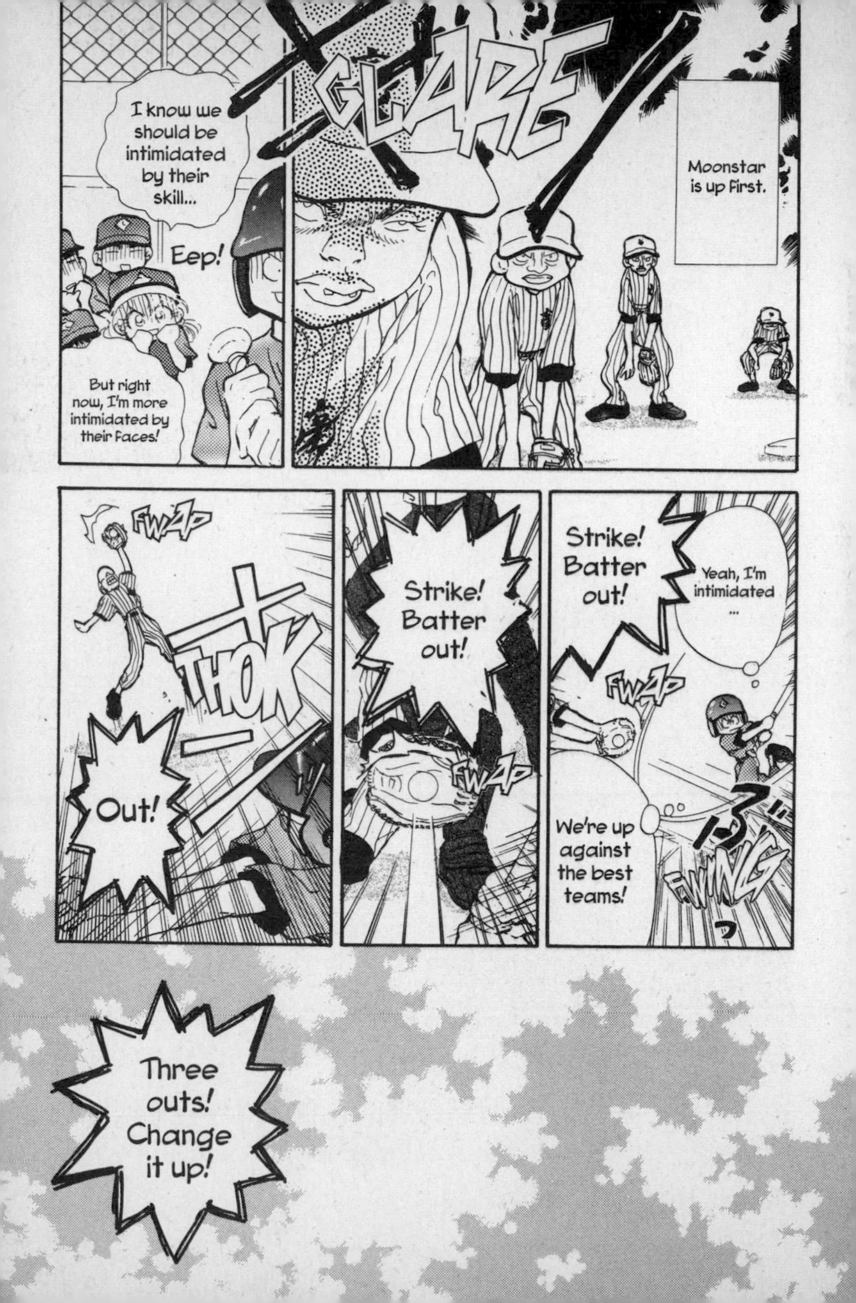
Moonstar is up first.
GLARE
I know we should be intimidated by their skill...
Eep!
But right now, I'm more intimidated by their faces!
Strike! Batter out!
Yeah, I'm intimidated ...
FWAP
FWING
We're up against the best teams!
Strike! Batter out!
FWAP
FWAP
THOK
Out!
Three outs! Change it up!

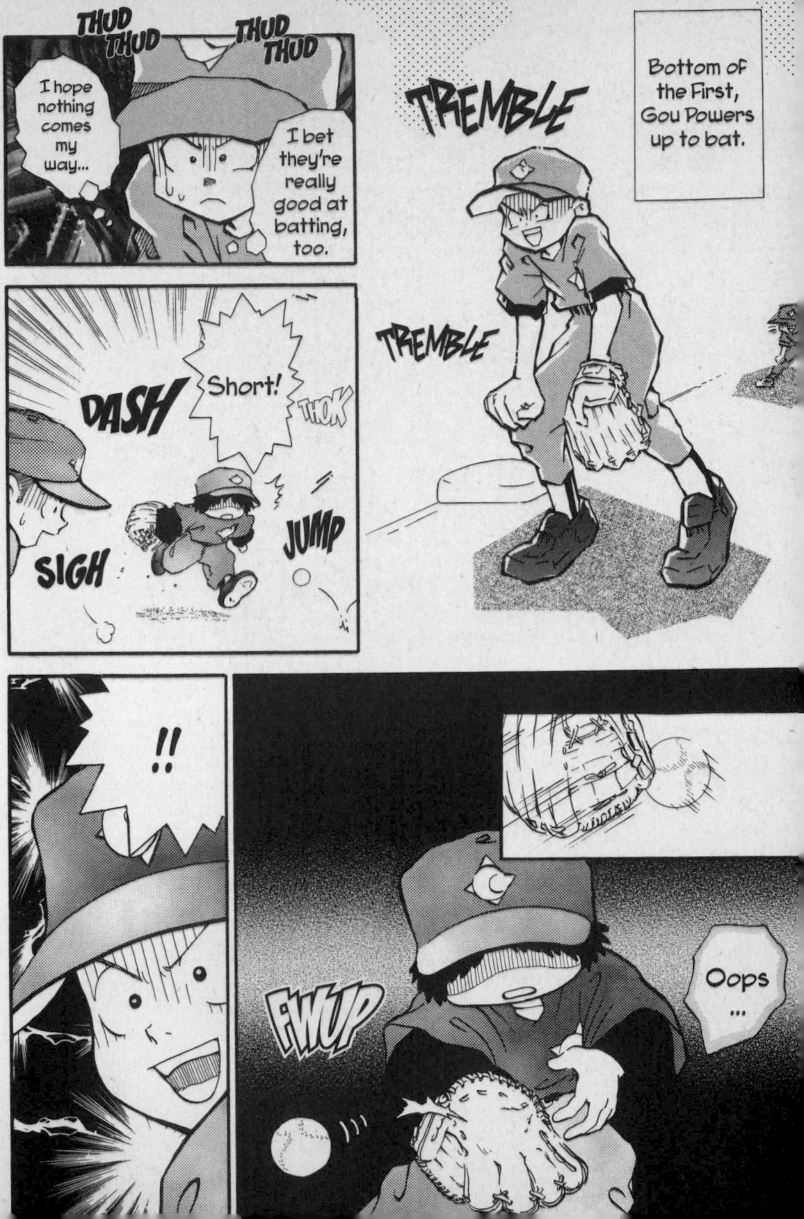
Bottom of the First, Gou Powers up to bat.
TREMBLE
TREMBLE
THUD THUD
THUD THUD
I bet they're really good at batting, too.
I hope nothing comes my way...
THOK
Short!
DASH
JUMP
SIGH
Oops ...
FWUP
!!

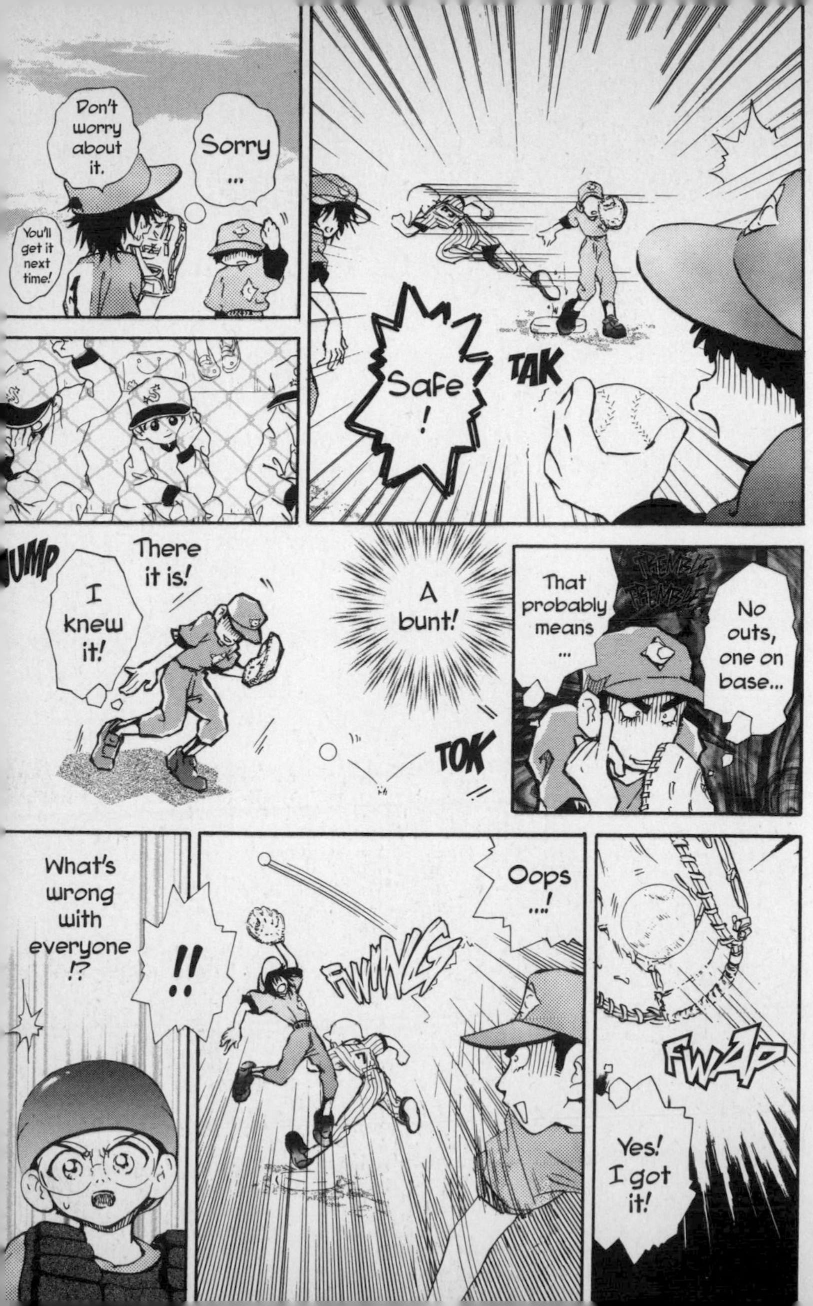

Safe !
TAK
Sorry ...
Don't worry about it.
You'll get it next time!
TREMBLE TREMBLE
No outs, one on base...
That probably means ...
A bunt!
TOK
JUMP
There it is!
I knew it!
FWAP
Yes! I got it!
Oops ...!
FWING
!!
What's wrong with everyone !?

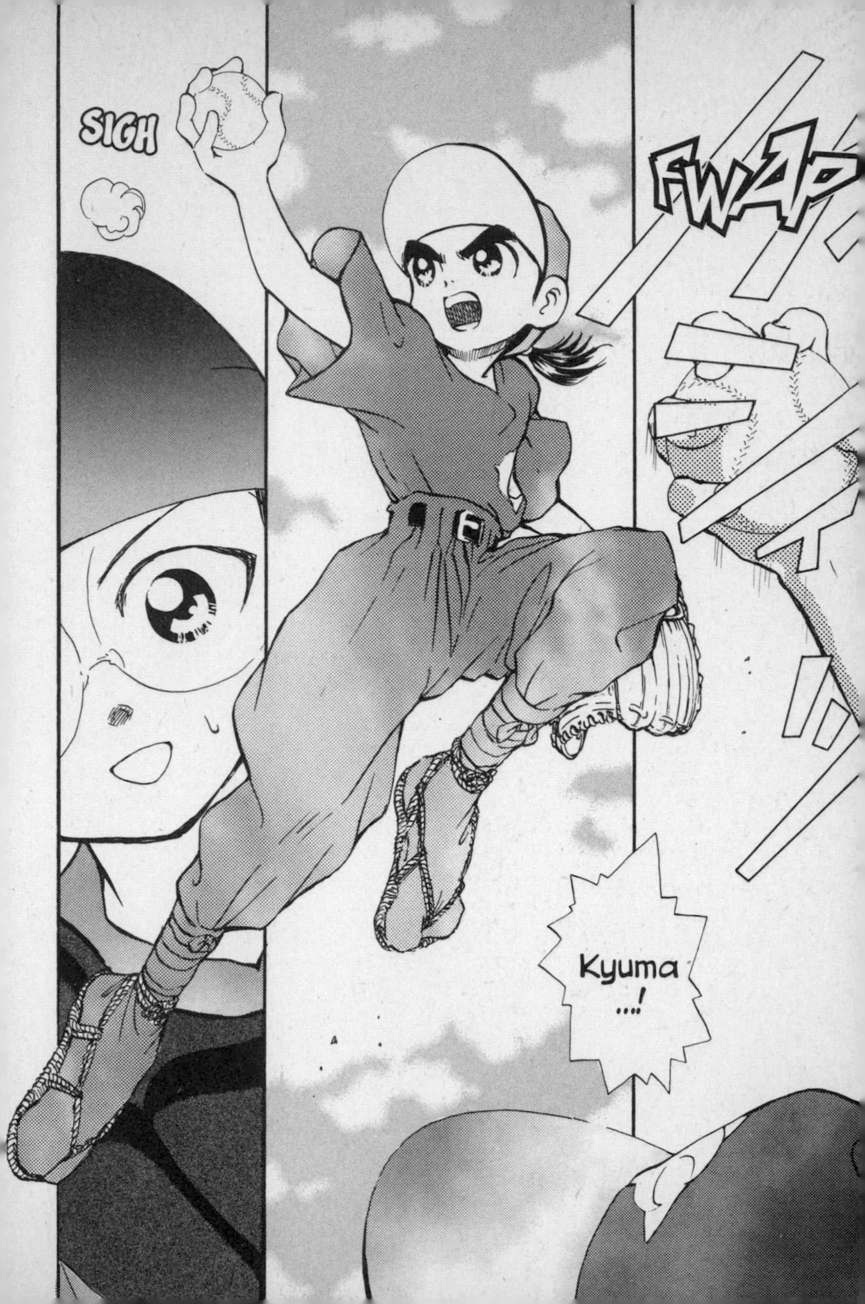
FWAP
Kyuma ...!
SIGH

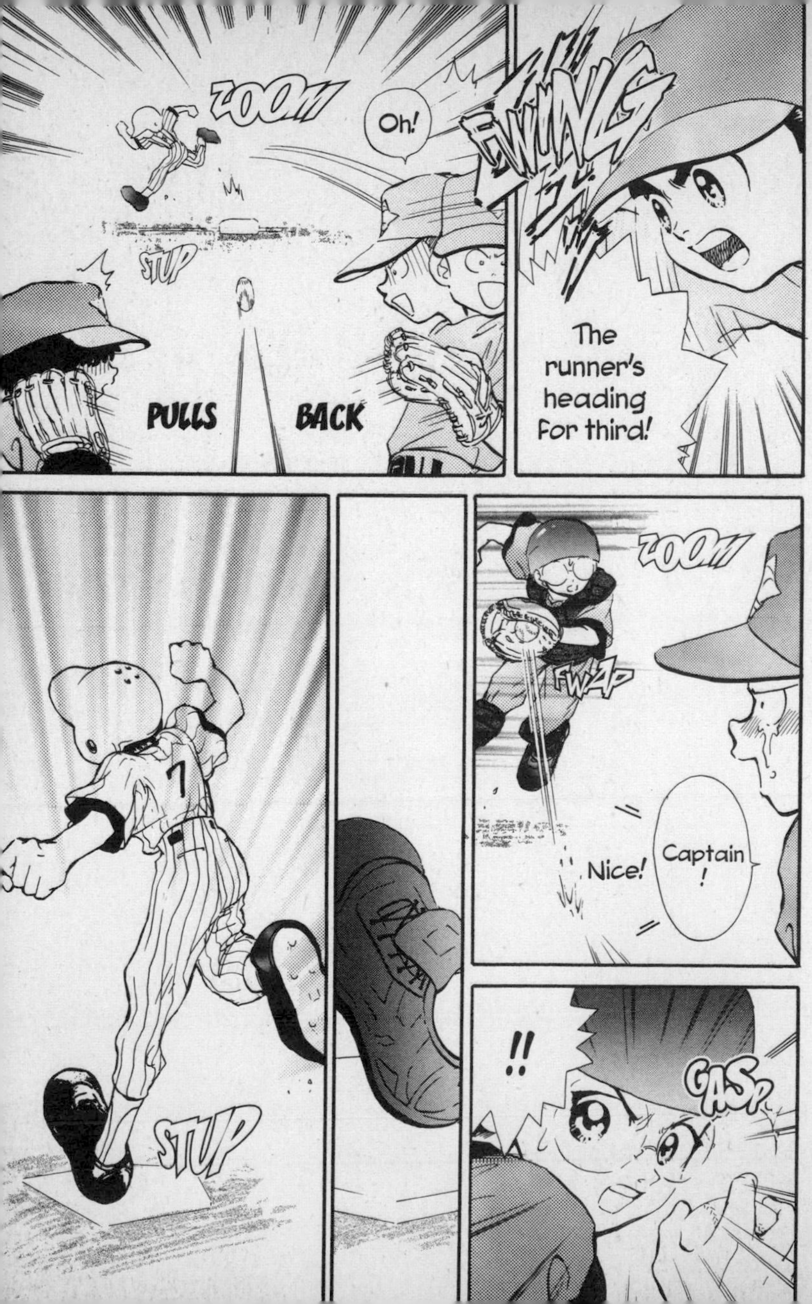
FWING
The runner's heading for third!
Oh!
ZOOM
STUP
PULLS BACK
ZOOM
FWAP
Captain!
Nice!
GASP
!!
STUP

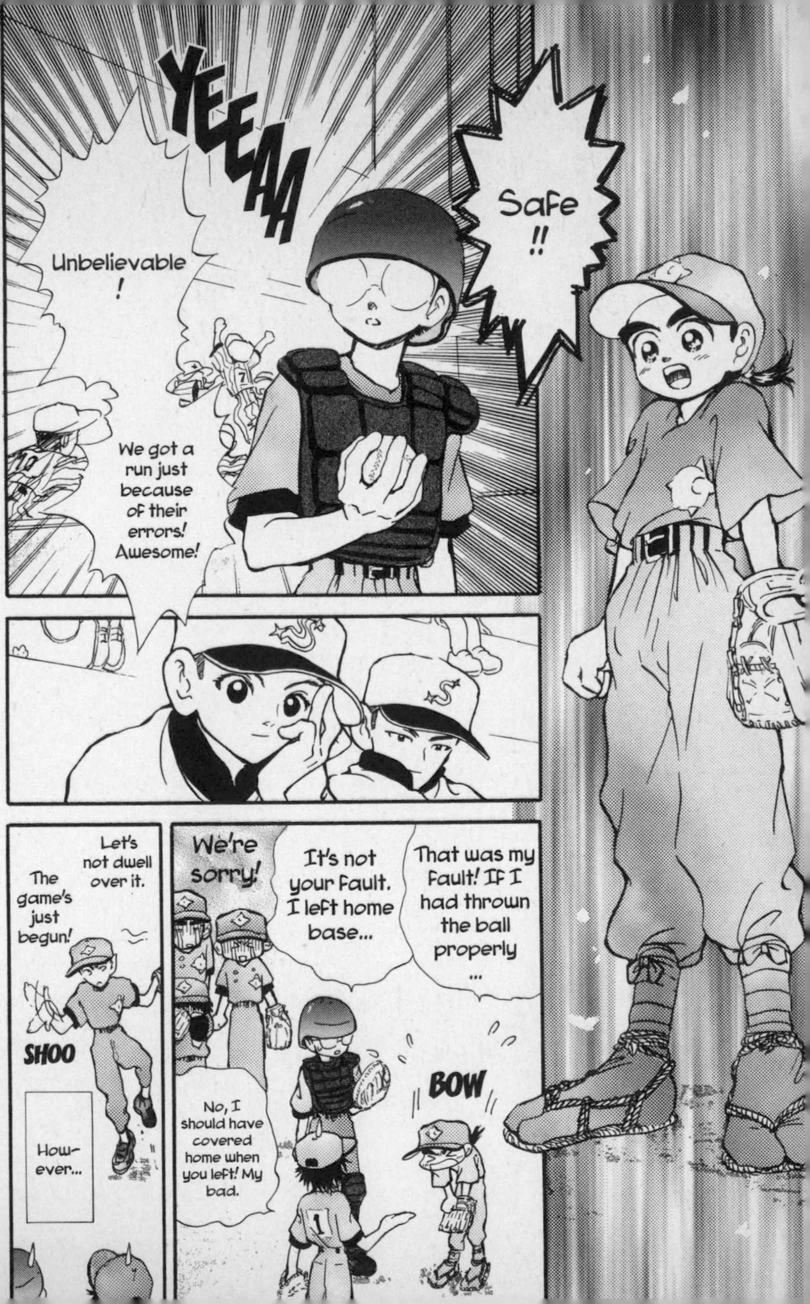
Safe !!
YEEAAA
Unbelievable !
We got a run just because of their errors! Awesome!
That was my fault! If I had thrown the ball properly ...
It's not your fault. I left home base...
We're sorry!
BOW
No, I should have covered home when you left! My bad.
Let's not dwell over it.
The game's just begun!
SHOO
How-ever...

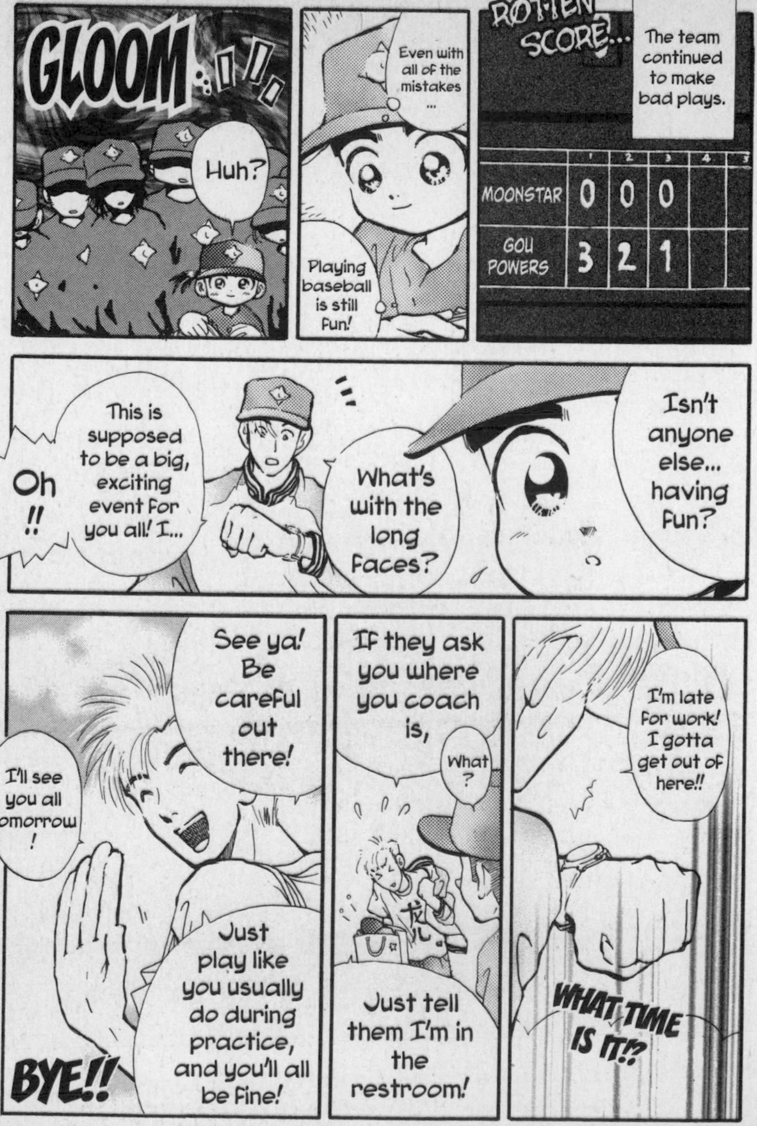
ROTTEN SCORE...
The team continued to make bad plays.
1 2 3 4 5
MOONSTAR 0 0 0
GOU POWERS 3 2 1
Even with all of the mistakes ...
Playing baseball is still fun!
GLOOM
Huh?
Isn't anyone else... having fun?
What's with the long faces?
This is supposed to be a big, exciting event for you all! I...
Oh !!
I'm late for work! I gotta get out of here!!
WHAT TIME IS IT!?
If they ask you where you coach is,
What ?
Just tell them I'm in the restroom!
See ya! Be careful out there!
I'll see you all tomorrow!
Just play like you usually do during practice, and you'll all be fine!
BYE!!

Read this way

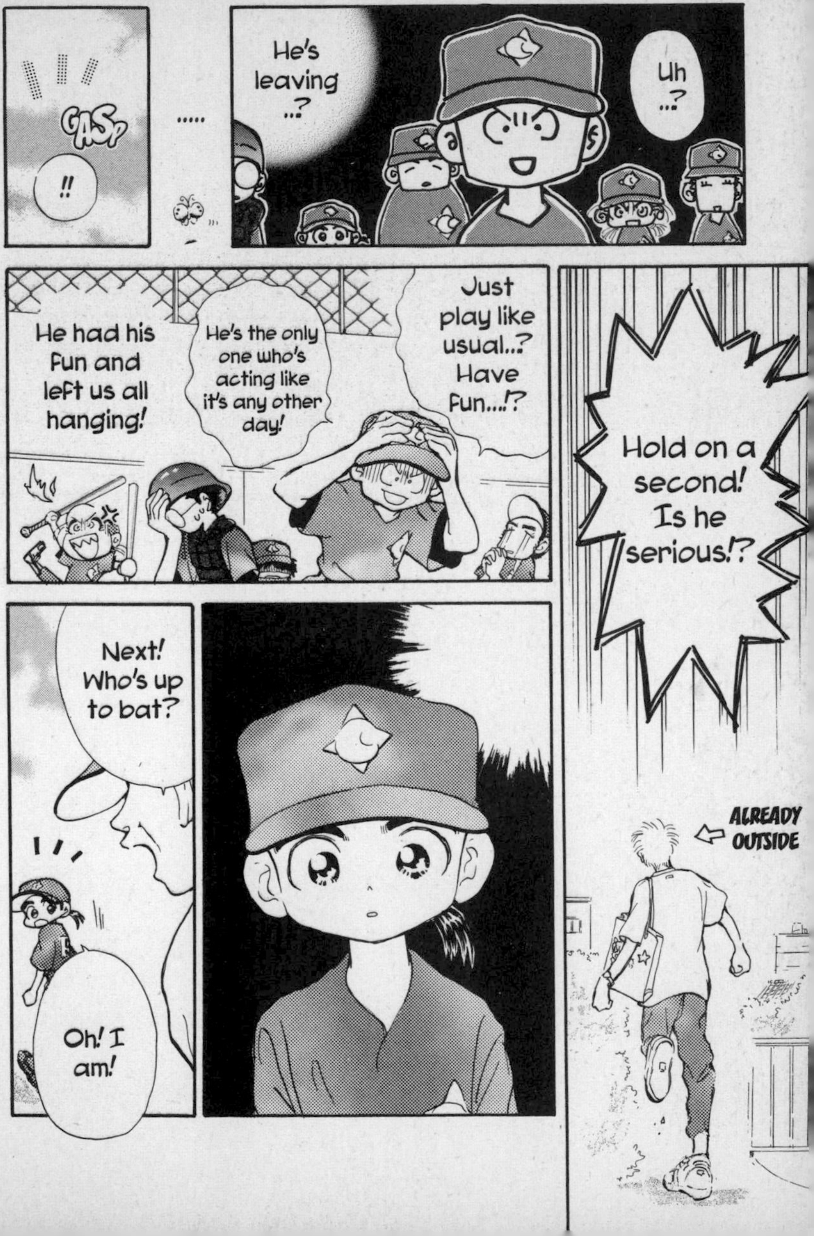

Uh ..?
He's leaving ..?
.....
GASP
!!
Hold on a second! Is he serious!?
ALREADY OUTSIDE
Just play like usual..? Have fun...!?
He's the only one who's acting like it's any other day!
He had his fun and left us all hanging!
Next! Who's up to bat?
Oh! I am!

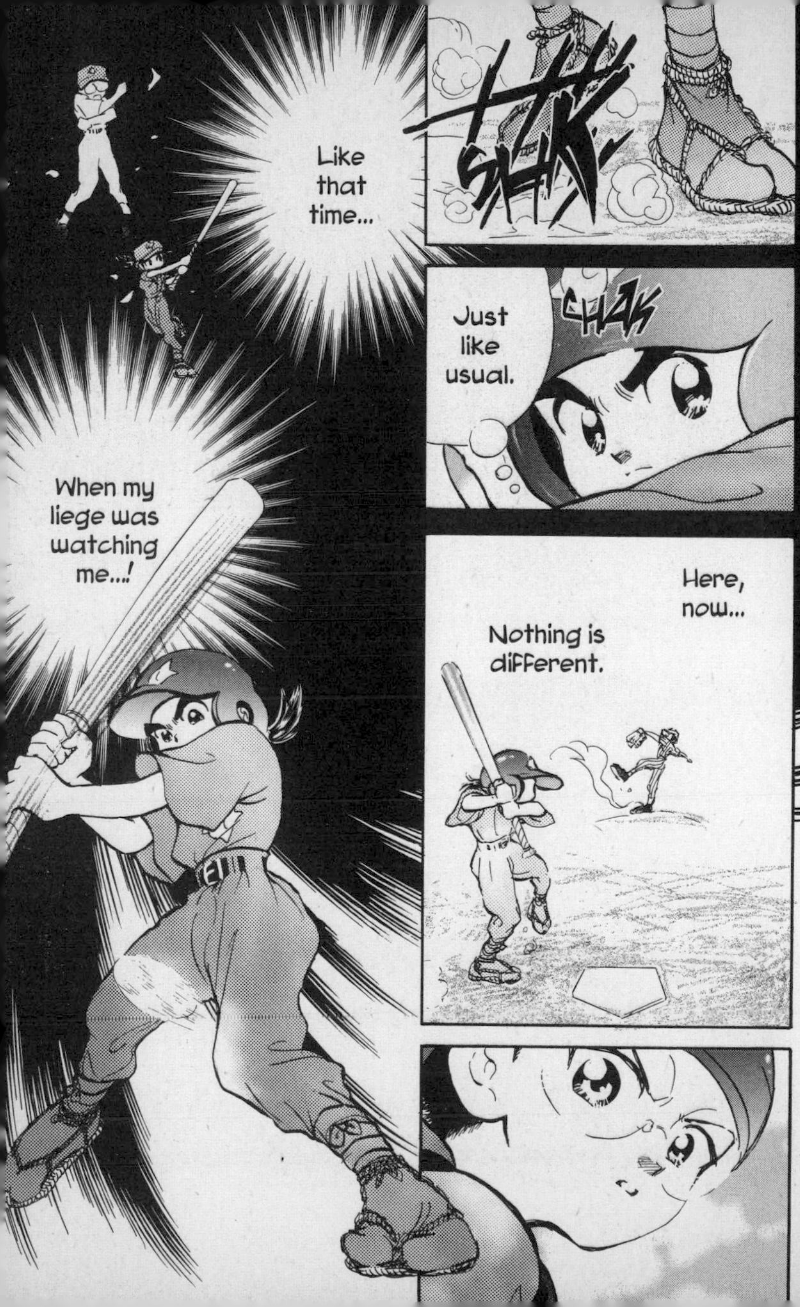
SHAK
CHAK
Just like usual.
Here, now...
Nothing is different.
Like that time...
When my liege was watching me...!

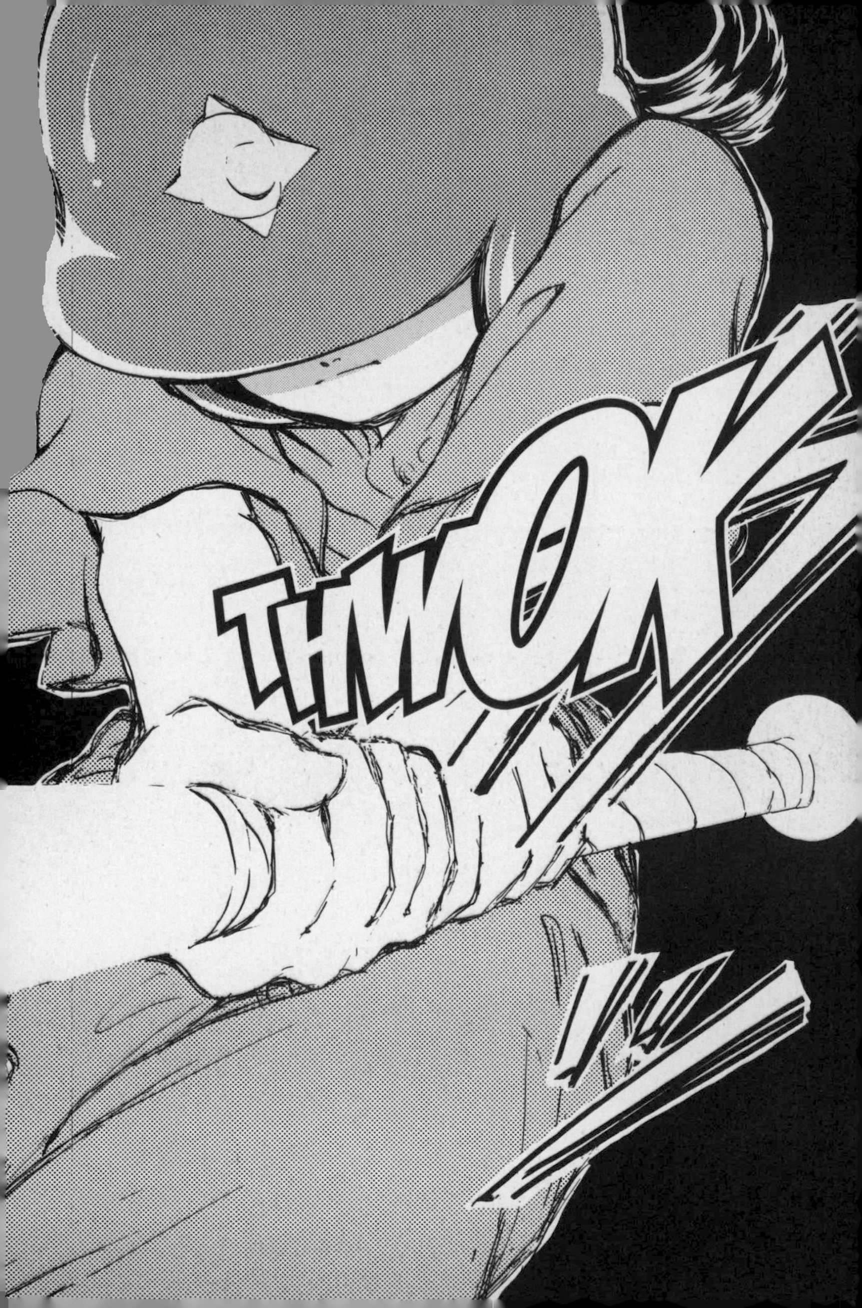
THWOK

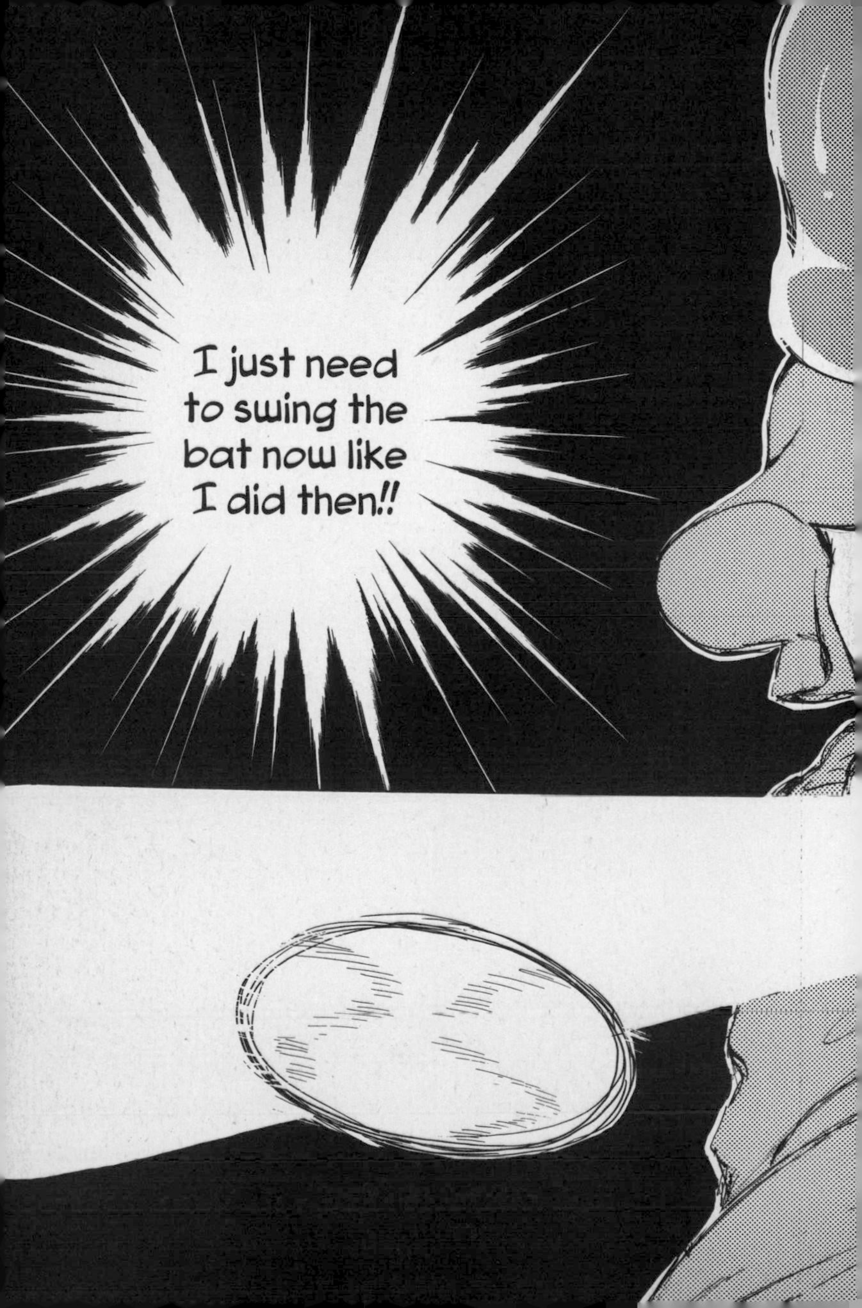
I just need to swing the bat now like I did then!!

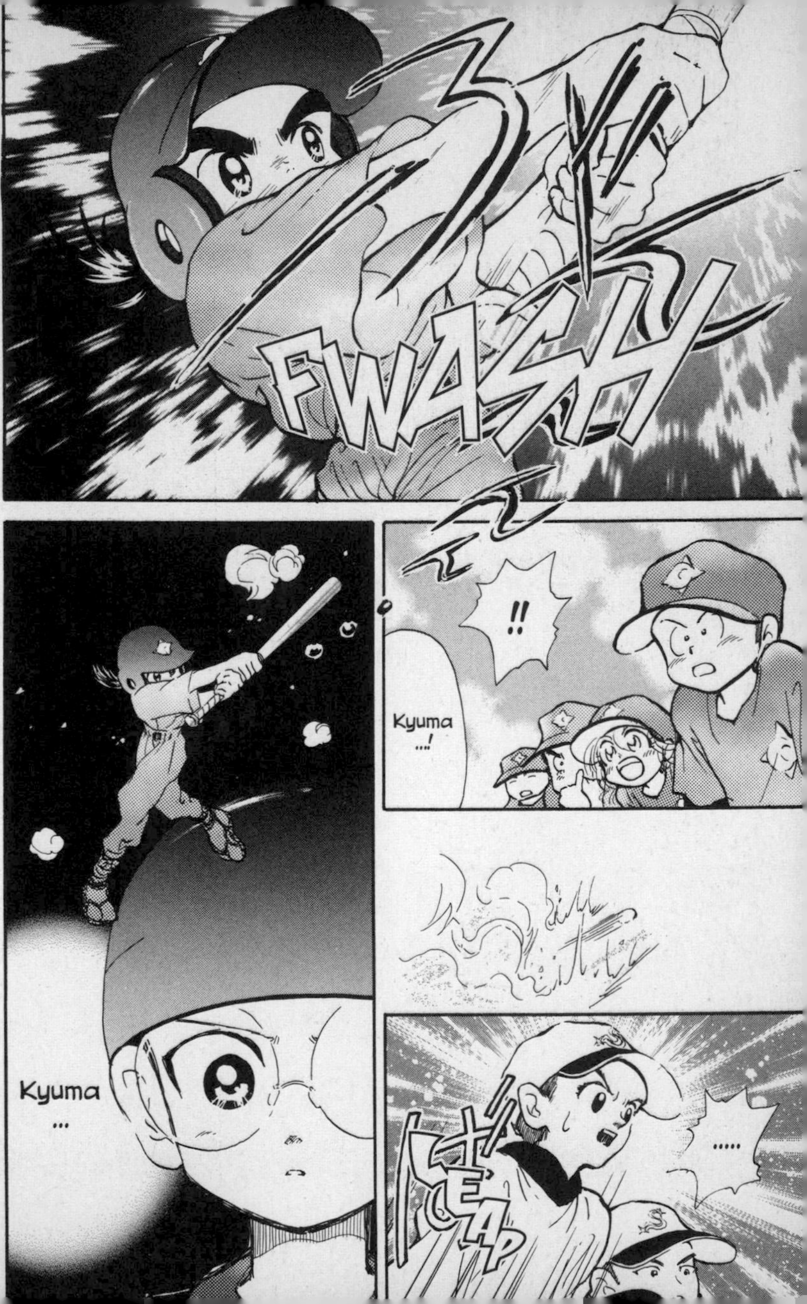
FWASH
!!
Kyuma ...!
LEAP
.....
Kyuma ...

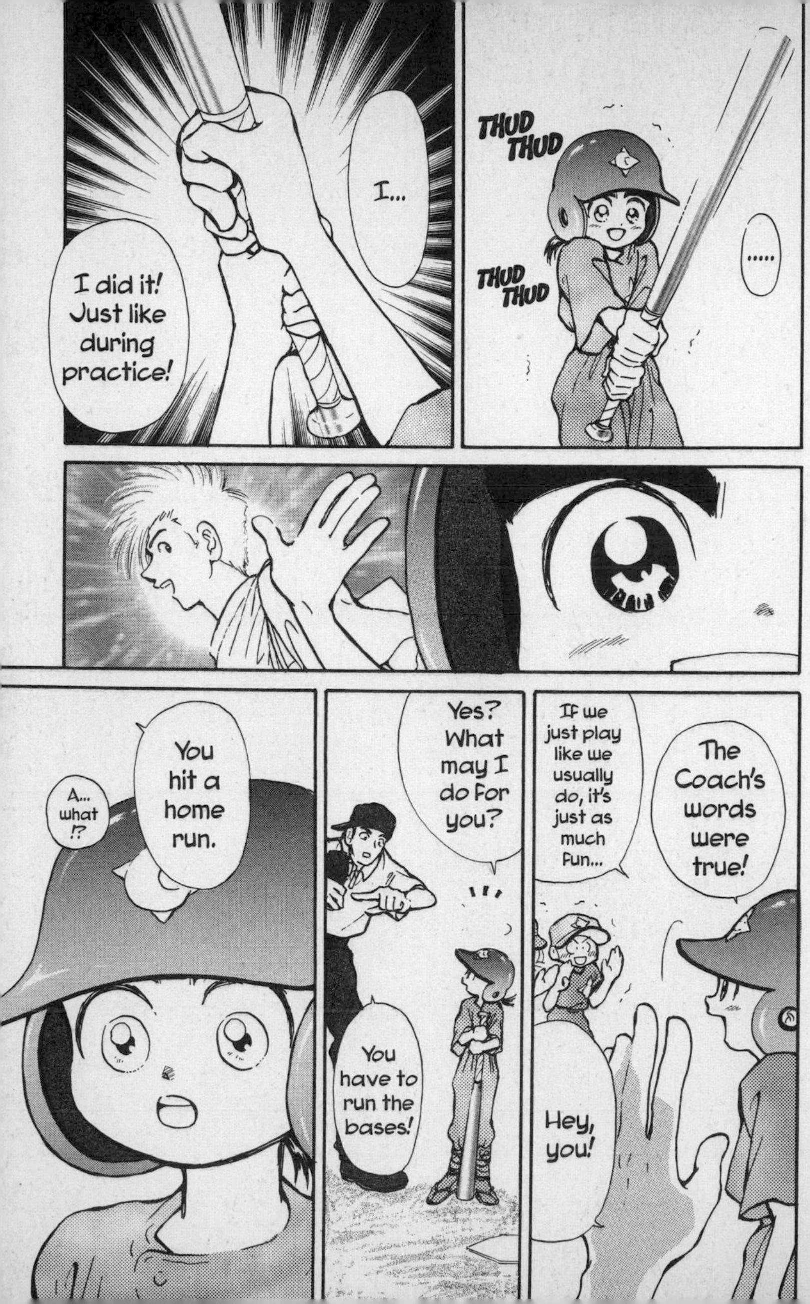
THUD THUD
THUD THUD
.....
I...
I did it! Just like during practice!
The Coach's words were true!
If we just play like we usually do, it's just as much fun...
Hey, you!
Yes? What may I do for you?
You have to run the bases!
You hit a home run.
A... what!?

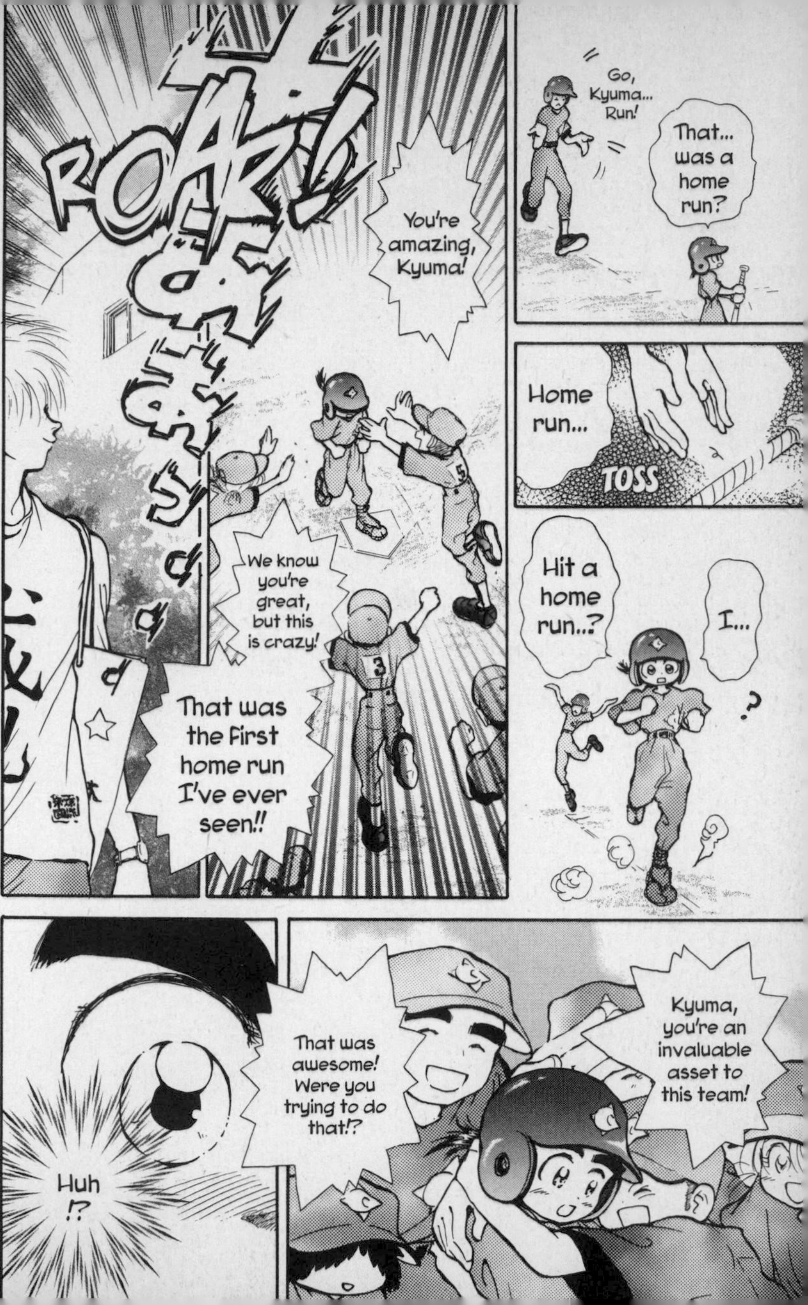
Go, Kyuma... Run!
That... was a home run?
Home run...
TOSS
I...
Hit a home run...?
?
ROAR!
You're amazing, Kyuma!
We know you're great, but this is crazy!
That was the first home run I've ever seen!!
Kyuma, you're an invaluable asset to this team!
That was awesome! Were you trying to do that!?
Huh!?

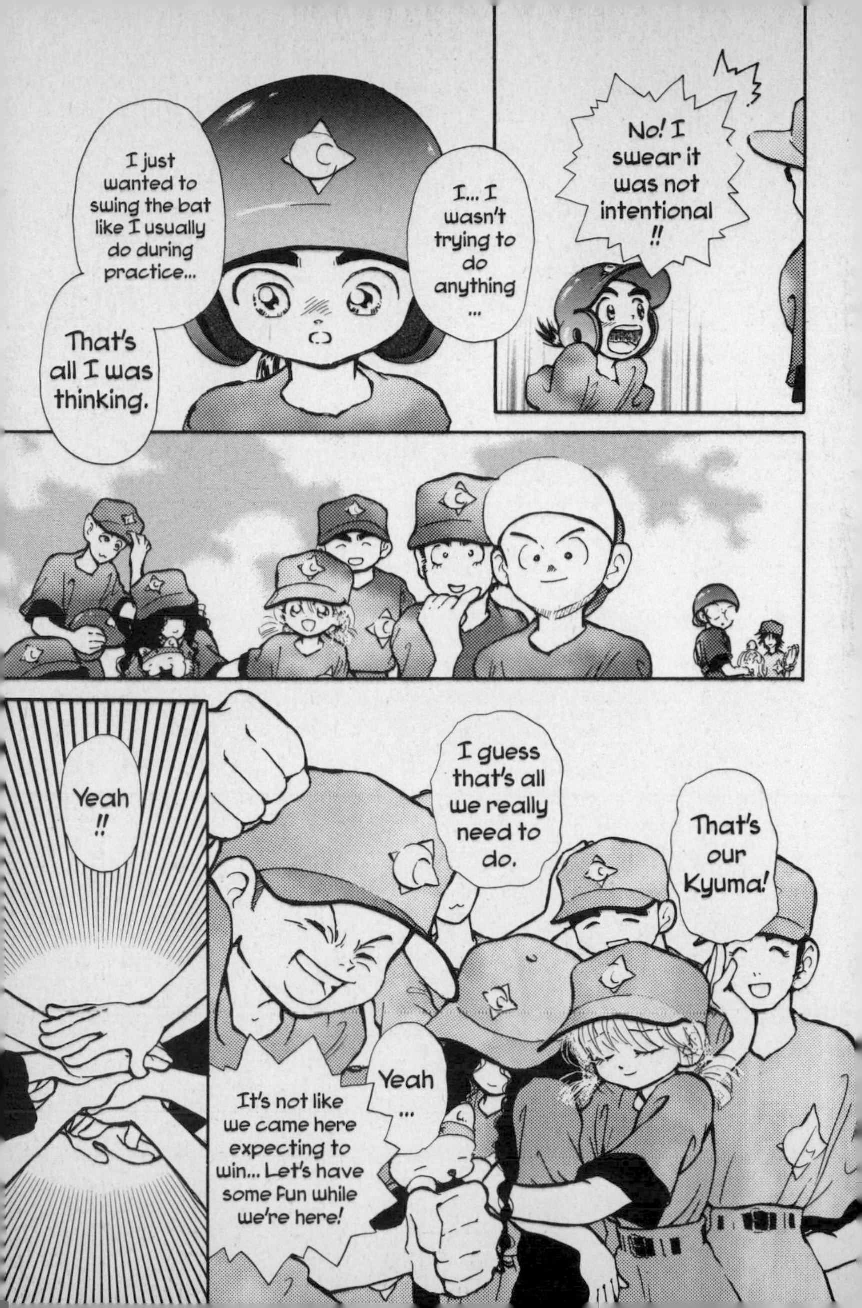
No! I swear it was not intentional!!
I... I wasn't trying to do anything...
I just wanted to swing the bat like I usually do during practice...
That's all I was thinking.
That's our Kyuma!
I guess that's all we really need to do.
Yeah...
It's not like we came here expecting to win... Let's have some fun while we're here!
Yeah!!

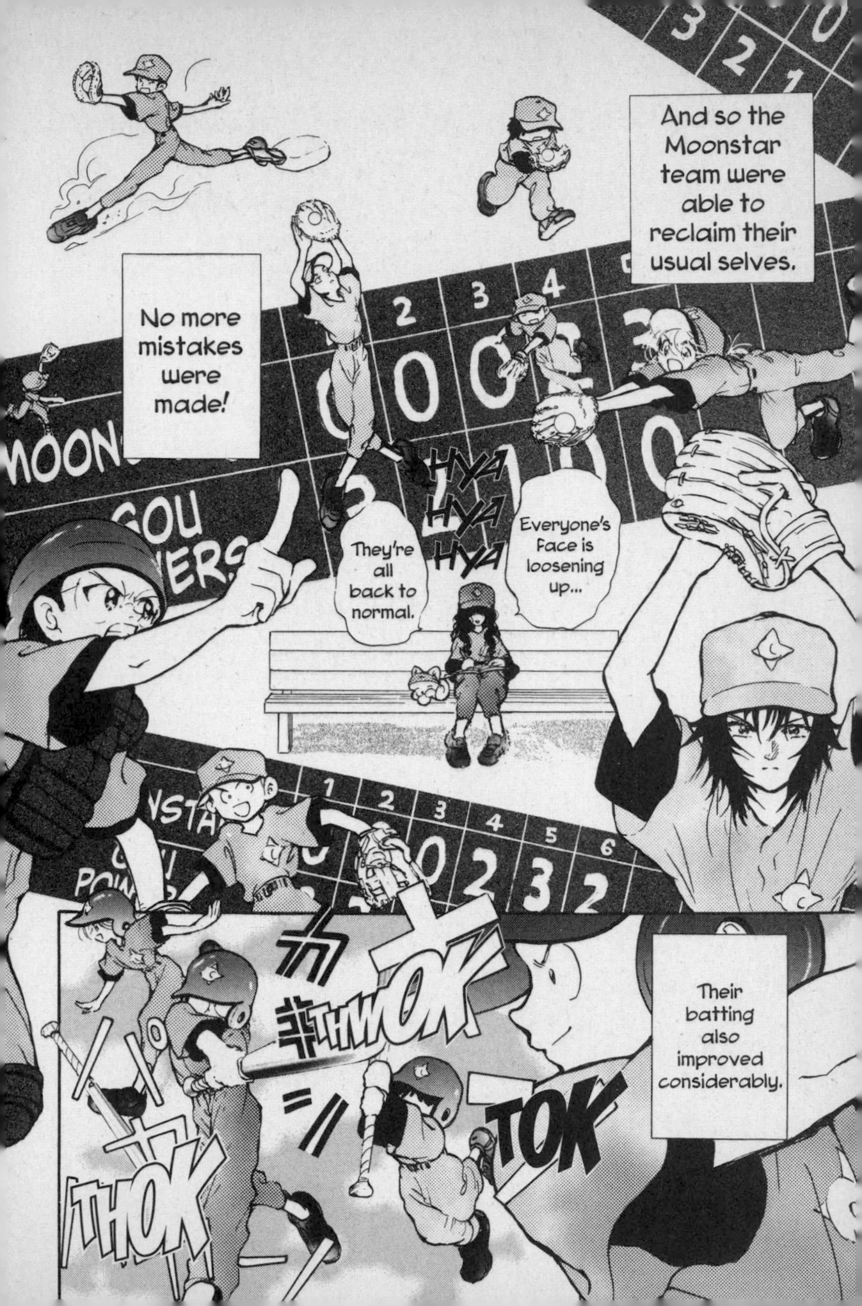
And so the Moonstar team were able to reclaim their usual selves.
No more mistakes were made!
Everyone's face is loosening up...
HYA HYA HYA
They're all back to normal.
Their batting also improved considerably.
TOK
THWOK
THOK

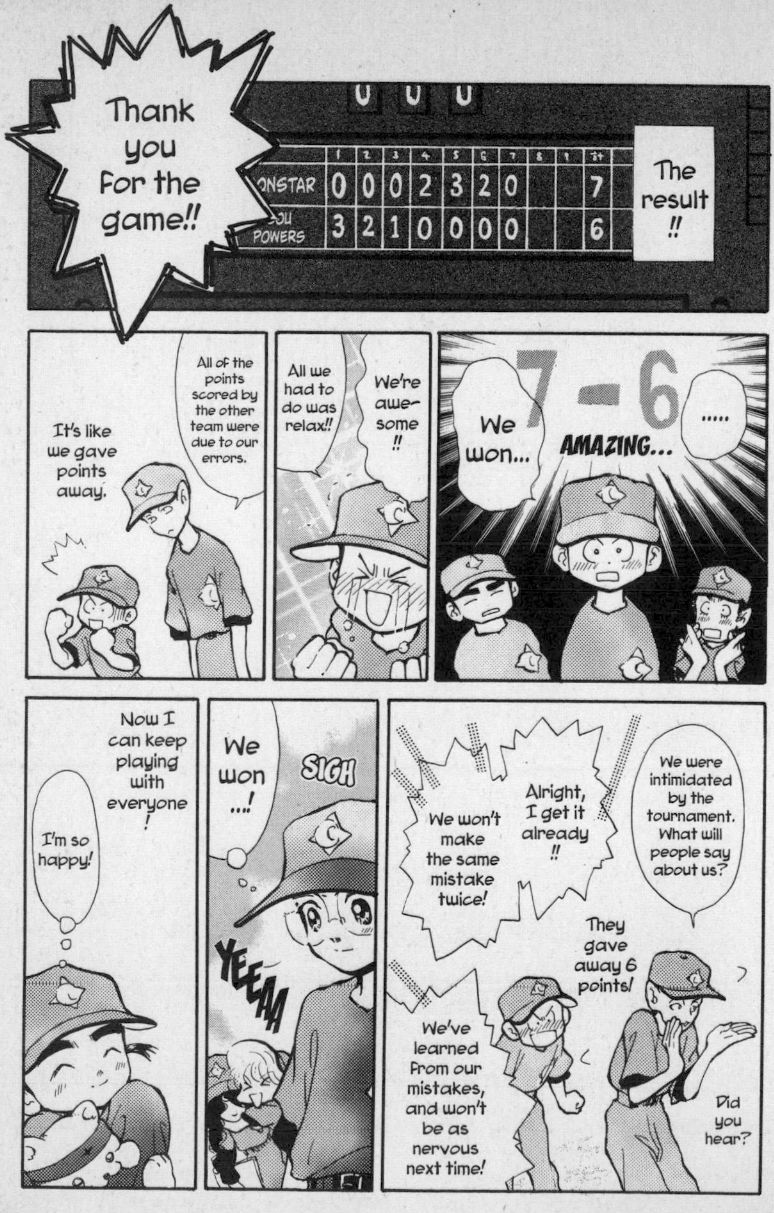

The result!!
Thank you for the game!!
.....
AMAZING...
We won...
7 - 6
We're awe-some!!
All we had to do was relax!!
All of the points scored by the other team were due to our errors.
It's like we gave points away.
We were intimidated by the tournament. What will people say about us?
Alright, I get it already!!
We won't make the same mistake twice!
They gave away 6 points!
Did you hear?
We've learned from our mistakes, and won't be as nervous next time!
SIGH
We won...!
YEEAAA
Now I can keep playing with everyone!
I'm so happy!

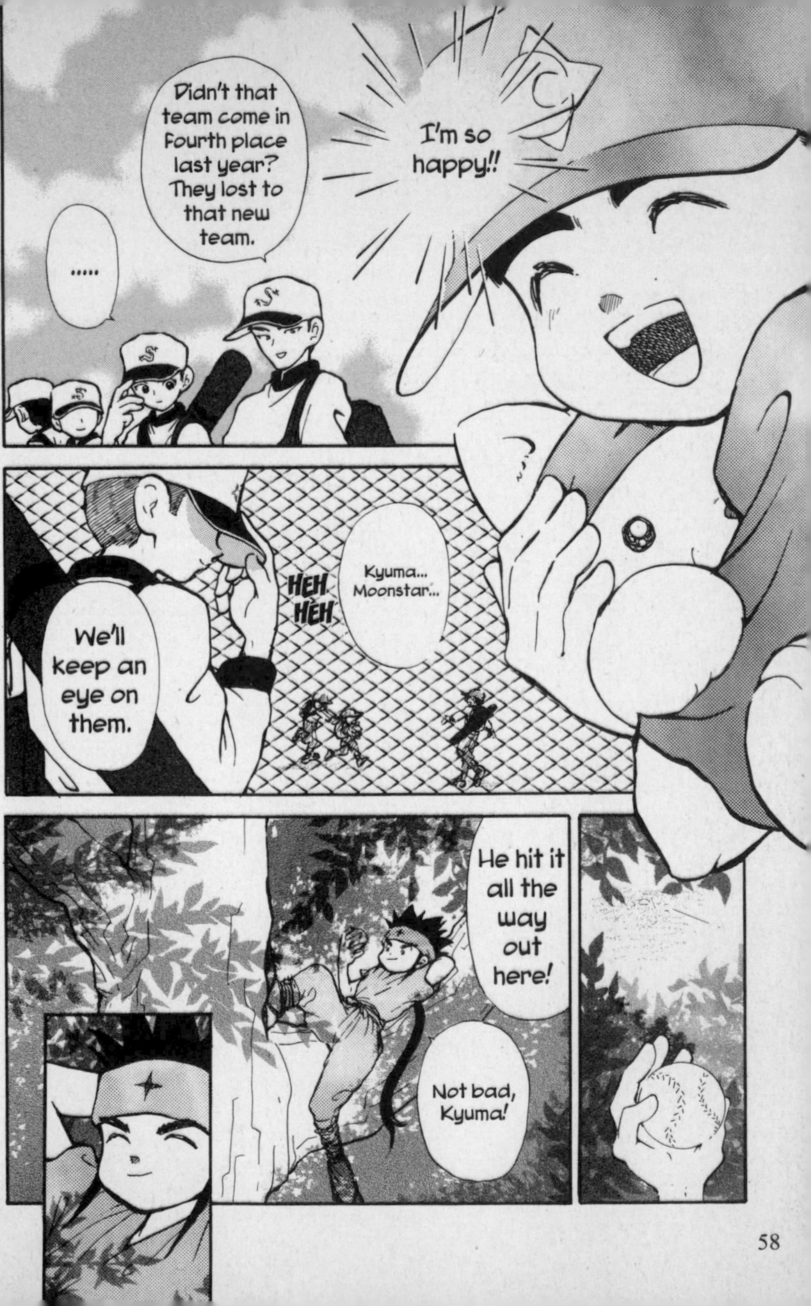
I'm so happy!!
Didn't that team come in fourth place last year? They lost to that new team.
.....
Kyuma... Moonstar...
HEH HEH
We'll keep an eye on them.
He hit it all the way out here!
Not bad, Kyuma!

PITCH 10 BYE FOR NOW!

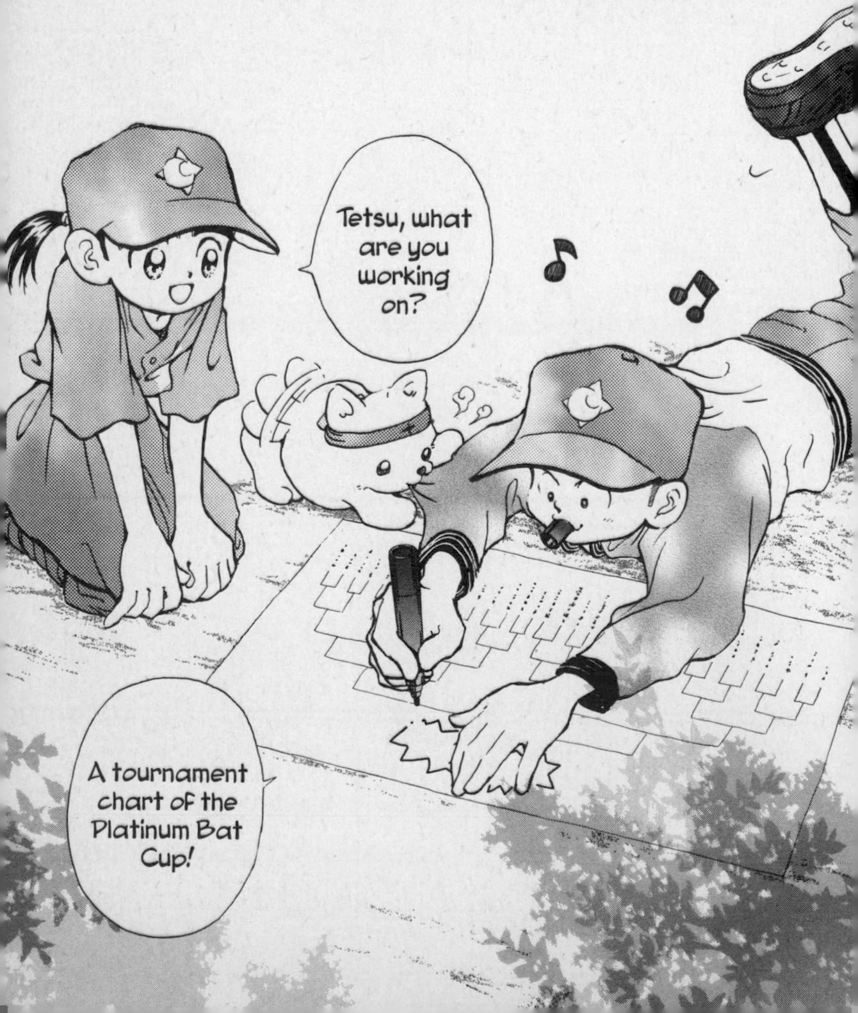
Tetsu, what are you working on?
A tournament chart of the Platinum Bat Cup!

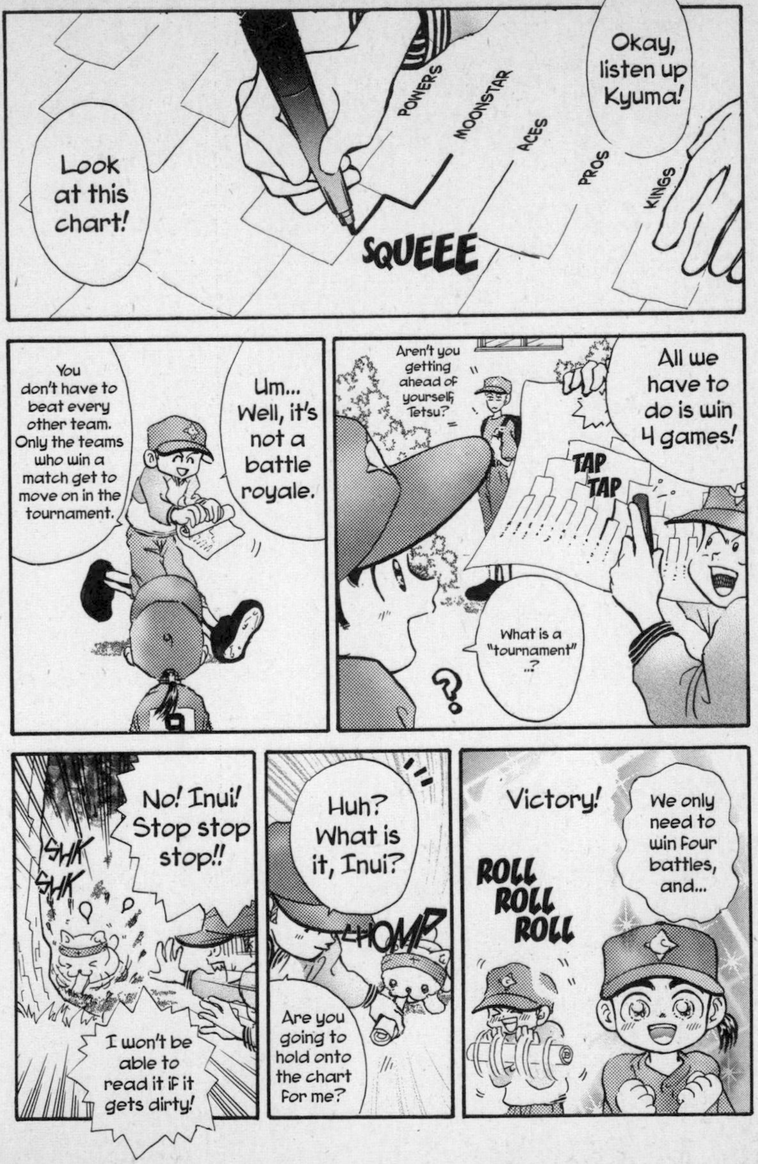
Okay, listen up Kyuma!
KINGS
PROS
ACES
MOONSTAR
POWERS
SQUEEE
Look at this chart!
All we have to do is win 4 games!
TAP TAP
Aren't you getting ahead of yourself, Tetsu?
What is a "tournament"...?
Um... Well, it's not a battle royale.
You don't have to beat every other team. Only the teams who win a match get to move on in the tournament.
We only need to win four battles, and...
Victory!
ROLL ROLL ROLL
Huh? What is it, Inui?
CHOMP
Are you going to hold onto the chart for me?
No! Inui! Stop stop stop!!
SHK SHK
I won't be able to read it if it gets dirty!

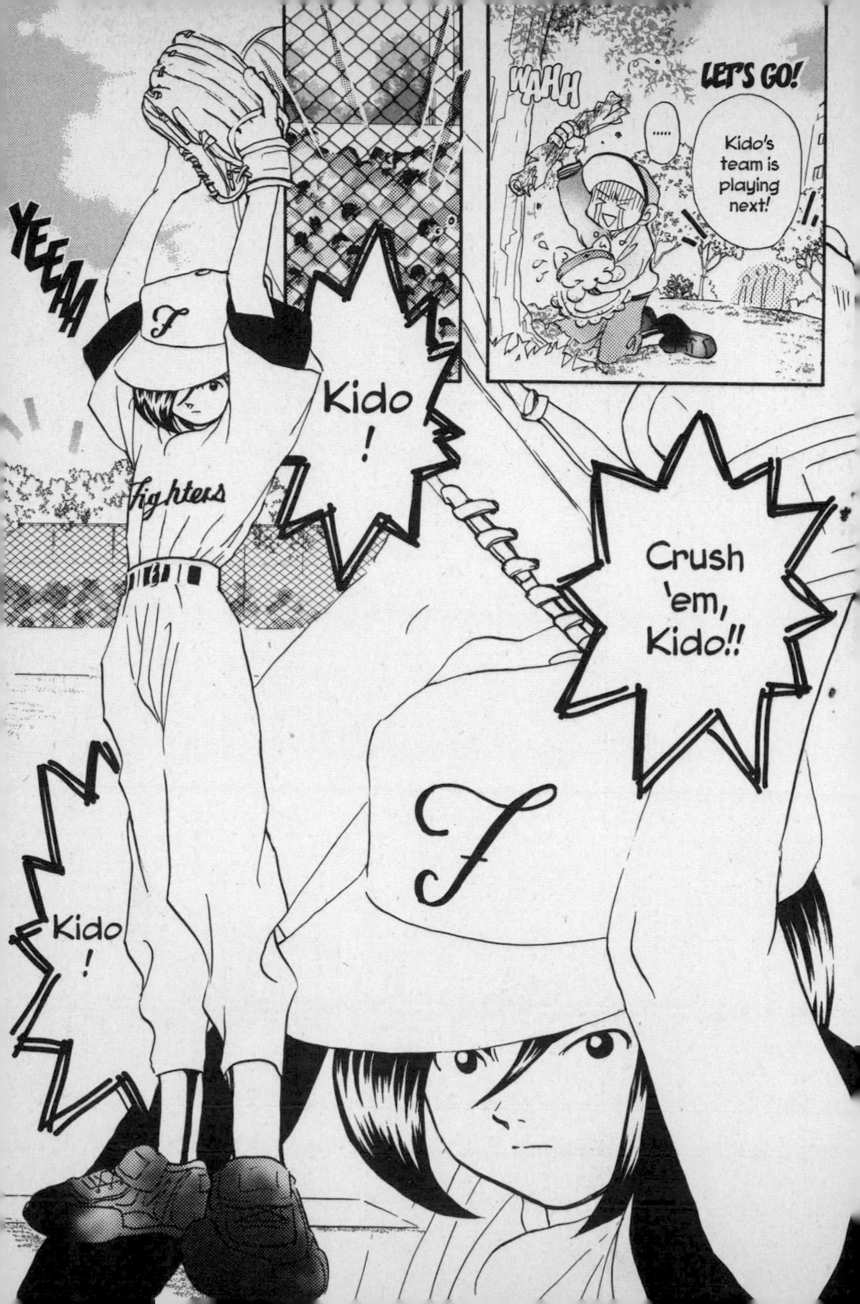
LET'S GO!
Kido's team is playing next!
.....
WAHH
Kido!
Crush 'em, Kido!!
YEEAAA
Kido!

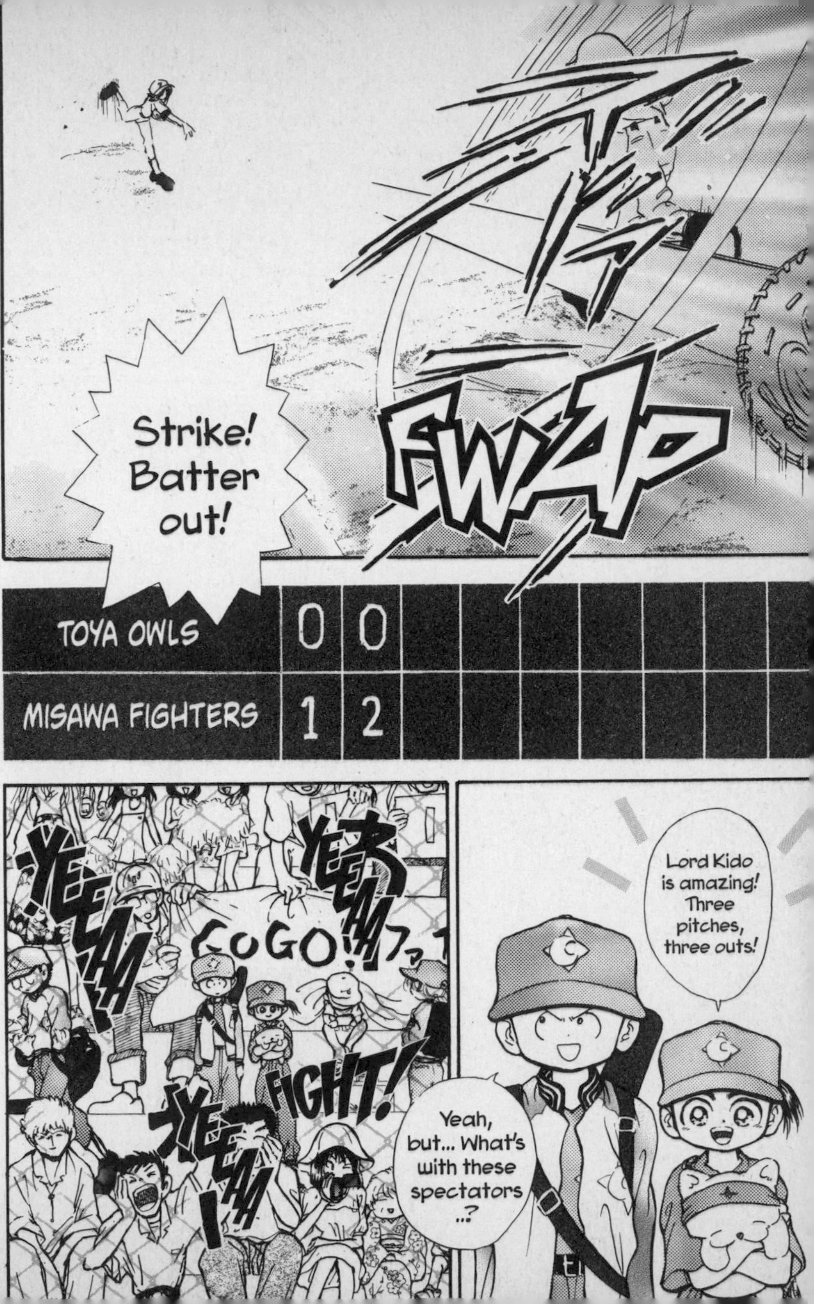
FWAP
Strike! Batter out!
TOYA OWLS 0 0
MISAWA FIGHTERS 1 2
Lord Kido is amazing! Three pitches, three outs!
Yeah, but... What's with these spectators ..?
YEEEAAA
YEEEAAA
GOGO!!
FIGHT!
YEEEAAA!

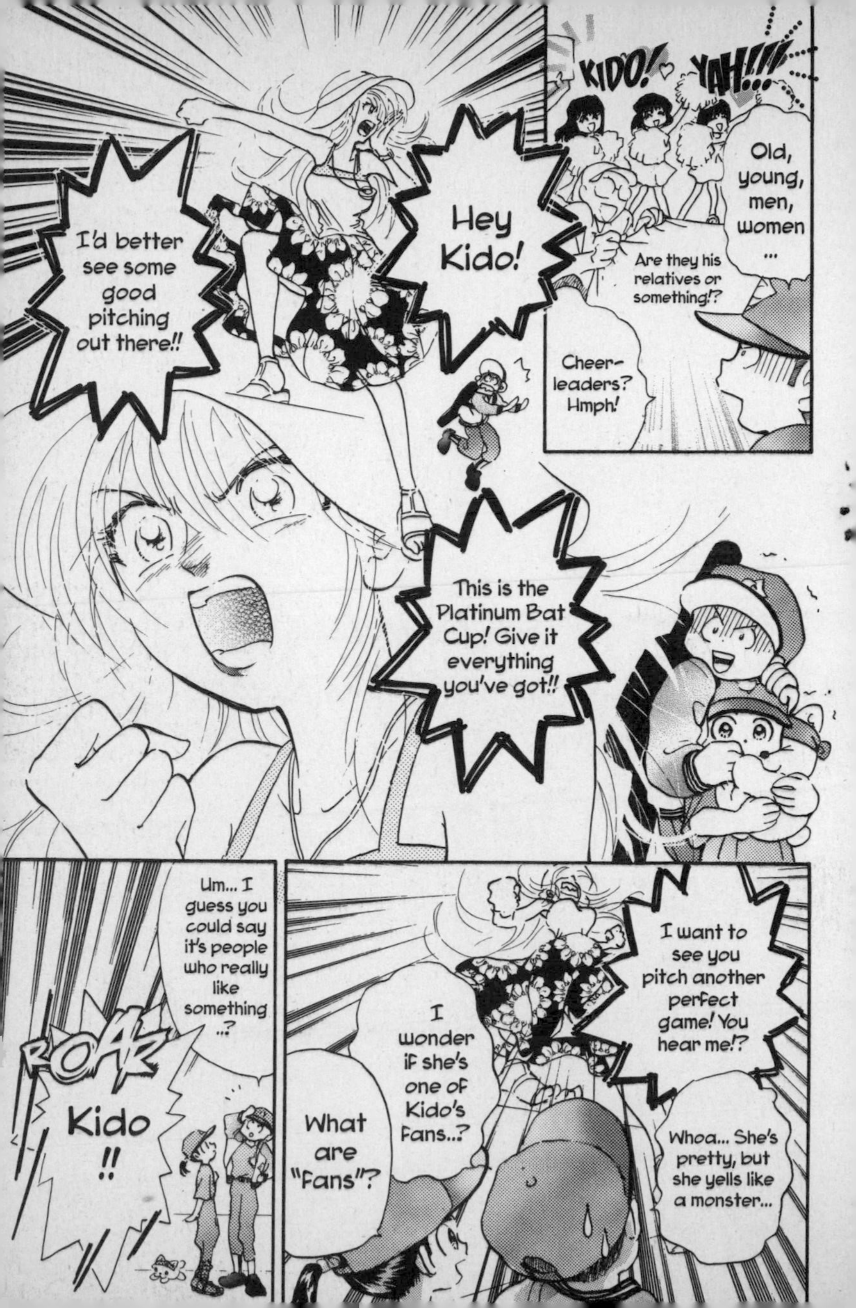

KIDO! YAH!!!!
Old, young, men, women ...
Are they his relatives or something!?
Cheer-leaders? Hmph!
Hey Kido!
I'd better see some good pitching out there!!
This is the Platinum Bat Cup! Give it everything you've got!!
I want to see you pitch another perfect game! You hear me!?
Whoa... She's pretty, but she yells like a monster...
I wonder if she's one of Kido's fans...?
What are "fans"?
Um... I guess you could say it's people who really like something ..?
ROAR
Kido !!

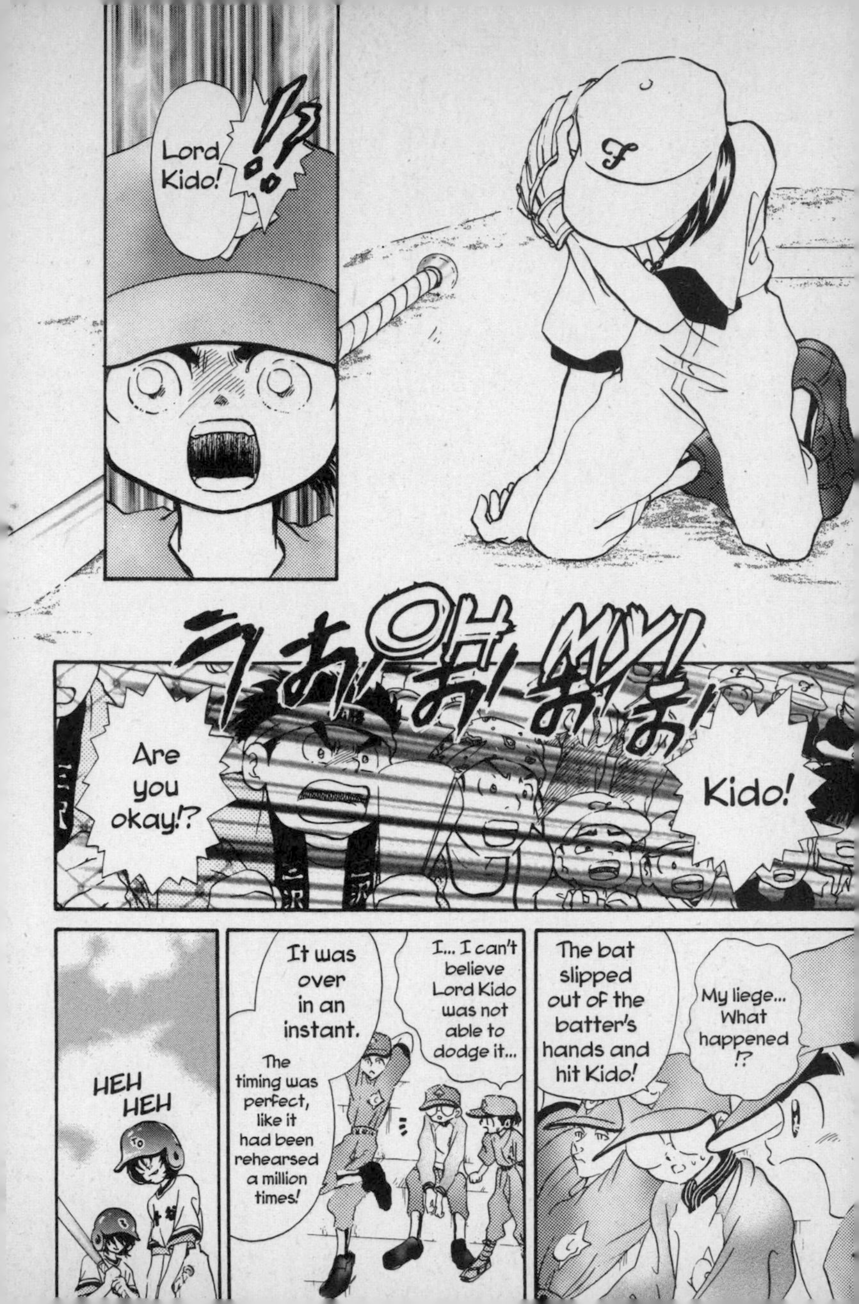
!?
Lord Kido!
OH MY!
Kido!
Are you okay!?
My liege... What happened!?
The bat slipped out of the batter's hands and hit Kido!
I... I can't believe Lord Kido was not able to dodge it...
It was over in an instant.
The timing was perfect, like it had been rehearsed a million times!
HEH HEH

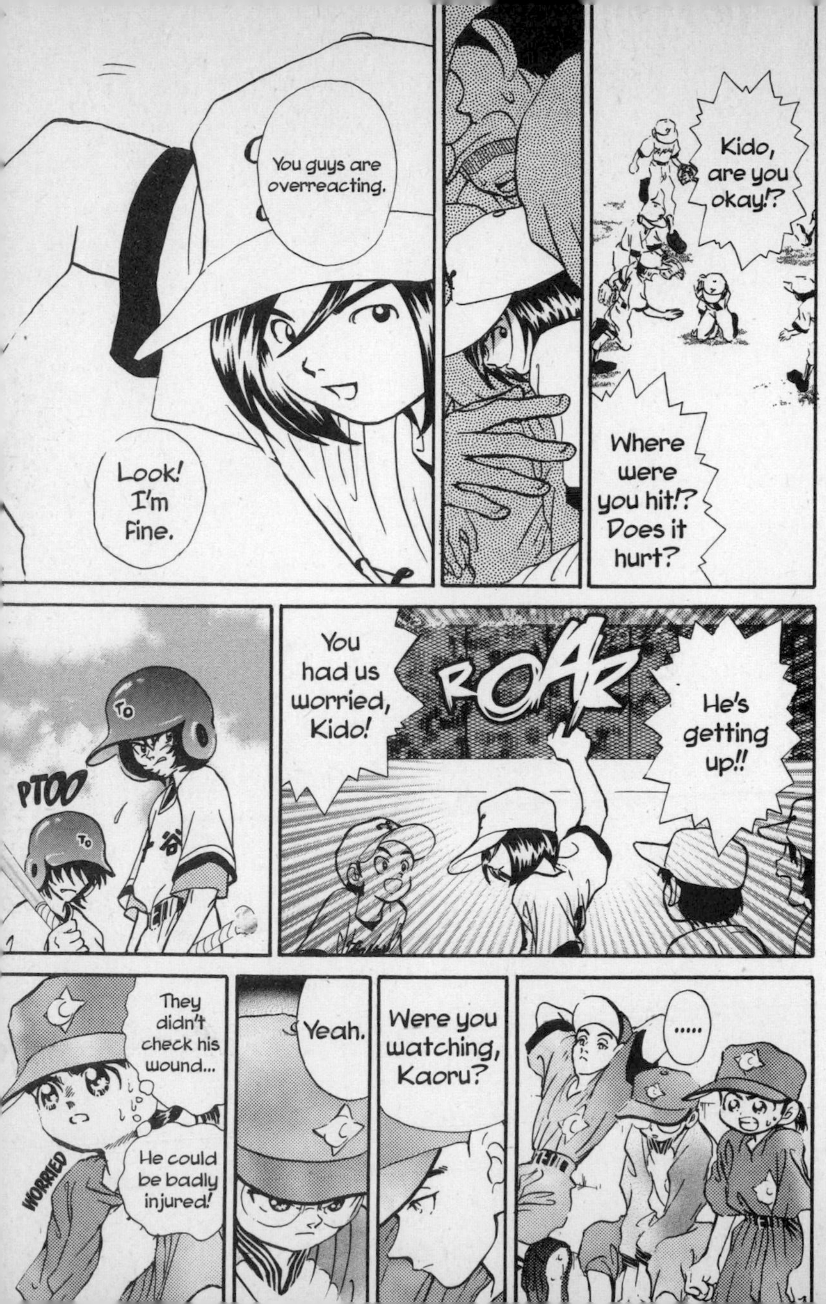

Kido, are you okay!?
Where were you hit!? Does it hurt?
You guys are overreacting.
Look! I'm fine.
He's getting up!!
ROAR
You had us worried, Kido!
PTOO
.....
Were you watching, Kaoru?
Yeah.
They didn't check his wound...
He could be badly injured!
WORRIED

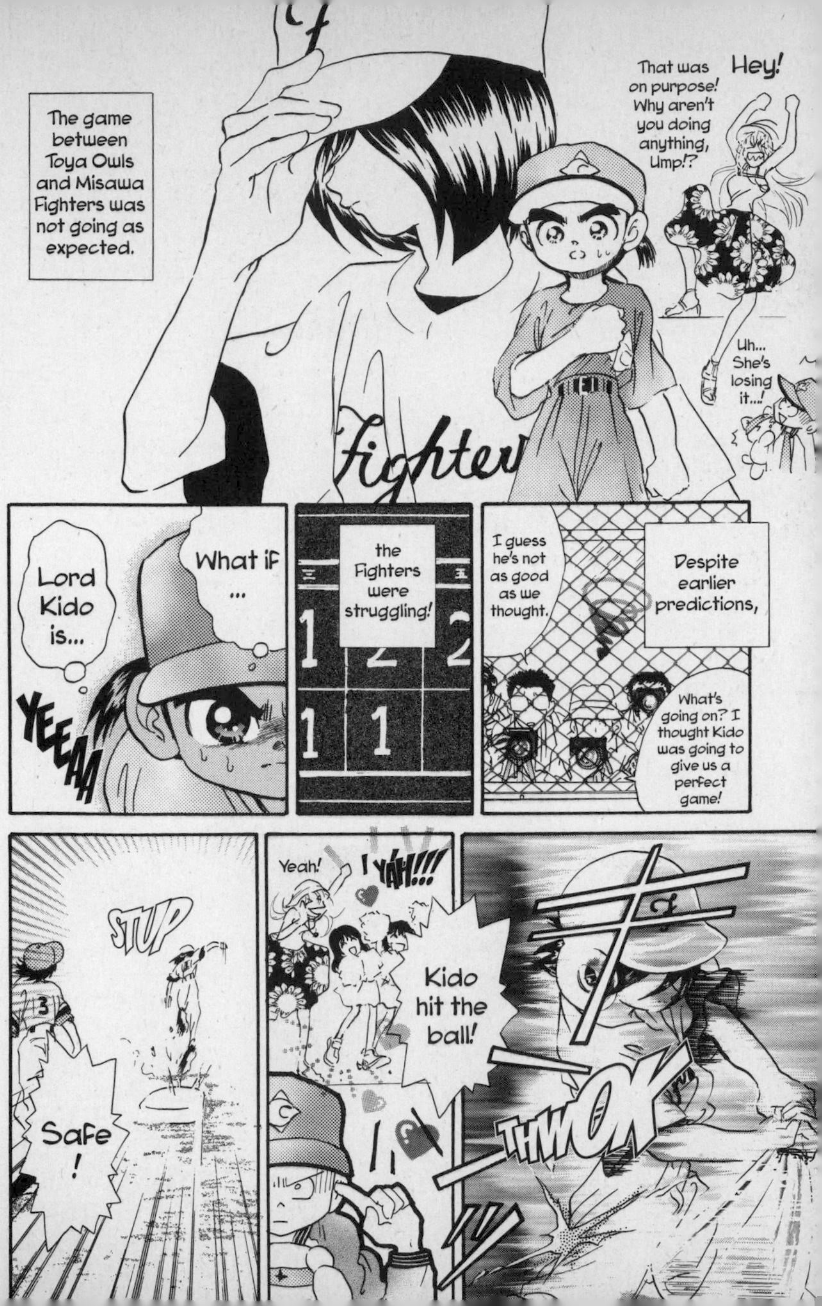
Hey!
That was on purpose! Why aren't you doing anything, Ump!?
Uh... She's losing it...!
The game between Toya Owls and Misawa Fighters was not going as expected.
Fighters
Despite earlier predictions,
I guess he's not as good as we thought.
What's going on? I thought Kido was going to give us a perfect game!
the Fighters were struggling!
What if ...
Lord Kido is...
YEEAAA
THWOK
I YAH!!!
Yeah!
Kido hit the ball!
STUP
Safe!

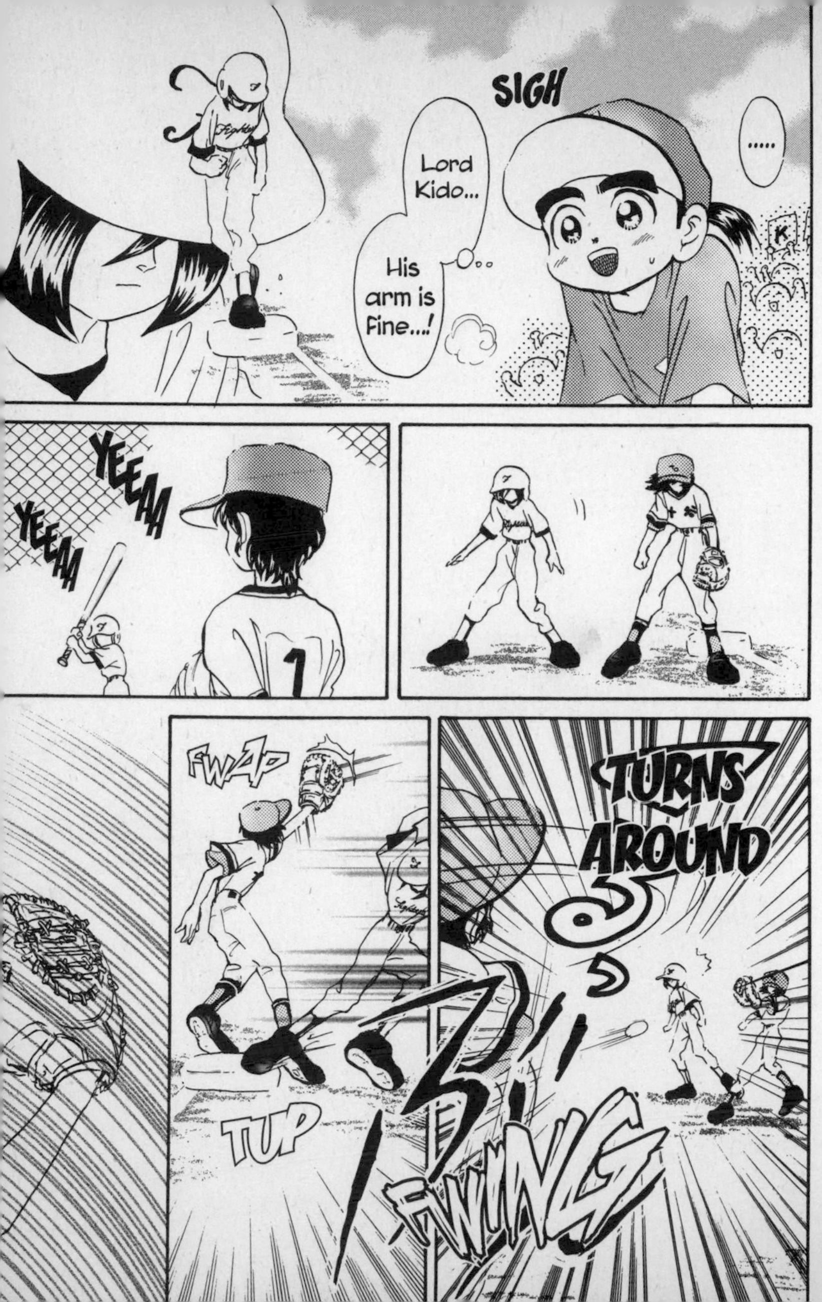
......
SIGH
Lord Kido...
His arm is fine...!
YEEAAA
YEEAAA
TURNS AROUND
SWING
FWAP
TUP

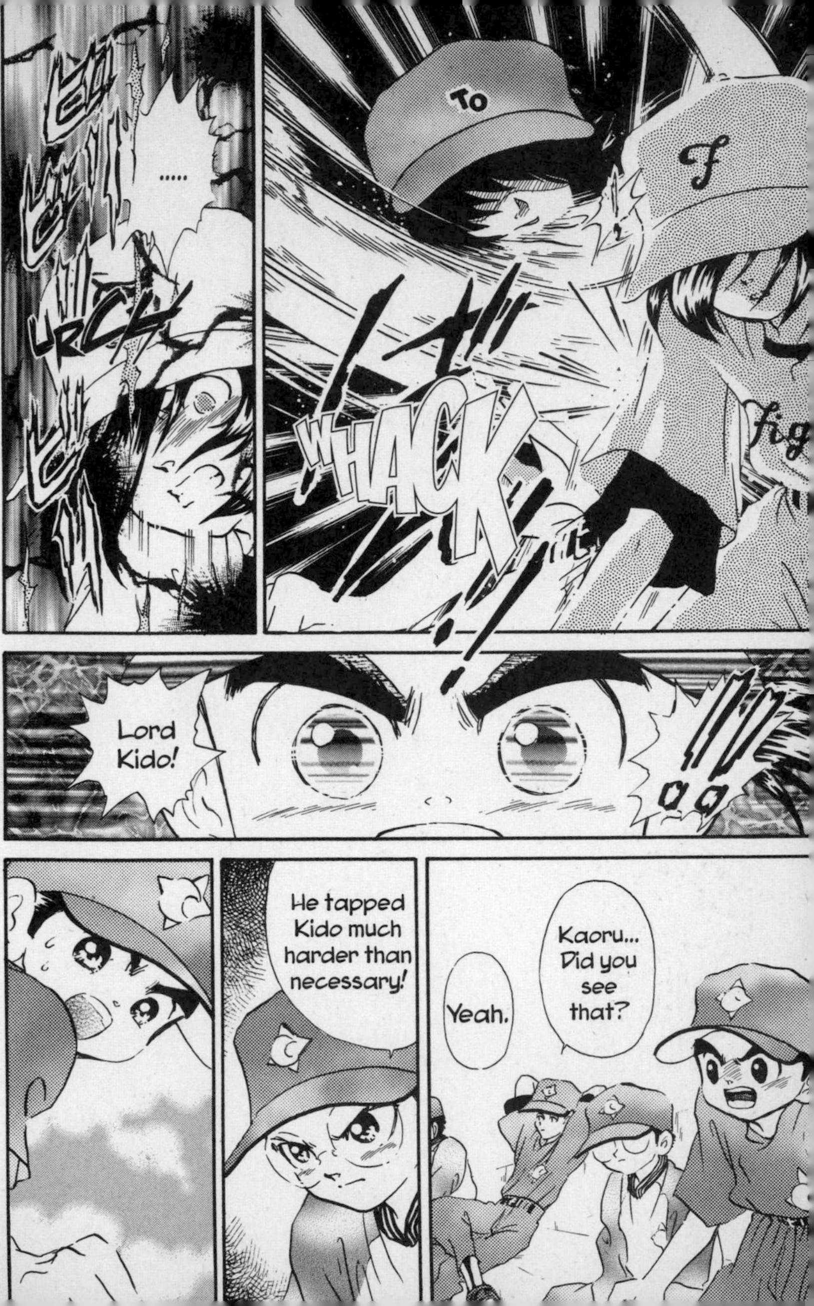
WHACK
.....
Lord Kido!
Kaoru... Did you see that?
Yeah.
He tapped Kido much harder than necessary!

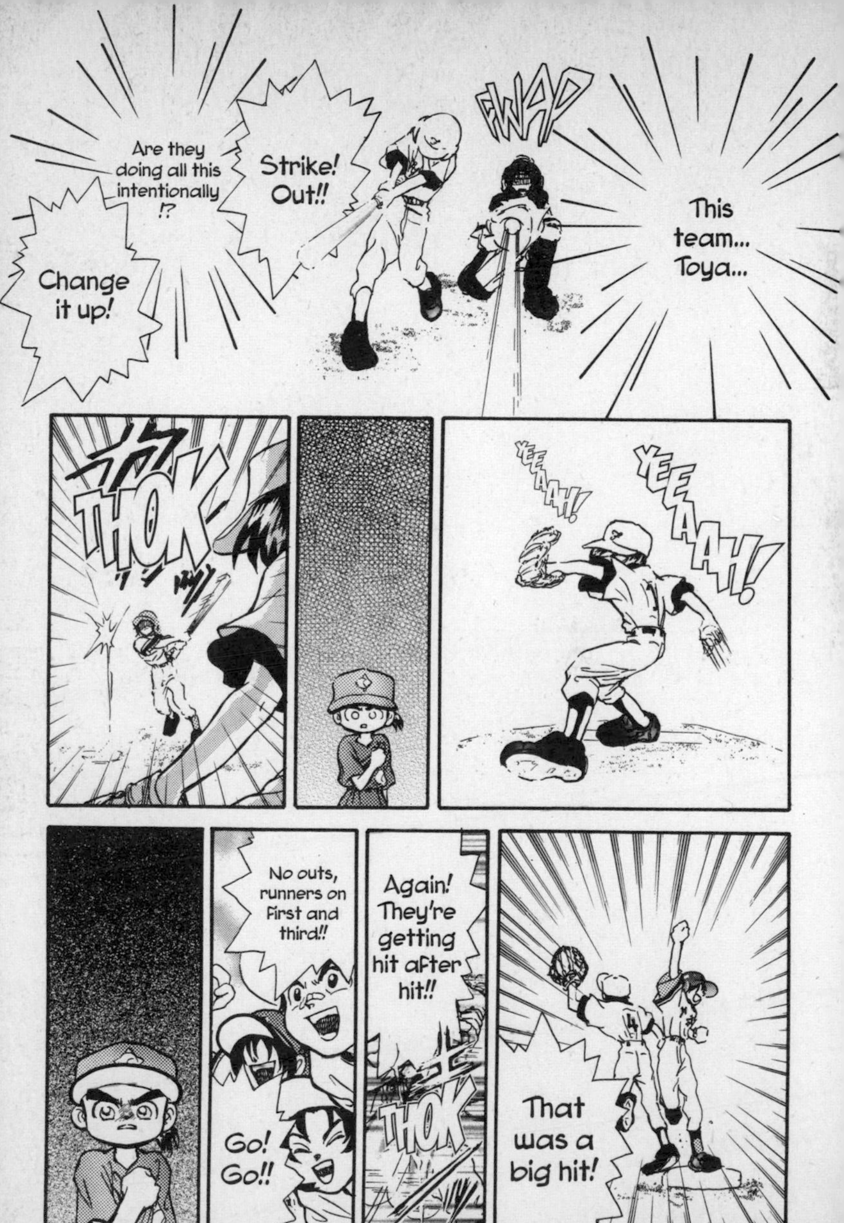
This team... Toya...
FWAP
Strike! Out!!
Are they doing all this intentionally!?
Change it up!
YEEAAAH!
YEEAAH!
THOK
That was a big hit!
Again! They're getting hit after hit!!
THOK
No outs, runners on first and third!!
Go! Go!!

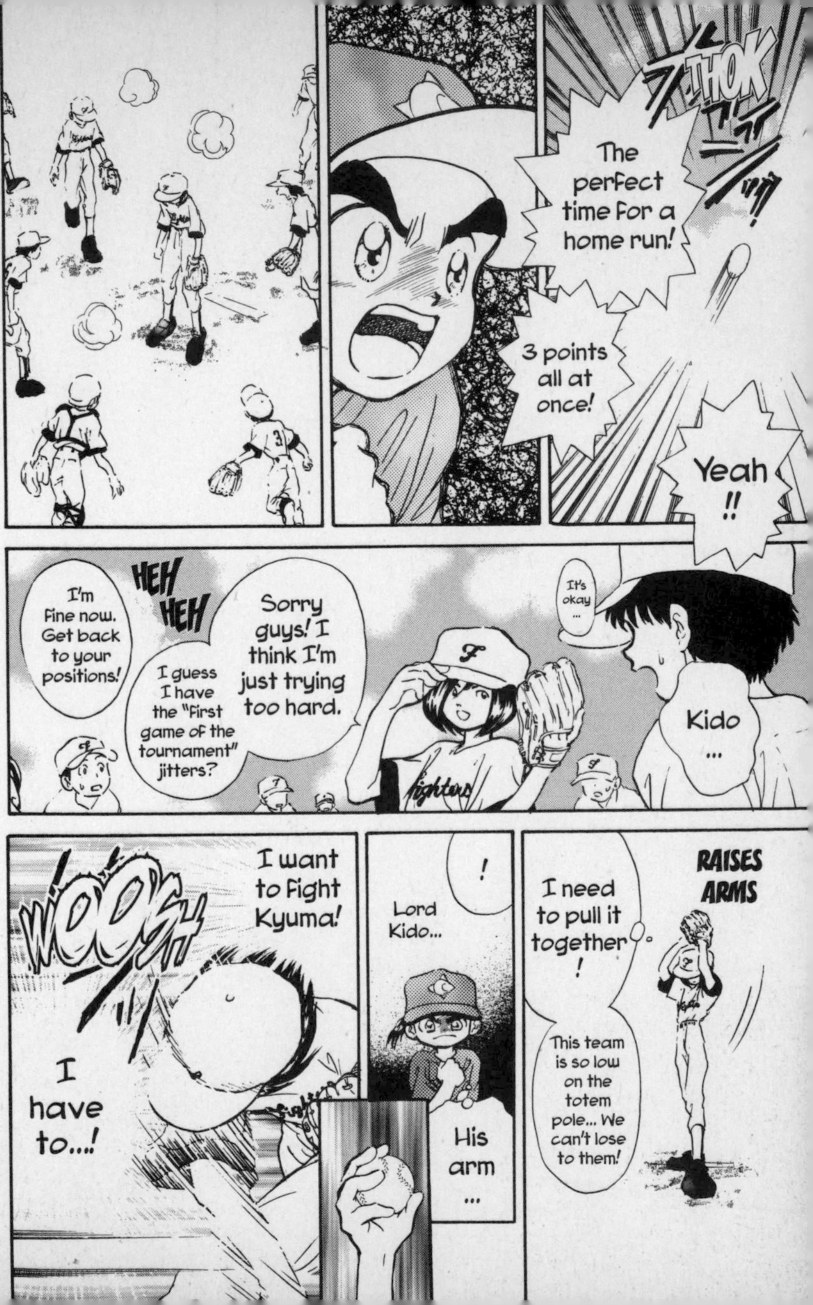
THOK
The perfect time for a home run!
3 points all at once!
Yeah !!
It's okay ...
Kido ...
Sorry guys! I think I'm just trying too hard.
HEH HEH
I guess I have the "first game of the tournament" jitters?
I'm fine now. Get back to your positions!
RAISES ARMS
I need to pull it together!
This team is so low on the totem pole... We can't lose to them!
!
Lord Kido...
His arm ...
I want to fight Kyuma!
WOOSH
I have to...!

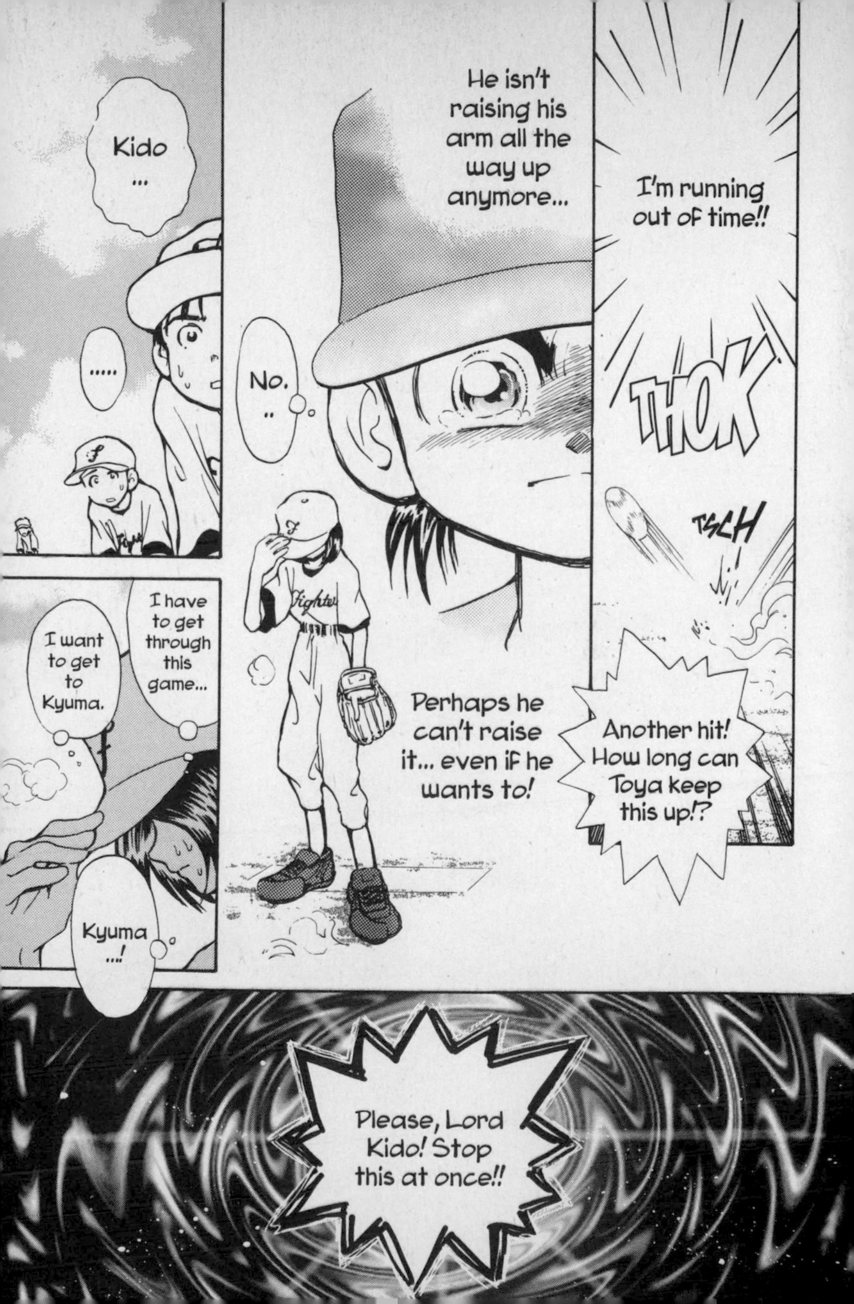
I'm running out of time!!
THOK
TSCH
Another hit! How long can Toya keep this up!?
He isn't raising his arm all the way up anymore...
No. ..
Perhaps he can't raise it... even if he wants to!
Kido ...
......
I have to get through this game...
I want to get to Kyuma.
Kyuma ...!
Please, Lord Kido! Stop this at once!!

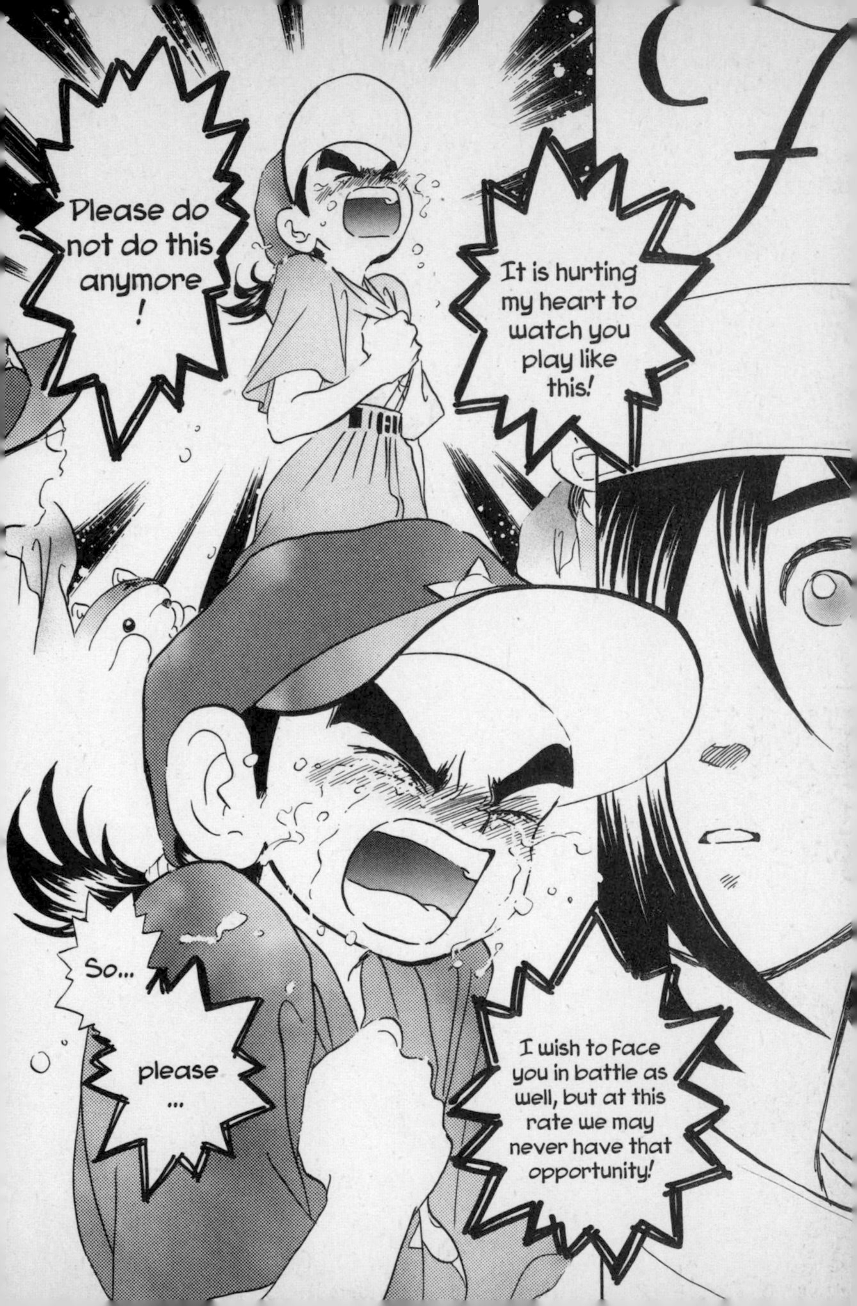
It is hurting my heart to watch you play like this!
Please do not do this anymore!
I wish to face you in battle as well, but at this rate we may never have that opportunity!
So...
please...

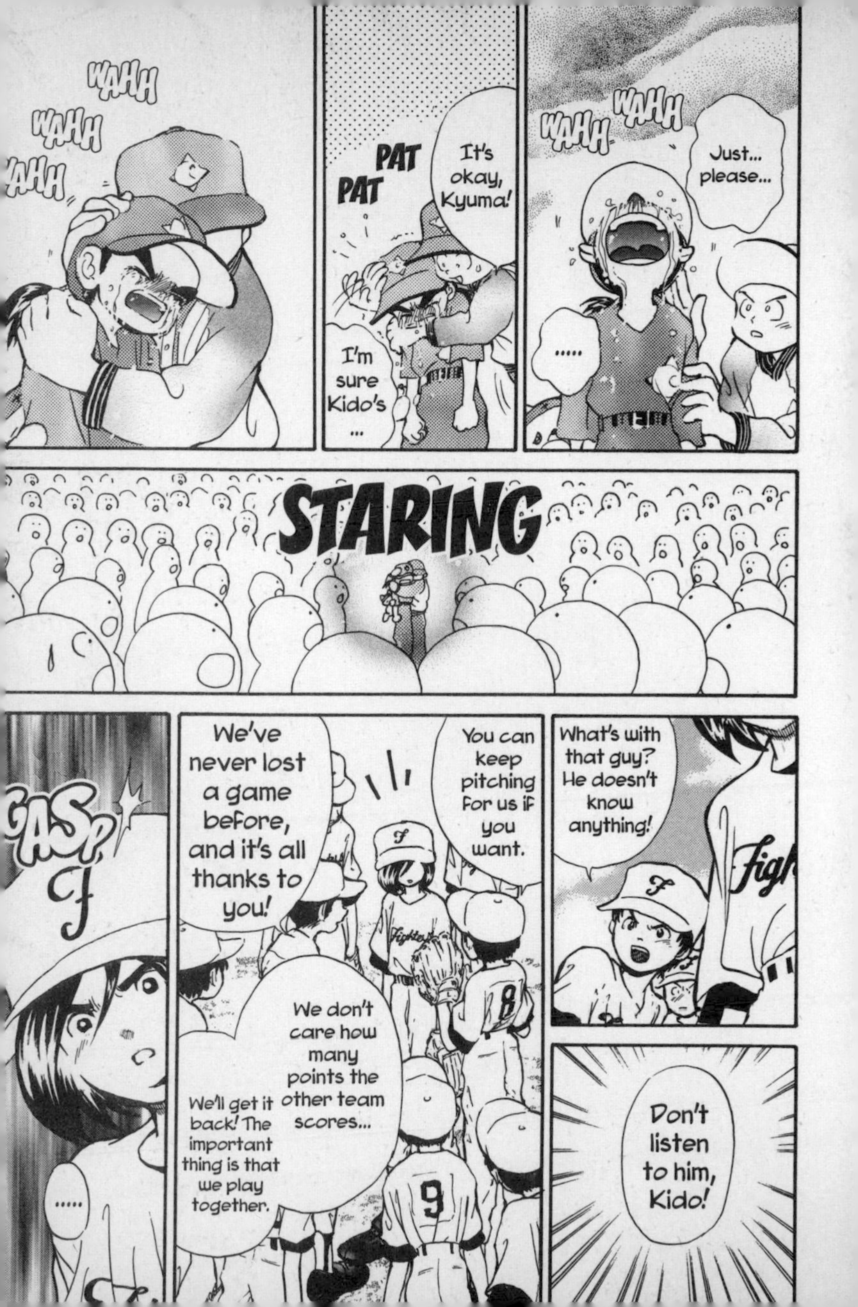
WAHH
WAHH
Just... please...
.....
It's okay, Kyuma!
PAT
PAT
I'm sure Kido's ...
WAHH
WAHH
STARING
What's with that guy? He doesn't know anything!
Don't listen to him, Kido!
You can keep pitching for us if you want.
We've never lost a game before, and it's all thanks to you!
We don't care how many points the other team scores...
We'll get it back! The important thing is that we play together.
GASP
.....

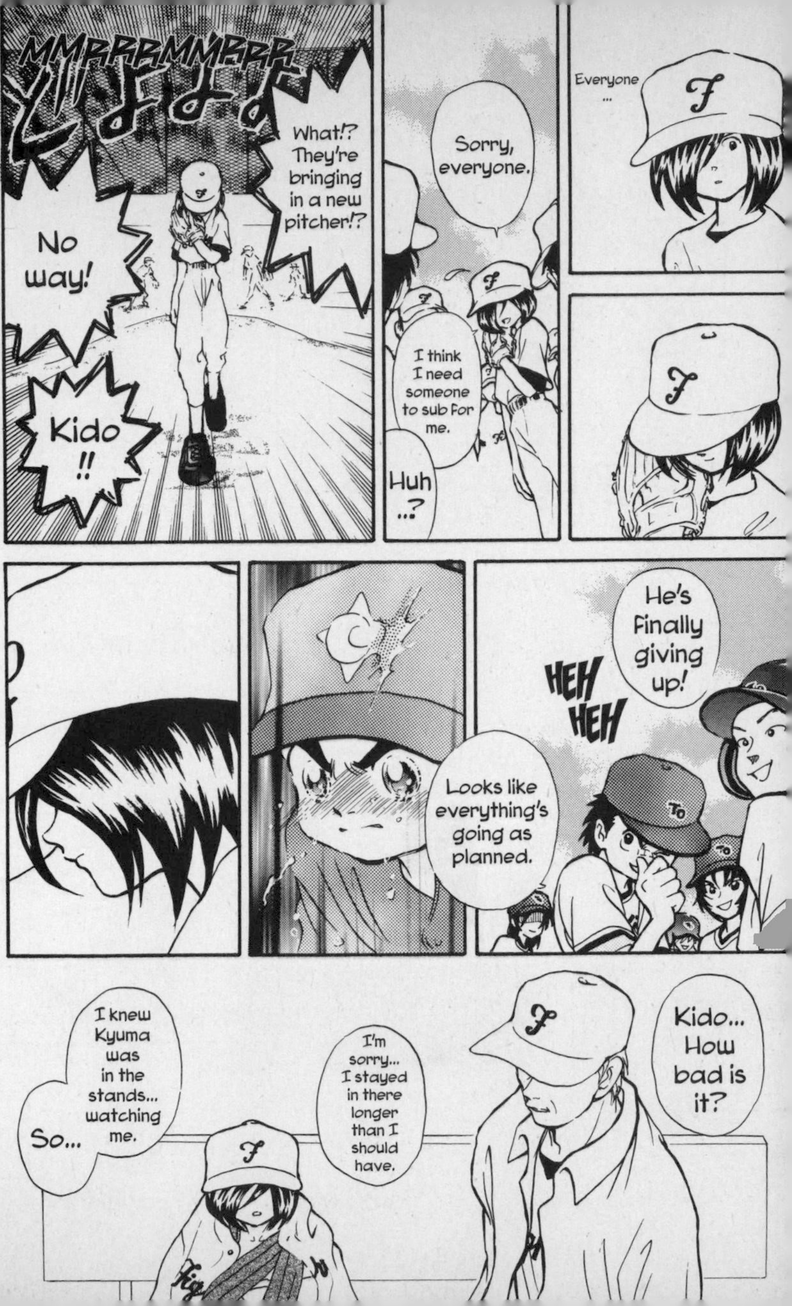

Everyone ...
Sorry, everyone.
I think I need someone to sub for me.
Huh ...?
MMRRRMMRRR
どよどよ
What!? They're bringing in a new pitcher!?
No way!
Kido !!
He's finally giving up!
HEH HEH
Looks like everything's going as planned.
Kido... How bad is it?
I'm sorry... I stayed in there longer than I should have.
I knew Kyuma was in the stands... watching me.
So...

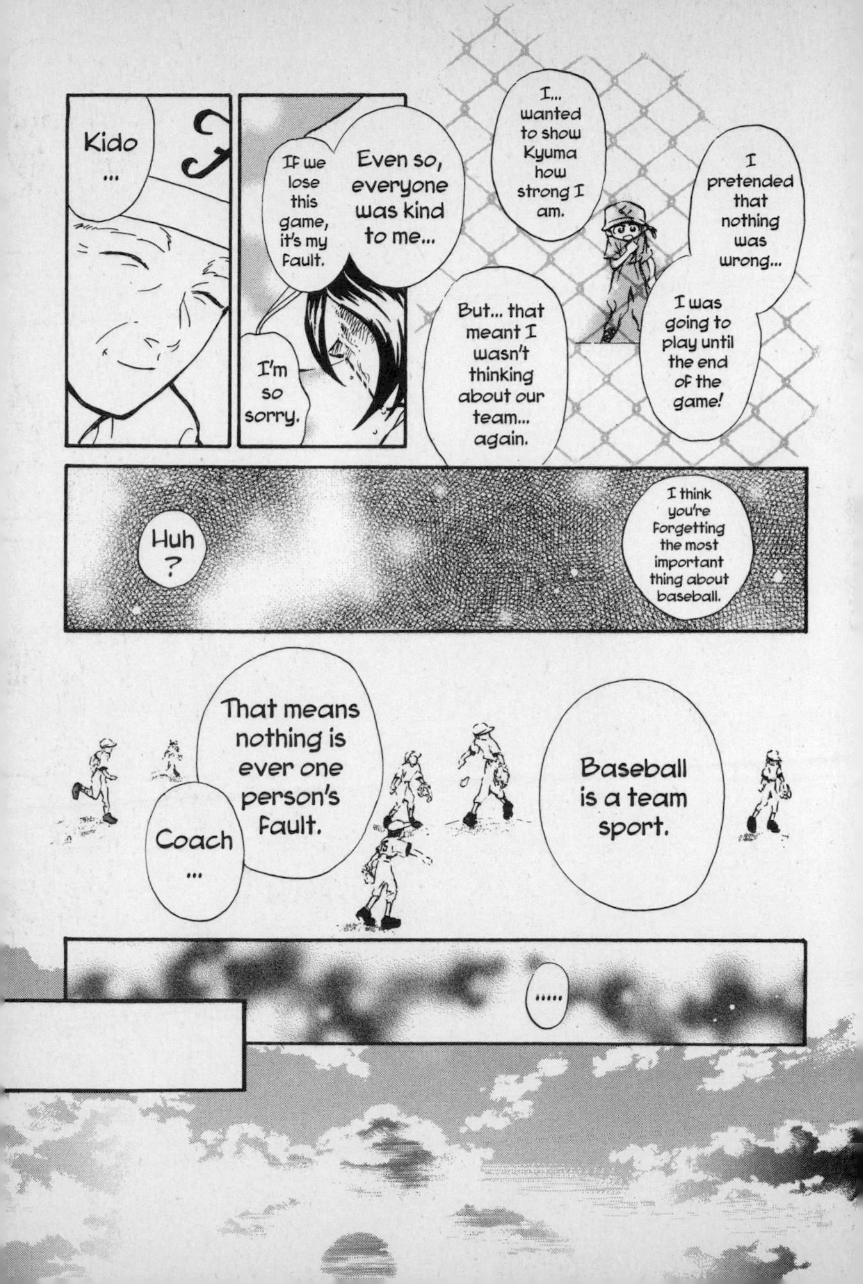

I... wanted to show Kyuma how strong I am.
I pretended that nothing was wrong...
I was going to play until the end of the game!
But... that meant I wasn't thinking about our team... again.
Even so, everyone was kind to me...
If we lose this game, it's my fault.
I'm so sorry.
Kido ...
I think you're forgetting the most important thing about baseball.
Huh ?
Baseball is a team sport.
That means nothing is ever one person's fault.
Coach ...
......

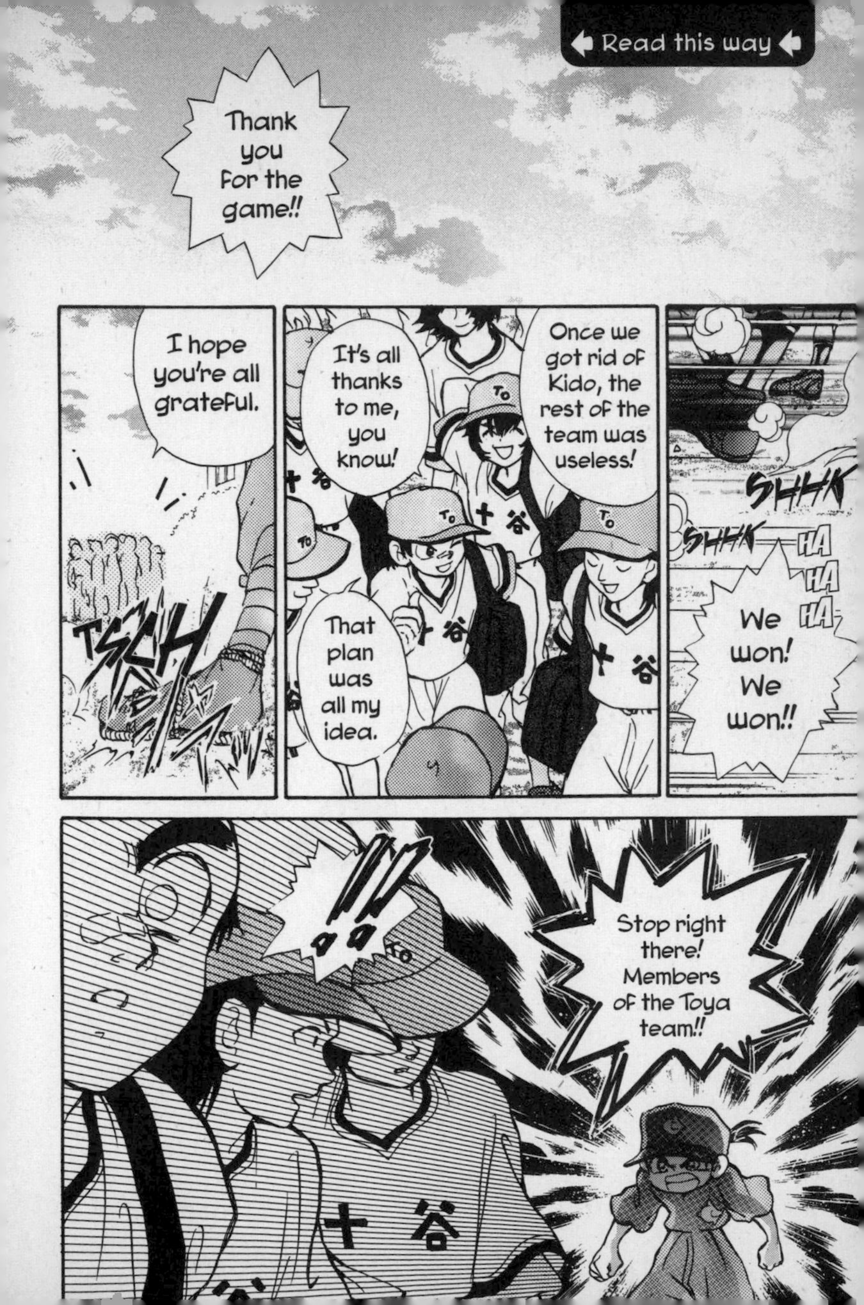
Read this way
Thank you for the game!!
SHHK
SHHK
HA HA HA
We won! We won!!
Once we got rid of Kido, the rest of the team was useless!
It's all thanks to me, you know!
That plan was all my idea.
I hope you're all grateful.
TSCH
Stop right there! Members of the Toya team!!

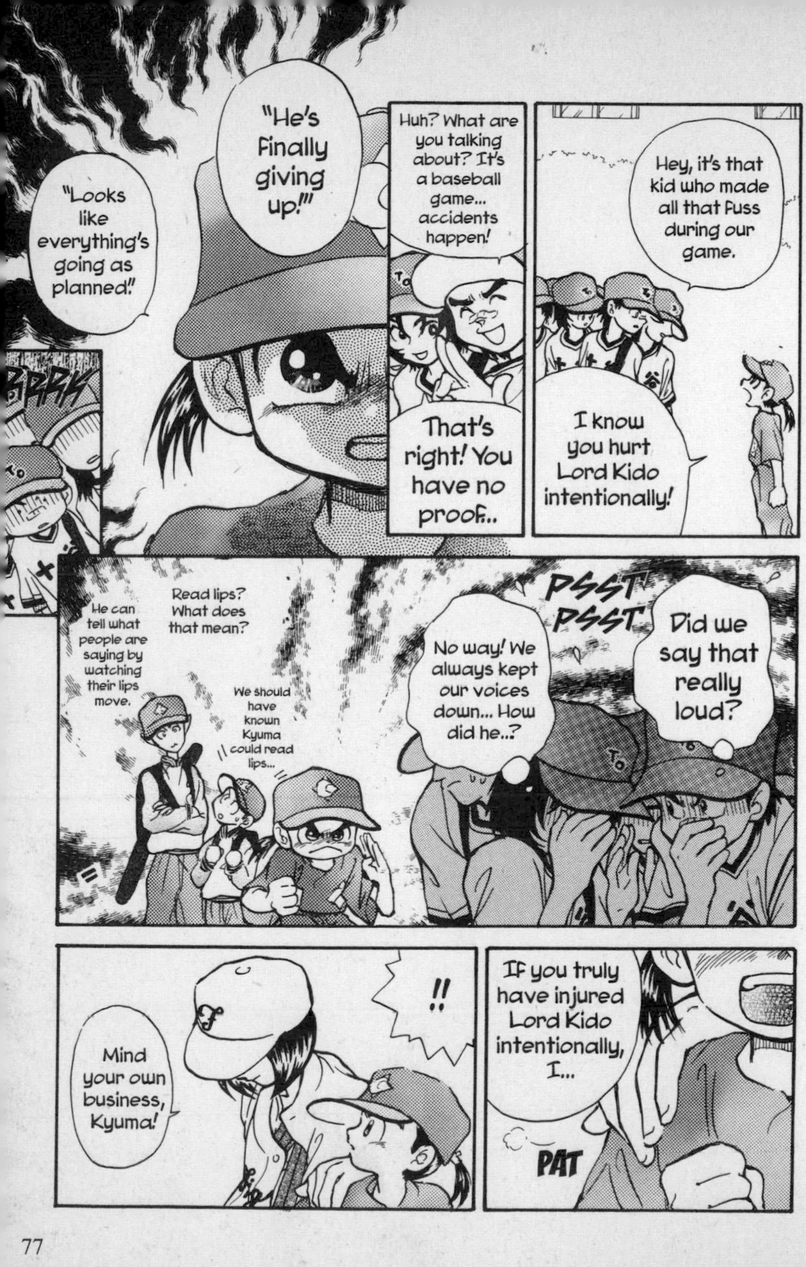

Hey, it's that kid who made all that fuss during our game.
I know you hurt Lord Kido intentionally!
Huh? What are you talking about? It's a baseball game... accidents happen!
That's right! You have no proof...
"He's finally giving up!"
"Looks like everything's going as planned!"
BRRK
PSST PSST
Did we say that really loud?
No way! We always kept our voices down... How did he..?
Read lips? What does that mean?
He can tell what people are saying by watching their lips move.
We should have known Kyuma could read lips...
If you truly have injured Lord Kido intentionally, I...
PAT
!!
Mind your own business, Kyuma!

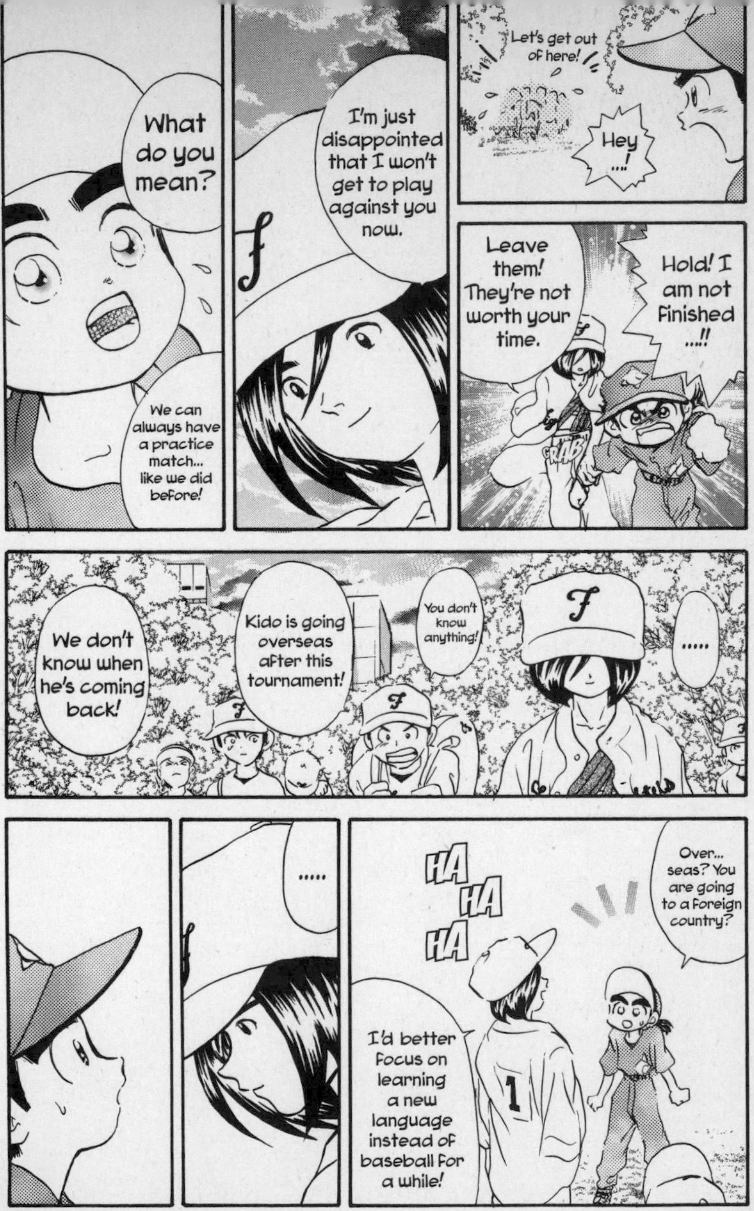
Let's get out of here!
Hey ...!
Hold! I am not finished ...!!
Leave them! They're not worth your time.
I'm just disappointed that I won't get to play against you now.
What do you mean?
We can always have a practice match... like we did before!
.....
You don't know anything!
Kido is going overseas after this tournament!
We don't know when he's coming back!
Over... seas? You are going to a foreign country?
HA HA HA
I'd better focus on learning a new language instead of baseball for a while!
.....

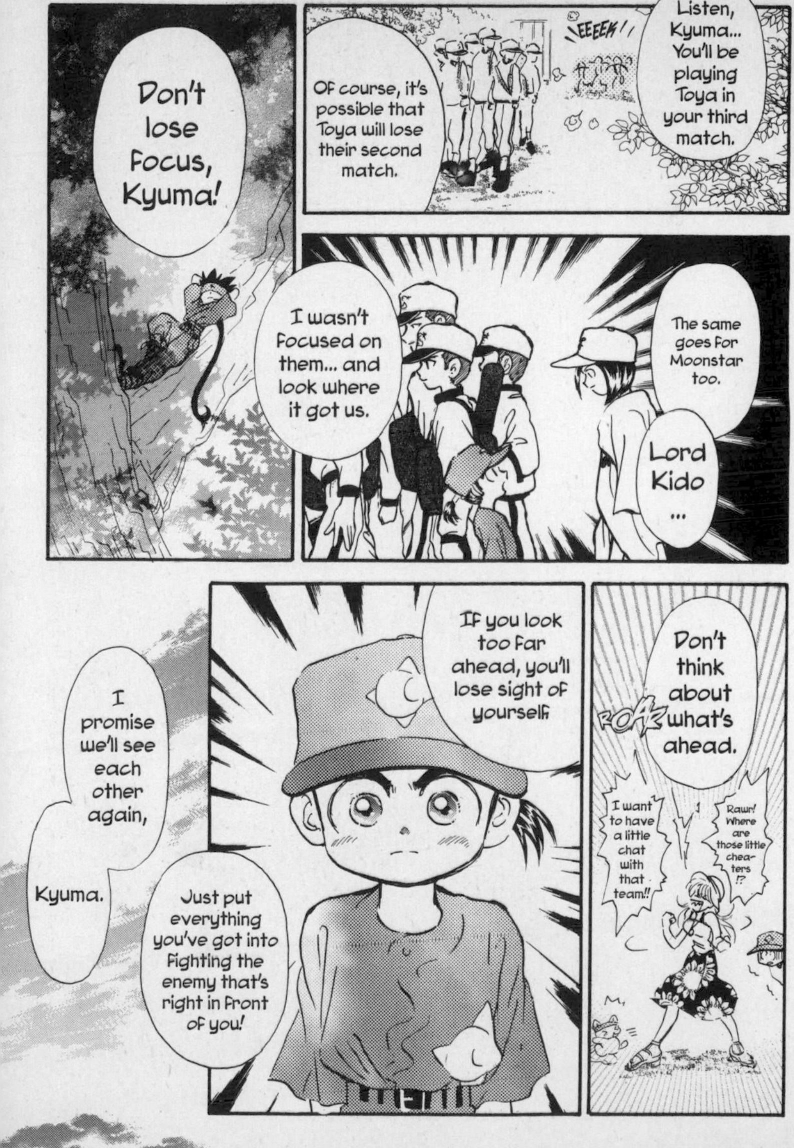
Listen, Kyuma... You'll be playing Toya in your third match.
EEEEK
Of course, it's possible that Toya will lose their second match.
The same goes for Moonstar too.
Lord Kido ...
I wasn't focused on them... and look where it got us.
Don't lose focus, Kyuma!
Don't think about what's ahead.
ROAR
Rawr! Where are those little cheaters !?
I want to have a little chat with that team!!
If you look too far ahead, you'll lose sight of yourself.
Just put everything you've got into fighting the enemy that's right in front of you!
I promise we'll see each other again,
Kyuma.

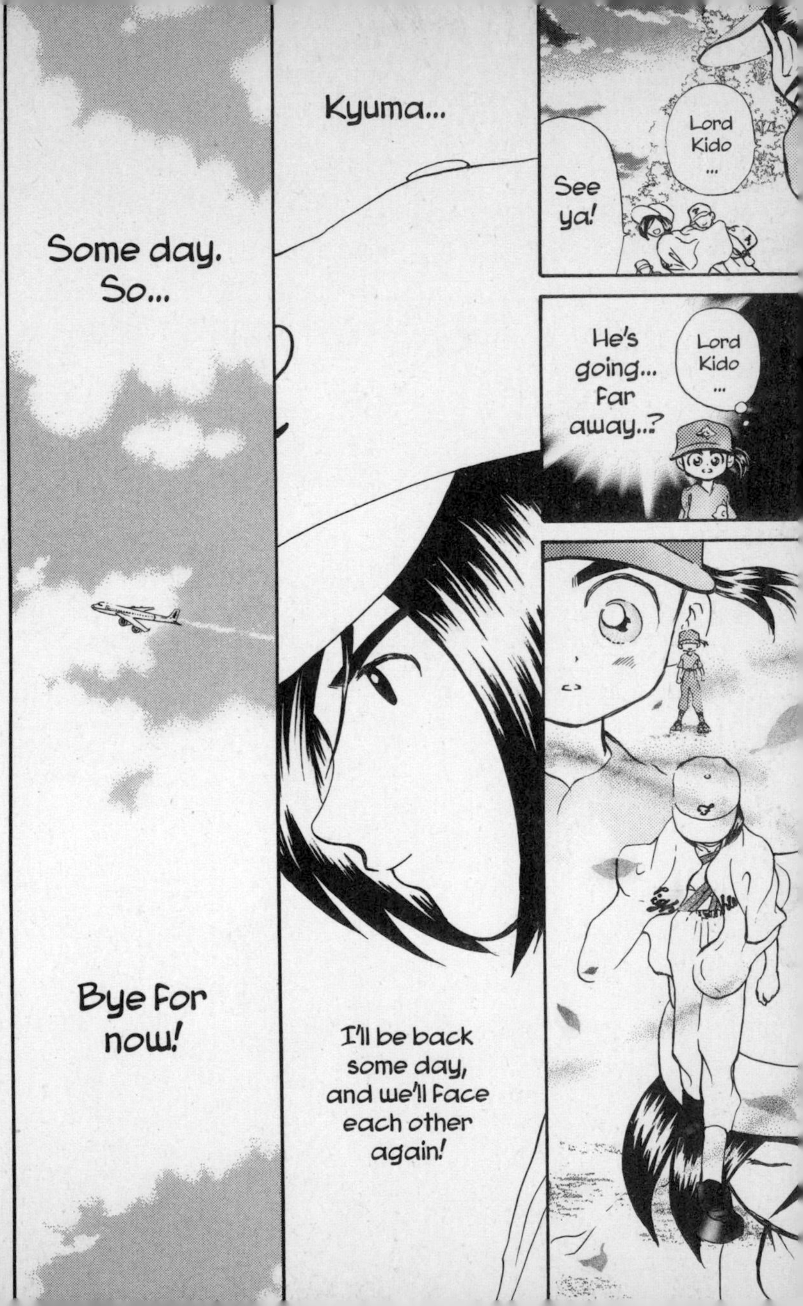
Lord Kido ...
See ya!
Lord Kido ...
He's going... far away...?
Kyuma...
I'll be back some day, and we'll face each other again!
Some day. So...
Bye for now!

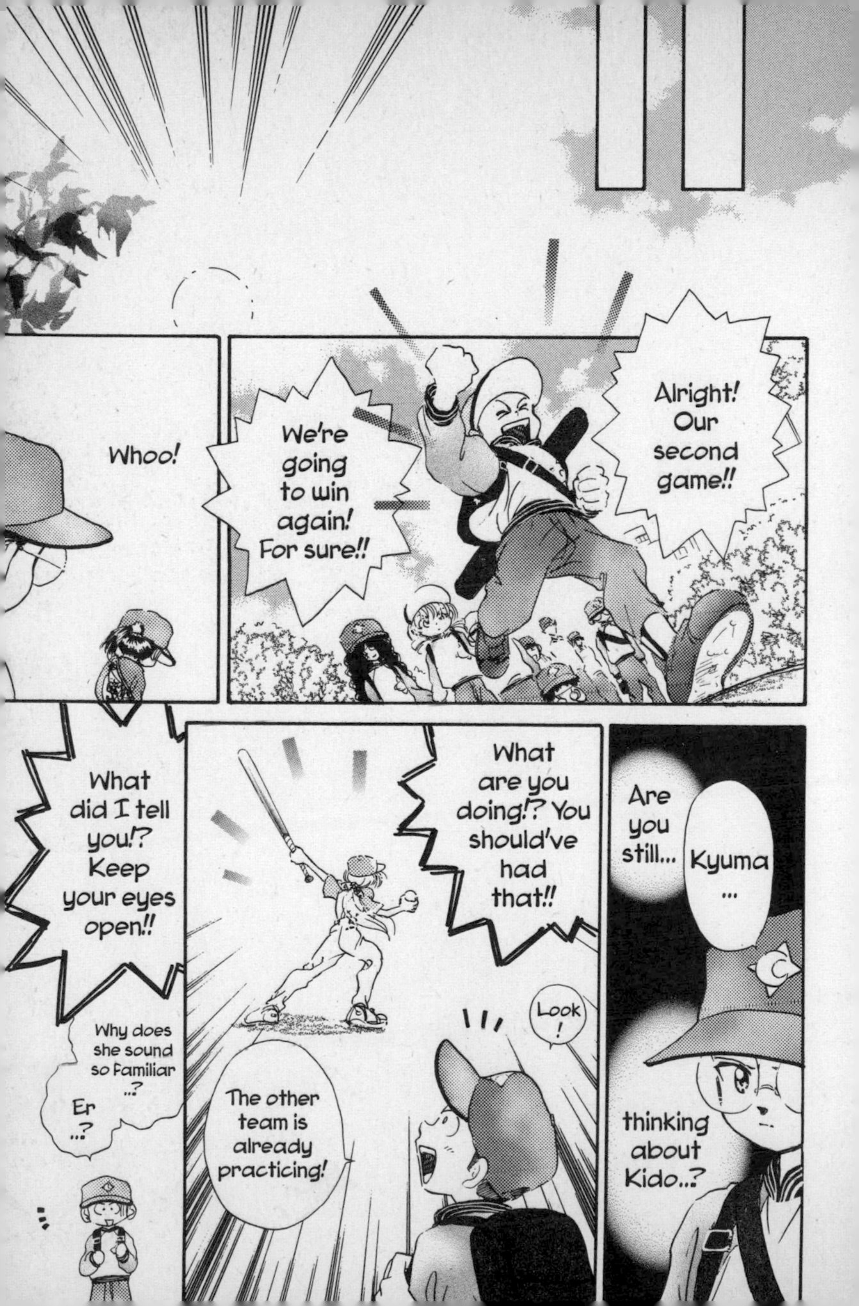
Alright! Our second game!!
We're going to win again! For sure!!
Whoo!
Kyuma...
Are you still...
thinking about Kido..?
What are you doing!? You should've had that!!
Look!
The other team is already practicing!
What did I tell you!? Keep your eyes open!!
Why does she sound so familiar..?
Er..?

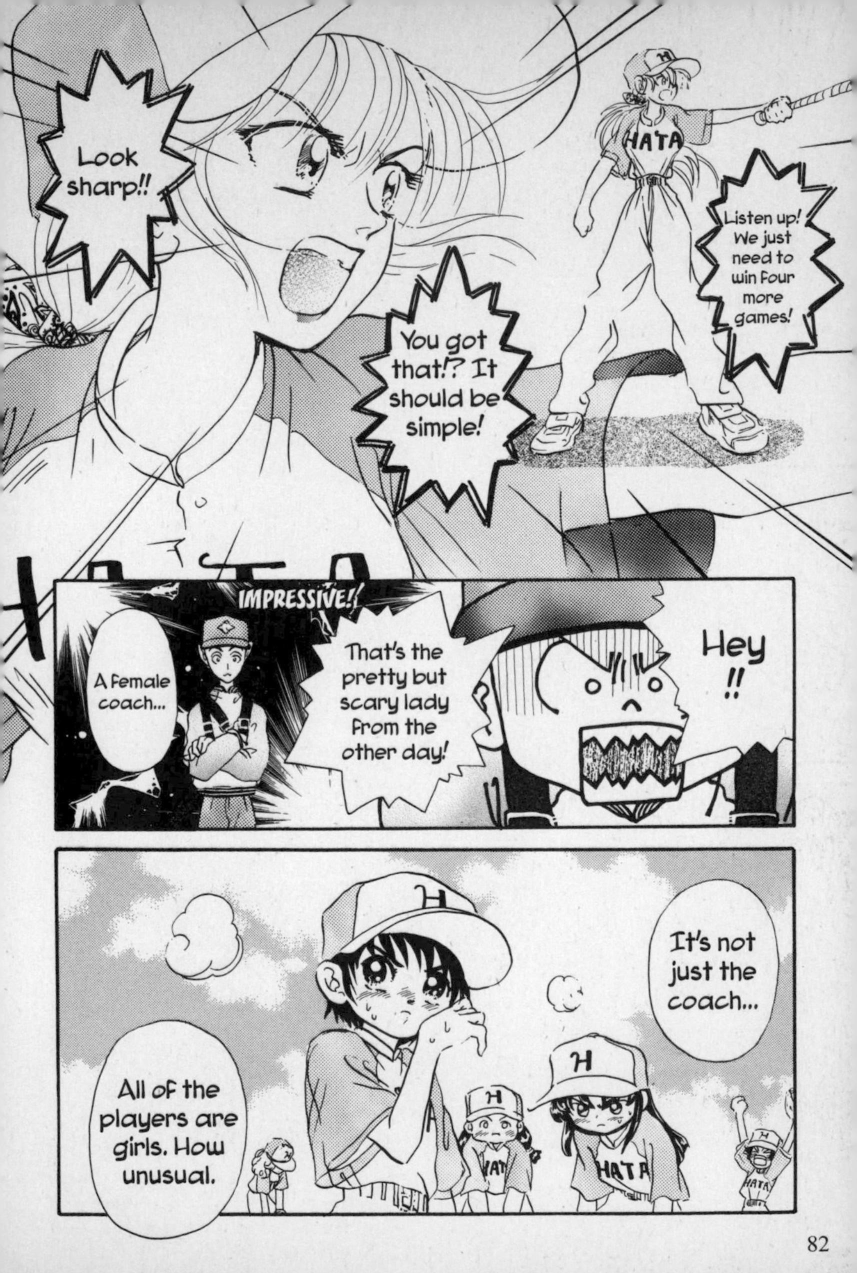
Listen up! We just need to win four more games!
You got that!? It should be simple!
Look sharp!!
Hey!!
That's the pretty but scary lady from the other day!
IMPRESSIVE!!
A female coach...
It's not just the coach...
All of the players are girls. How unusual.

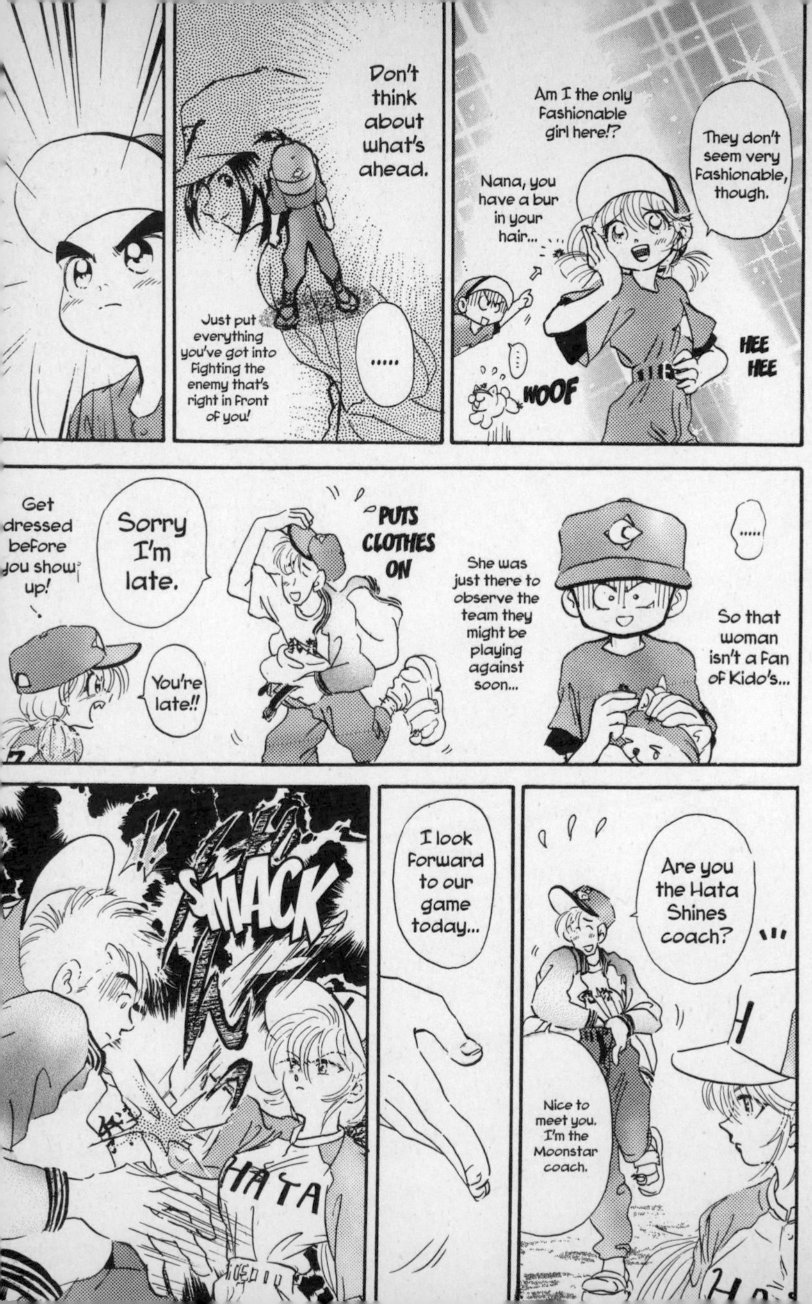
They don't seem very fashionable, though.
Am I the only fashionable girl here!?
HEE HEE
Nana, you have a bur in your hair...
...
WOOF
Don't think about what's ahead.
.....
Just put everything you've got into fighting the enemy that's right in front of you!
.....
So that woman isn't a fan of Kido's...
She was just there to observe the team they might be playing against soon...
PUTS CLOTHES ON
Sorry I'm late.
Get dressed before you show up!
You're late!!
Are you the Hata Shines coach?
Nice to meet you. I'm the Moonstar coach.
I look forward to our game today...
SMACK
HATA

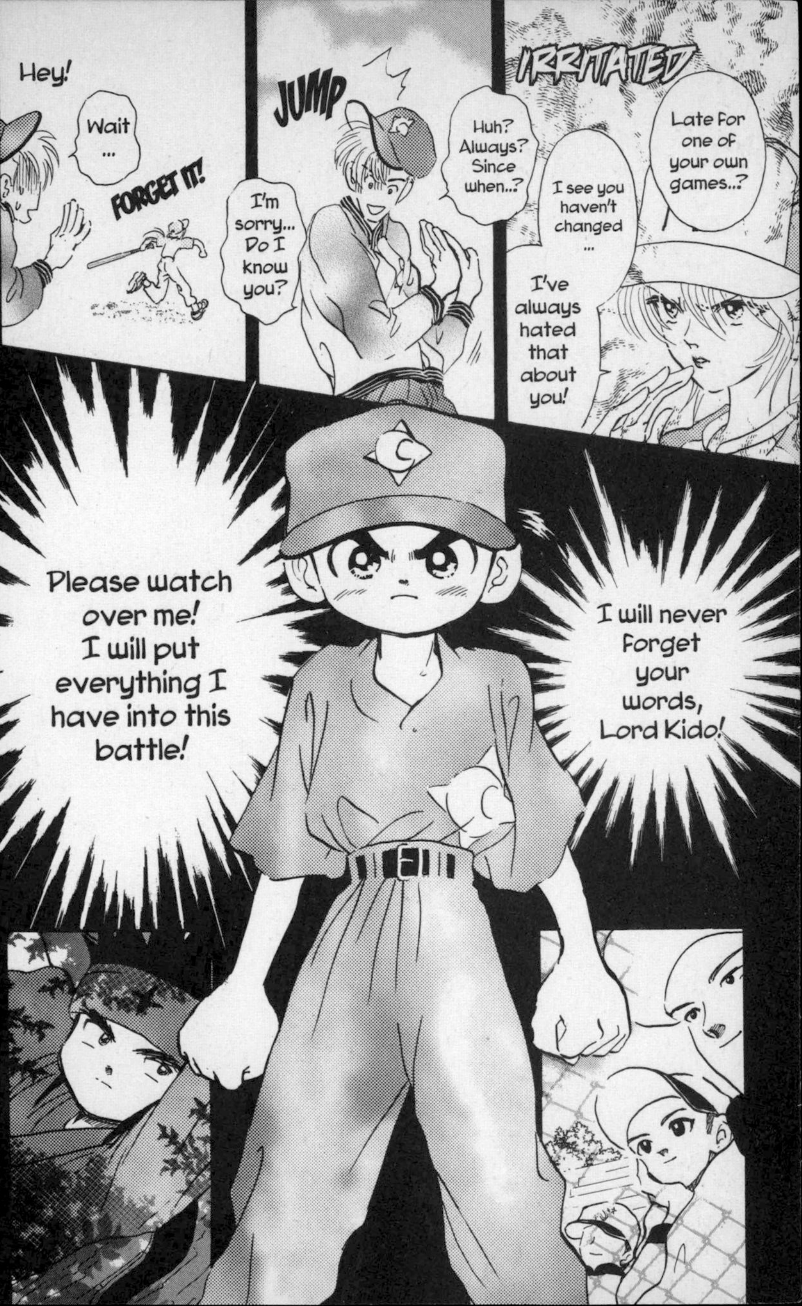
IRRITATED
Late for one of your own games..?
I see you haven't changed ...
I've always hated that about you!
JUMP
Huh? Always? Since when..?
I'm sorry... Do I know you?
Hey!
Wait ...
FORGET IT!
I will never forget your words, Lord Kido!
Please watch over me! I will put everything I have into this battle!

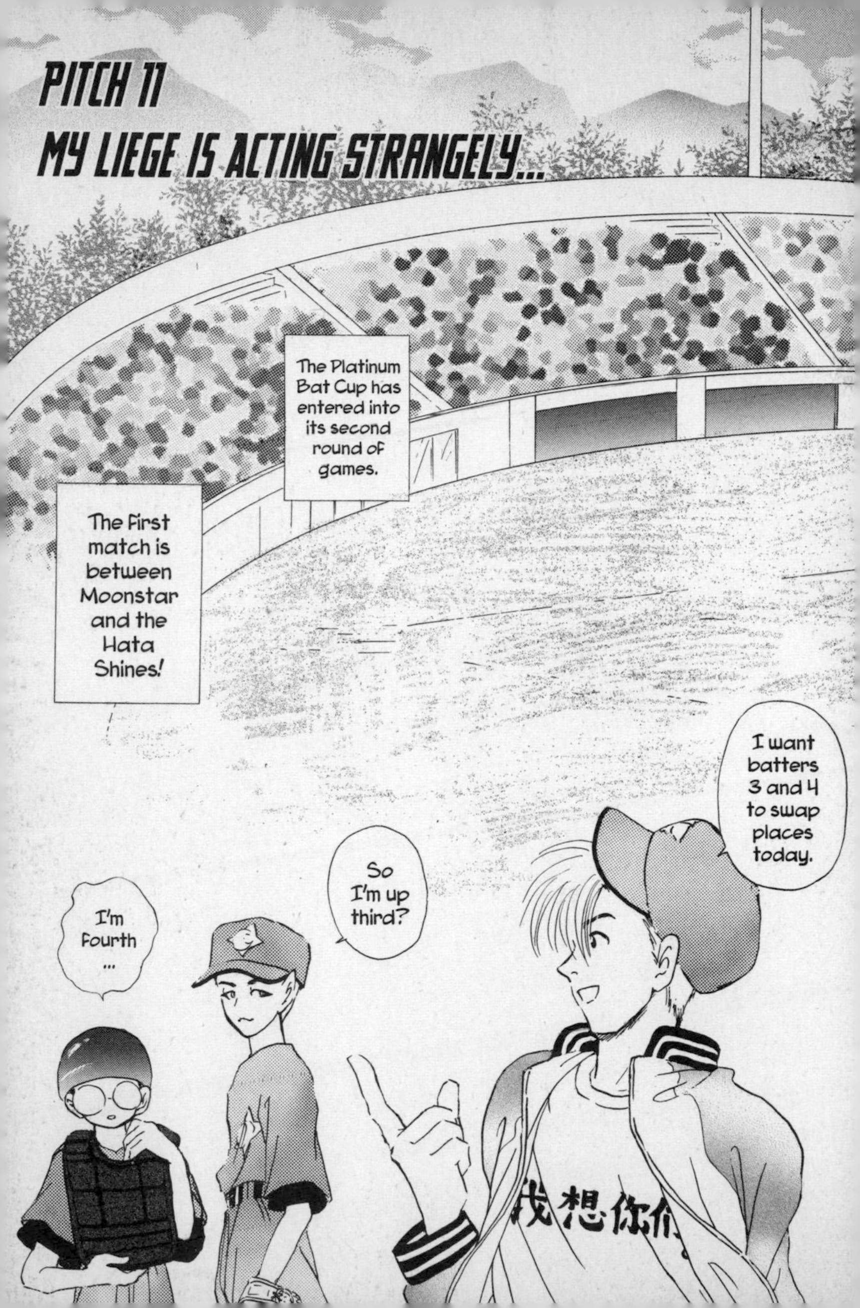

PITCH 11
MY LIEGE IS ACTING STRANGELY...
The Platinum Bat Cup has entered into its second round of games.
The first match is between Moonstar and the Hata Shines!
I want batters 3 and 4 to swap places today.
So I'm up third?
I'm fourth ...
我想你(

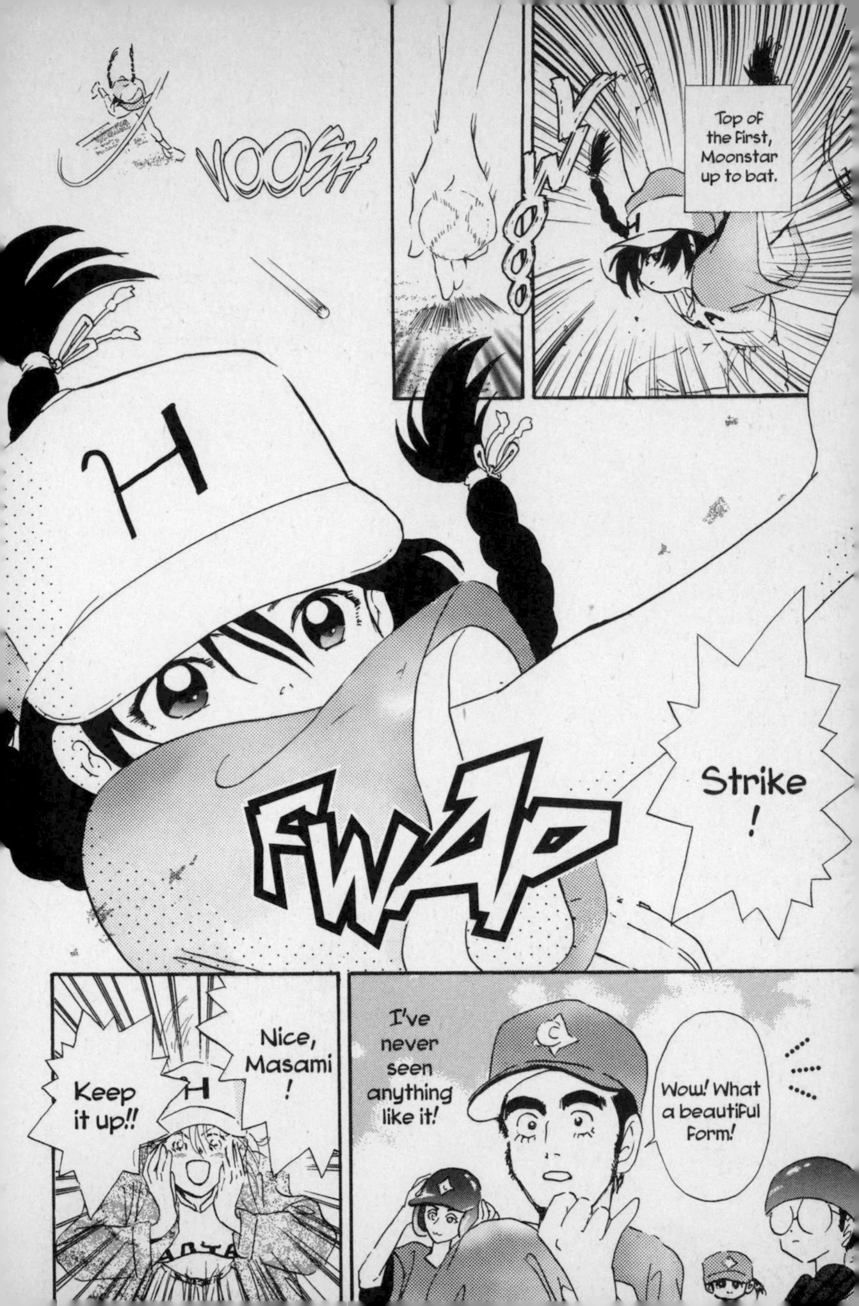
Top of the First, Moonstar up to bat.
VOOSH
FWAP
Strike!
......
Wow! What a beautiful form!
I've never seen anything like it!
Nice, Masami!
Keep it up!!

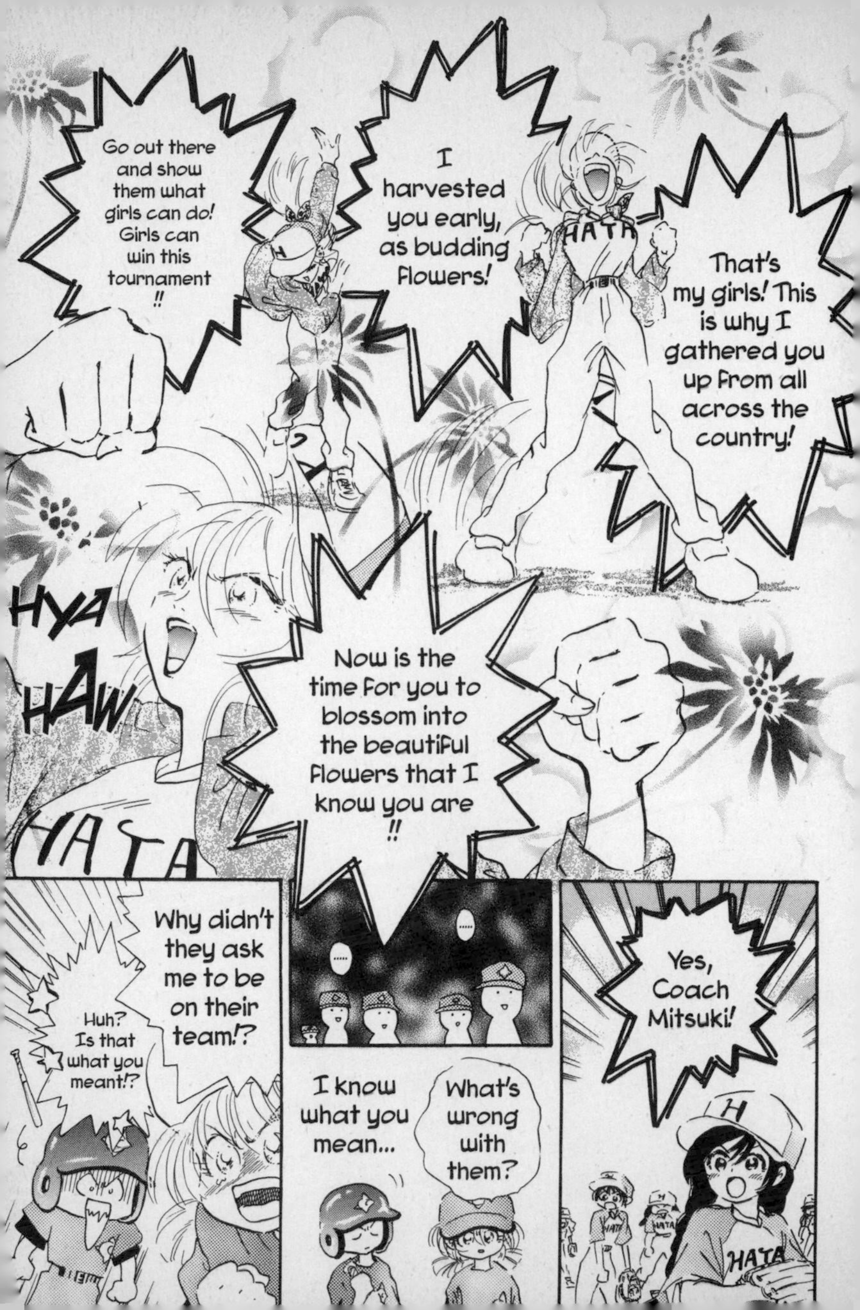

That's my girls! This is why I gathered you up from all across the country!
I harvested you early, as budding flowers!
Go out there and show them what girls can do! Girls can win this tournament!!
Now is the time for you to blossom into the beautiful flowers that I know you are!!
HYA
HAW
HATA
Yes, Coach Mitsuki!
......
......
What's wrong with them?
I know what you mean...
Why didn't they ask me to be on their team!?
Huh? Is that what you meant!?

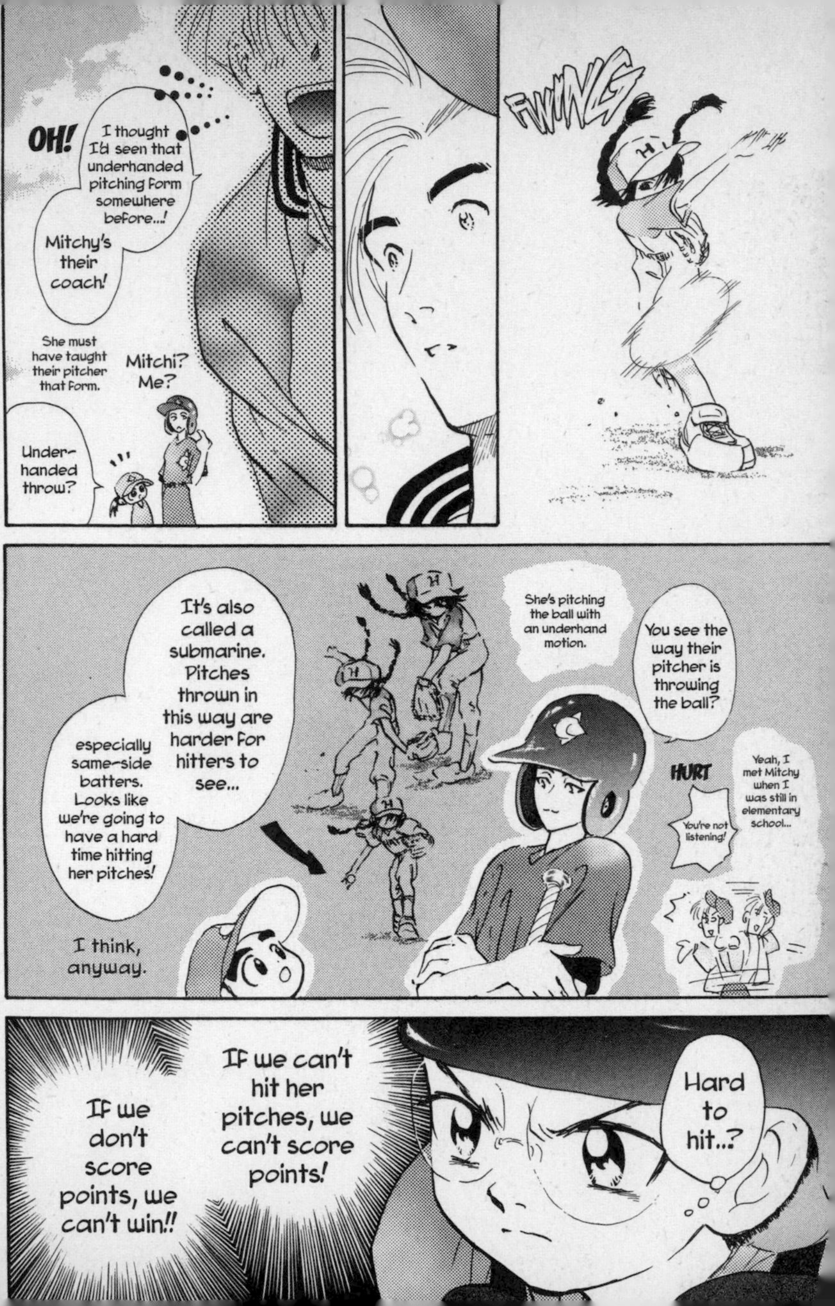
FWING
OH!
I thought I'd seen that underhanded pitching form somewhere before...!
Mitchy's their coach!
Mitchi? Me?
She must have taught their pitcher that form.
Under-handed throw?
You see the way their pitcher is throwing the ball?
She's pitching the ball with an underhand motion.
Yeah, I met Mitchy when I was still in elementary school...
HURT
You're not listening!
It's also called a submarine. Pitches thrown in this way are harder for hitters to see...
especially same-side batters. Looks like we're going to have a hard time hitting her pitches!
I think, anyway.
Hard to hit...?
If we can't hit her pitches, we can't score points!
If we don't score points, we can't win!!

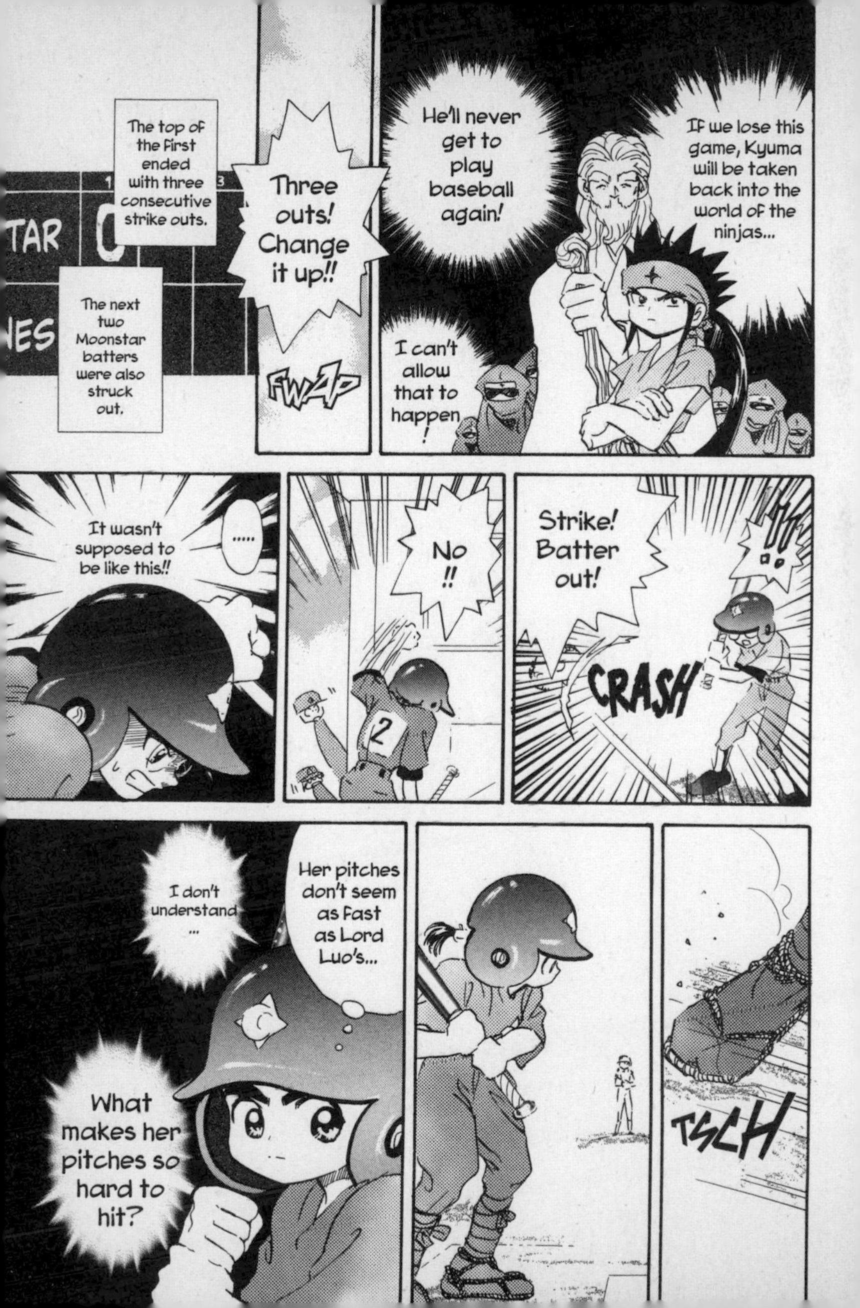
The top of the first ended with three consecutive strike outs.
Three outs! Change it up!!
The next two Moonstar batters were also struck out.
FWAP
If we lose this game, Kyuma will be taken back into the world of the ninjas...
He'll never get to play baseball again!
I can't allow that to happen!
It wasn't supposed to be like this!!
......
No!!
Strike! Batter out!
CRASH
!!
I don't understand...
Her pitches don't seem as fast as Lord Luo's...
What makes her pitches so hard to hit?
TSCH

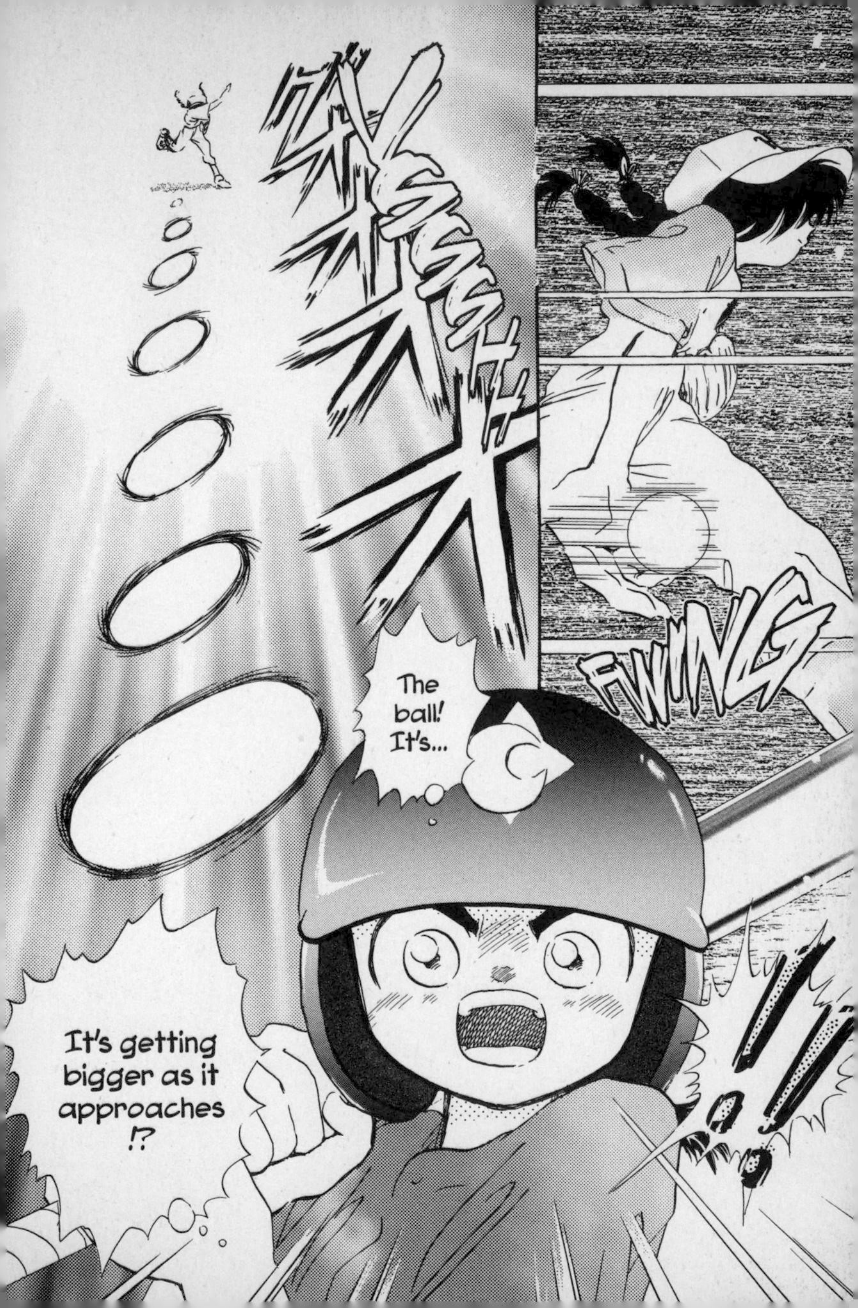
FWING
SSSSHH
The ball! It's...
It's getting bigger as it approaches!?
!!

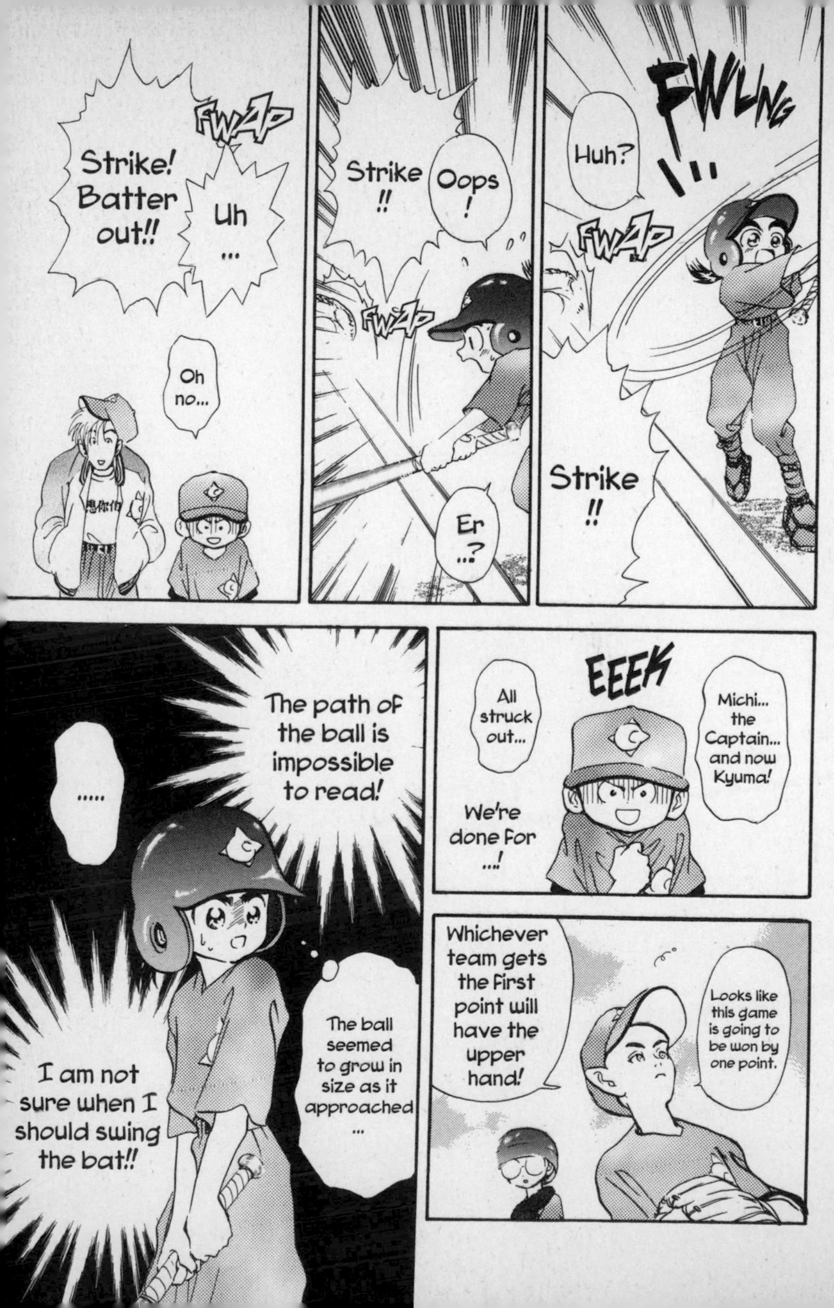
FWUNG
Huh?
FWAP
Strike !!
Oops !
Strike !!
FWAP
Er ...?
FWAP
Uh ...
Strike! Batter out!!
Oh no...
Michi... the Captain... and now Kyuma!
EEEK
All struck out...
We're done for ...!
Looks like this game is going to be won by one point.
Whichever team gets the first point will have the upper hand!
The path of the ball is impossible to read!
.....
The ball seemed to grow in size as it approached ...
I am not sure when I should swing the bat!!

Read this way

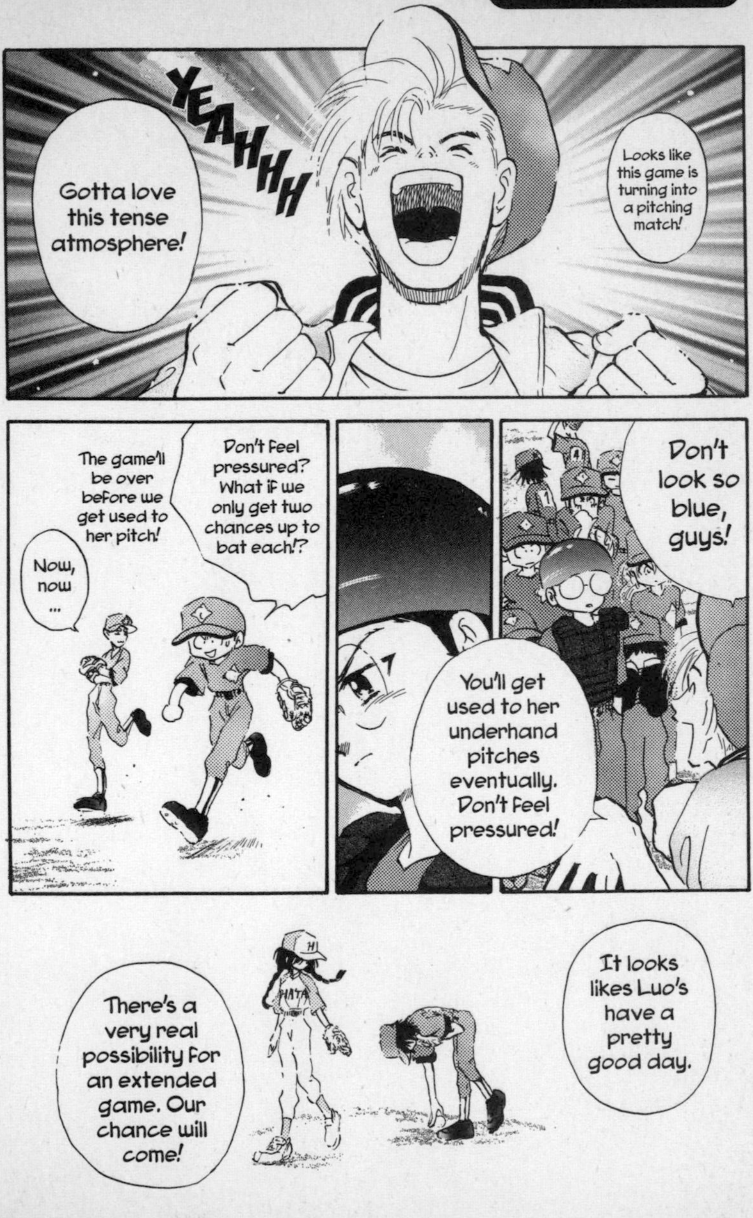

Looks like this game is turning into a pitching match!
YEAHHHH
Gotta love this tense atmosphere!
Don't look so blue, guys!
You'll get used to her underhand pitches eventually. Don't feel pressured!
Don't feel pressured? What if we only get two chances up to bat each!?
The game'll be over before we get used to her pitch!
Now, now ...
It looks likes Luo's have a pretty good day.
There's a very real possibility for an extended game. Our chance will come!

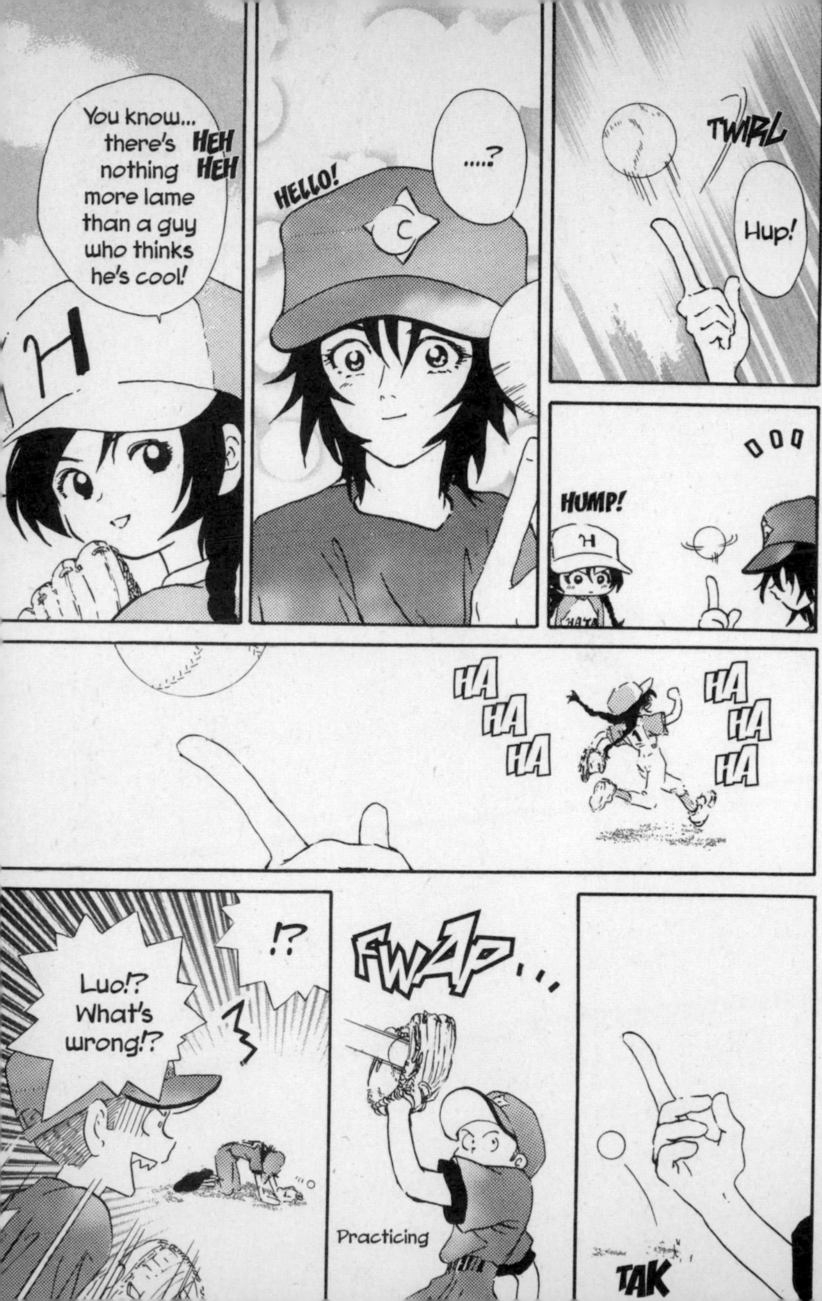
TWIRL
Hup!
HUMP!
....?
HELLO!
You know... there's nothing more lame than a guy who thinks he's cool!
HEH HEH
HA HA HA
HA HA HA
TAK
FWAP...
Practicing
!?
Luo!? What's wrong!?

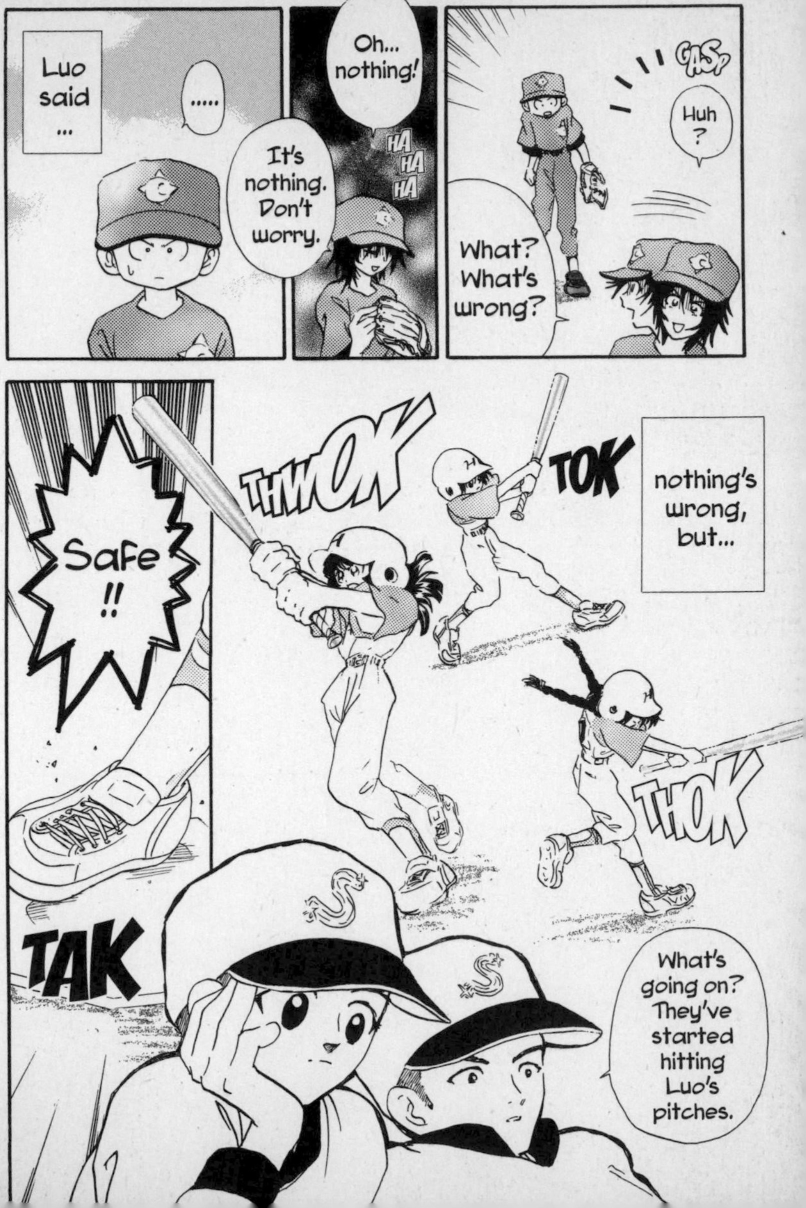
GASP
Huh ?
What? What's wrong?
Oh... nothing!
HA HA HA
It's nothing. Don't worry.
Luo said ...
.....
nothing's wrong, but...
TOK
THWOK
THOK
What's going on? They've started hitting Luo's pitches.
Safe !!
TAK

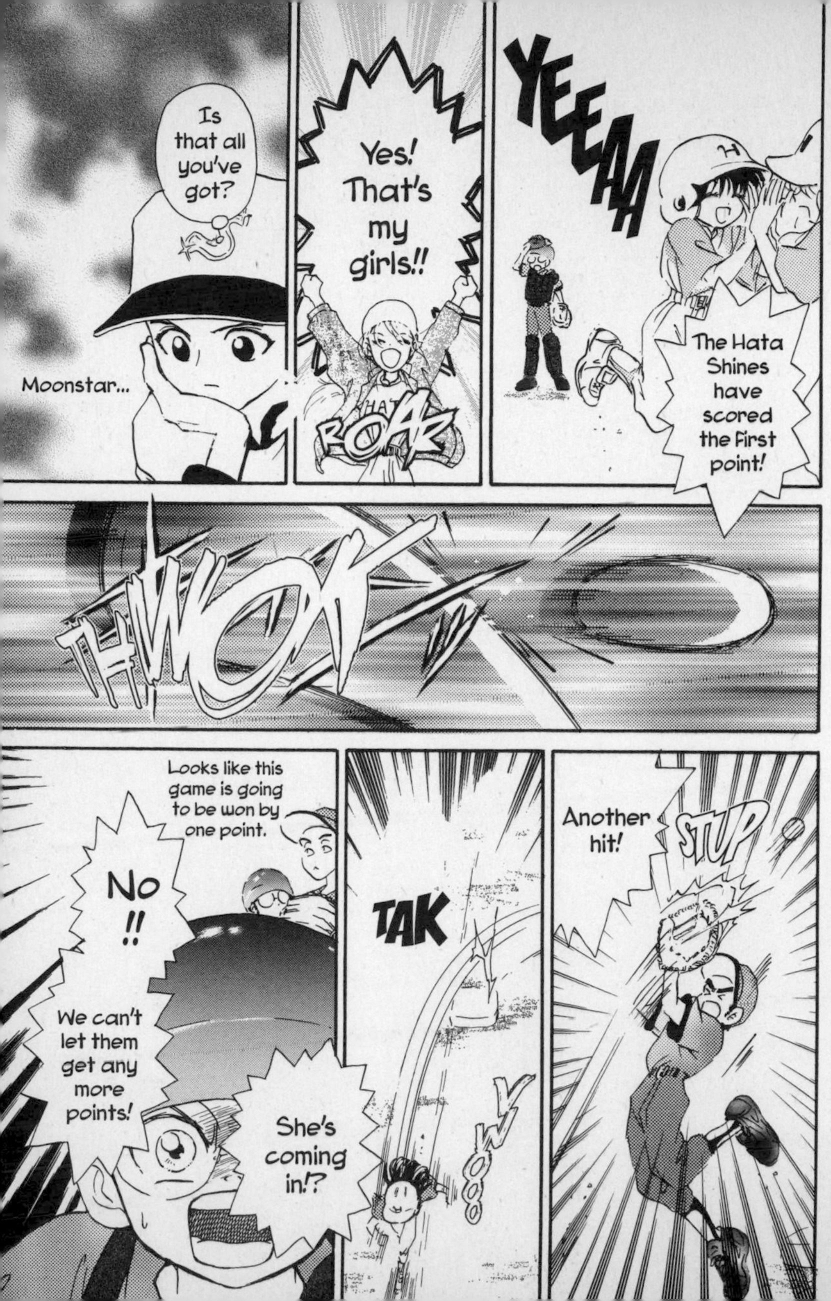

YEEAAA
The Hata Shines have scored the first point!
Yes! That's my girls!!
ROAR
Is that all you've got?
Moonstar...
THWOK
Another hit!
STUP
TAK
Wooo
Looks like this game is going to be won by one point.
No !!
We can't let them get any more points!
She's coming in!?

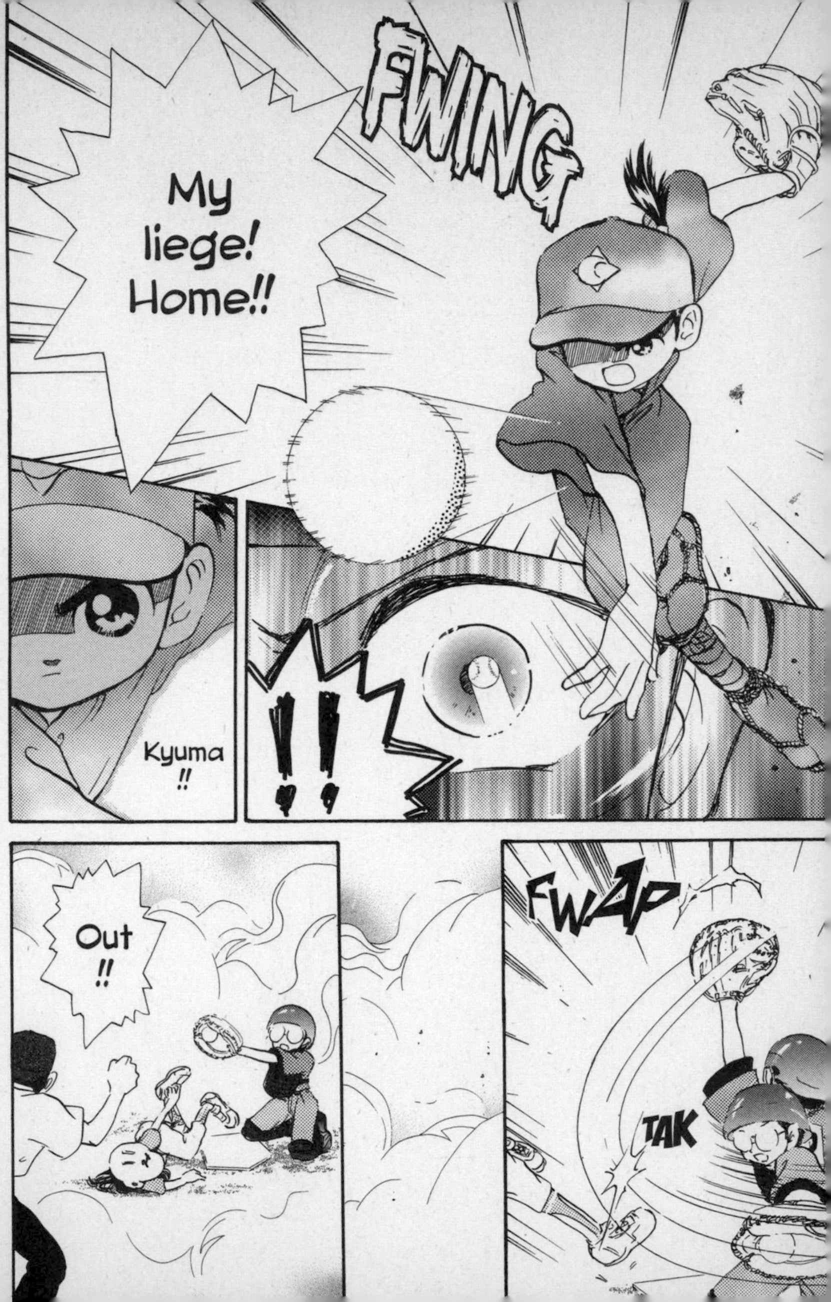
FWING
My liege! Home!!
!!
Kyuma!!
FWAP
TAK
Out!!

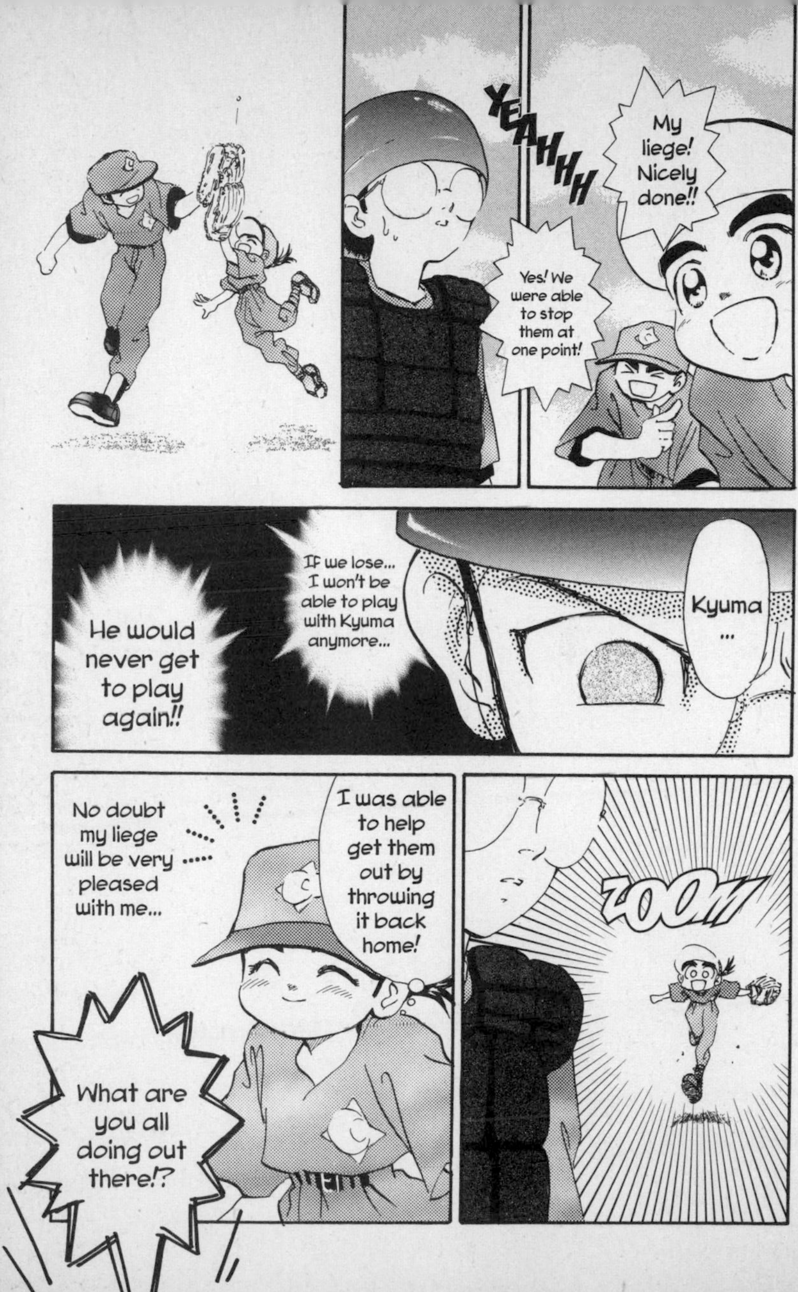
My liege! Nicely done!!
Yes! We were able to stop them at one point!
YEAHHHH
Kyuma ...
If we lose... I won't be able to play with Kyuma anymore...
He would never get to play again!!
ZOOM
I was able to help get them out by throwing it back home!
No doubt my liege will be very pleased with me...
What are you all doing out there!?

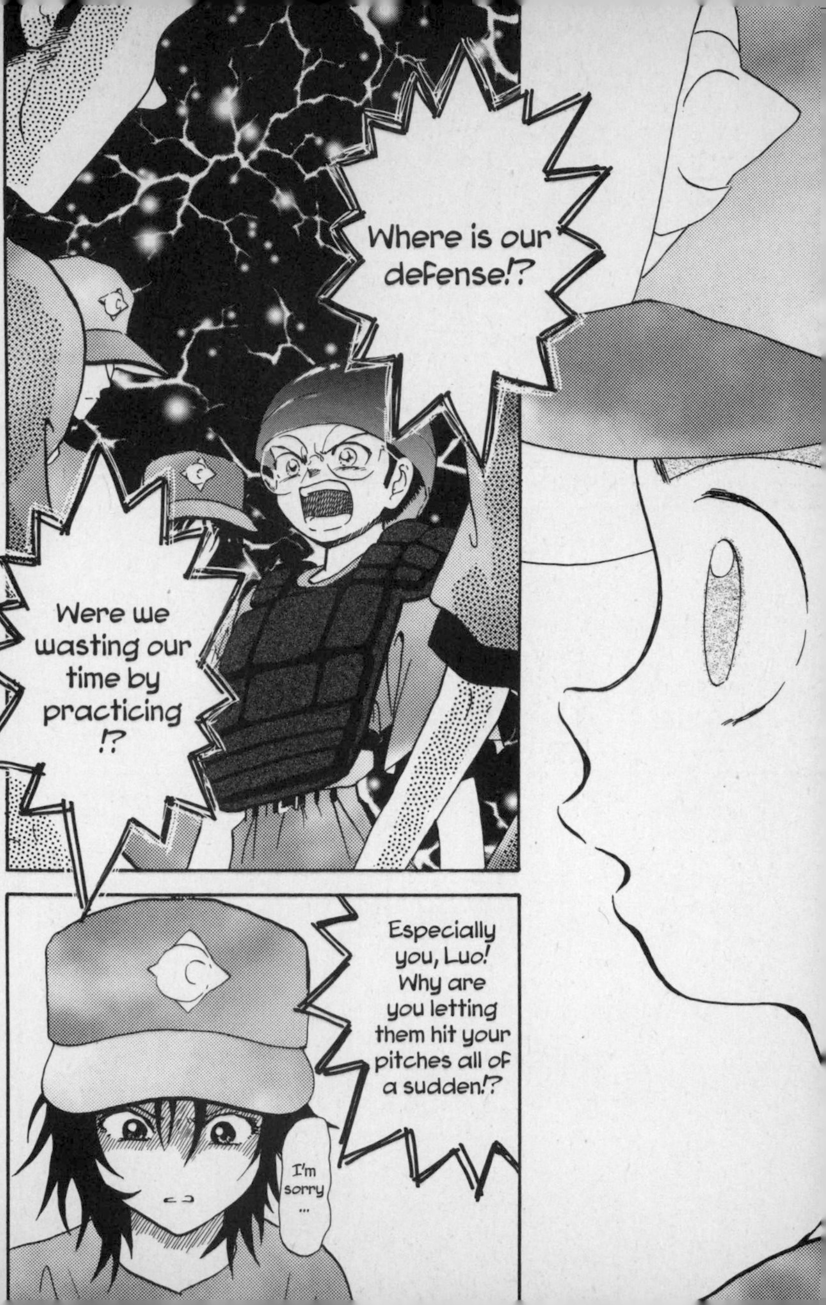
Where is our defense!?
Were we wasting our time by practicing!?
Especially you, Luo! Why are you letting them hit your pitches all of a sudden!?
I'm sorry ...

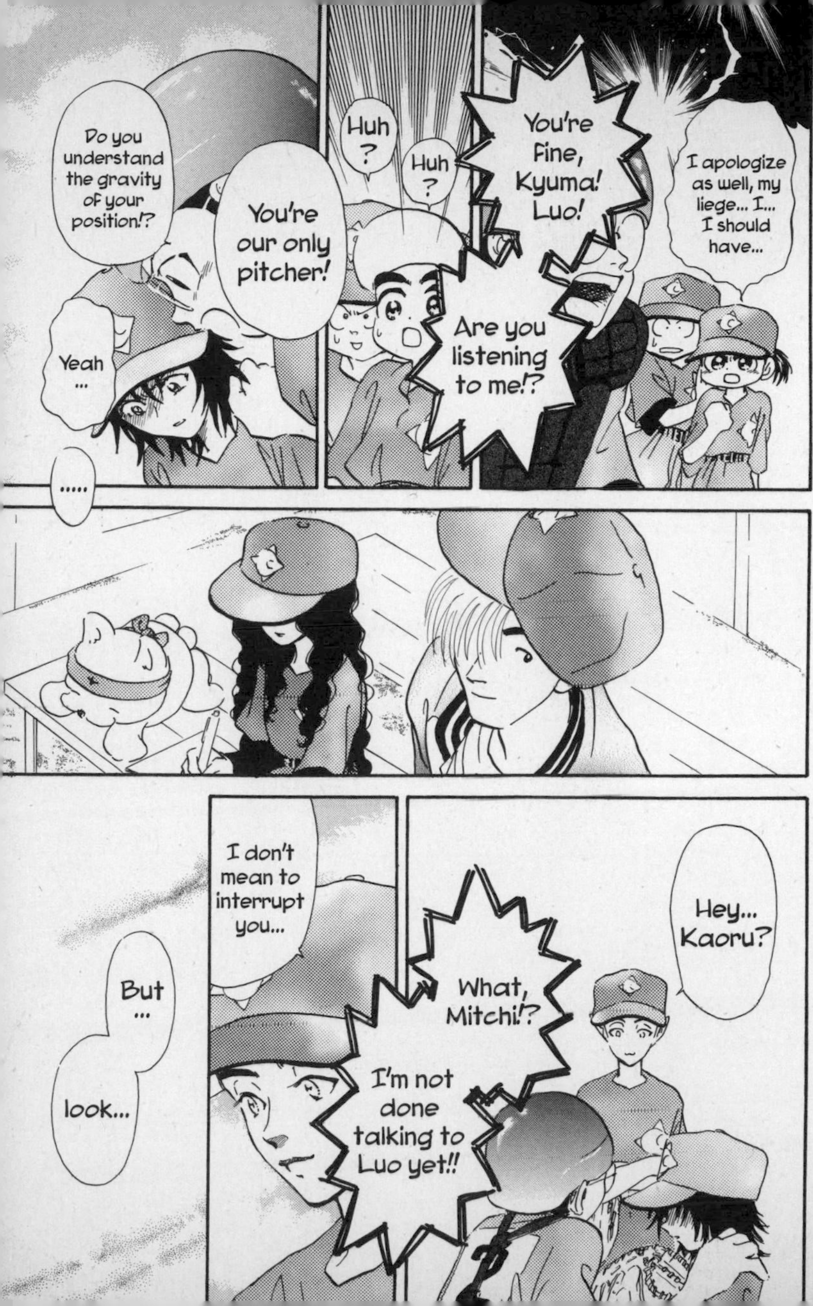
I apologize as well, my liege... I... I should have...
You're fine, Kyuma! Luo!
Are you listening to me!?
Huh ?
Huh ?
You're our only pitcher!
Do you understand the gravity of your position!?
Yeah ...
......
Hey... Kaoru?
What, Mitchi!?
I'm not done talking to Luo yet!!
I don't mean to interrupt you...
But ...
look...

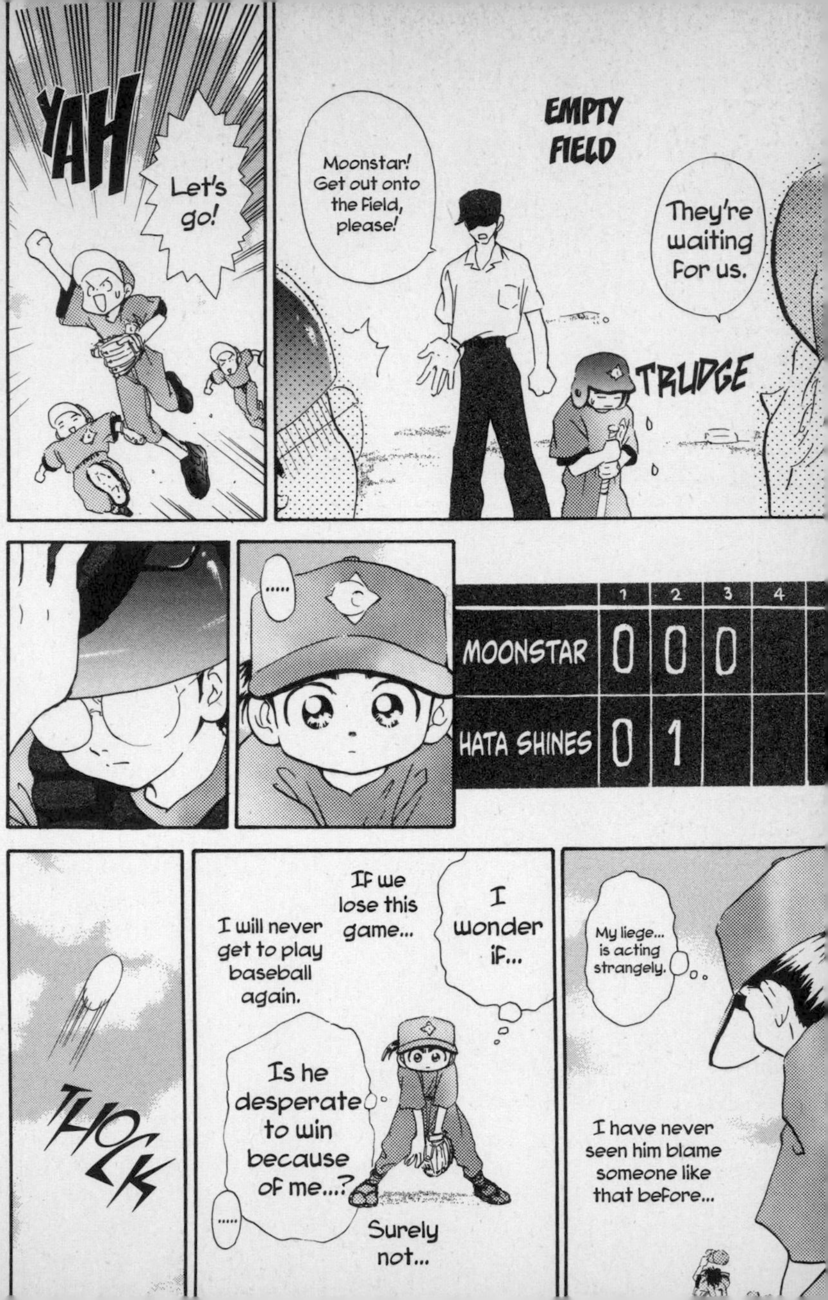
EMPTY FIELD
They're waiting for us.
Moonstar! Get out onto the field, please!
TRUDGE
YAH
Let's go!
1 2 3 4
MOONSTAR 0 0 0
HATA SHINES 0 1
......
My liege... is acting strangely.
I have never seen him blame someone like that before...
I wonder if...
If we lose this game...
I will never get to play baseball again.
Is he desperate to win because of me...?
......
Surely not...
THOCK

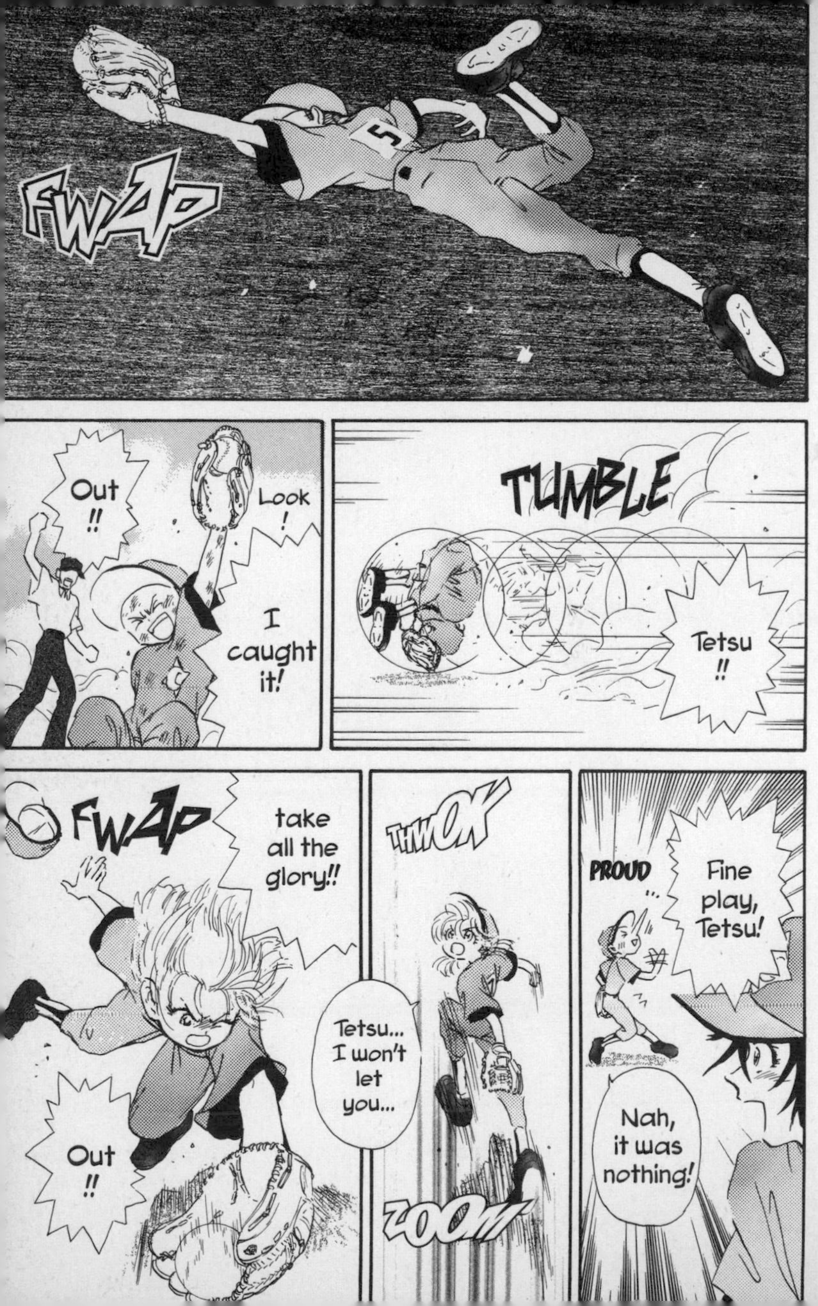
FWAP
TUMBLE
Tetsu!!
Look!
I caught it!
Out!!
Fine play, Tetsu!
PROUD...
Nah, it was nothing!
THWOK
Tetsu... I won't let you...
ZOOM
take all the glory!!
FWAP
Out!!

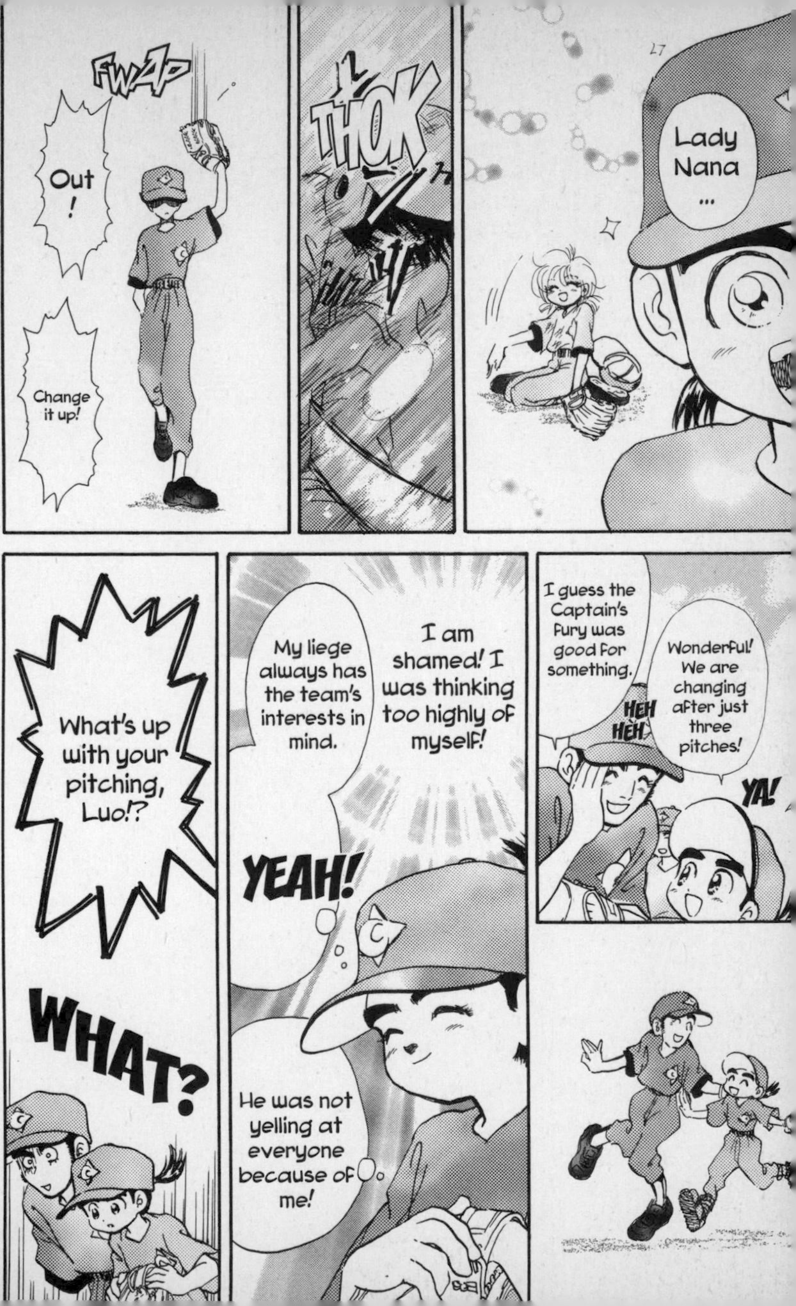
Lady Nana ...
THOK
FWAP
Out!
Change it up!
Wonderful! We are changing after just three pitches!
YA!
I guess the Captain's fury was good for something.
HEH HEH
I am shamed! I was thinking too highly of myself!
My liege always has the team's interests in mind.
YEAH!
He was not yelling at everyone because of me!
What's up with your pitching, Luo!?
WHAT?

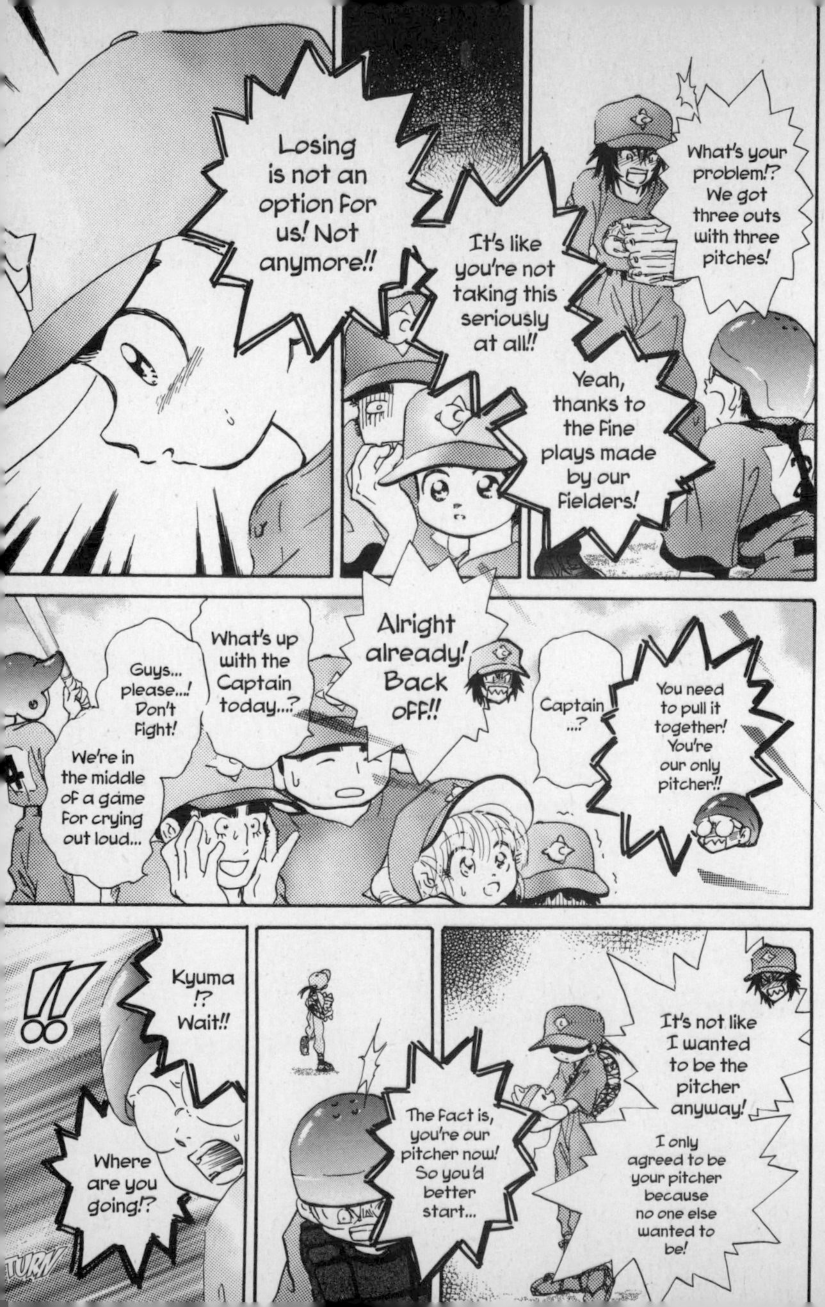
What's your problem!? We got three outs with three pitches!
Yeah, thanks to the fine plays made by our fielders!
It's like you're not taking this seriously at all!!
Losing is not an option for us! Not anymore!!
You need to pull it together! You're our only pitcher!!
Captain ...?
Alright already! Back off!!
What's up with the Captain today...?
Guys... please...! Don't fight!
We're in the middle of a game for crying out loud...
It's not like I wanted to be the pitcher anyway!
I only agreed to be your pitcher because no one else wanted to be!
The fact is, you're our pitcher now! So you'd better start...
!!
Kyuma!? Wait!!
Where are you going!?

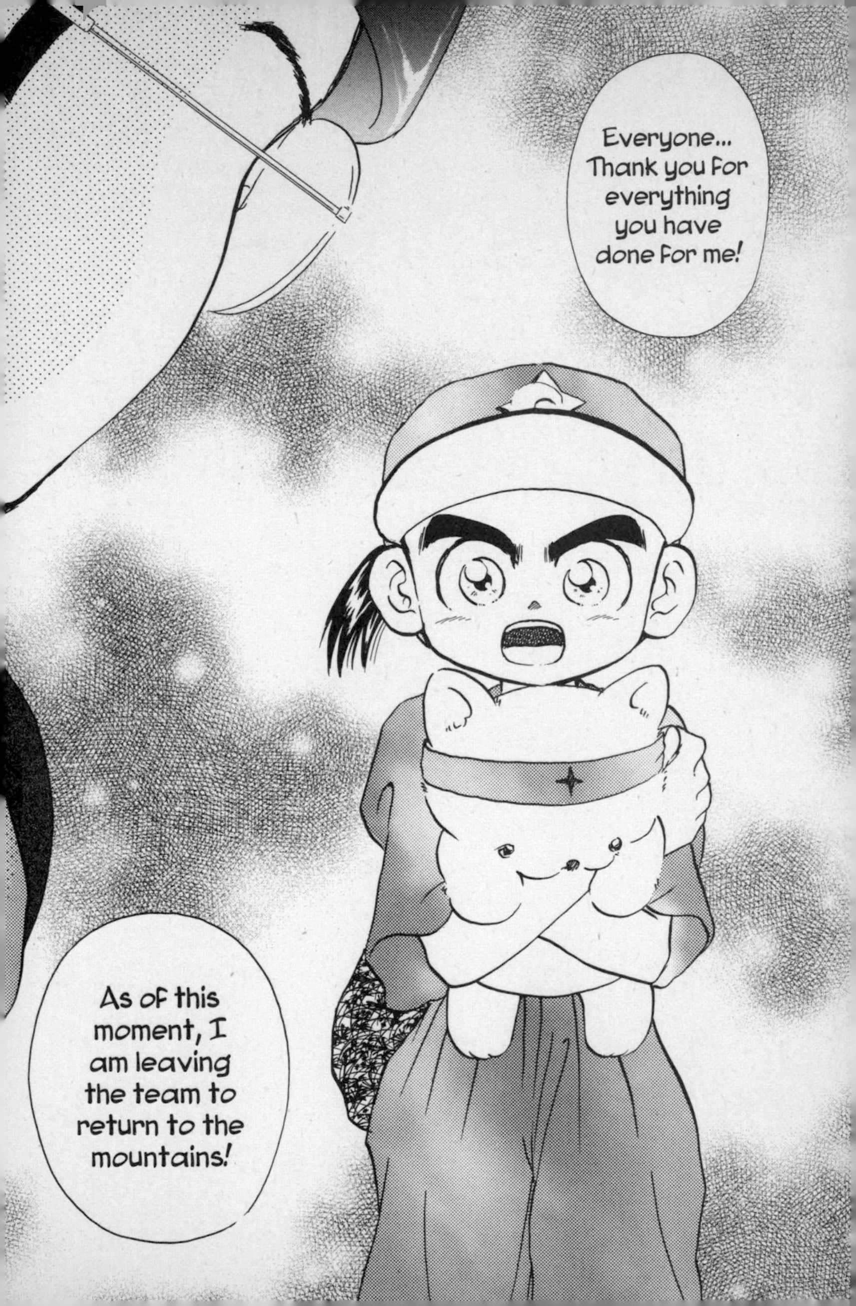
Everyone... Thank you for everything you have done for me!
As of this moment, I am leaving the team to return to the mountains!

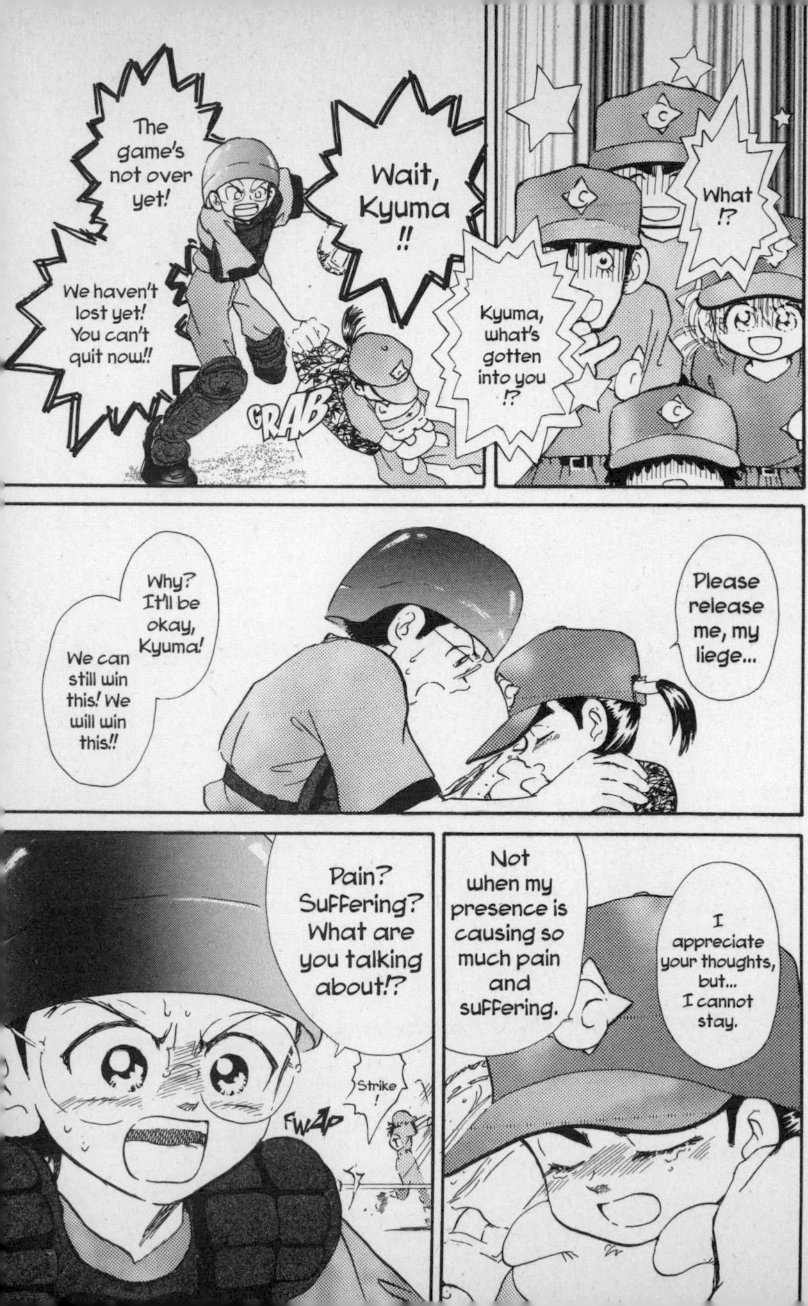
What!?
Kyuma, what's gotten into you!?
Wait, Kyuma!!
The game's not over yet!
We haven't lost yet! You can't quit now!!
GRAB
Please release me, my liege...
Why? It'll be okay, Kyuma!
We can still win this! We will win this!!
I appreciate your thoughts, but... I cannot stay.
Not when my presence is causing so much pain and suffering.
Pain? Suffering? What are you talking about!?
Strike!
FWAP

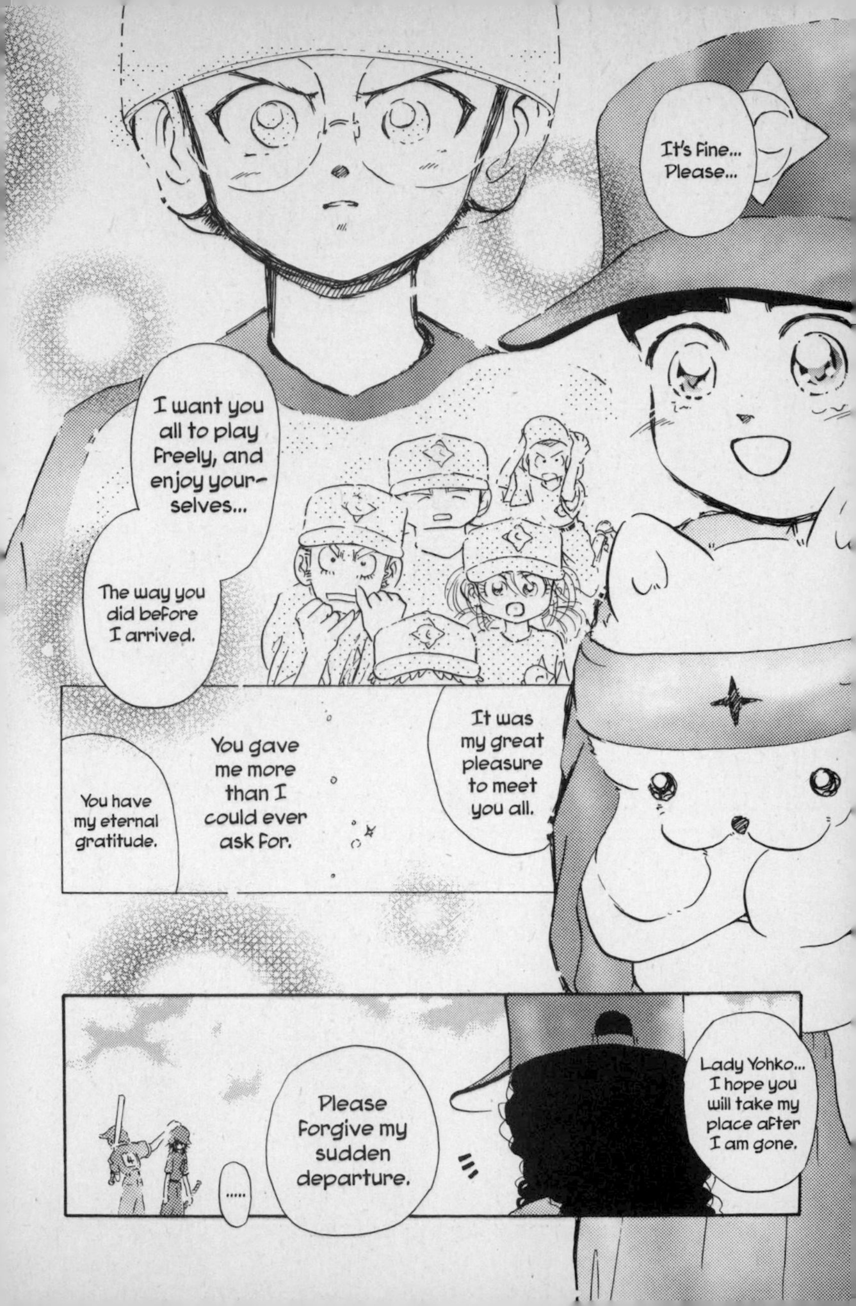
It's fine... Please...
I want you all to play freely, and enjoy your-selves...
The way you did before I arrived.
It was my great pleasure to meet you all.
You gave me more than I could ever ask for.
You have my eternal gratitude.
Lady Yohko... I hope you will take my place after I am gone.
Please forgive my sudden departure.
.....

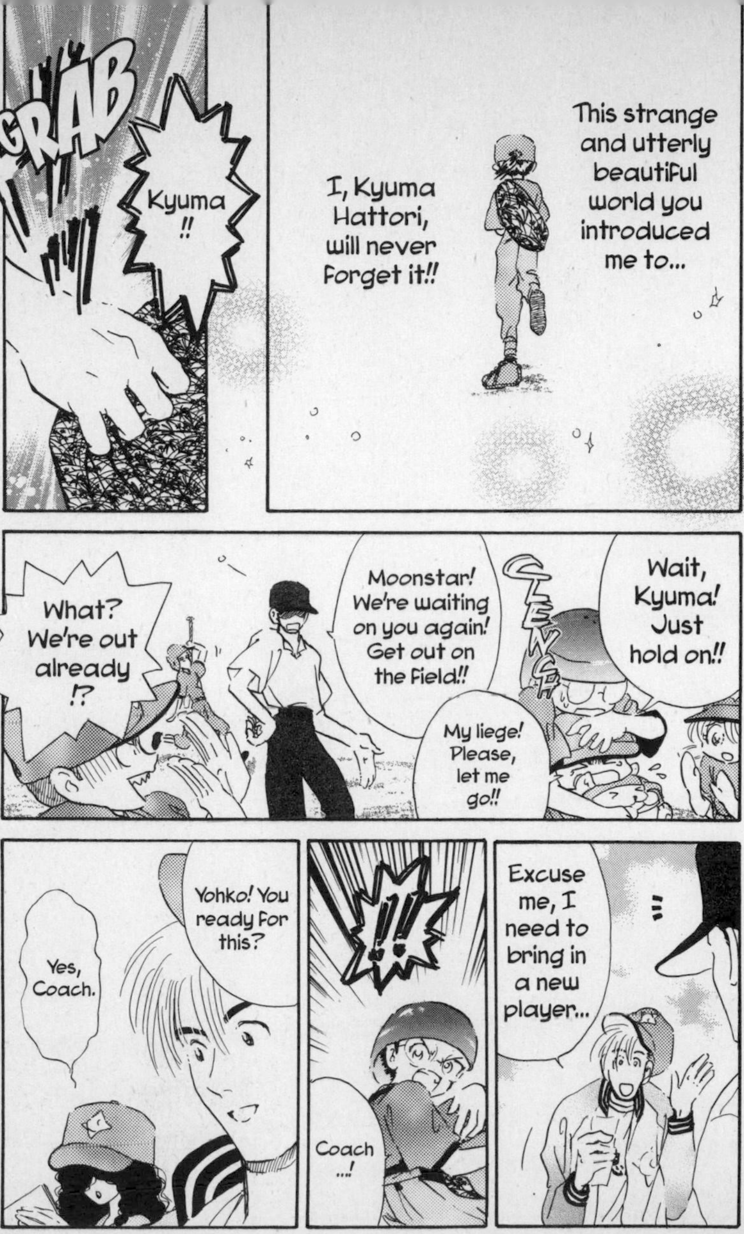
This strange and utterly beautiful world you introduced me to...
I, Kyuma Hattori, will never forget it!!
GRAB
Kyuma !!
Wait, Kyuma! Just hold on!!
CLENCH
Moonstar! We're waiting on you again! Get out on the field!!
My liege! Please, let me go!!
What? We're out already !?
Excuse me, I need to bring in a new player...
!!
Coach ...!
Yohko! You ready for this?
Yes, Coach.

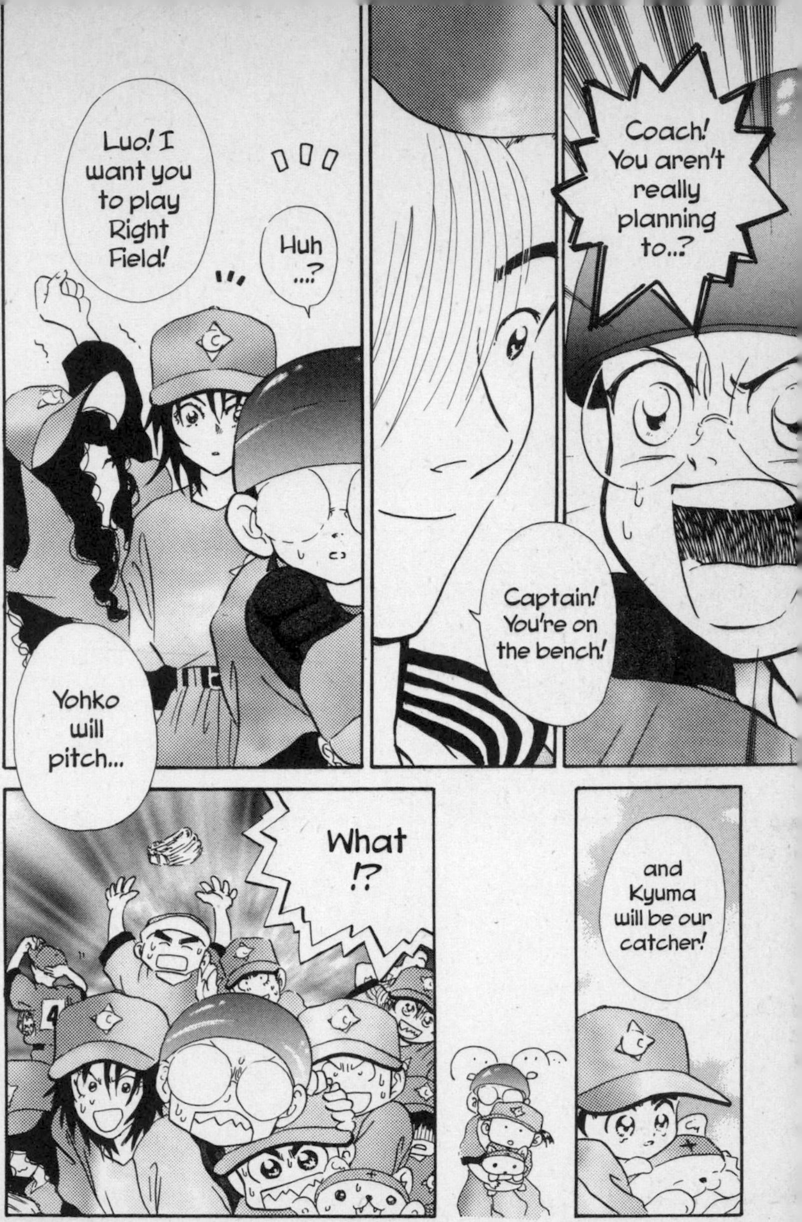
Coach! You aren't really planning to..?
Captain! You're on the bench!
Luo! I want you to play Right Field!
Huh ...?
Yohko will pitch...
and Kyuma will be our catcher!
What !?

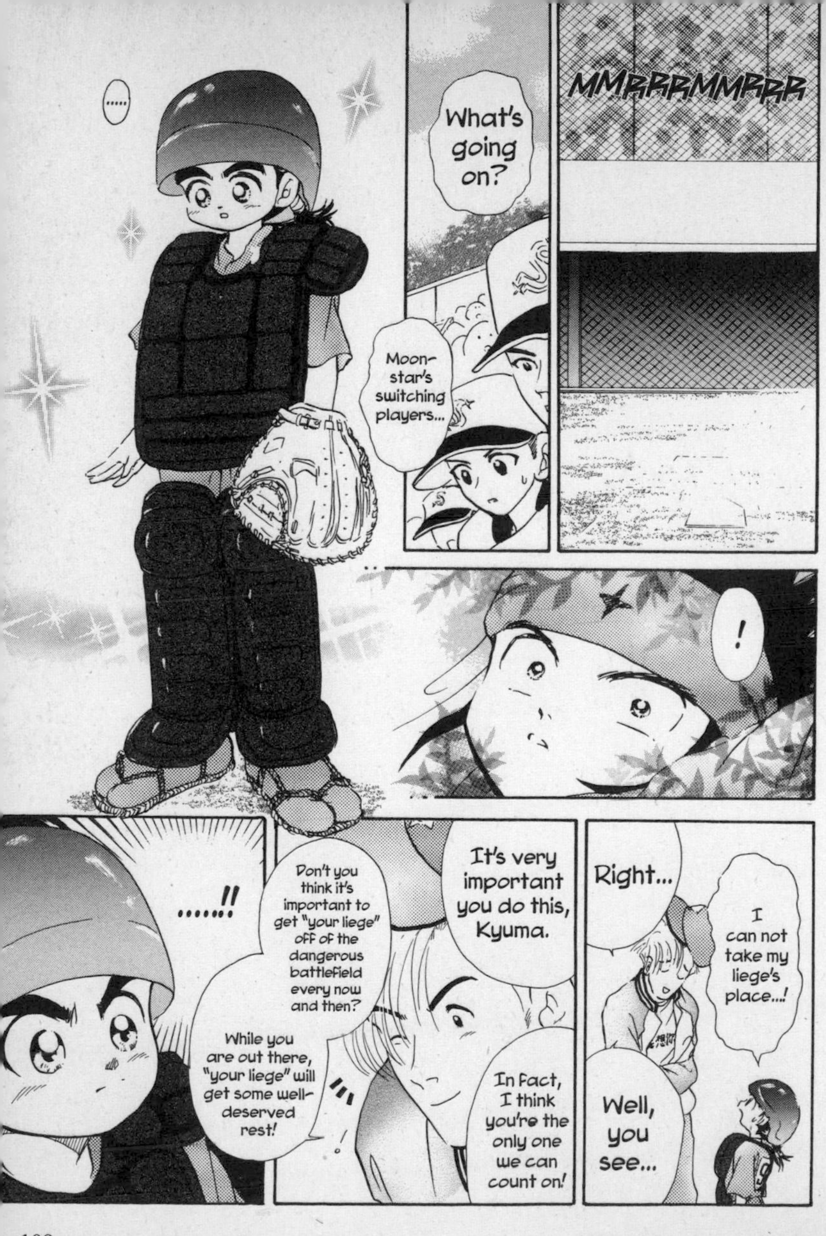

MMRRRMMRRR
What's going on?
Moon-star's switching players...
..
!
......
Right...
I can not take my liege's place...!
Well, you see...
It's very important you do this, Kyuma.
Don't you think it's important to get "your liege" off of the dangerous battlefield every now and then?
While you are out there, "your liege" will get some well-deserved rest!
In fact, I think you're the only one we can count on!
......!!

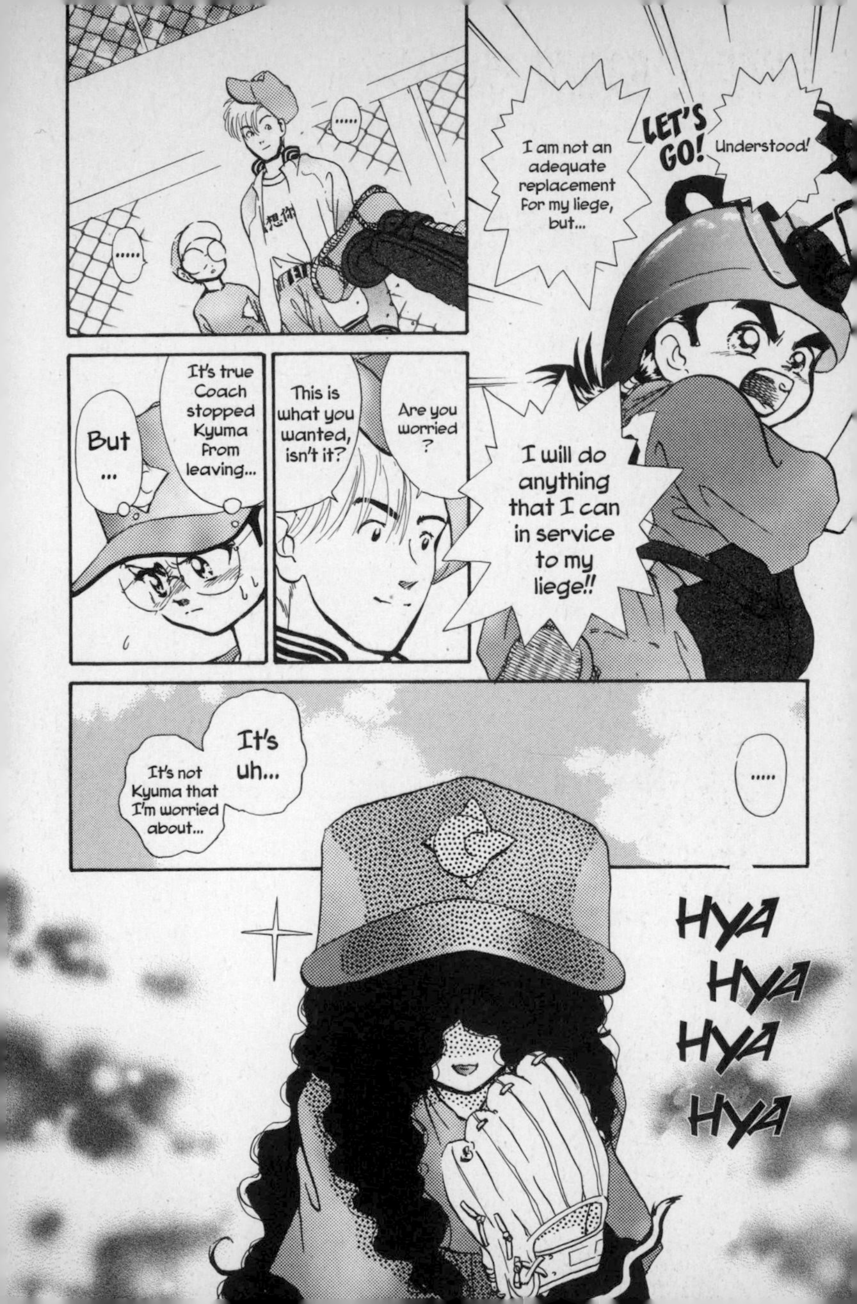
Understood!
LET'S GO!
I am not an adequate replacement for my liege, but...
I will do anything that I can in service to my liege!!
.....
......
Are you worried?
This is what you wanted, isn't it?
It's true Coach stopped Kyuma from leaving...
But ...
.....
It's uh...
It's not Kyuma that I'm worried about...
HYA HYA HYA HYA

PITCH 12 YOHKO PITCHES

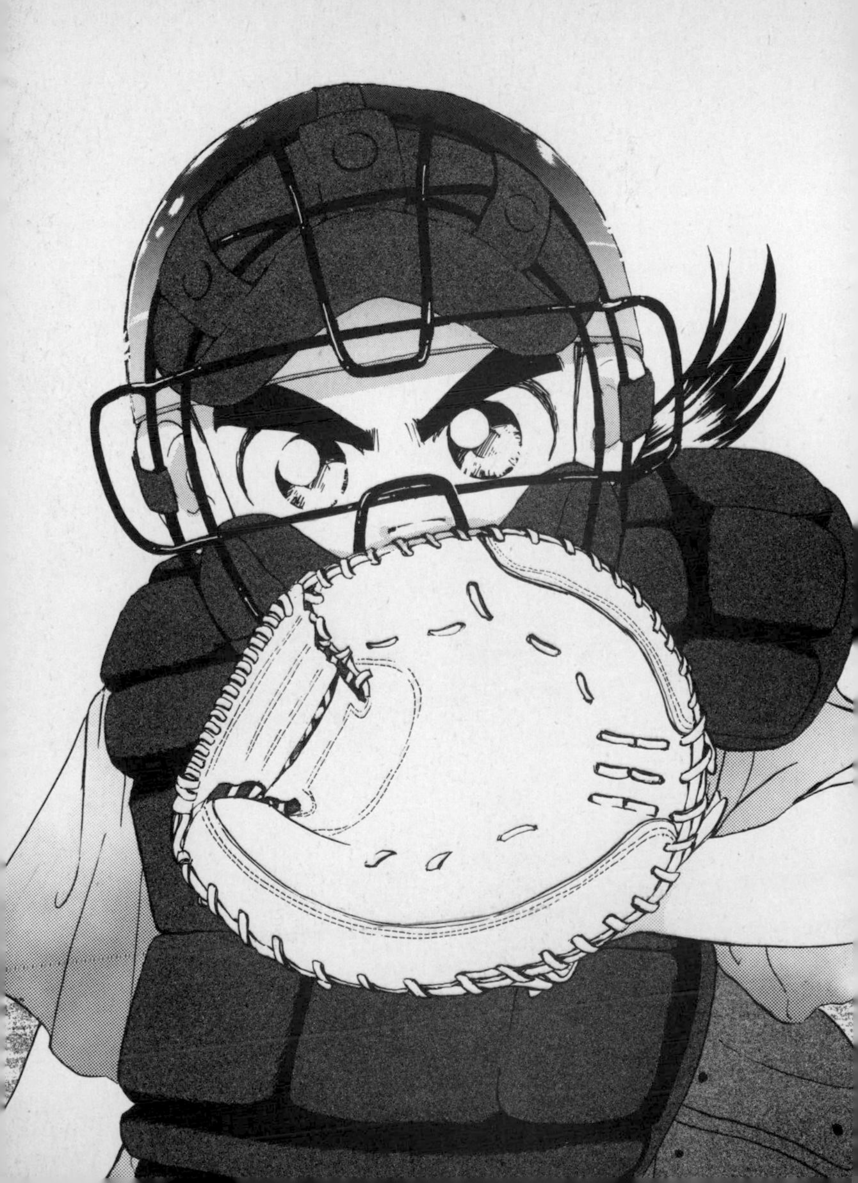

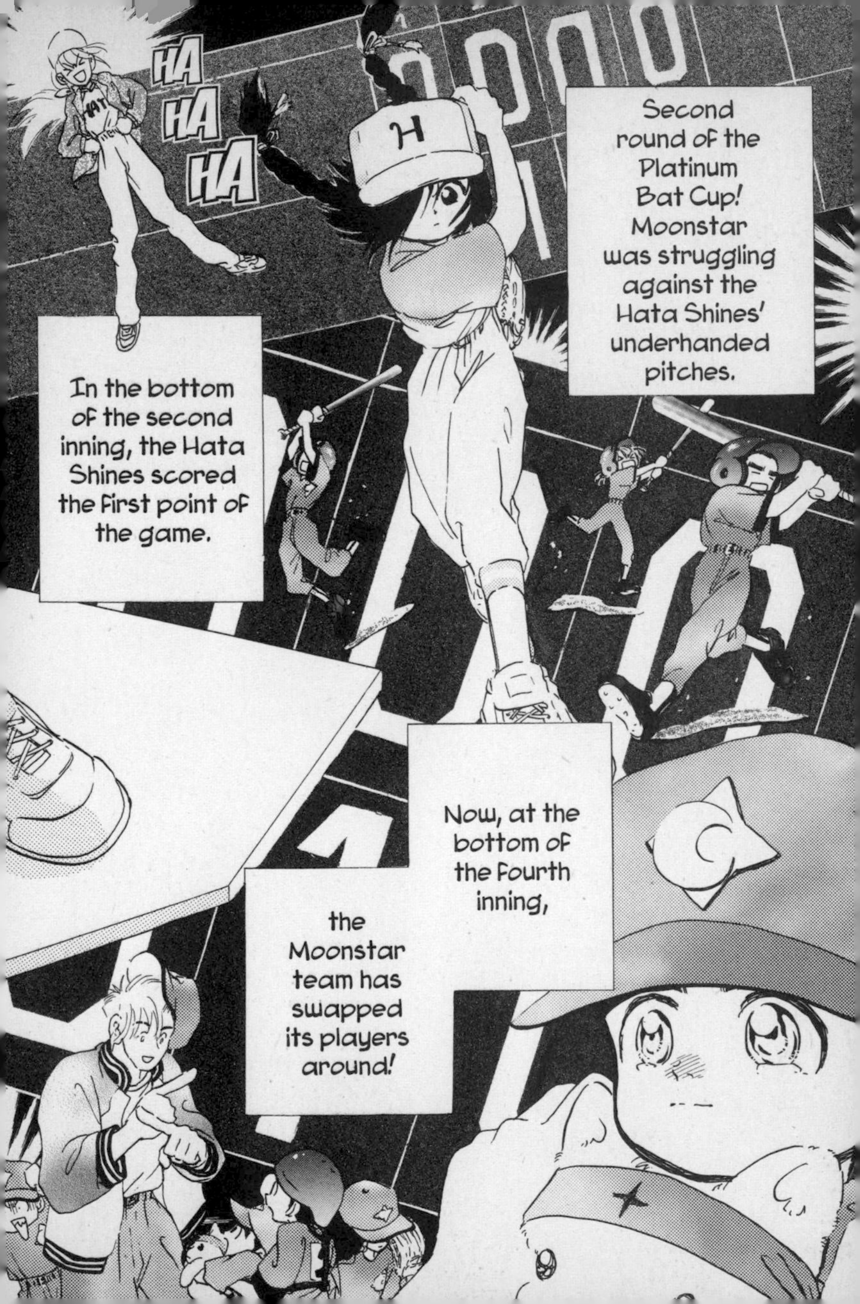
Second round of the Platinum Bat Cup! Moonstar was struggling against the Hata Shines' underhanded pitches.
HA HA HA
In the bottom of the second inning, the Hata Shines scored the first point of the game.
Now, at the bottom of the fourth inning,
the Moonstar team has swapped its players around!

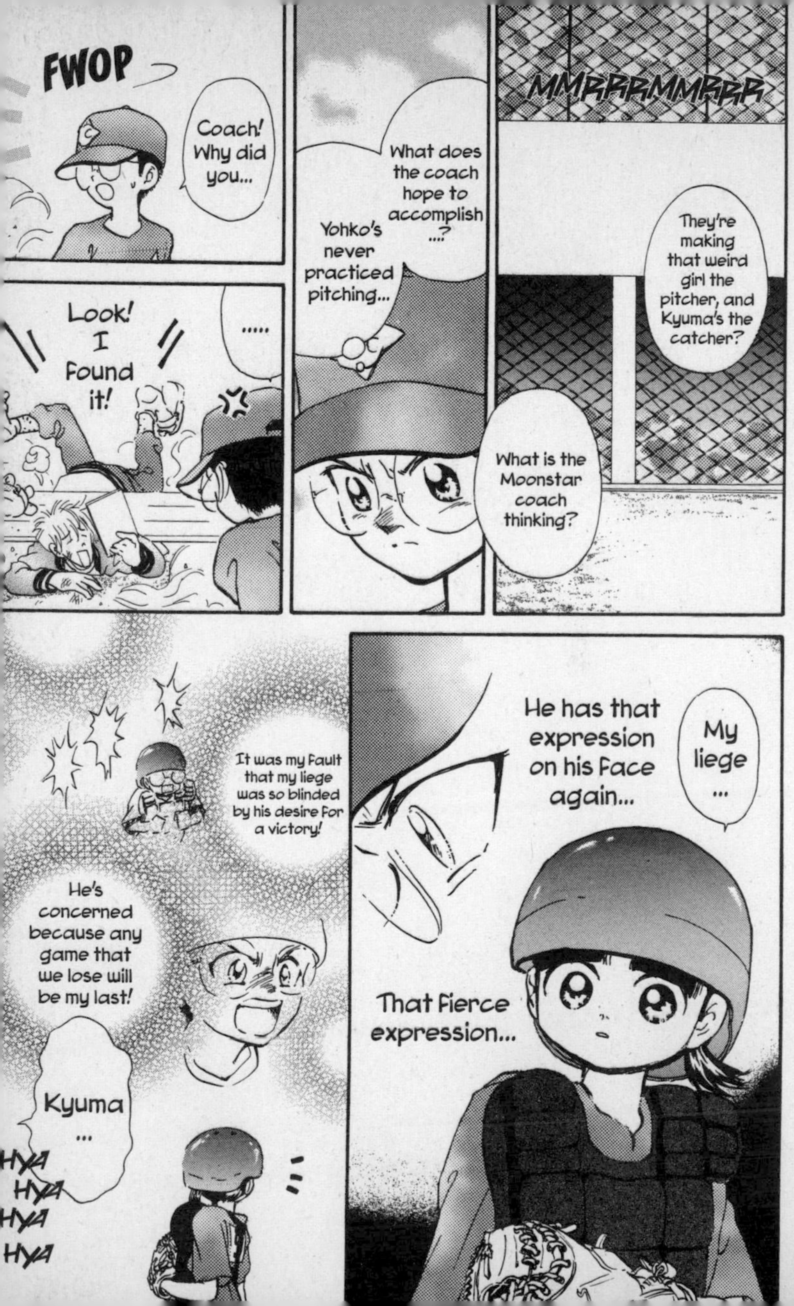
MMRRRMMRRR
They're making that weird girl the pitcher, and Kyuma's the catcher?
What is the Moonstar coach thinking?
What does the coach hope to accomplish ...?
Yohko's never practiced pitching...
Coach! Why did you...
FWOP
.....
Look! I found it!
My liege ...
He has that expression on his face again...
That fierce expression...
It was my fault that my liege was so blinded by his desire for a victory!
He's concerned because any game that we lose will be my last!
Kyuma ...
HYA HYA HYA HYA

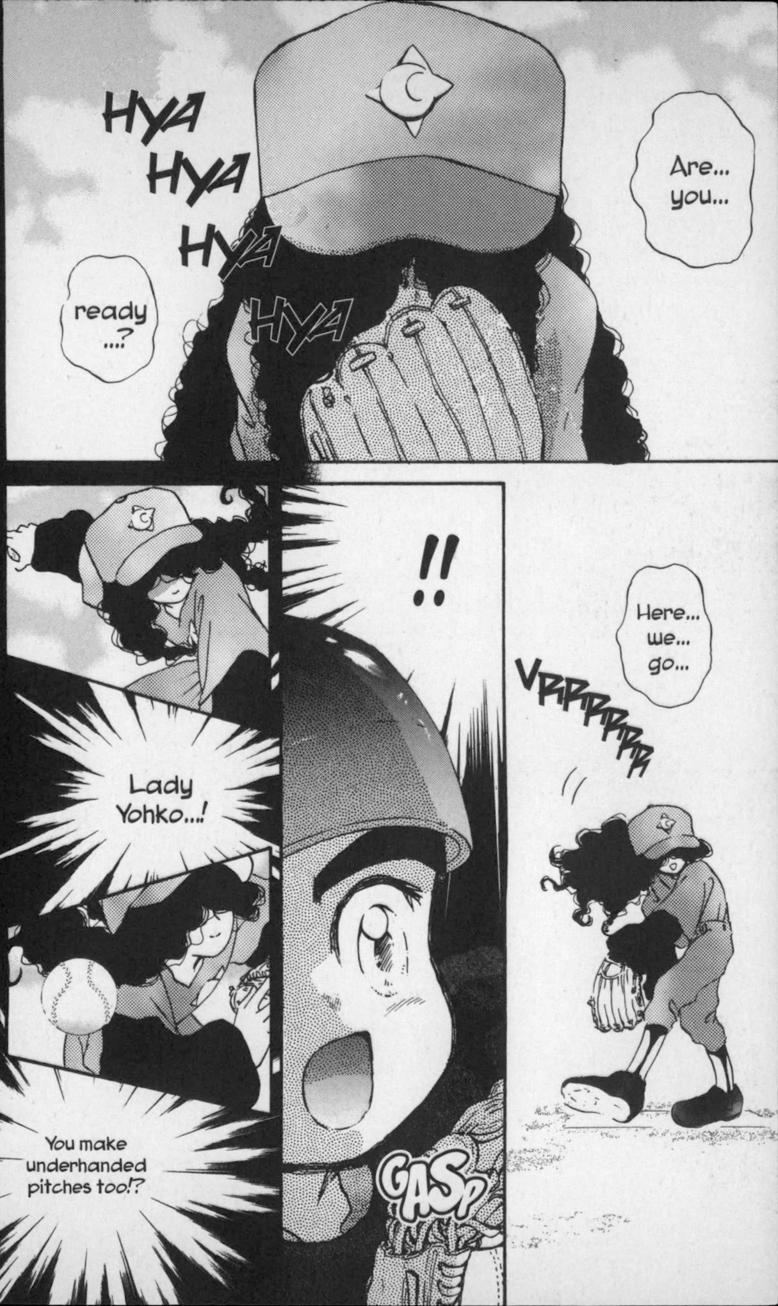
Are... you...
HYA
HYA
HYA
HYA
ready ...?
Here... we... go...
VRRRRRRR
!!
GASP
Lady Yohko...!
You make underhanded pitches too!?

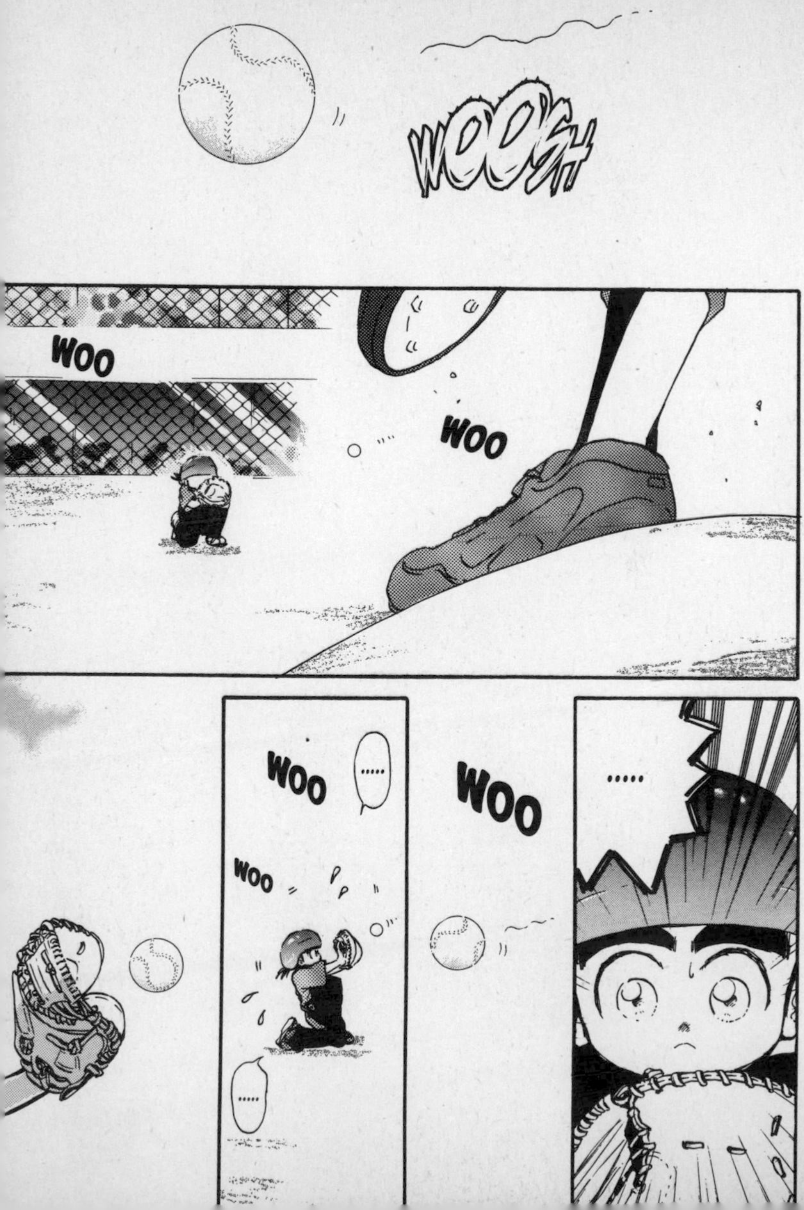
WOOSH
WOO
WOO
......
WOO
......
WOO
WOO
......

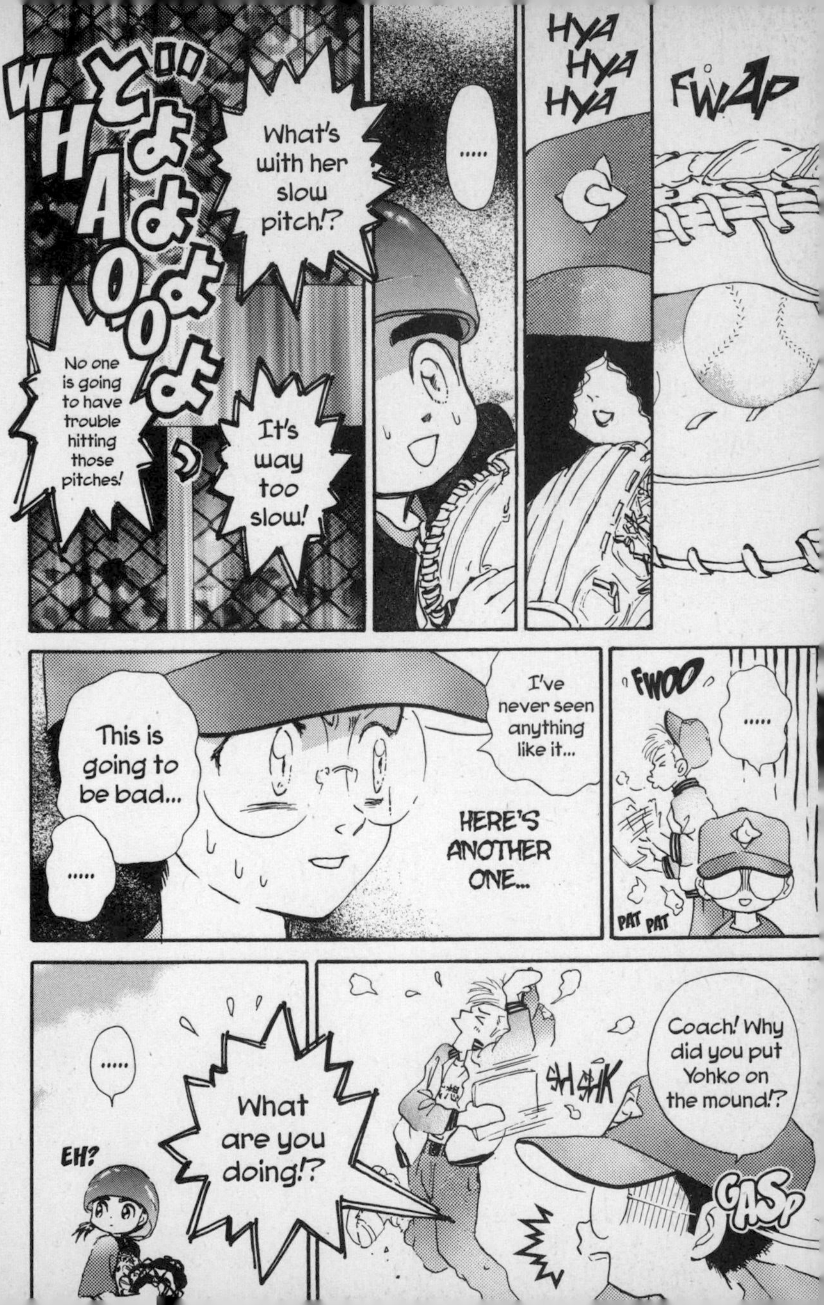
FWAP
HYA HYA HYA
.....
WHAOO
What's with her slow pitch!?
It's way too slow!
No one is going to have trouble hitting those pitches!
FWOO
.....
PAT PAT
I've never seen anything like it...
HERE'S ANOTHER ONE...
This is going to be bad...
.....
GASP
Coach! Why did you put Yohko on the mound!?
SHK SHK
What are you doing!?
EH?
.....

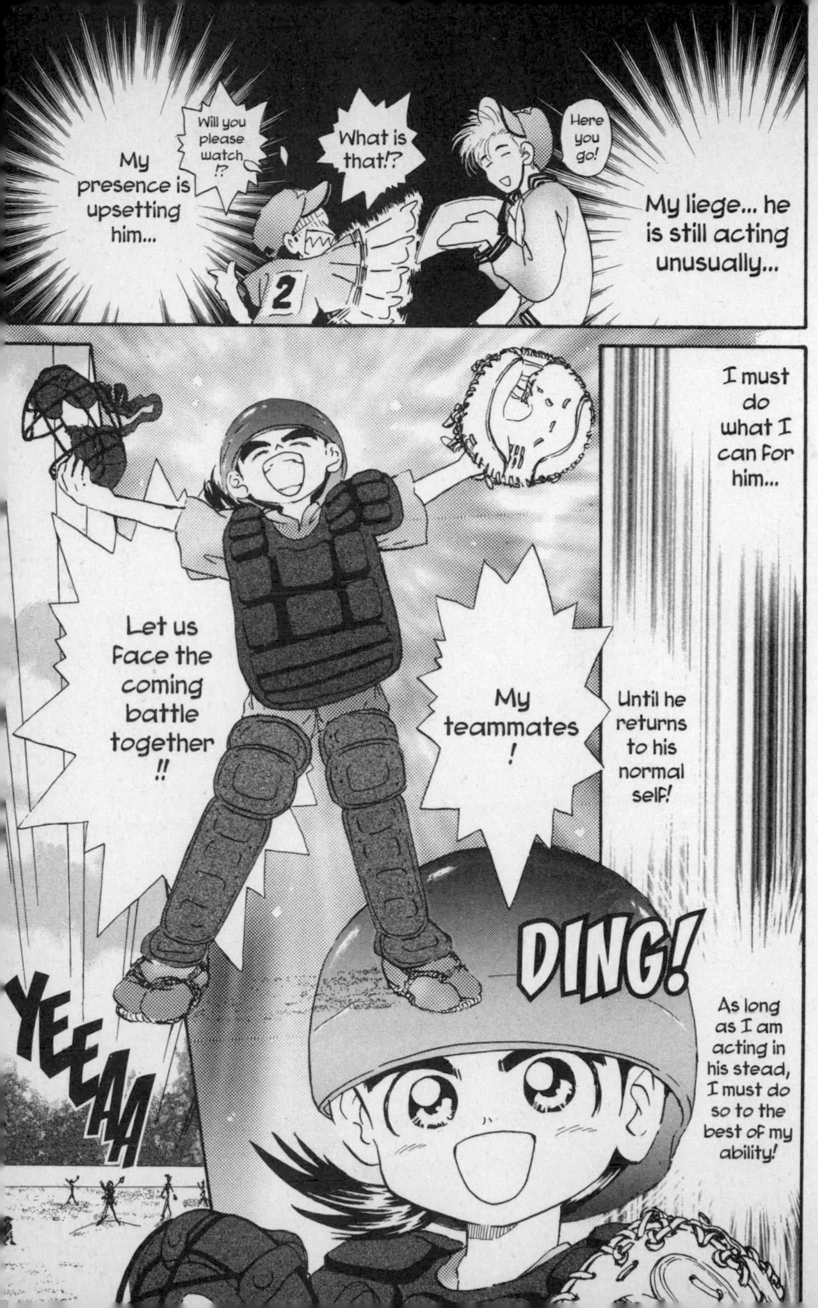
My liege... he is still acting unusually...
Here you go!
What is that!?
Will you please watch!?
My presence is upsetting him...
I must do what I can for him...
Until he returns to his normal self!
My teammates!
Let us face the coming battle together!!
DING!
As long as I am acting in his stead, I must do so to the best of my ability!
YEEAAA

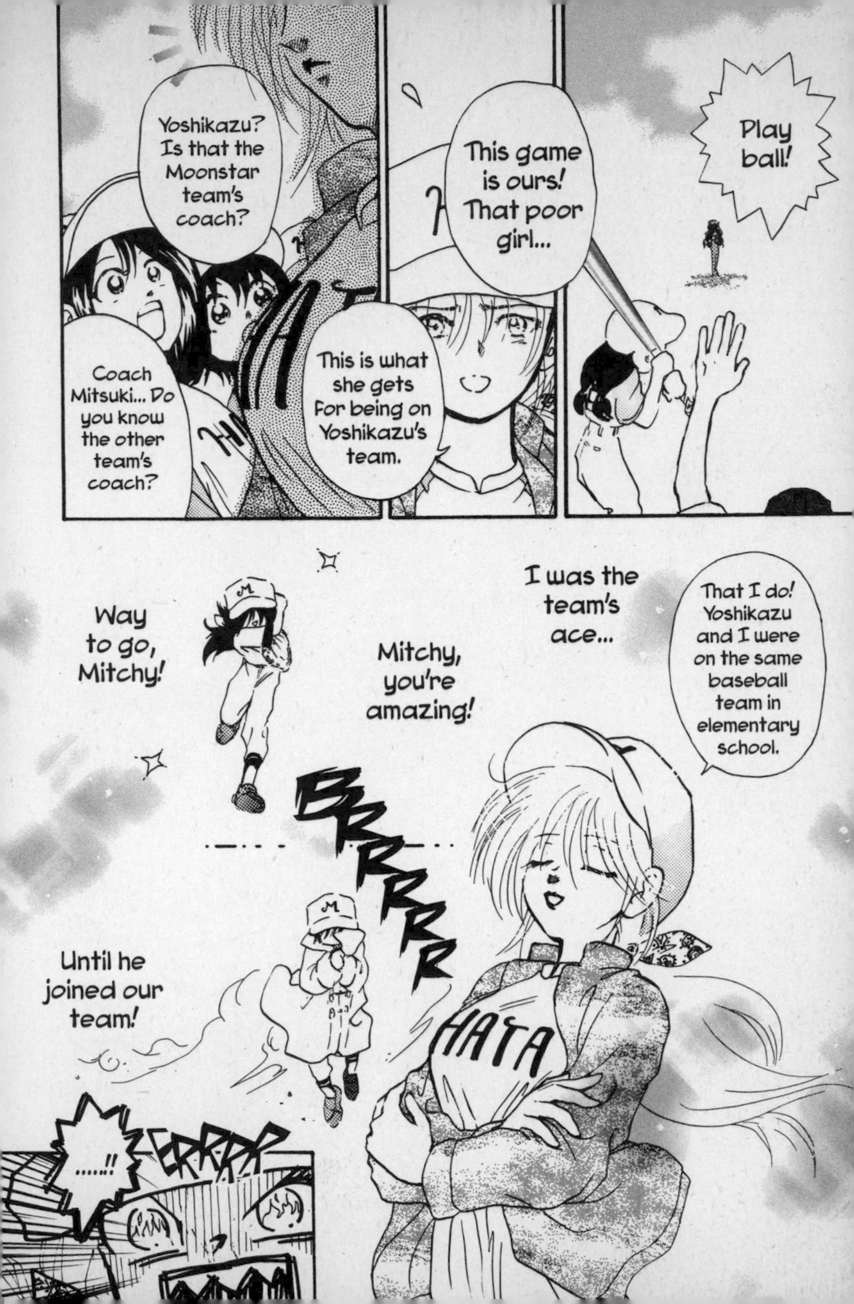

Play ball!
This game is ours! That poor girl...
This is what she gets for being on Yoshikazu's team.
Yoshikazu? Is that the Moonstar team's coach?
Coach Mitsuki... Do you know the other team's coach?
That I do! Yoshikazu and I were on the same baseball team in elementary school.
I was the team's ace...
Mitchy, you're amazing!
Way to go, Mitchy!
BRRRRRR
Until he joined our team!
ERRRRR
......!!

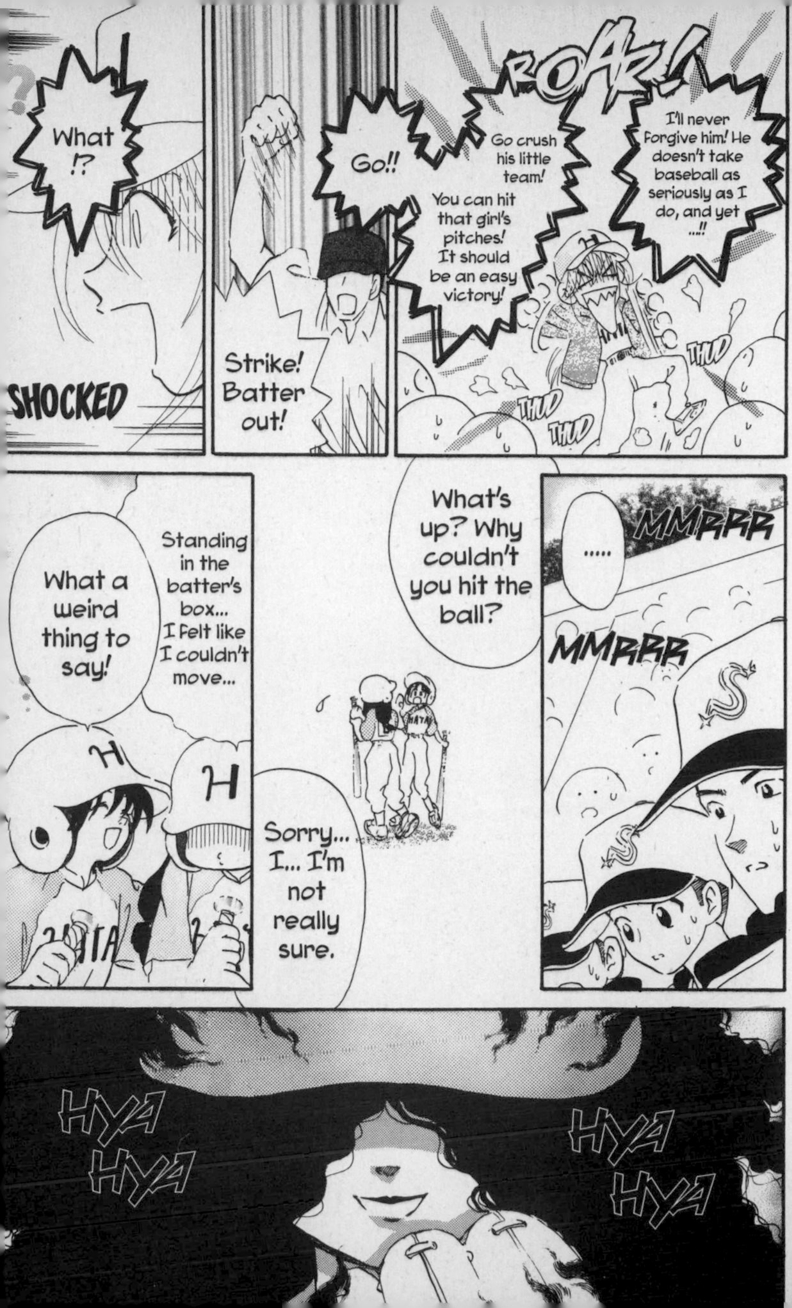
ROAR!
I'll never forgive him! He doesn't take baseball as seriously as I do, and yet ...!!
Go crush his little team!
You can hit that girl's pitches! It should be an easy victory!
THUD
THUD
THUD
Go!!
Strike! Batter out!
What !?
SHOCKED
MMRRR
.....
MMRRR
What's up? Why couldn't you hit the ball?
Sorry... I... I'm not really sure.
Standing in the batter's box... I felt like I couldn't move...
What a weird thing to say!
HYA HYA
HYA HYA

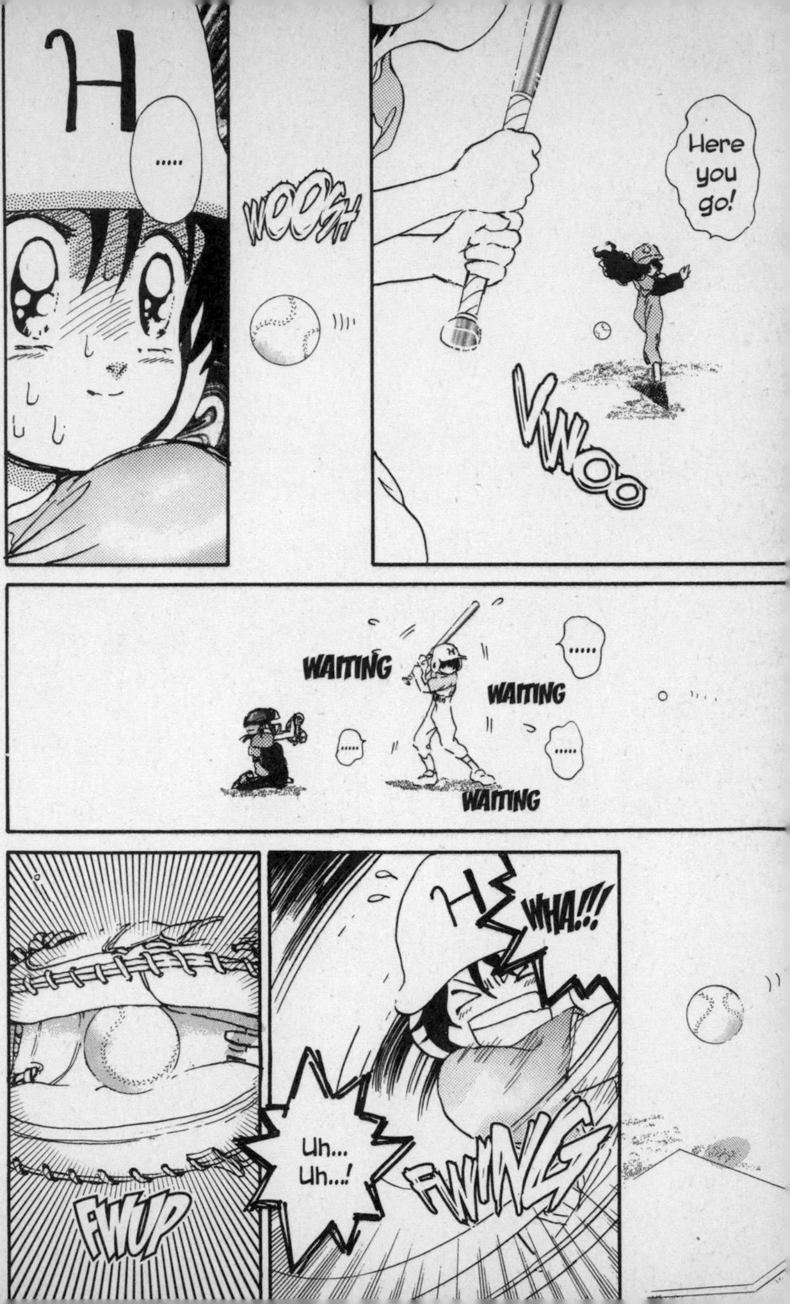
Here you go!
VWOO
WOOSH
......
......
WAITING
WAITING
......
......
WAITING
WHA!!!
Uh... Uh...!
FWING
FWUP

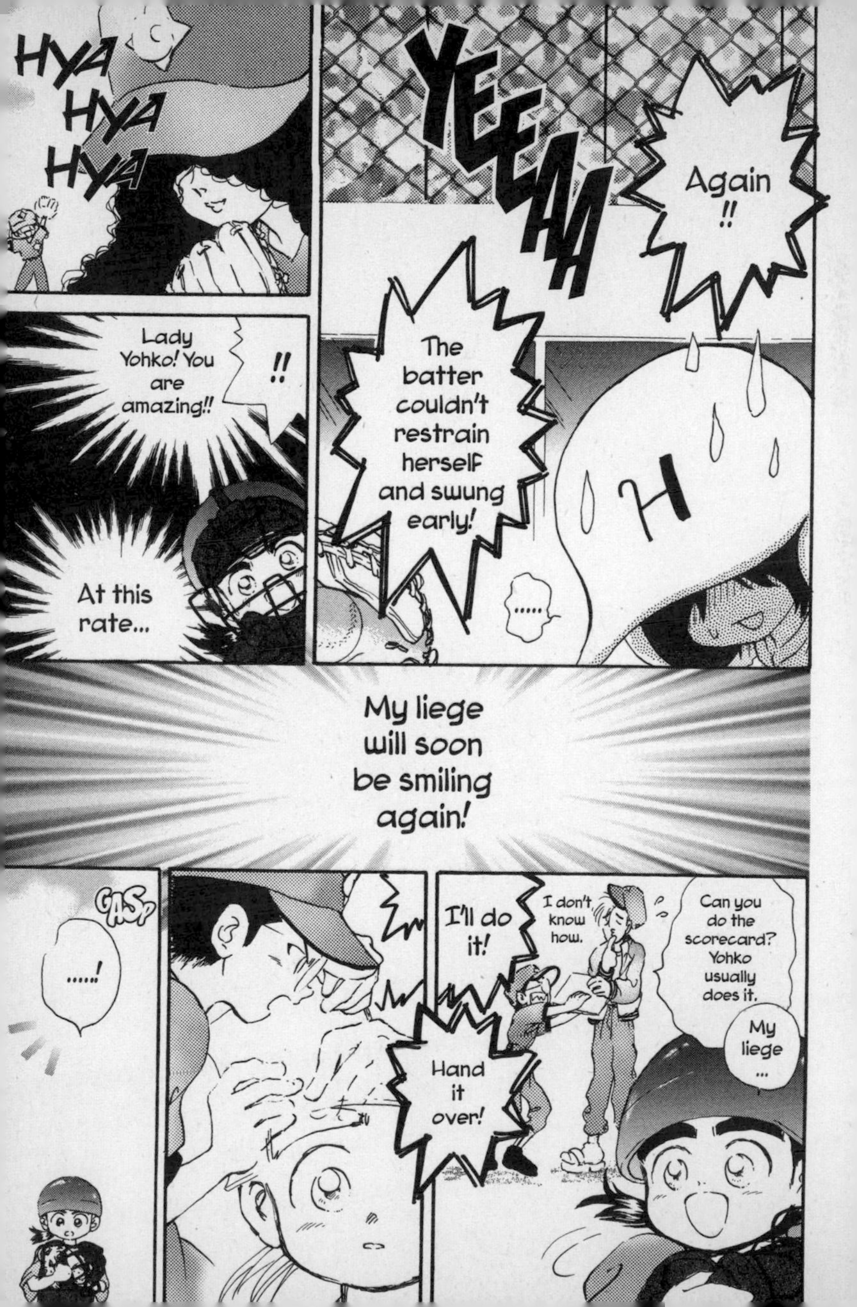

YEEAA
Again!!
HYA HYA HYA
The batter couldn't restrain herself and swung early!
......
Lady Yohko! You are amazing!!
!!
At this rate...
My liege will soon be smiling again!
Can you do the scorecard? Yohko usually does it.
I don't know how.
My liege ...
I'll do it!
Hand it over!
GASP
......!

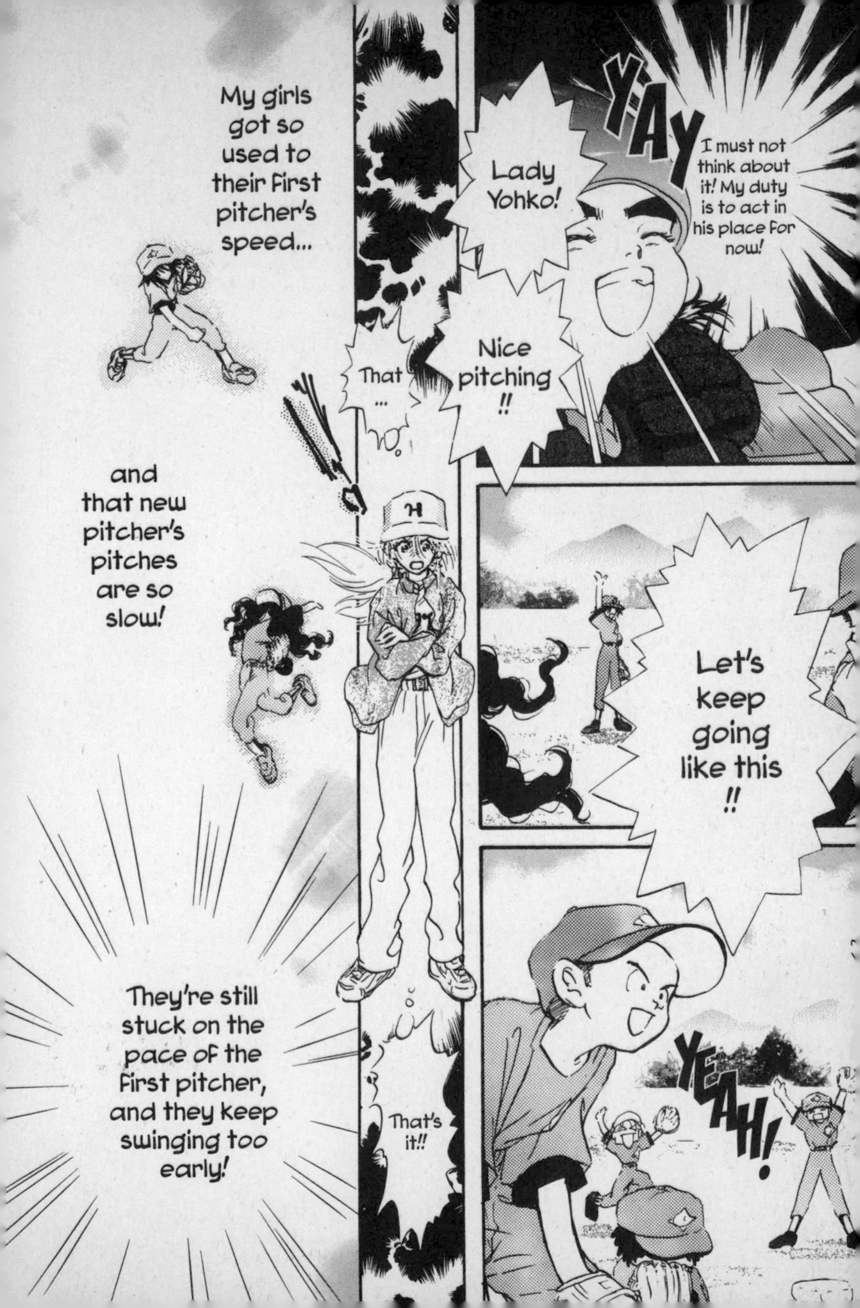

YAY
I must not think about it! My duty is to act in his place for now!
Lady Yohko!
Nice pitching!!
Let's keep going like this!!
YEAH!
That ...
That's it!!
My girls got so used to their first pitcher's speed...
and that new pitcher's pitches are so slow!
They're still stuck on the pace of the first pitcher, and they keep swinging too early!

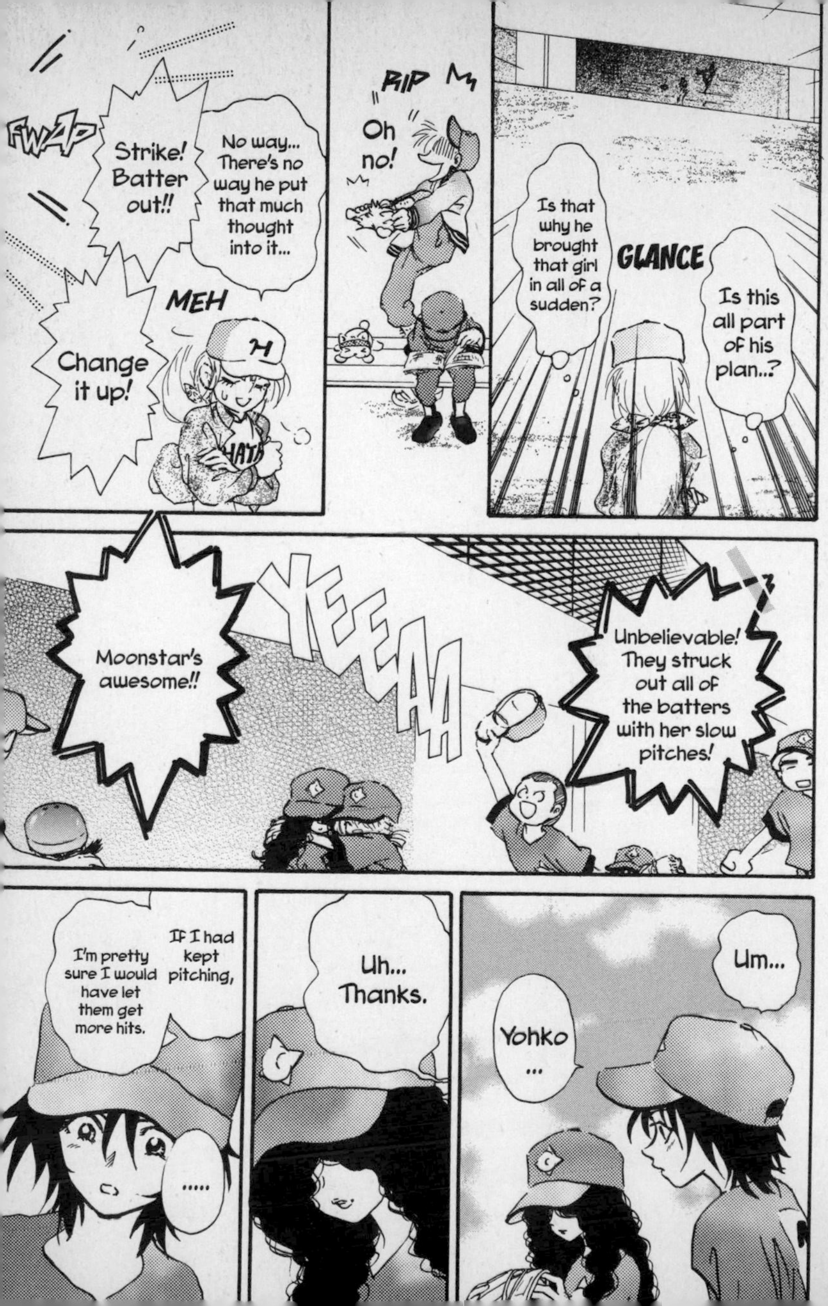
GLANCE
Is this all part of his plan..?
Is that why he brought that girl in all of a sudden?
RIP
Oh no!
FWAP
Strike! Batter out!!
No way... There's no way he put that much thought into it...
MEH
Change it up!
Unbelievable! They struck out all of the batters with her slow pitches!
YEEAA
Moonstar's awesome!!
Um...
Yohko ...
Uh... Thanks.
If I had kept pitching,
I'm pretty sure I would have let them get more hits.
.....

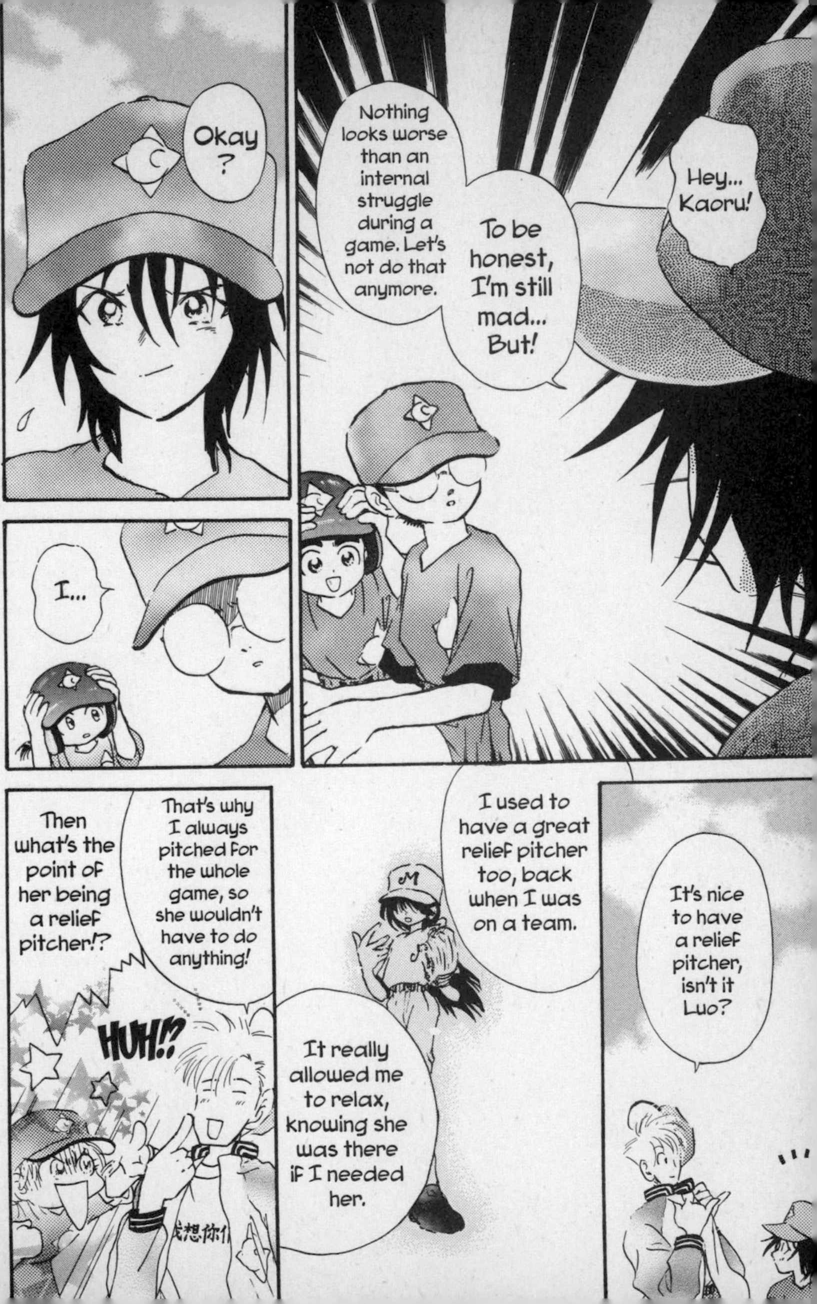

Hey... Kaoru!
To be honest, I'm still mad... But!
Nothing looks worse than an internal struggle during a game. Let's not do that anymore.
Okay?
I...
It's nice to have a relief pitcher, isn't it Luo?
...
I used to have a great relief pitcher too, back when I was on a team.
It really allowed me to relax, knowing she was there if I needed her.
That's why I always pitched for the whole game, so she wouldn't have to do anything!
Then what's the point of her being a relief pitcher!?
HUH!?

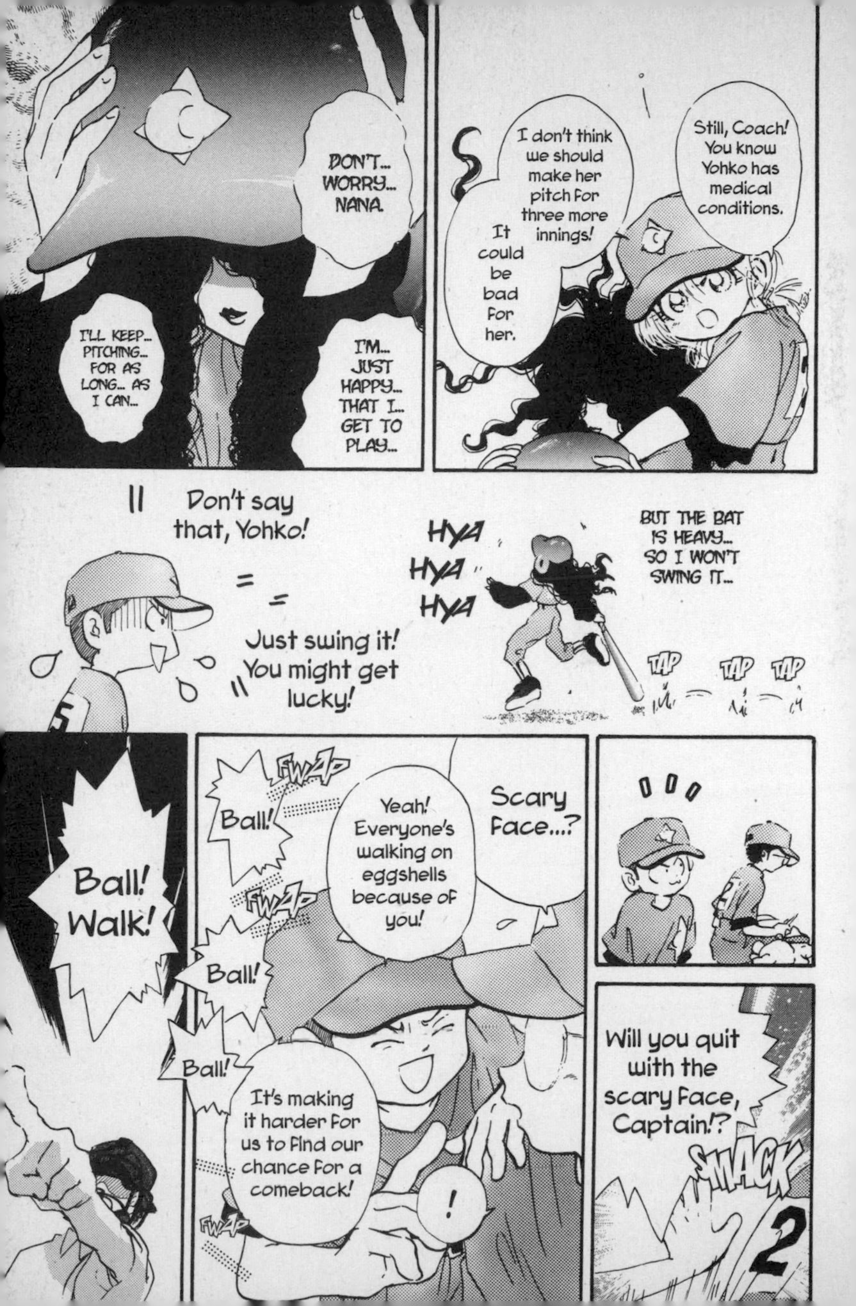
Still, Coach! You know Yohko has medical conditions.
I don't think we should make her pitch for three more innings! It could be bad for her.
DON'T... WORRY... NANA.
I'M... JUST HAPPY... THAT I... GET TO PLAY...
I'LL KEEP... PITCHING... FOR AS LONG... AS I CAN...
BUT THE BAT IS HEAVY... SO I WON'T SWING IT...
HYA
HYA
HYA
TAP
TAP
TAP
Don't say that, Yohko!
Just swing it! You might get lucky!
Will you quit with the scary face, Captain!?
SMACK
2
Scary face...?
Yeah! Everyone's walking on eggshells because of you!
FWAP
Ball!
FWAP
Ball!
Ball!
It's making it harder for us to find our chance for a comeback!
!
FWAP
Ball! Walk!

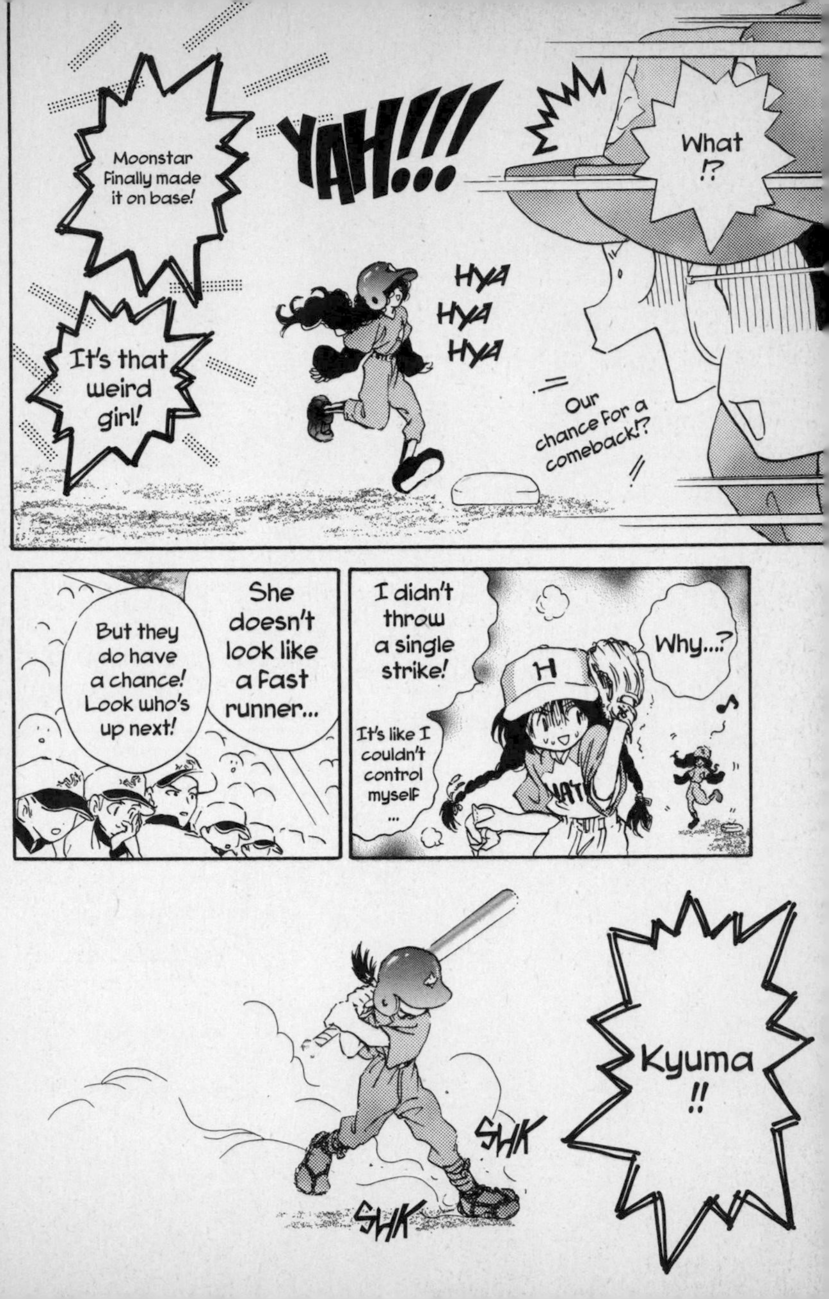
What!?
YAH!!!!...
Moonstar finally made it on base!
Hya Hya Hya
Our chance for a comeback!?
It's that weird girl!
Why...?
I didn't throw a single strike!
It's like I couldn't control myself ...
She doesn't look like a fast runner...
But they do have a chance! Look who's up next!
Kyuma!!
SHK
SHK

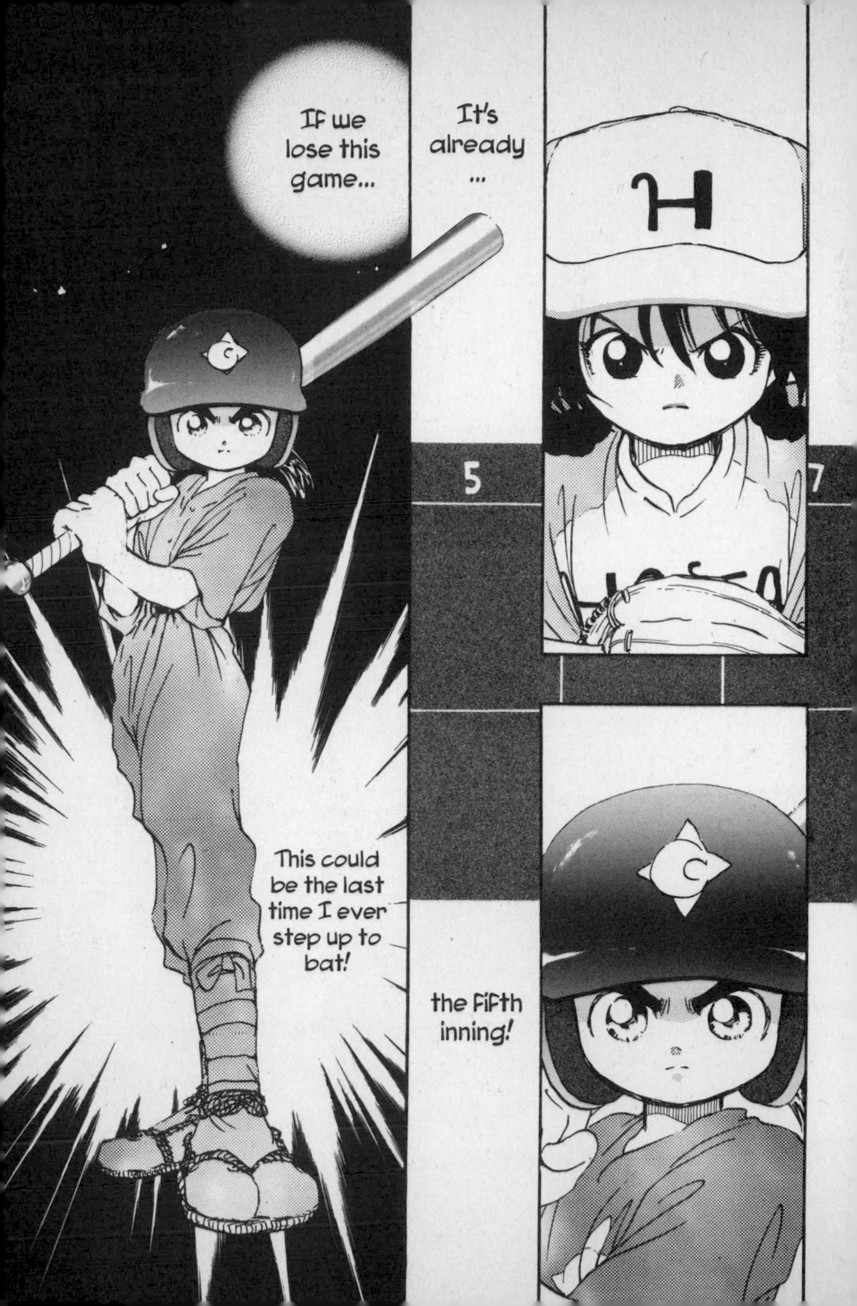
It's already ...
the fifth inning!
If we lose this game...
This could be the last time I ever step up to bat!

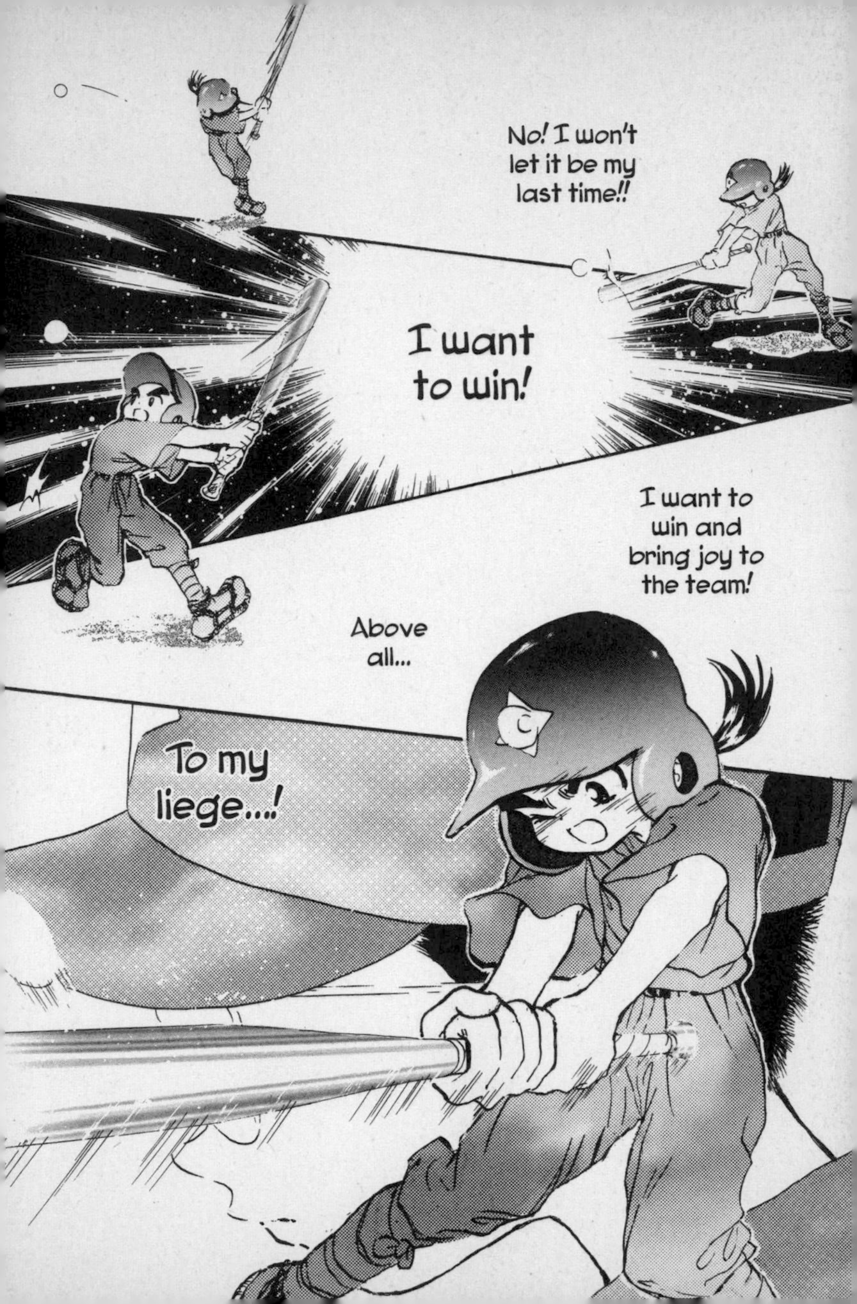
No! I won't let it be my last time!!
I want to win!
I want to win and bring joy to the team!
Above all...
To my liege...!

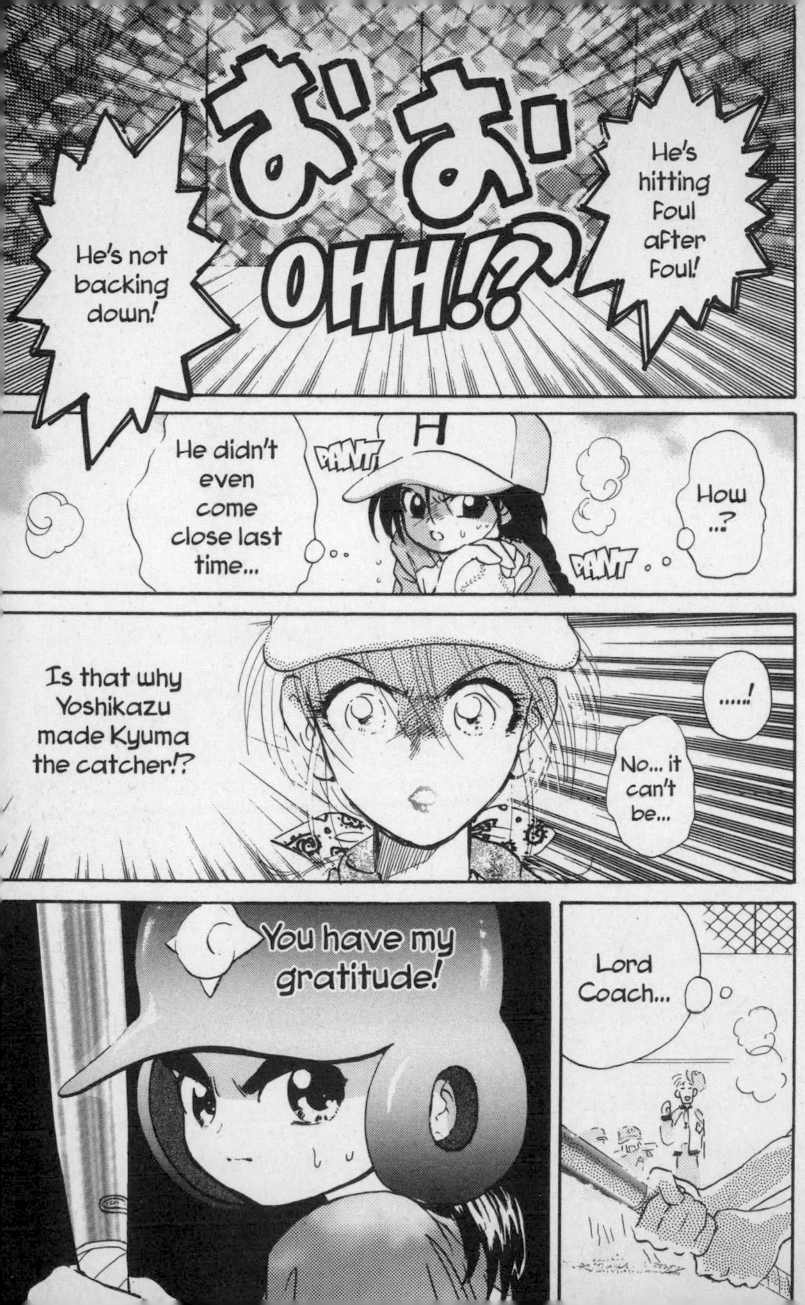

He's hitting foul after foul!
おお OHH!?
He's not backing down!
How ...?
PANT
He didn't even come close last time...
PANT
......!
No... it can't be...
Is that why Yoshikazu made Kyuma the catcher!?
Lord Coach...
You have my gratitude!

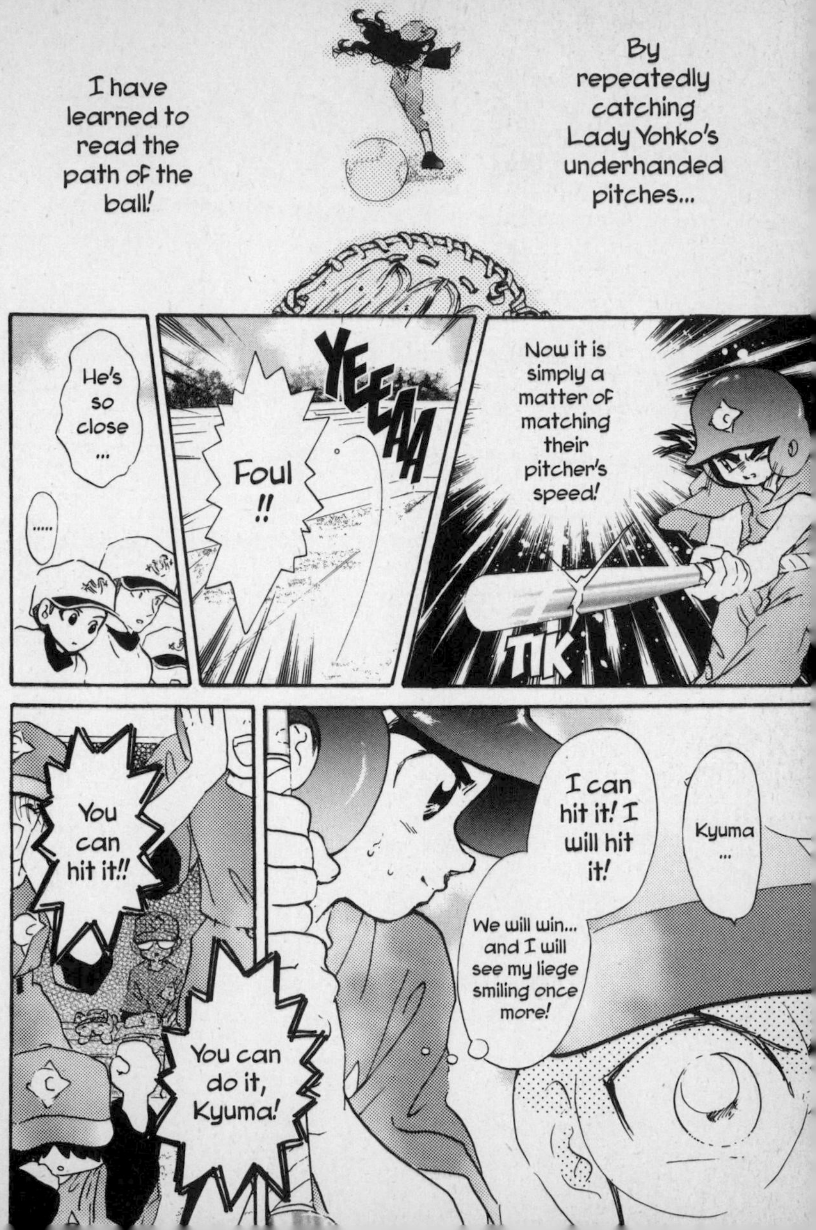
By repeatedly catching Lady Yohko's underhanded pitches...
I have learned to read the path of the ball!
Now it is simply a matter of matching their pitcher's speed!
TIK
YEEAAA
Foul !!
He's so close ...
.....
Kyuma ...
I can hit it! I will hit it!
We will win... and I will see my liege smiling once more!
You can hit it!!
You can do it, Kyuma!

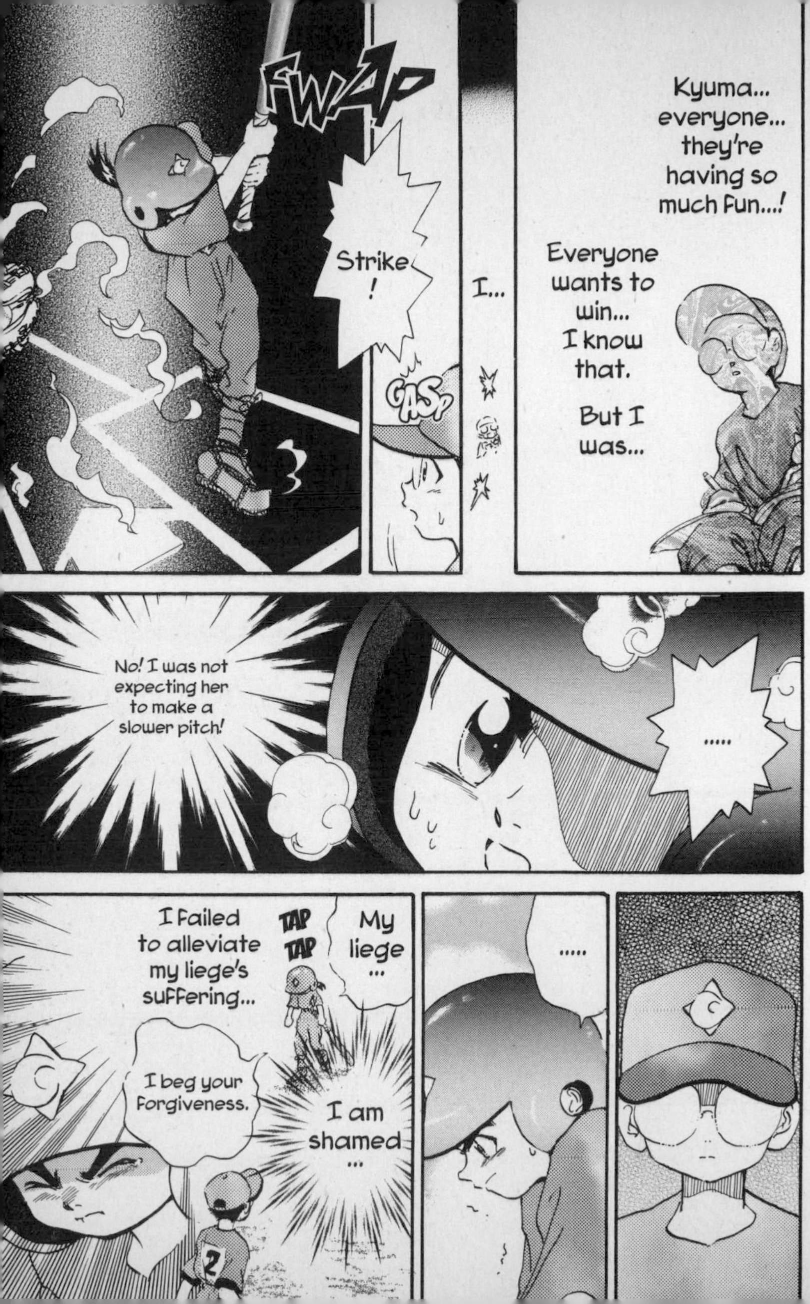
Kyuma... everyone... they're having so much fun...!
Everyone wants to win... I know that.
But I was...
I...
GASP
FWAP
Strike!
.....
No! I was not expecting her to make a slower pitch!
.....
My liege...
TAP TAP
I failed to alleviate my liege's suffering...
I am shamed...
I beg your forgiveness.

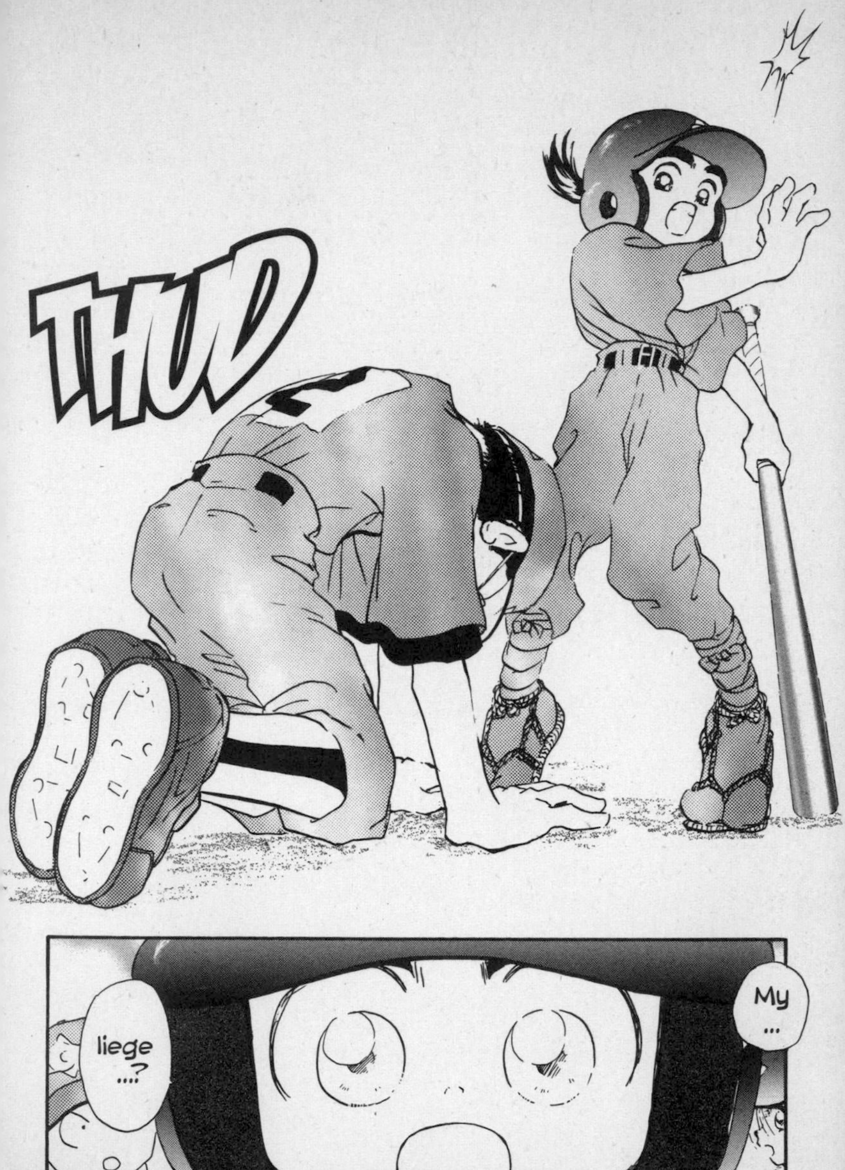
THUD
My ...
liege ....?

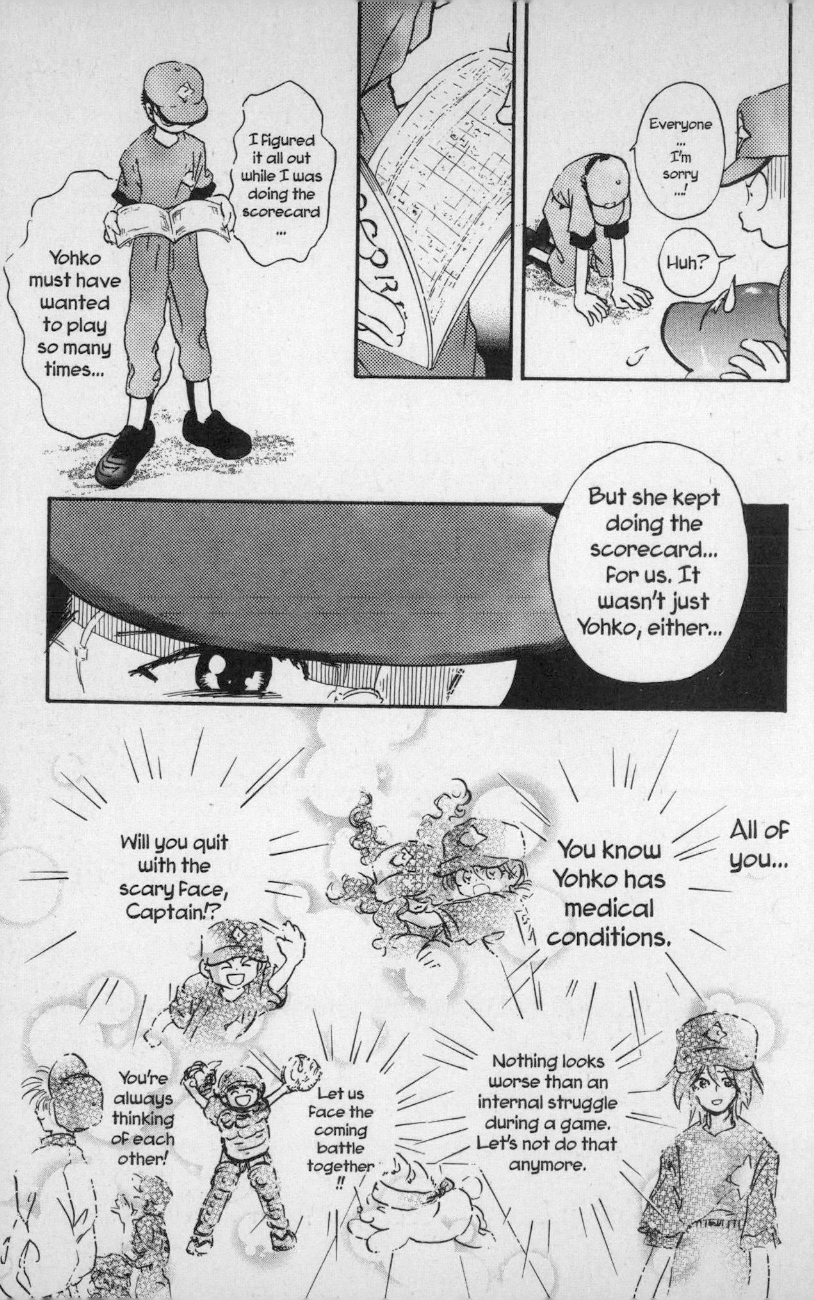
Everyone ... I'm sorry ...!
Huh?
I figured it all out while I was doing the scorecard ...
Yohko must have wanted to play so many times...
But she kept doing the scorecard... for us. It wasn't just Yohko, either...
All of you...
You know Yohko has medical conditions.
Will you quit with the scary face, Captain!?
Nothing looks worse than an internal struggle during a game. Let's not do that anymore.
Let us face the coming battle together!!
You're always thinking of each other!

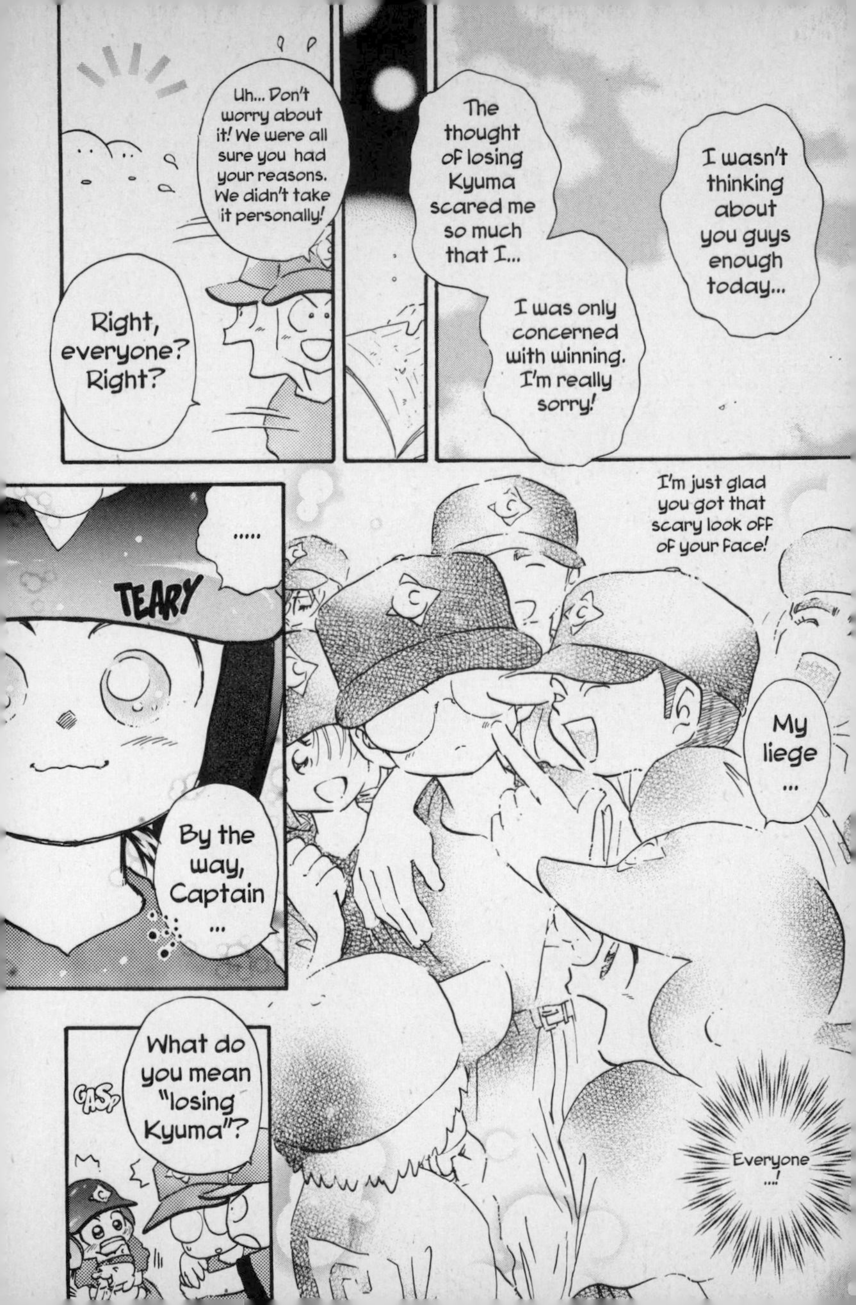
I wasn't thinking about you guys enough today...
The thought of losing Kyuma scared me so much that I...
I was only concerned with winning. I'm really sorry!
Uh... Don't worry about it! We were all sure you had your reasons. We didn't take it personally!
Right, everyone? Right?
I'm just glad you got that scary look off of your face!
My liege ...
Everyone ...!
.....
TEARY
By the way, Captain ...
GASP
What do you mean "losing Kyuma"?

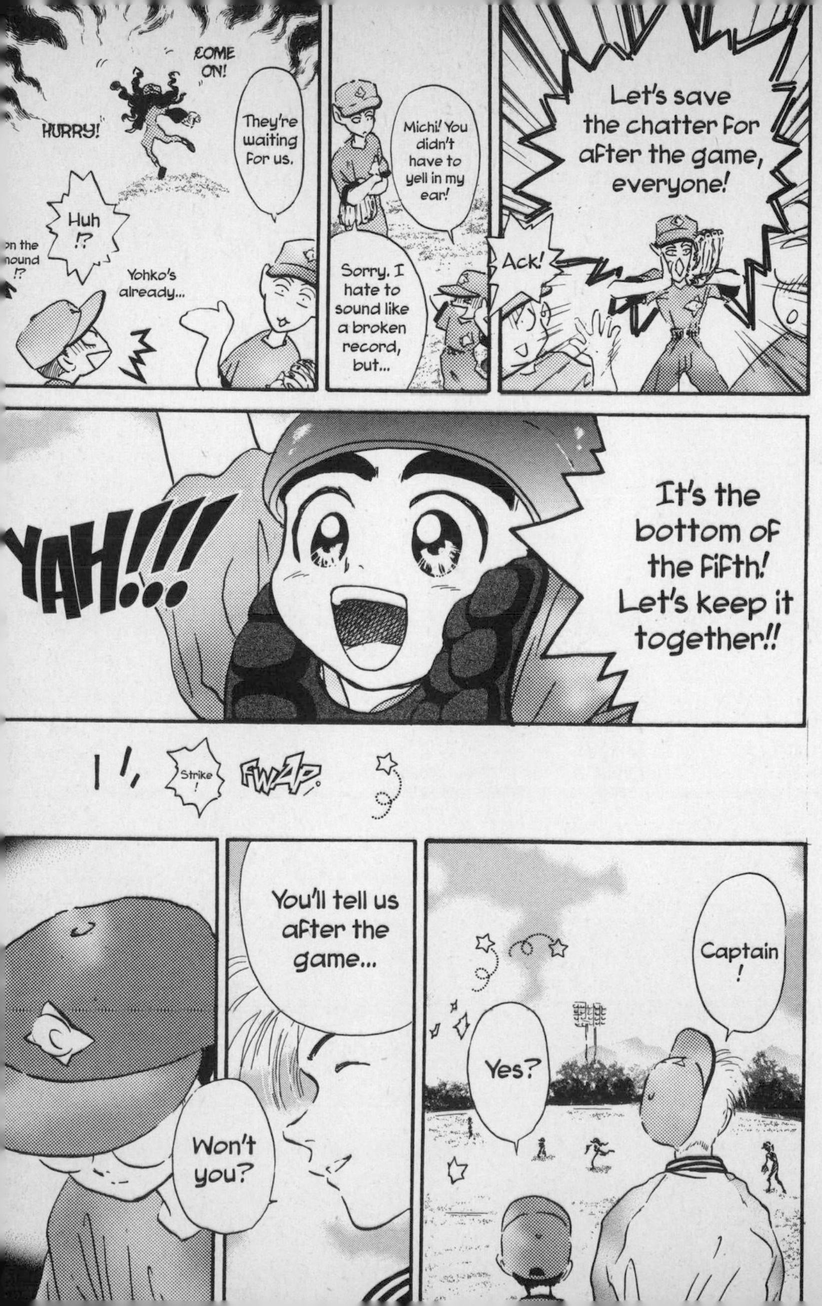
Let's save the chatter for after the game, everyone!
Ack!
Michi! You didn't have to yell in my ear!
Sorry. I hate to sound like a broken record, but...
They're waiting for us.
COME ON!
HURRY!
Huh !?
Yohko's already...
on the
ound !?
It's the bottom of the fifth! Let's keep it together!!
YAH!!!
Strike !
FWAP
Captain !
Yes?
You'll tell us after the game...
Won't you?

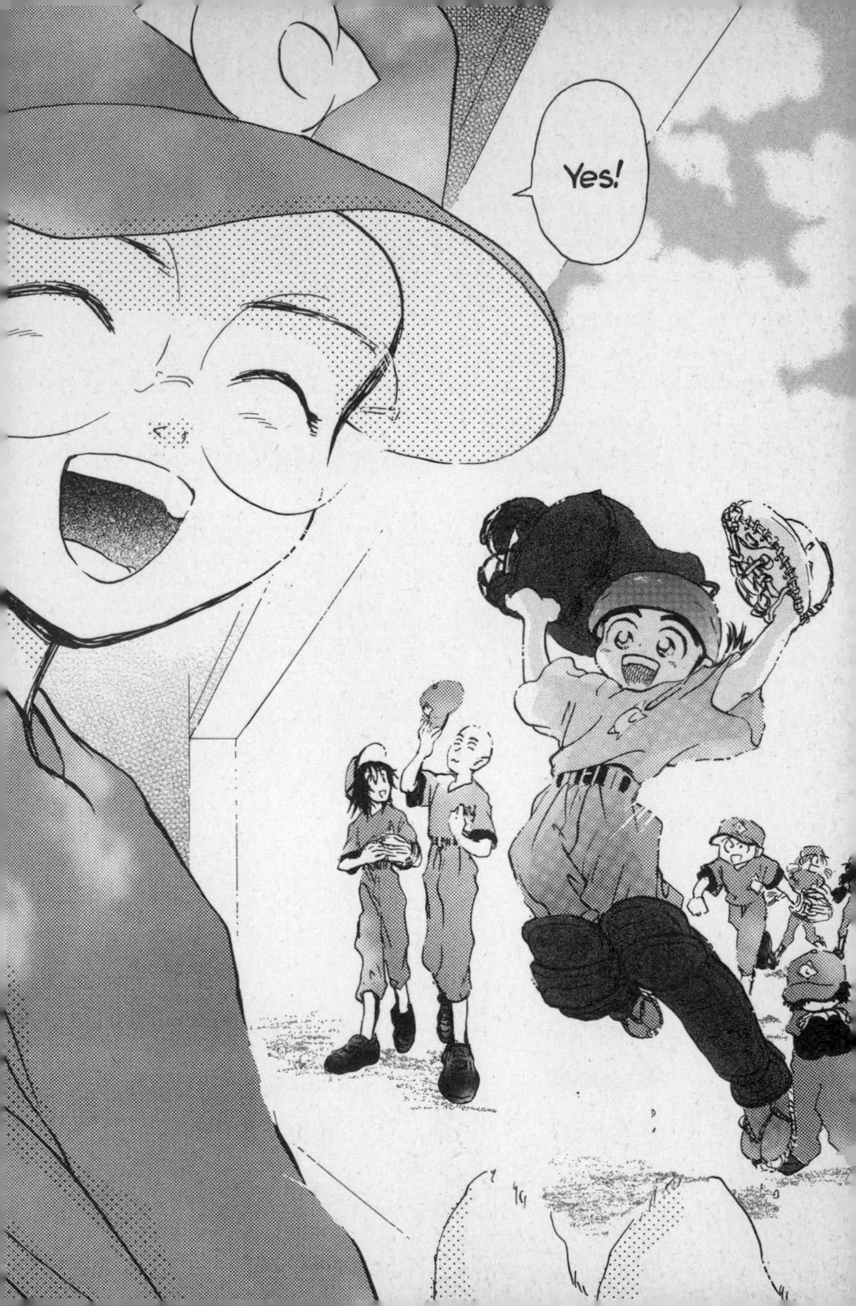
Yes!

PITCH 13 LAST UP TO BAT

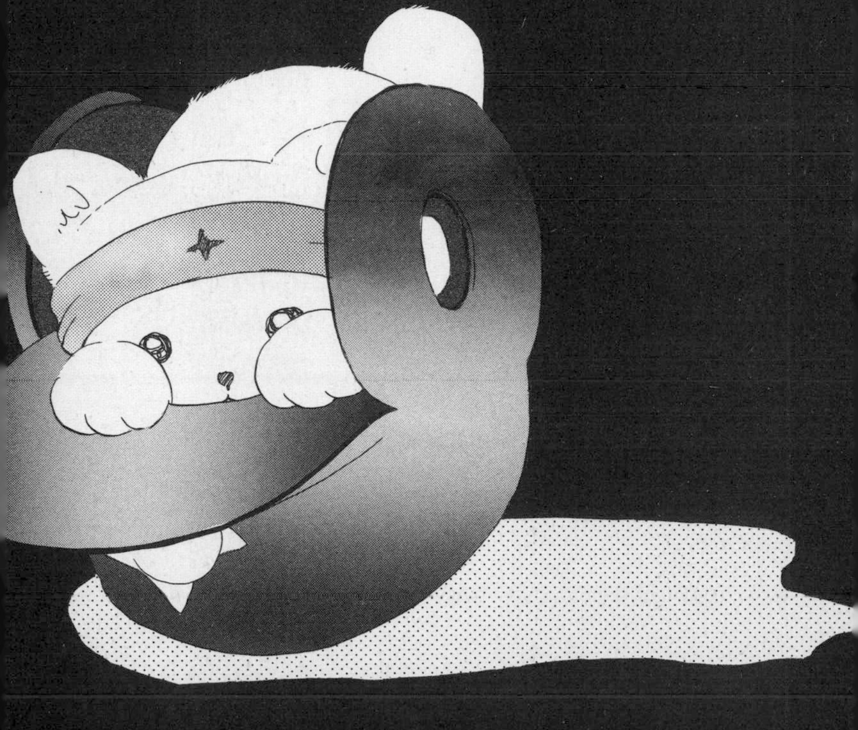

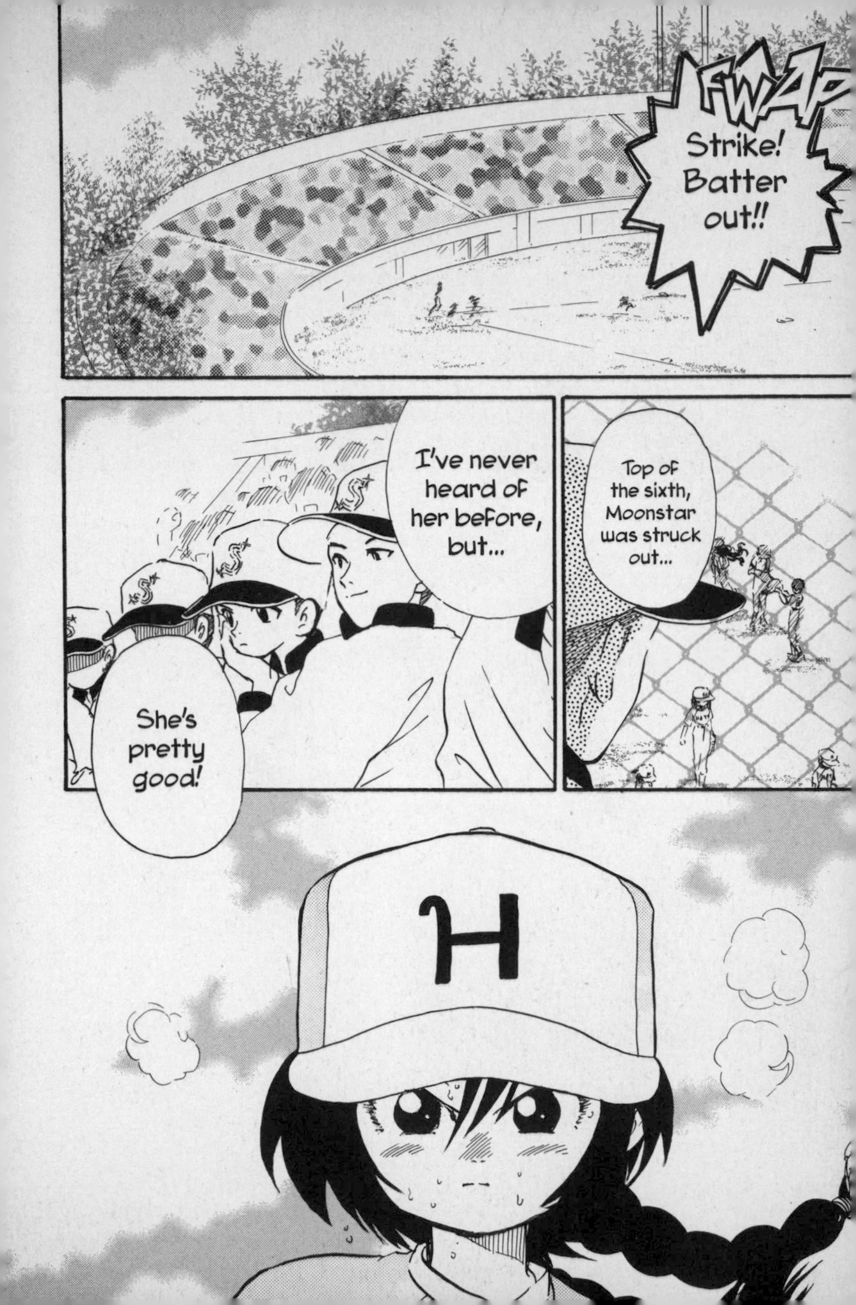
FWAP
Strike! Batter out!!
Top of the sixth, Moonstar was struck out...
I've never heard of her before, but...
She's pretty good!

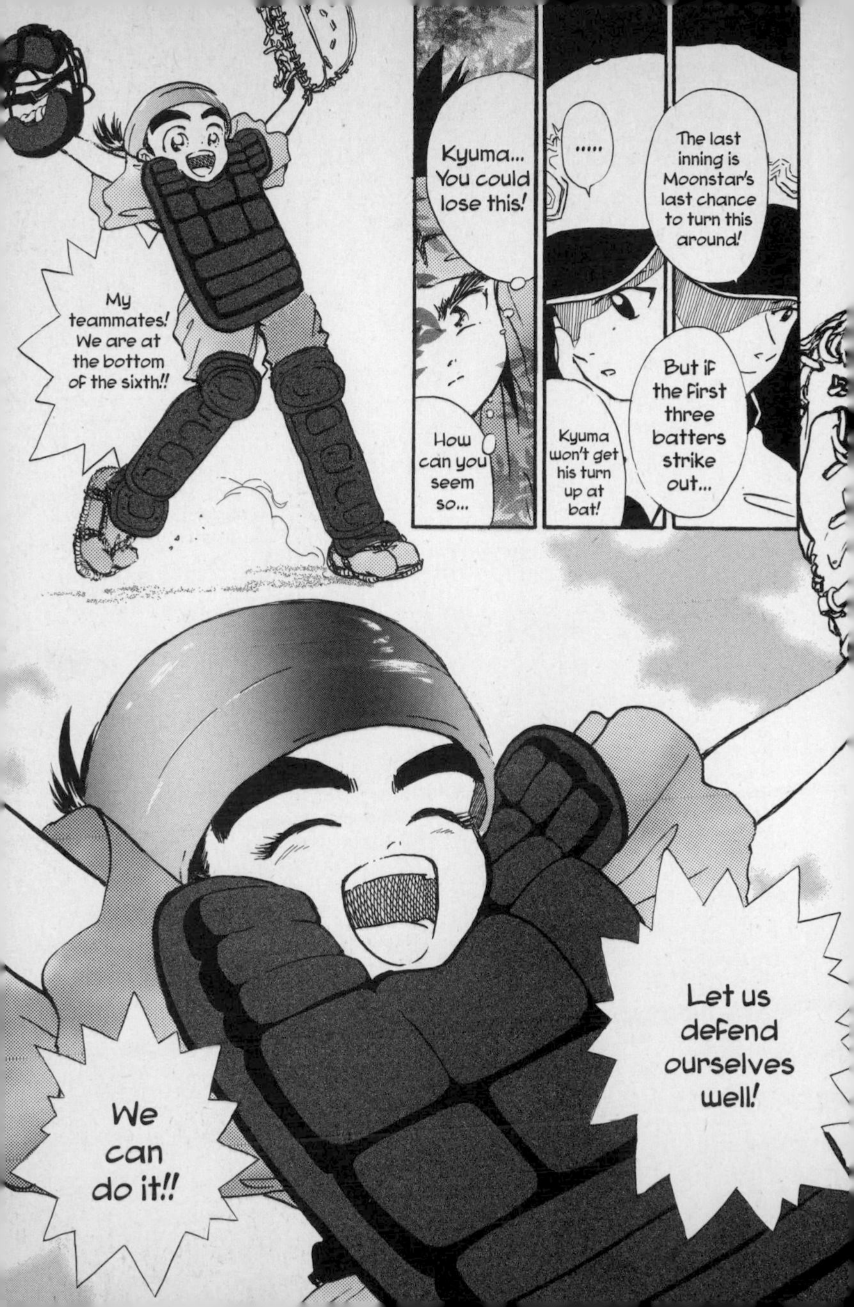
The last inning is Moonstar's last chance to turn this around!
But if the first three batters strike out...
.....
Kyuma won't get his turn up at bat!
Kyuma... You could lose this!
How can you seem so...
My teammates! We are at the bottom of the sixth!!
Let us defend ourselves well!
We can do it!!

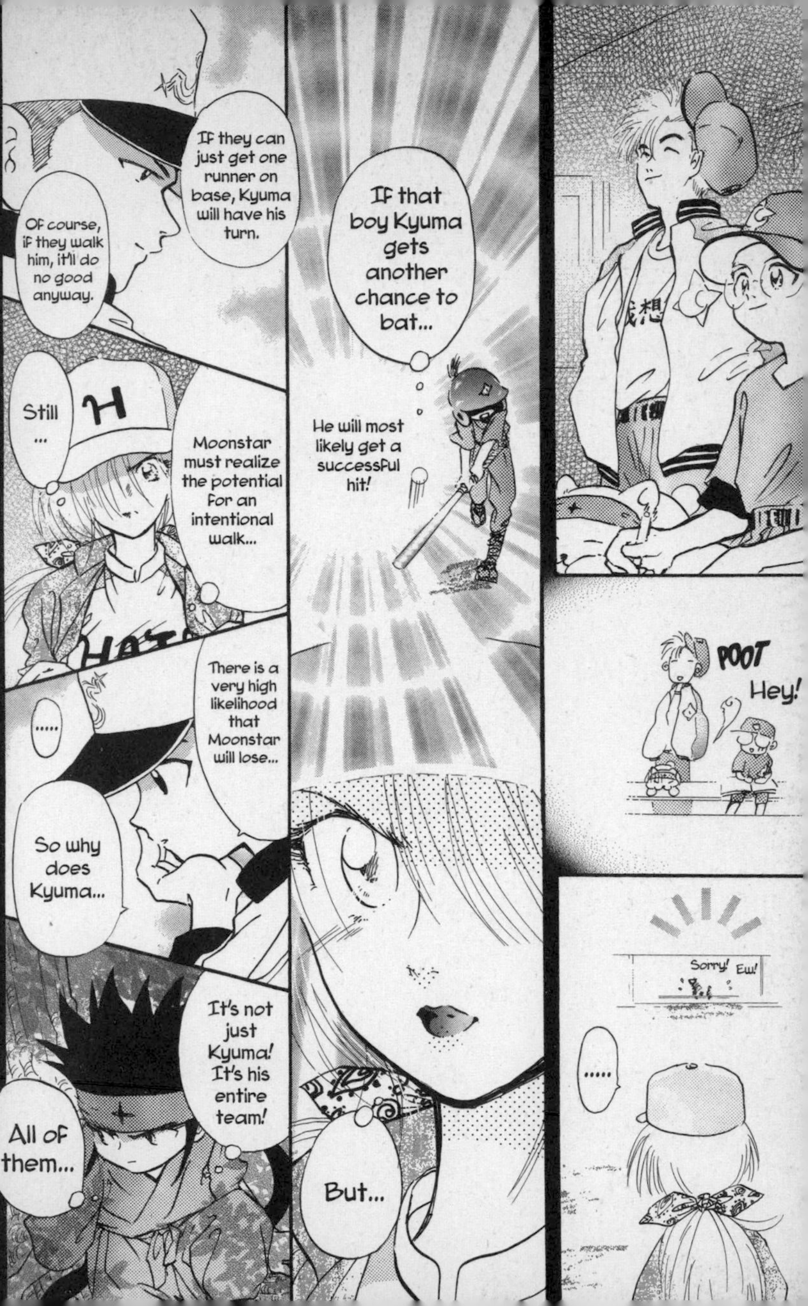
POOT
Hey!
Ew!
Sorry!
......
If that boy Kyuma gets another chance to bat...
He will most likely get a successful hit!
But...
If they can just get one runner on base, Kyuma will have his turn.
Of course, if they walk him, it'll do no good anyway.
Moonstar must realize the potential for an intentional walk...
Still ...
There is a very high likelihood that Moonstar will lose...
......
So why does Kyuma...
It's not just Kyuma! It's his entire team!
All of them...

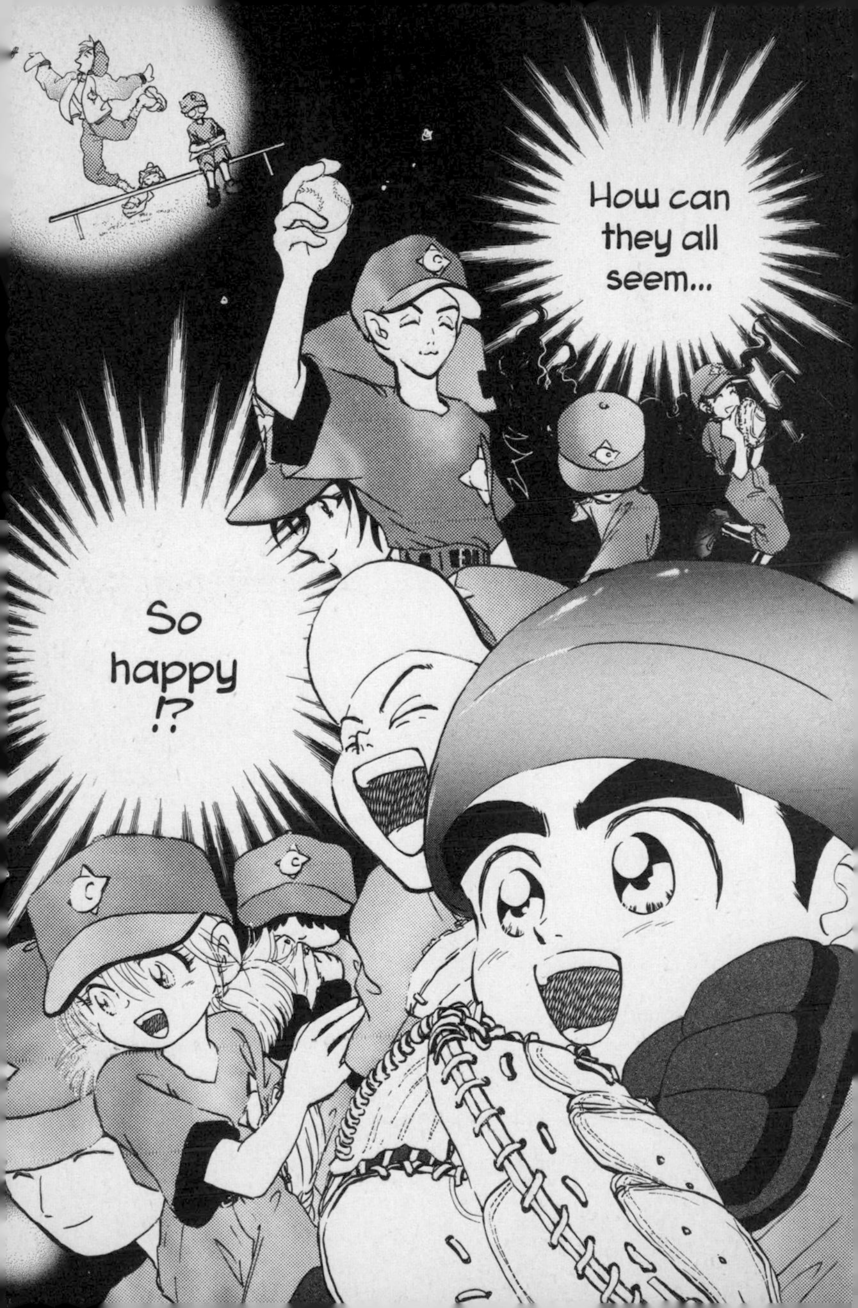
How can they all seem...
So happy!?

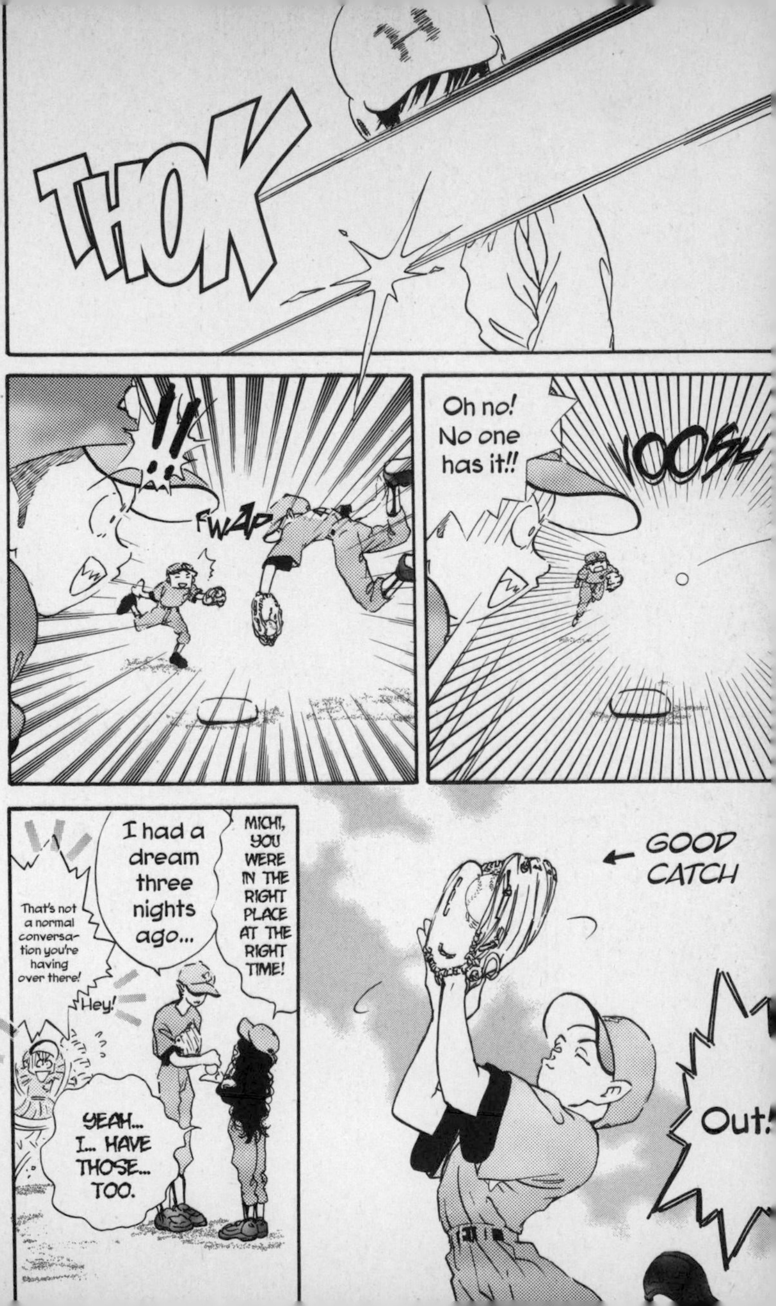
THOK
Oh no! No one has it!!
VOOSH
!!
FWAP
GOOD CATCH
Out!
MICHI, YOU WERE IN THE RIGHT PLACE AT THE RIGHT TIME!
I had a dream three nights ago...
That's not a normal conversation you're having over there!
Hey!
YEAH... I... HAVE THOSE... TOO.

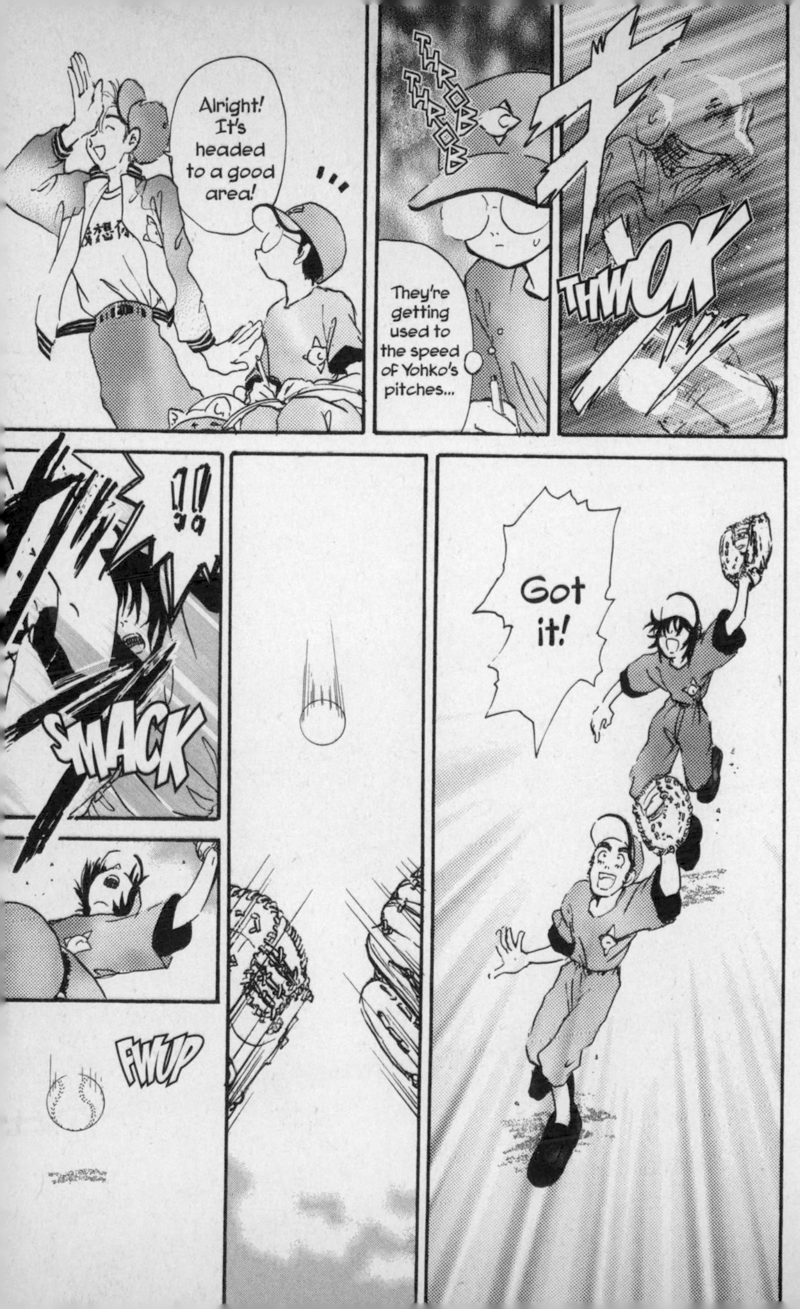
THWOK
THROB THROB
They're getting used to the speed of Yohko's pitches...
Alright! It's headed to a good area!
...
Got it!
!!
SMACK
FWUP

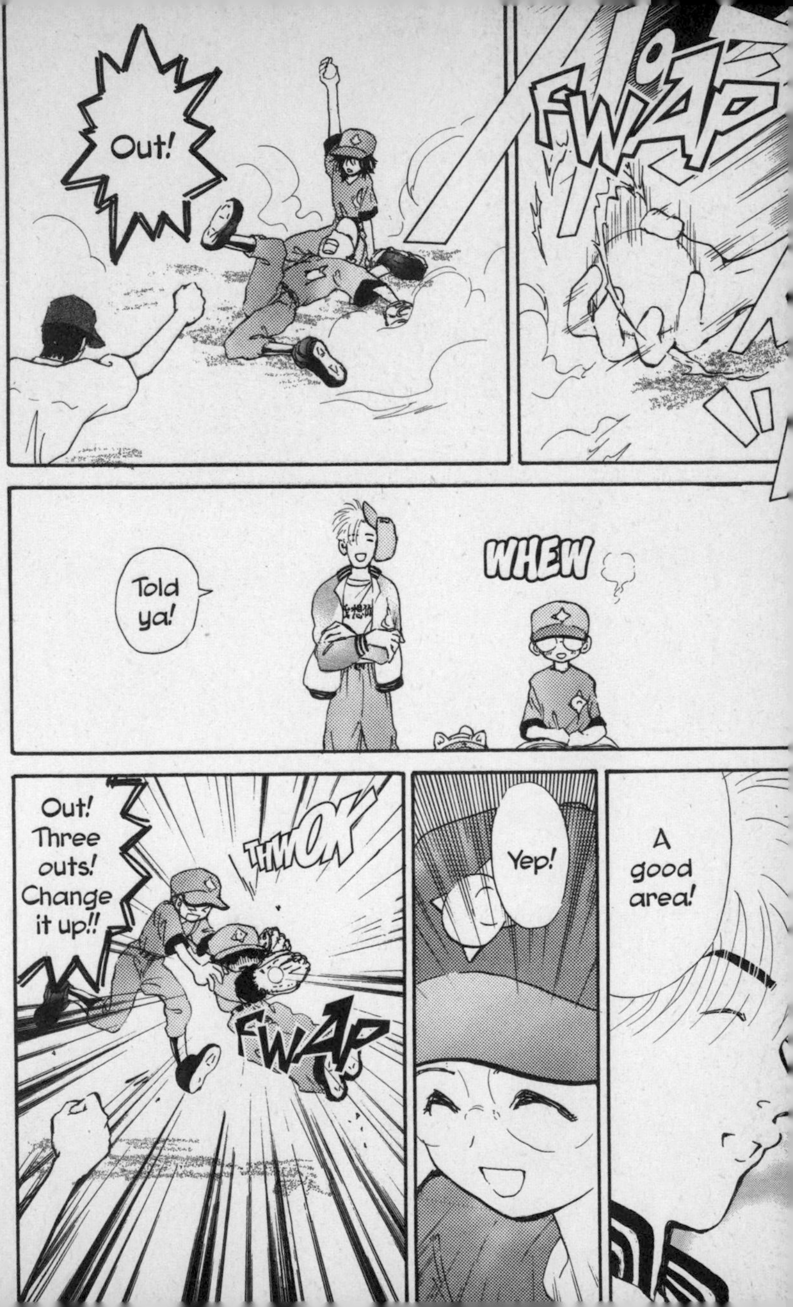
FWAP
Out!
WHEW
Told ya!
A good area!
Yep!
THWOK
Out! Three outs! Change it up!!
FWAP

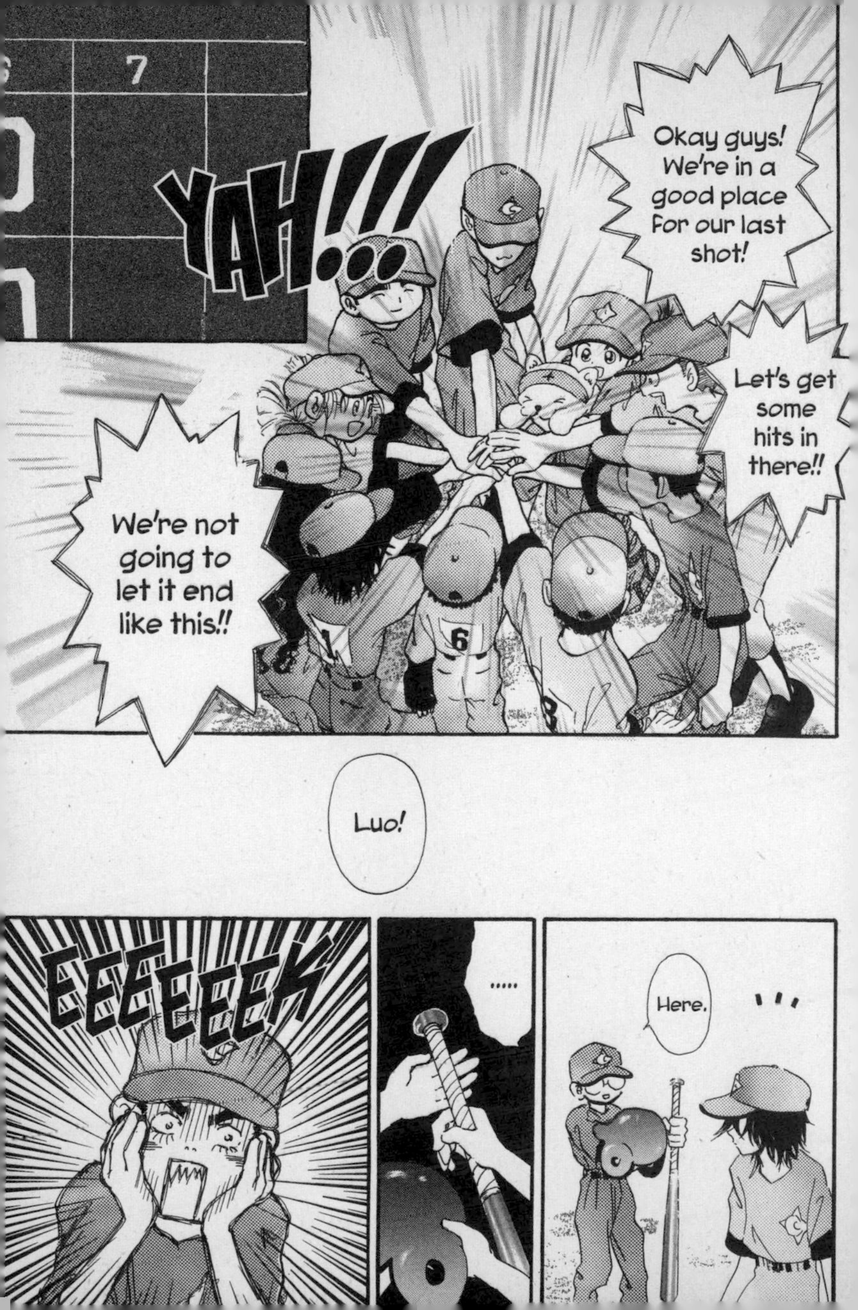
Okay guys! We're in a good place for our last shot!
YAH!!!
Let's get some hits in there!!
We're not going to let it end like this!!
Luo!
Here.
.....
EEEEEEK

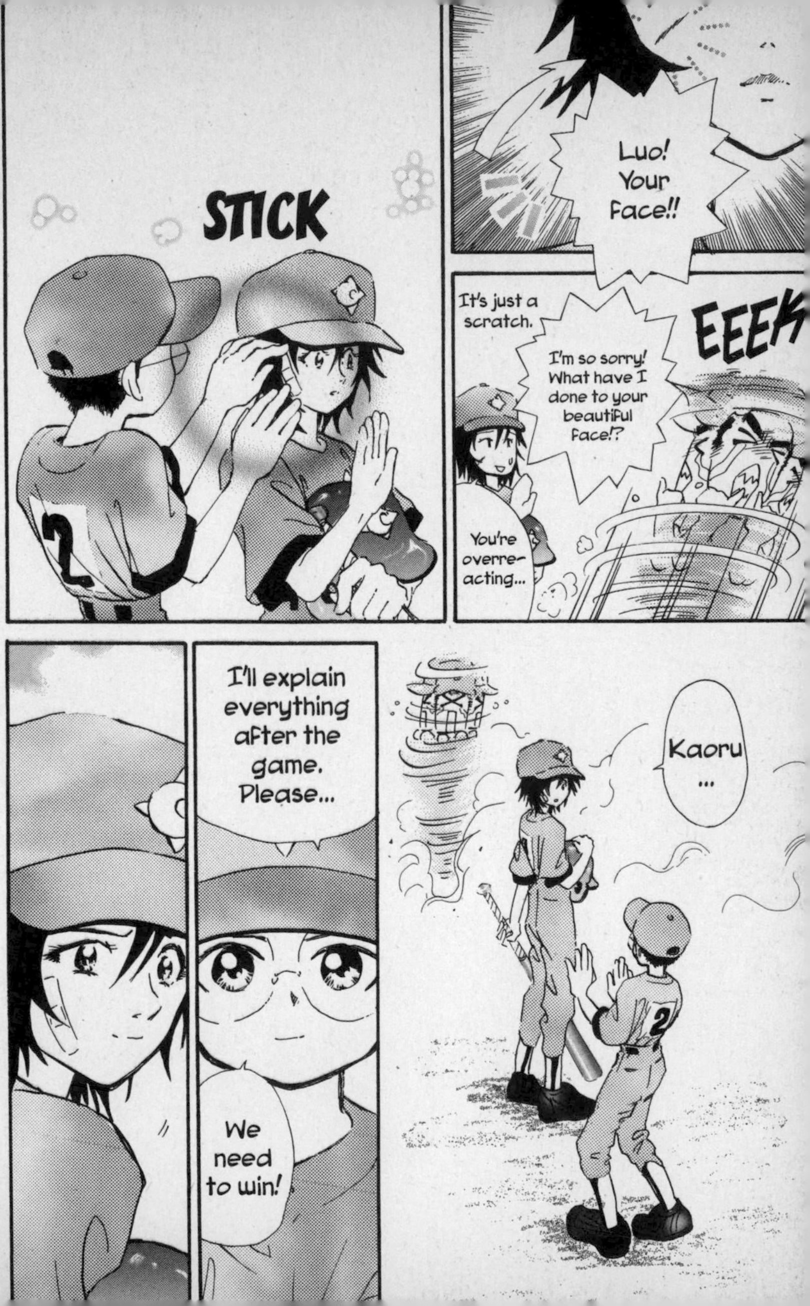
Luo! Your Face!!
EEEK
I'm so sorry! What have I done to your beautiful face!?
It's just a scratch.
You're overre-acting...
STICK
Kaoru ...
I'll explain everything after the game. Please...
We need to win!

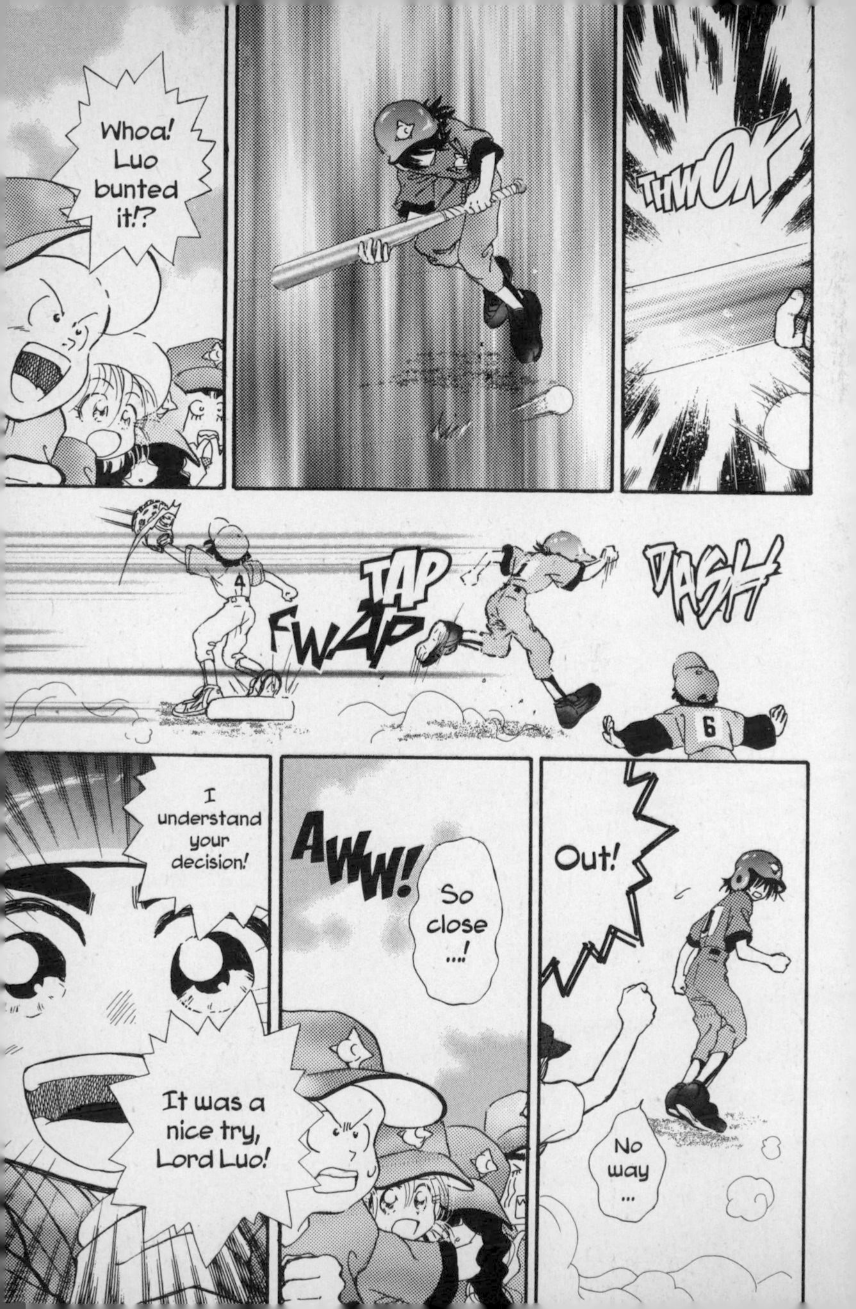

THWOK
Whoa! Luo bunted it!?
DASH
TAP
FWAP
Out!
No way ...
AWW!
So close ...!
I understand your decision!
It was a nice try, Lord Luo!

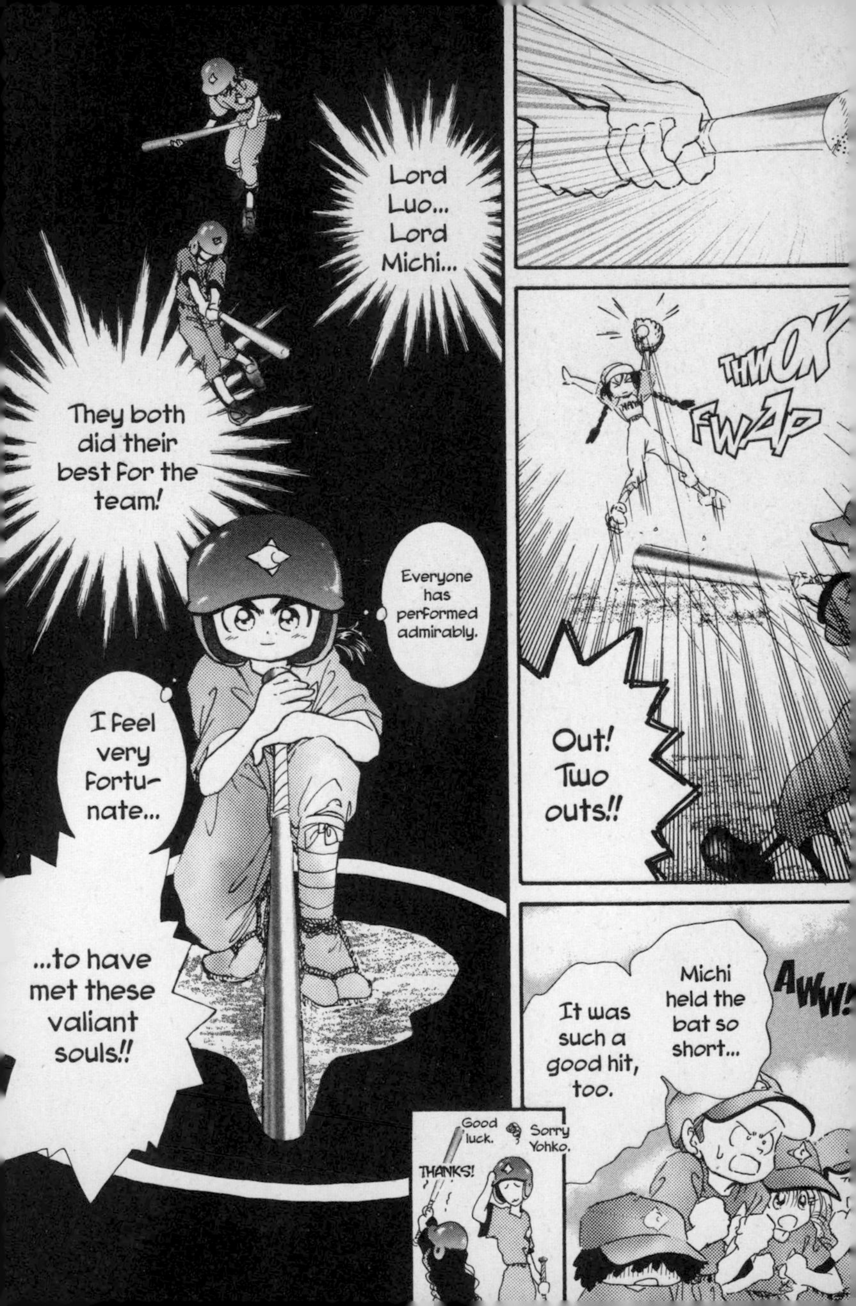
THWOK
FWAP
Out! Two outs!!
Michi held the bat so short...
AWW!
It was such a good hit, too.
Sorry Yohko.
Good luck.
THANKS!
Lord Luo... Lord Michi...
They both did their best for the team!
Everyone has performed admirably.
I feel very fortu-nate...
...to have met these valiant souls!!

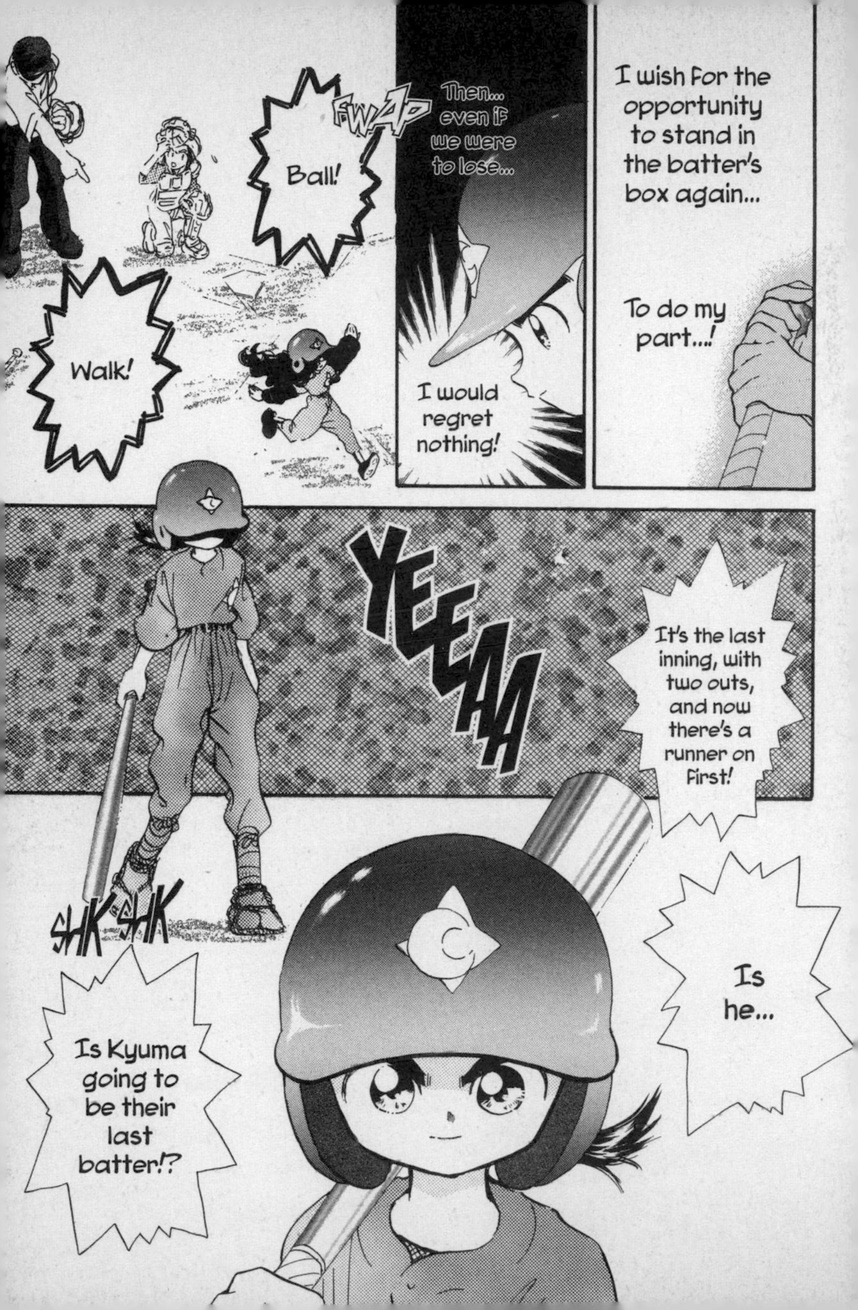

I wish for the opportunity to stand in the batter's box again...
To do my part...!
Then... even if we were to lose...
I would regret nothing!
FWAP
Ball!
Walk!
YEEAAA
It's the last inning, with two outs, and now there's a runner on first!
SHK SHK
Is he...
Is Kyuma going to be their last batter!?

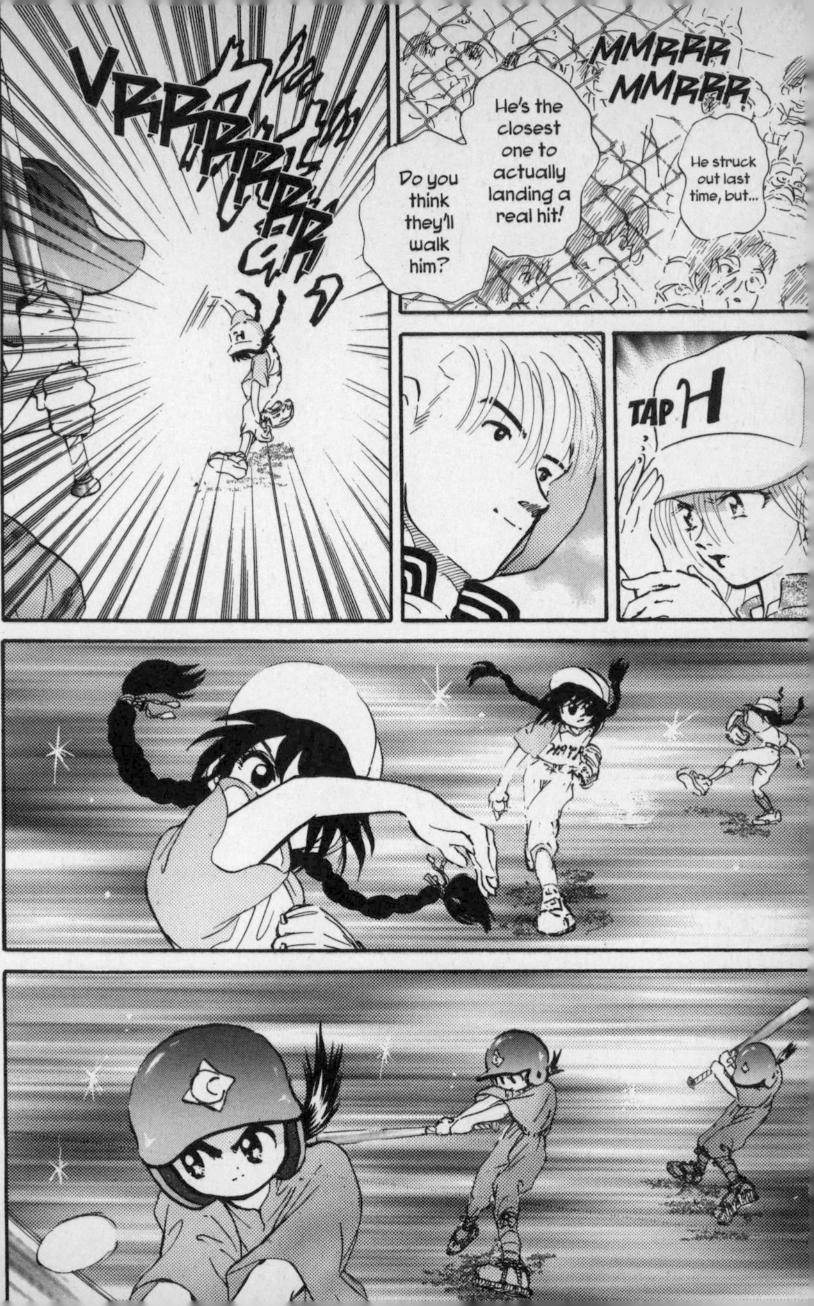
MMRRR MMRRR
He struck out last time, but...
He's the closest one to actually landing a real hit!
Do you think they'll walk him?
TAP
VRRRRRRR

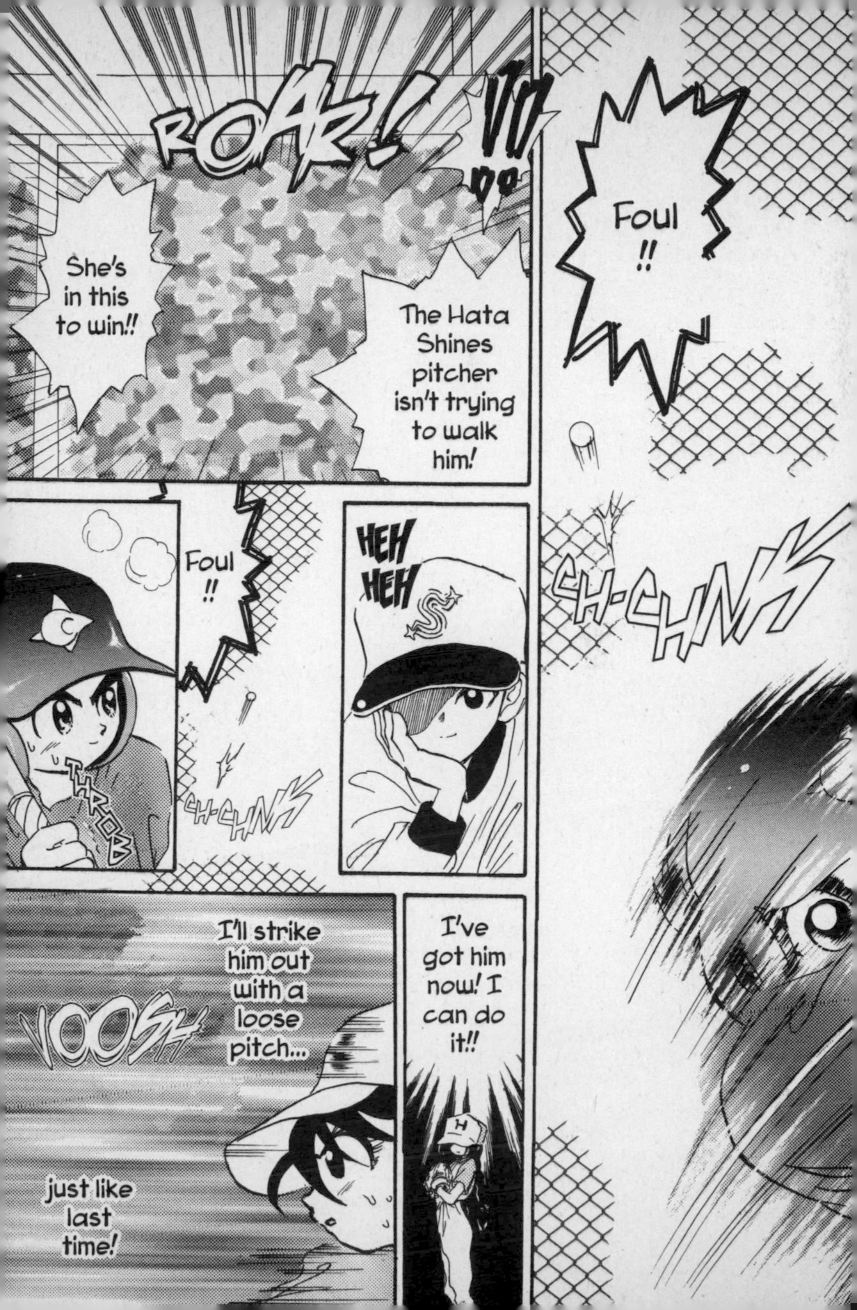

Foul !!
CH-CHN
ROAR!!!
The Hata Shines pitcher isn't trying to walk him!
She's in this to win!!
HEH HEH
Foul !!
CH-CHN
THROB
I've got him now! I can do it!!
I'll strike him out with a loose pitch...
VOOSH
just like last time!

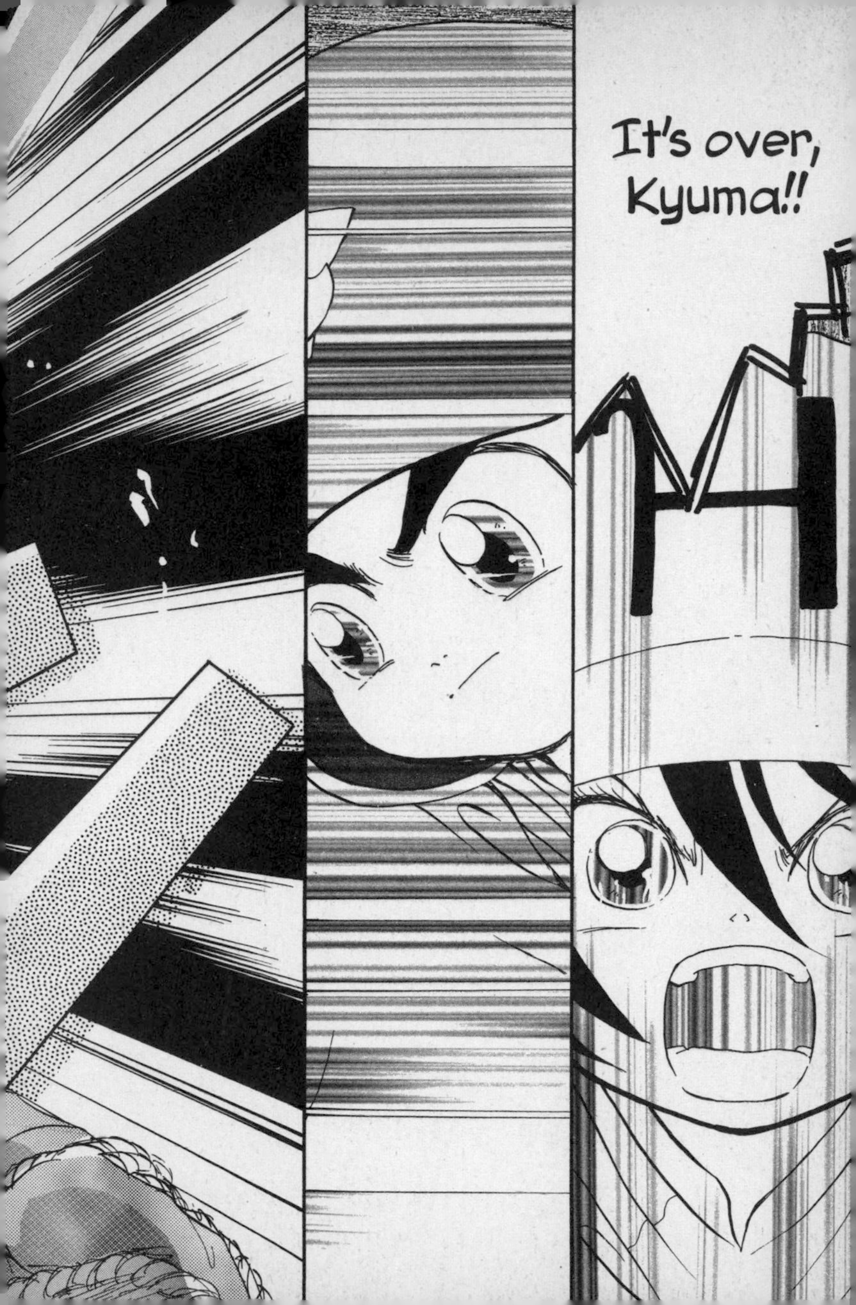
It's over, Kyuma!!
AH

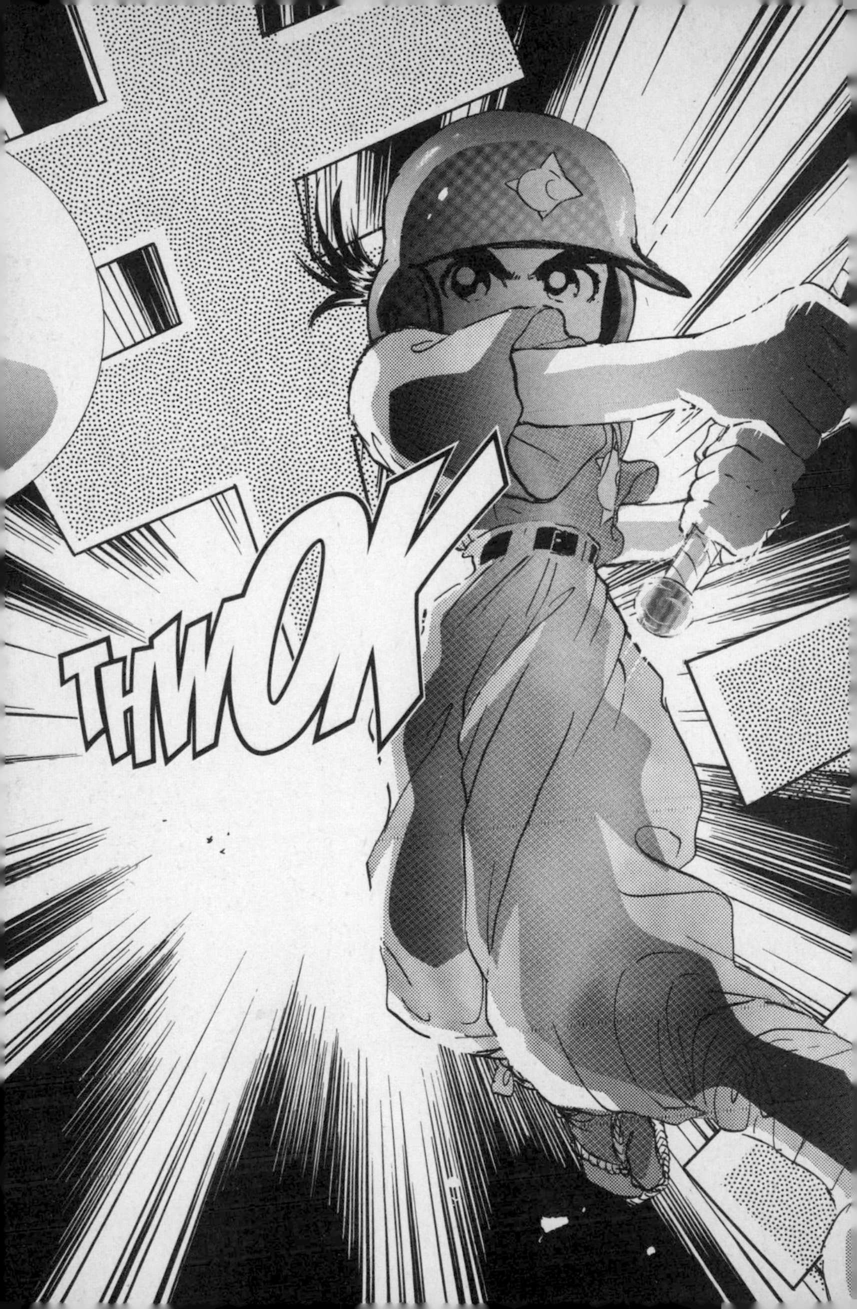
THWOCK

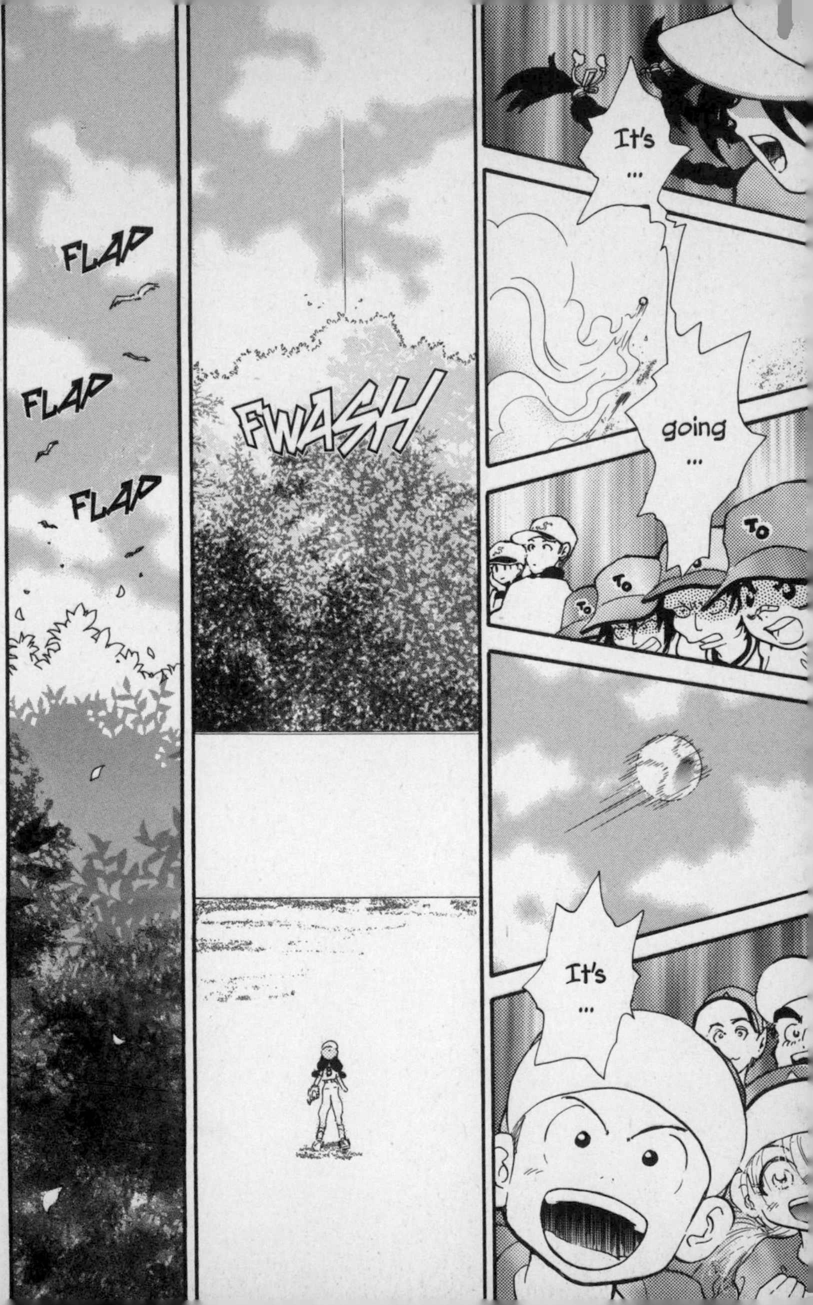
It's ...
going ...
It's ...
FWASH
FLAP
FLAP
FLAP

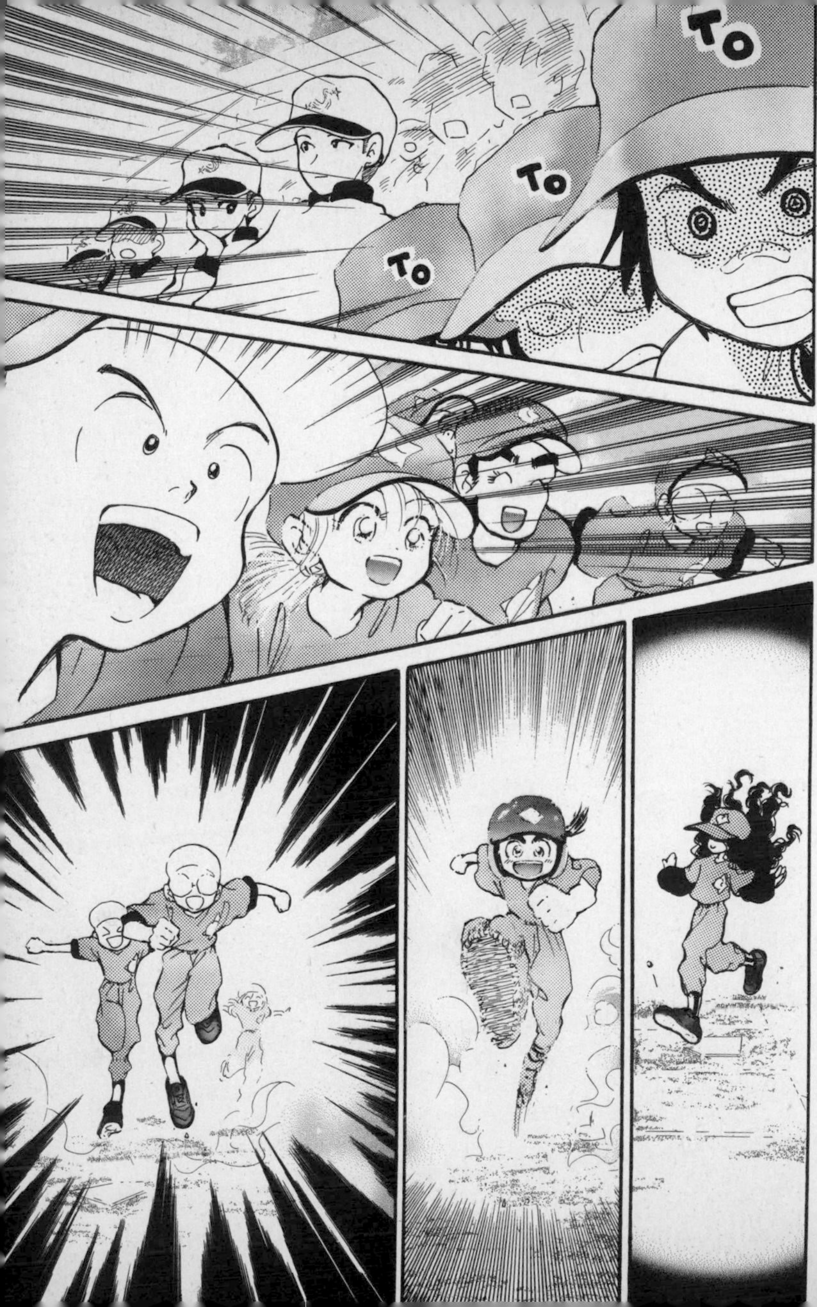
TO
TO
TO

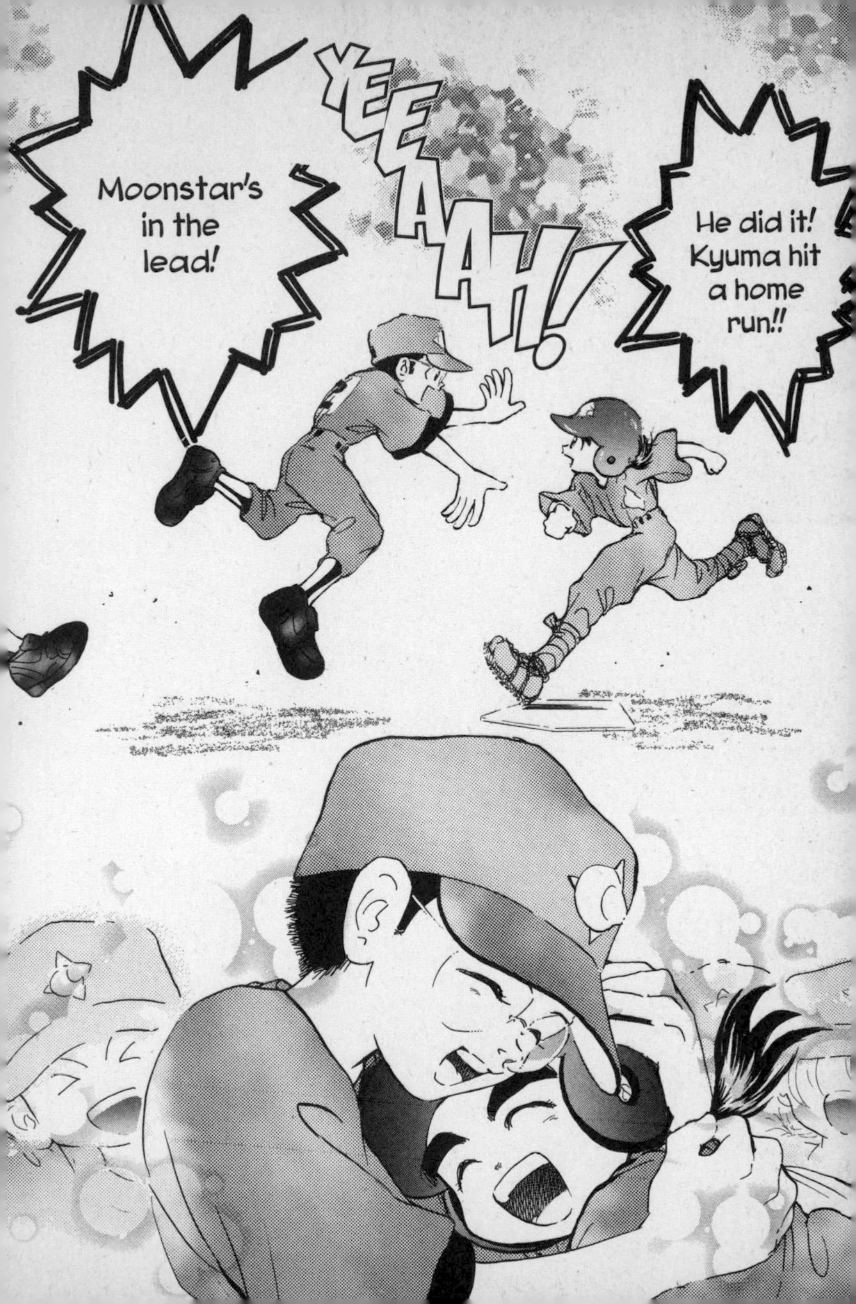
He did it! Kyuma hit a home run!!
YEEAAH!
Moonstar's in the lead!

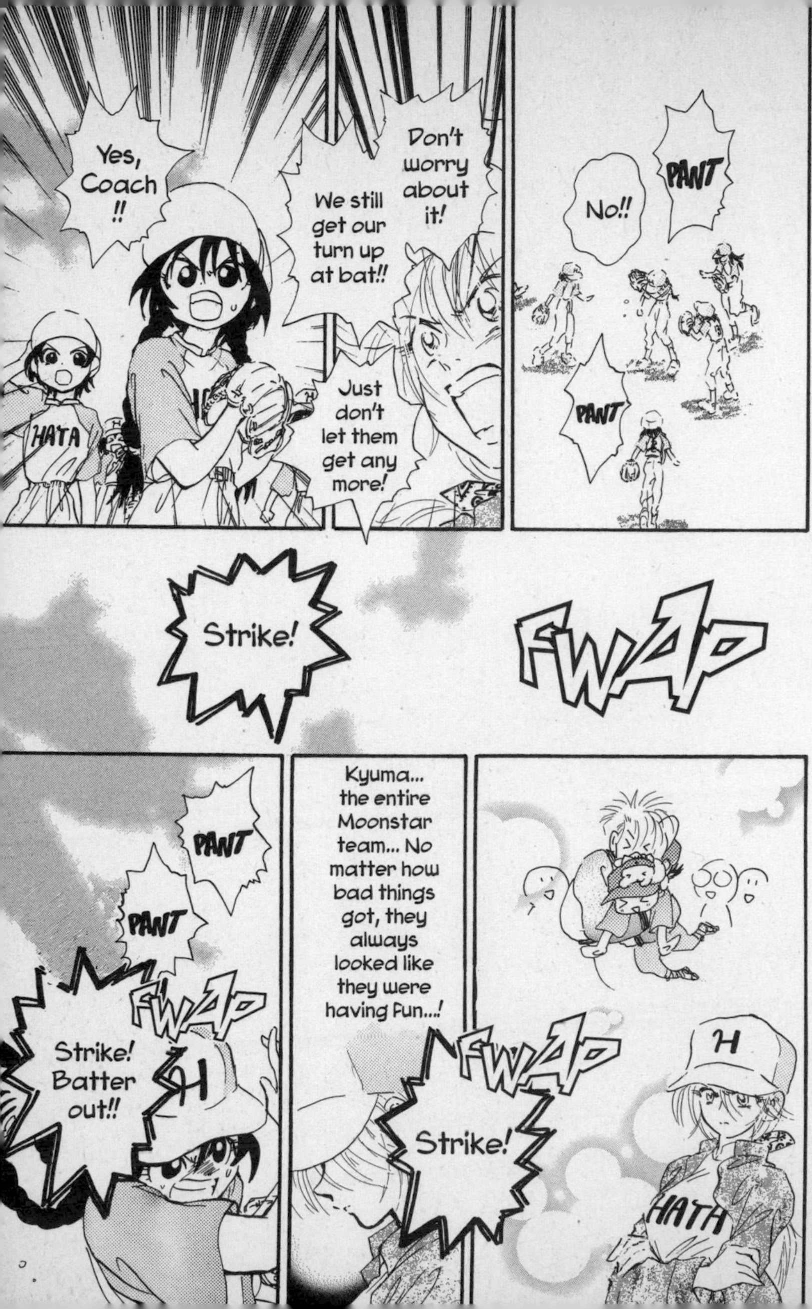
PANT
No!!
PANT
Don't worry about it!
We still get our turn up at bat!!
Just don't let them get any more!
Yes, Coach!!
FWAP
Strike!
Kyuma... the entire Moonstar team... No matter how bad things got, they always looked like they were having fun...!
FWAP
Strike!
PANT
PANT
FWAP
Strike! Batter out!!

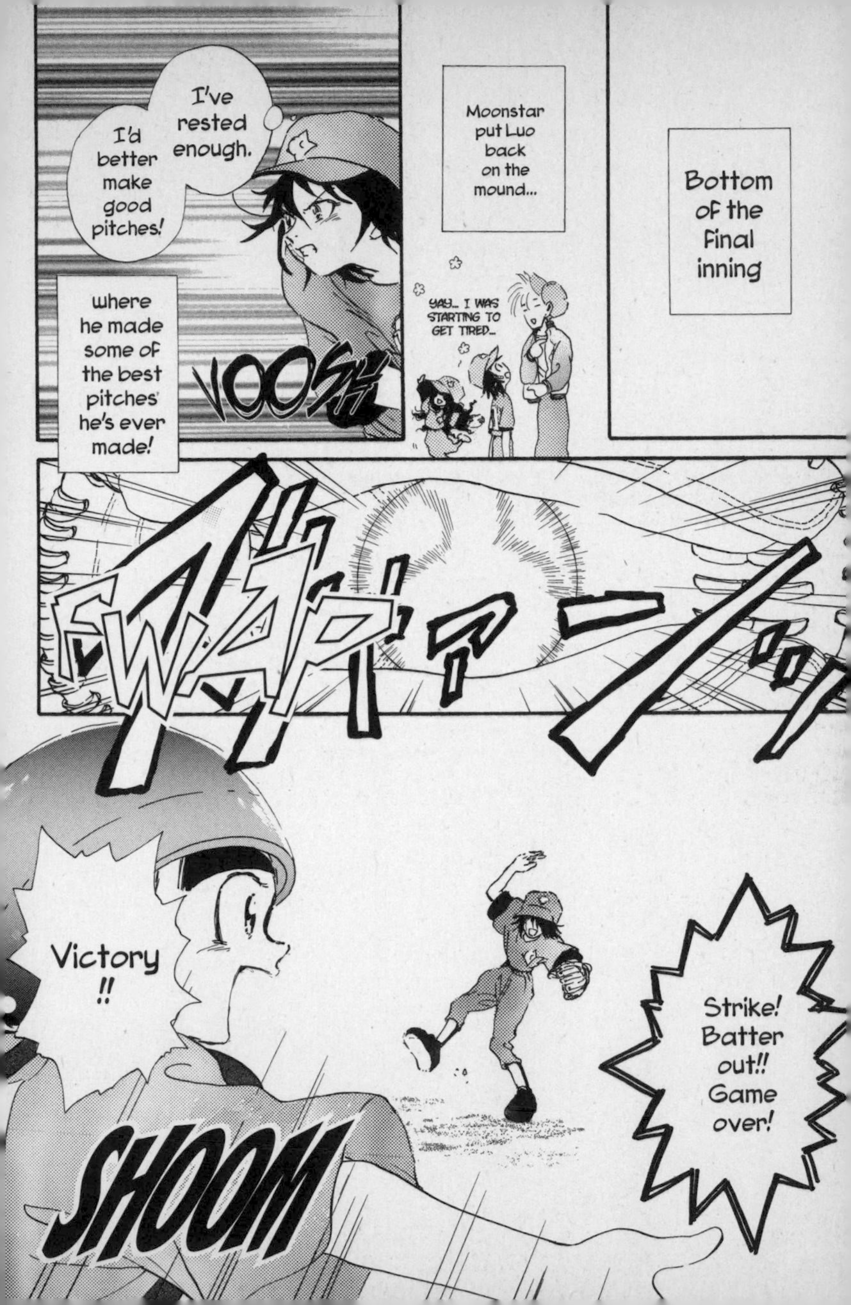
Bottom of the final inning
Moonstar put Luo back on the mound...
YAY... I WAS STARTING TO GET TIRED...
I've rested enough.
I'd better make good pitches!
VOOSH
where he made some of the best pitches he's ever made!
SWAP
Strike! Batter out!! Game over!
Victory!!
SHOOM

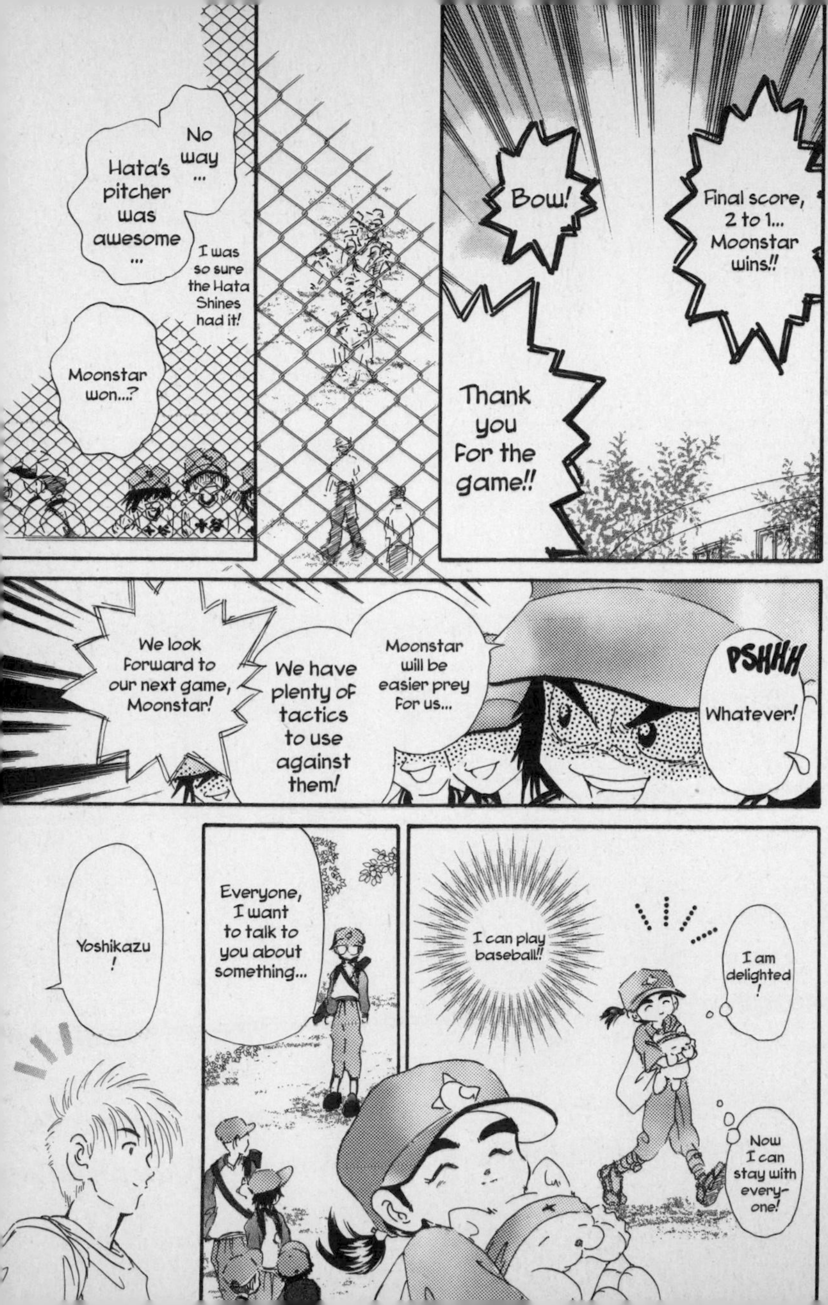
Final score, 2 to 1... Moonstar wins!!
Bow!
Thank you for the game!!
No way ...
Hata's pitcher was awesome ...
I was so sure the Hata Shines had it!
Moonstar won...?
PSHHH
Whatever!
Moonstar will be easier prey for us...
We have plenty of tactics to use against them!
We look forward to our next game, Moonstar!
I am delighted!
I can play baseball!!
Now I can stay with every-one!
Everyone, I want to talk to you about something...
Yoshikazu!

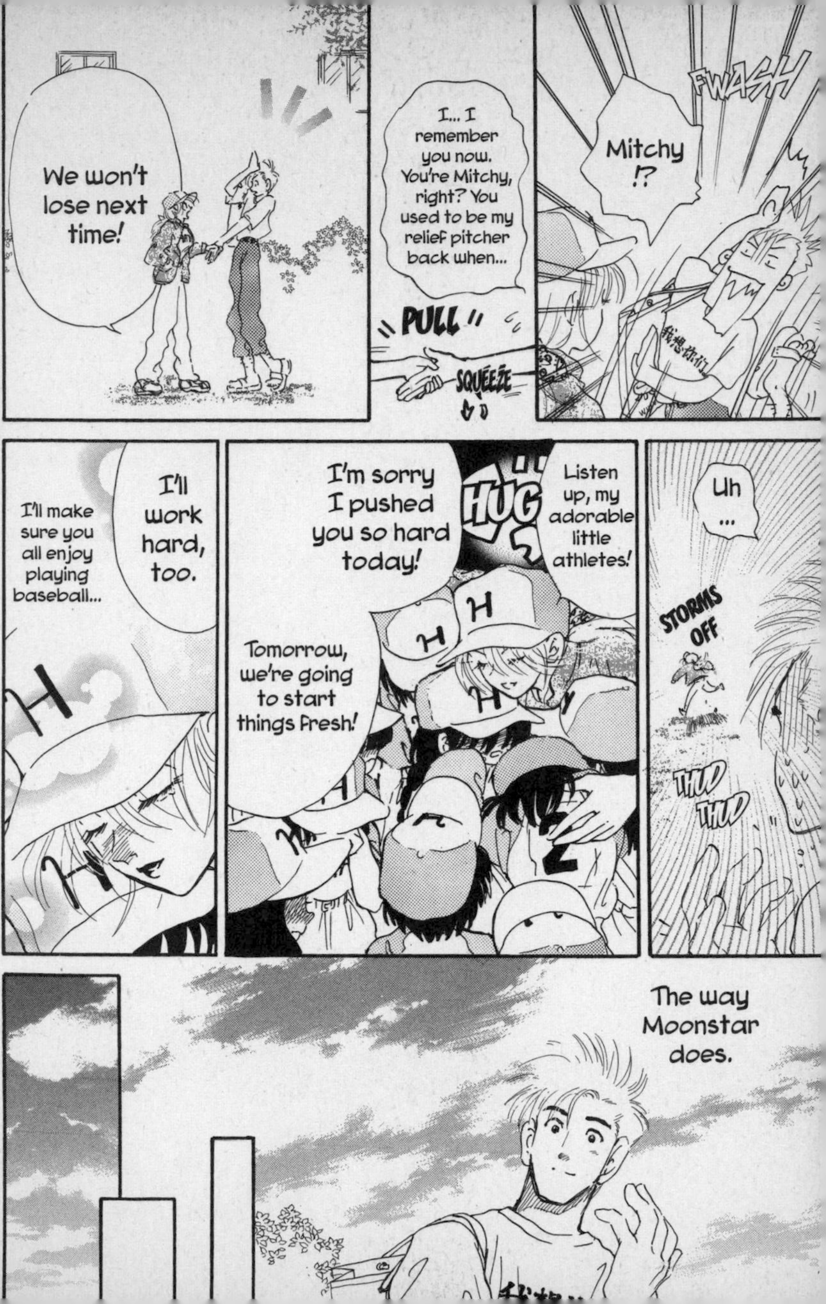
FWASH
Mitchy !?
我想你们
I... I remember you now. You're Mitchy, right? You used to be my relief pitcher back when...
PULL
SQUEEZE
We won't lose next time!
Uh ...
STORMS OFF
THUD
THUD
Listen up, my adorable little athletes!
HUG
I'm sorry I pushed you so hard today!
Tomorrow, we're going to start things fresh!
I'll work hard, too.
I'll make sure you all enjoy playing baseball...
The way Moonstar does.

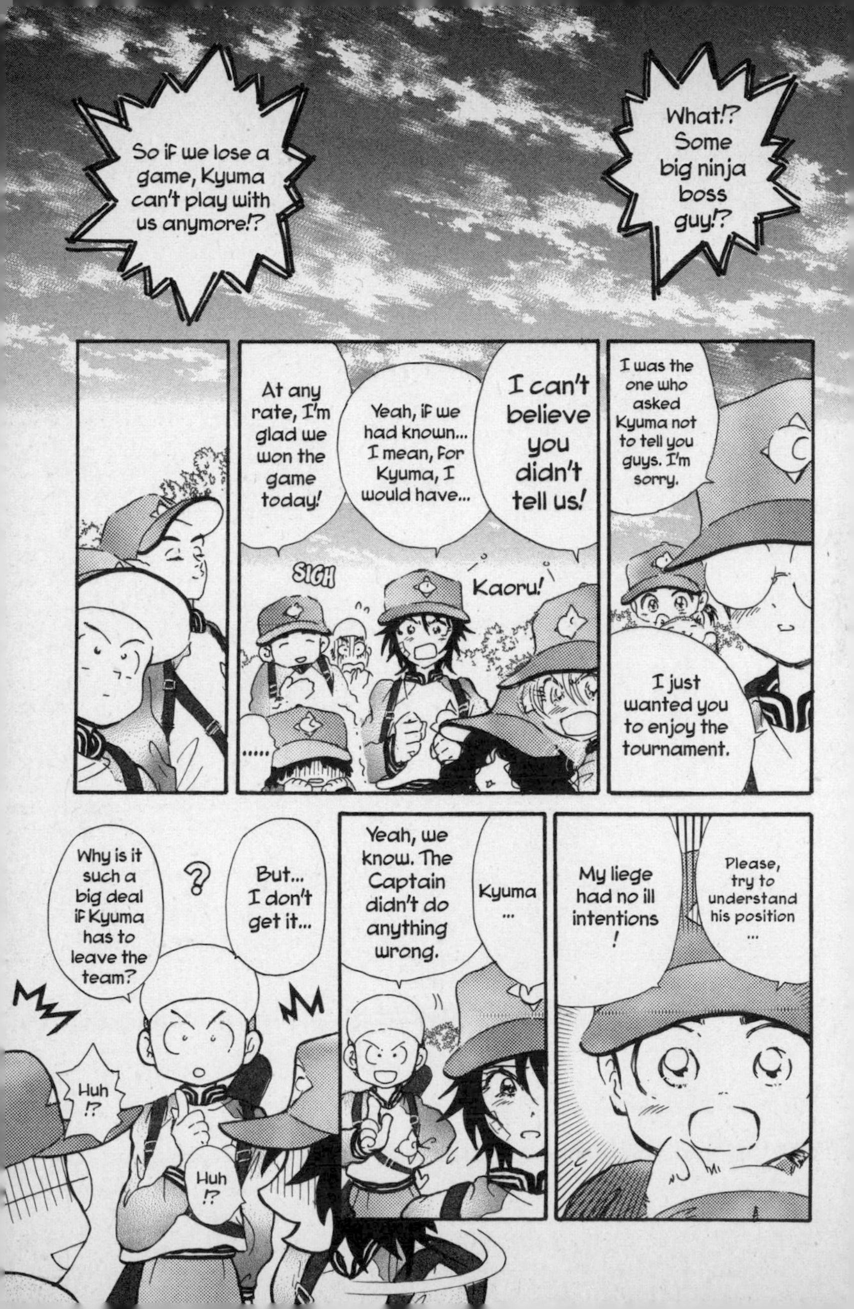
What!? Some big ninja boss guy!?
So if we lose a game, Kyuma can't play with us anymore!?
I was the one who asked Kyuma not to tell you guys. I'm sorry.
I just wanted you to enjoy the tournament.
I can't believe you didn't tell us!
Yeah, if we had known... I mean, for Kyuma, I would have...
At any rate, I'm glad we won the game today!
SIGH
Kaoru!
.....
Please, try to understand his position ...
My liege had no ill intentions !
Kyuma ...
Yeah, we know. The Captain didn't do anything wrong.
But... I don't get it...
?
Why is it such a big deal if Kyuma has to leave the team?
Huh !?
Huh !?

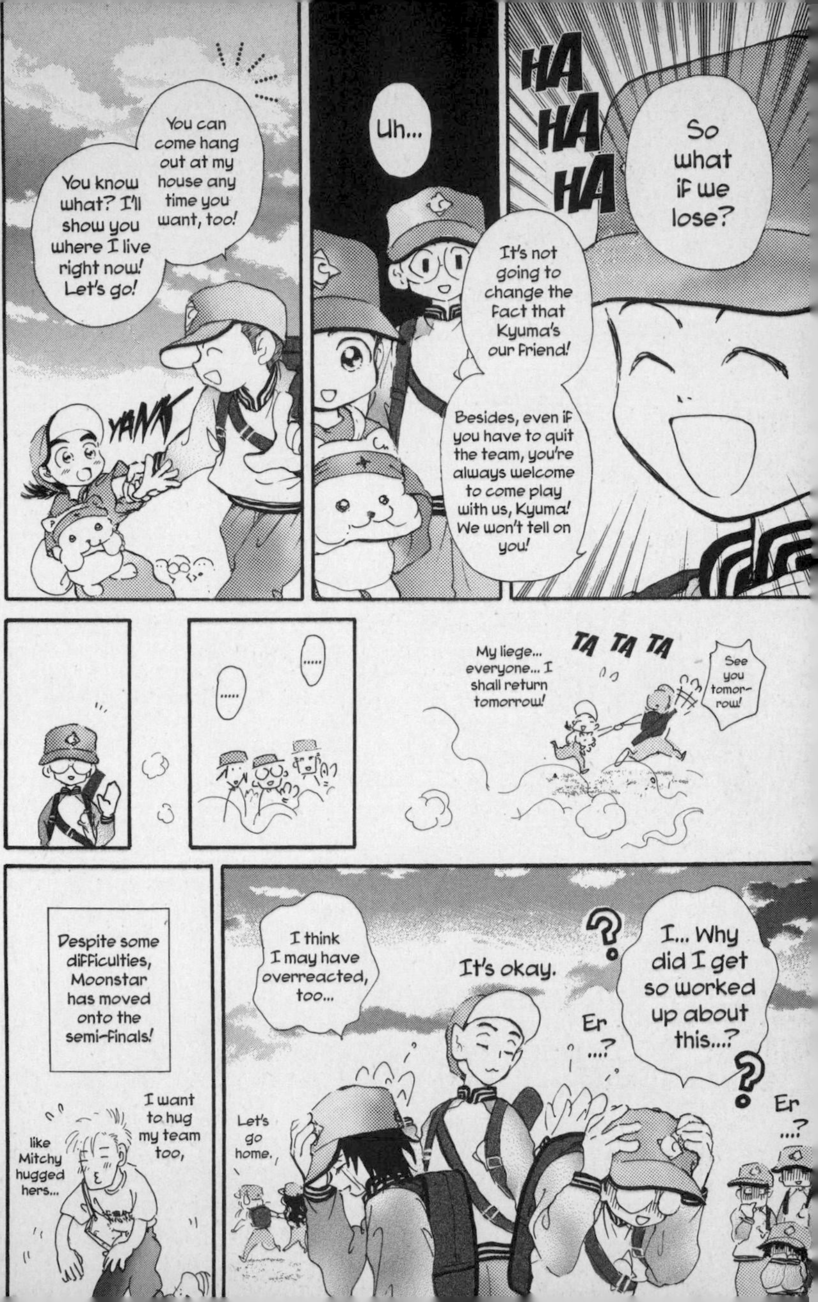
HA HA HA
So what if we lose?
Uh...
It's not going to change the fact that Kyuma's our friend!
Besides, even if you have to quit the team, you're always welcome to come play with us, Kyuma! We won't tell on you!
You can come hang out at my house any time you want, too!
You know what? I'll show you where I live right now! Let's go!
YANK
TA TA TA
See you tomorrow!
My liege... everyone... I shall return tomorrow!
......
......
I... Why did I get so worked up about this...?
Er ...?
Er ...?
It's okay.
I think I may have overreacted, too...
Let's go home.
Despite some difficulties, Moonstar has moved onto the semi-finals!
I want to hug my team too,
like Mitchy hugged hers...

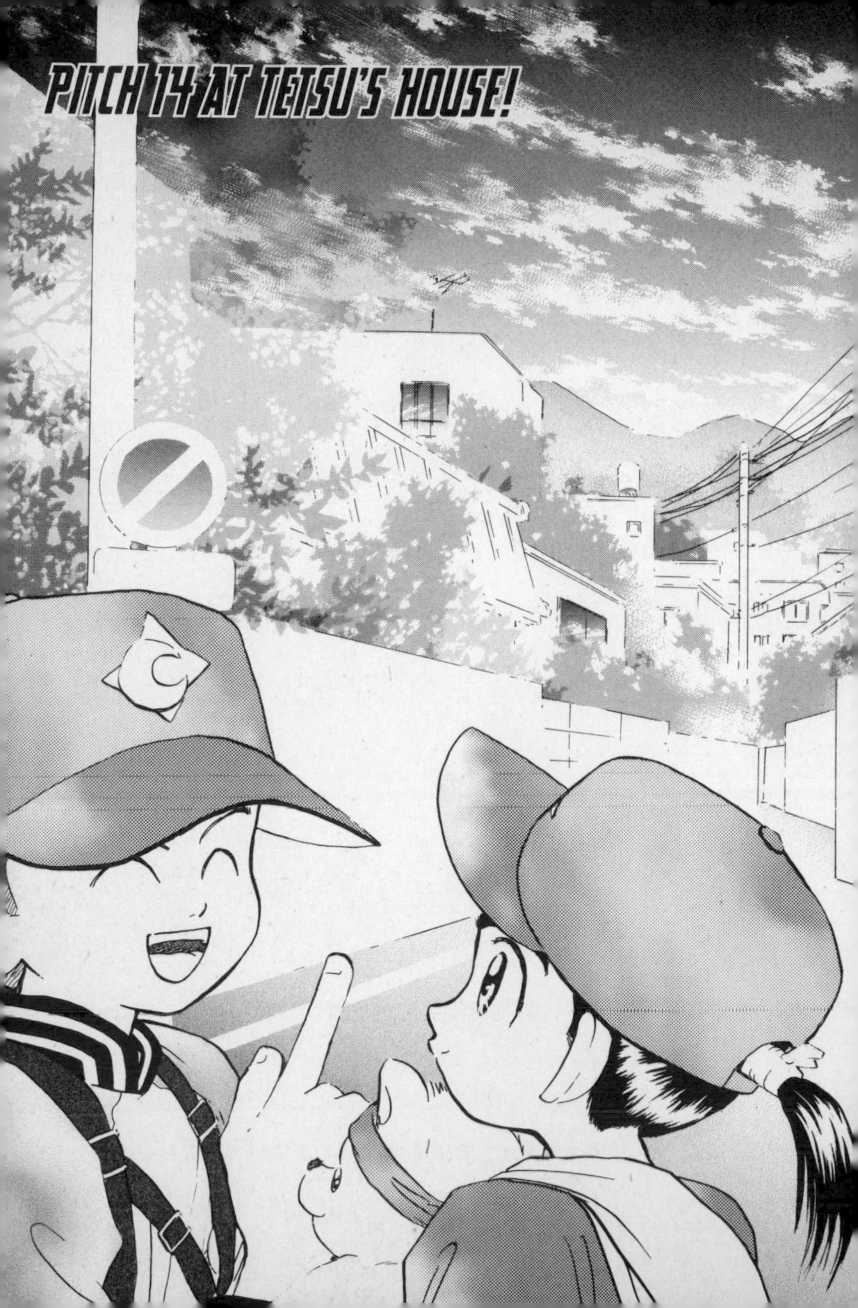
PITCH 14 AT TETSU'S HOUSE!

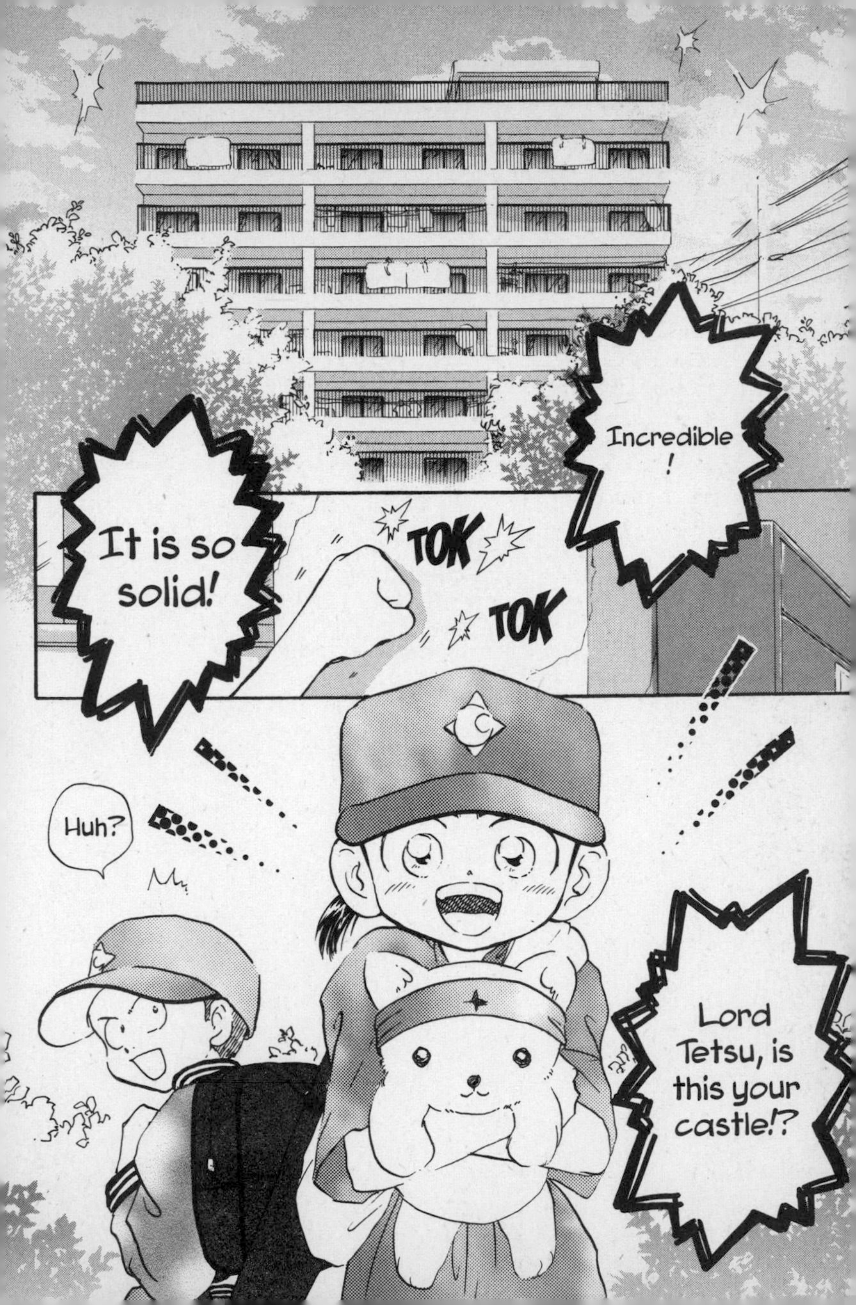
Incredible!
TOK
TOK
It is so solid!
Lord Tetsu, is this your castle!?
Huh?

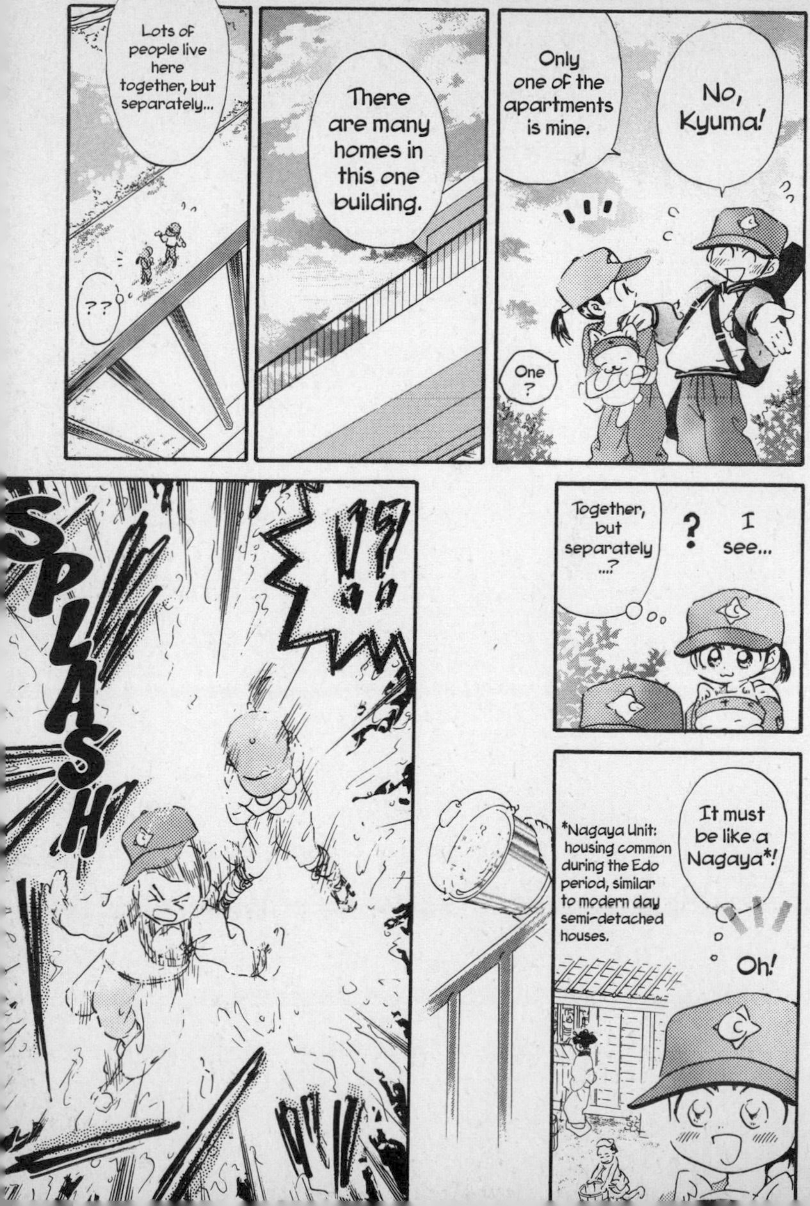
No, Kyuma!
Only one of the apartments is mine.
One?
There are many homes in this one building.
Lots of people live here together, but separately...
??
I see...
?
Together, but separately...?
Oh!
It must be like a Nagaya*!
*Nagaya Unit: housing common during the Edo period, similar to modern day semi-detached houses.
!?
SPLASH

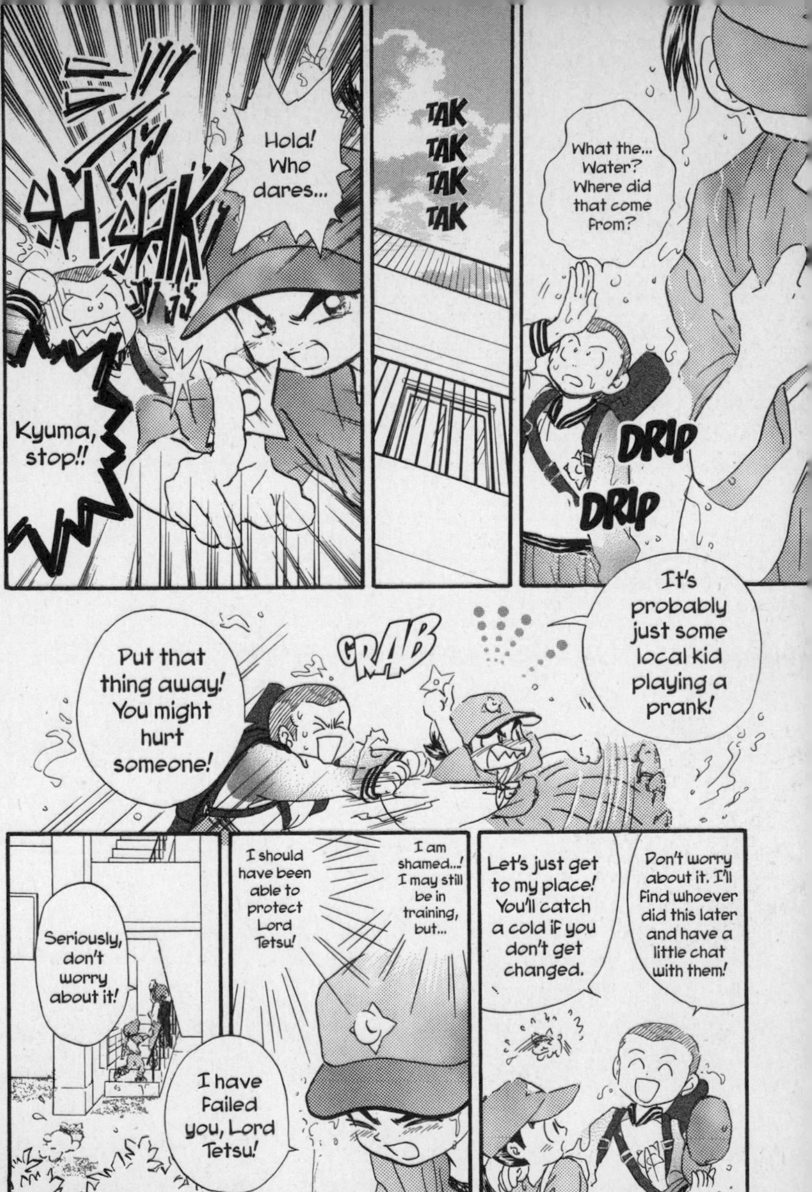
What the... Water? Where did that come from?
DRIP
DRIP
TAK
TAK
TAK
TAK
Hold! Who dares...
SH SHK
Kyuma, stop!!
It's probably just some local kid playing a prank!
GRAB
Put that thing away! You might hurt someone!
Don't worry about it. I'll find whoever did this later and have a little chat with them!
Let's just get to my place! You'll catch a cold if you don't get changed.
I am shamed...! I may still be in training, but...
I should have been able to protect Lord Tetsu!
I have failed you, Lord Tetsu!
Seriously, don't worry about it!

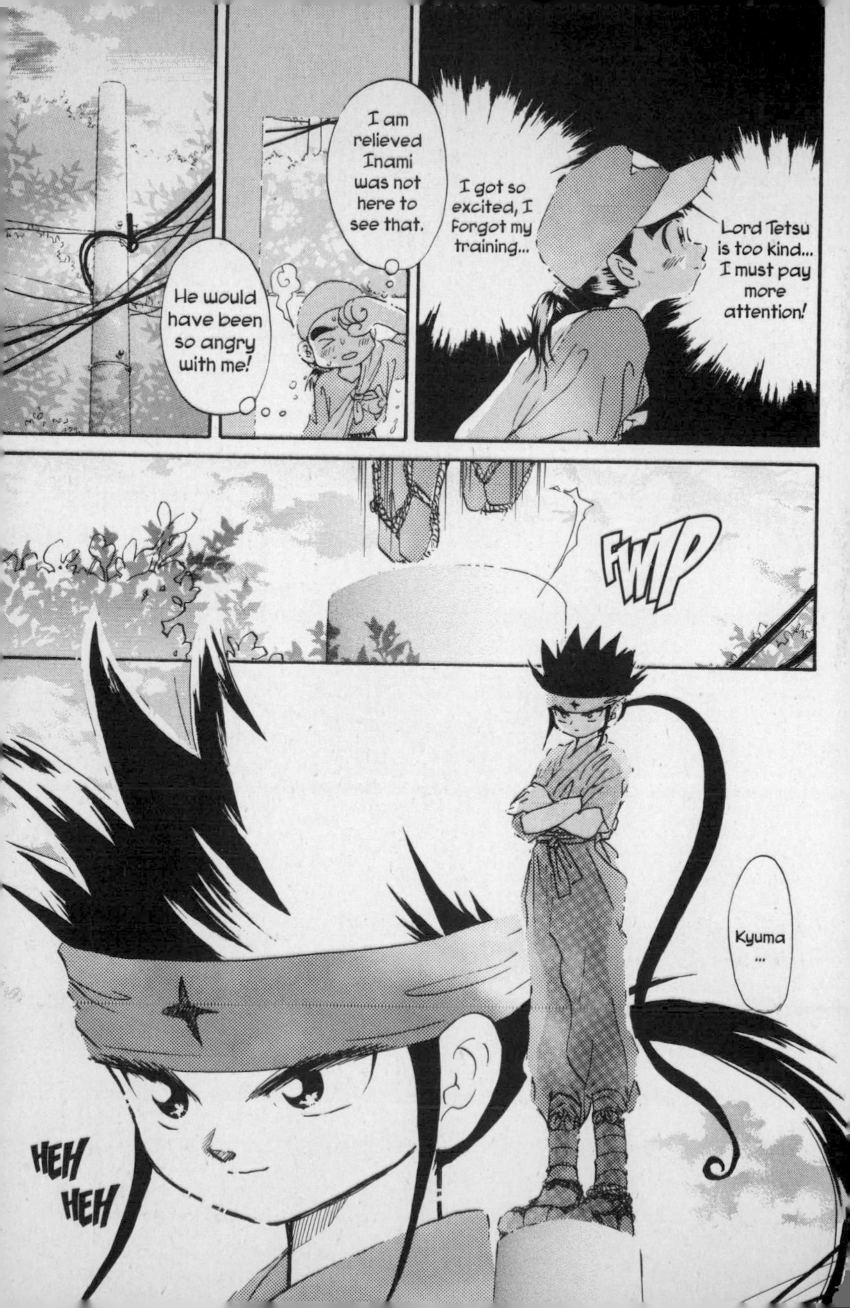
Lord Tetsu is too kind... I must pay more attention!
I got so excited, I forgot my training...
I am relieved Inami was not here to see that.
He would have been so angry with me!
FWIP
Kyuma ...
HEH HEH

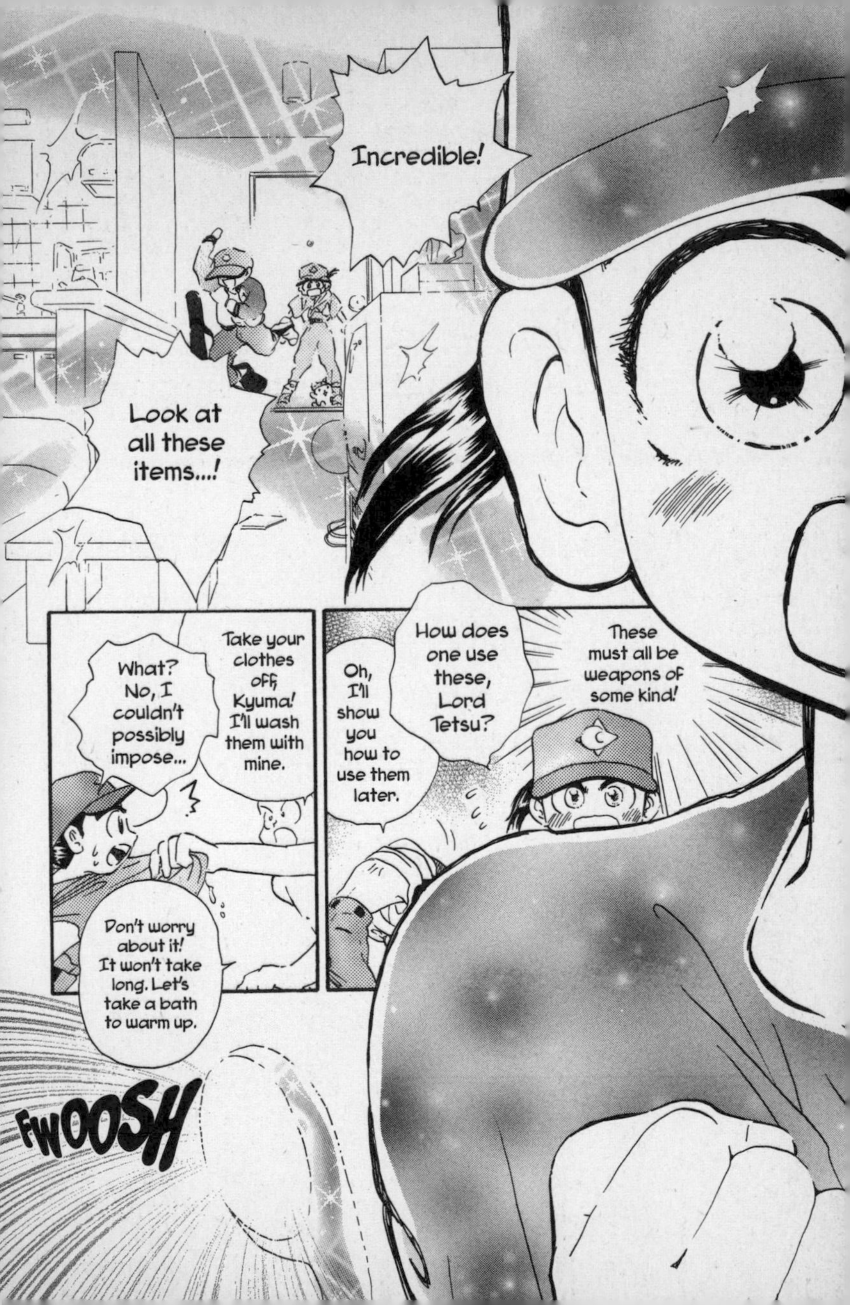
Incredible!
Look at all these items...!
These must all be weapons of some kind!
How does one use these, Lord Tetsu?
Oh, I'll show you how to use them later.
Take your clothes off, Kyuma! I'll wash them with mine.
What? No, I couldn't possibly impose...
Don't worry about it! It won't take long. Let's take a bath to warm up.
FWOOSH

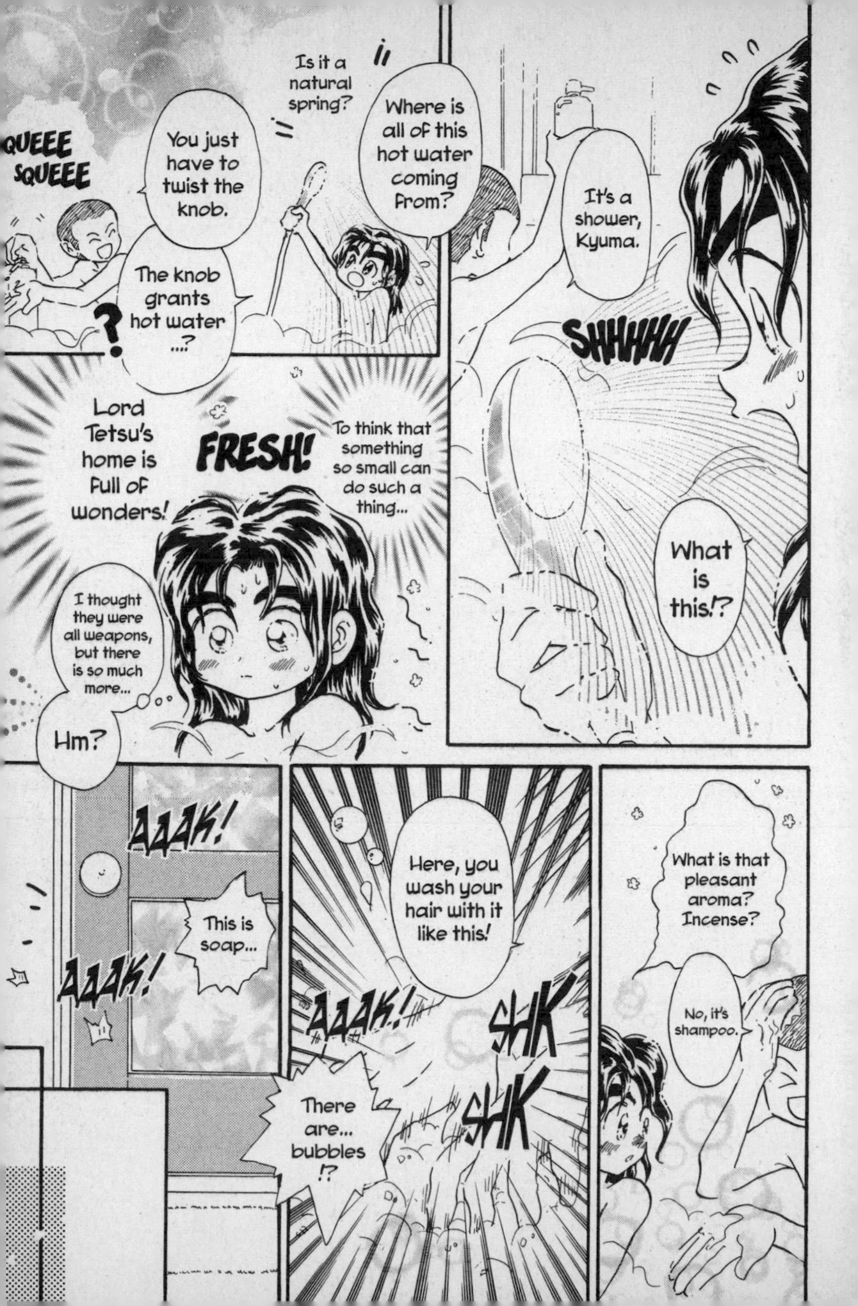
It's a shower, Kyuma.
SHHHHH
What is this!?
Where is all of this hot water coming from?
Is it a natural spring?
You just have to twist the knob.
QUEEE SQUEEE
The knob grants hot water ...?
To think that something so small can do such a thing...
FRESH!
Lord Tetsu's home is full of wonders!
I thought they were all weapons, but there is so much more...
Hm?
What is that pleasant aroma? Incense?
No, it's shampoo.
Here, you wash your hair with it like this!
SHK
SHK
AAAK!
There are... bubbles!?
AAAK!
This is soap...
AAAK!

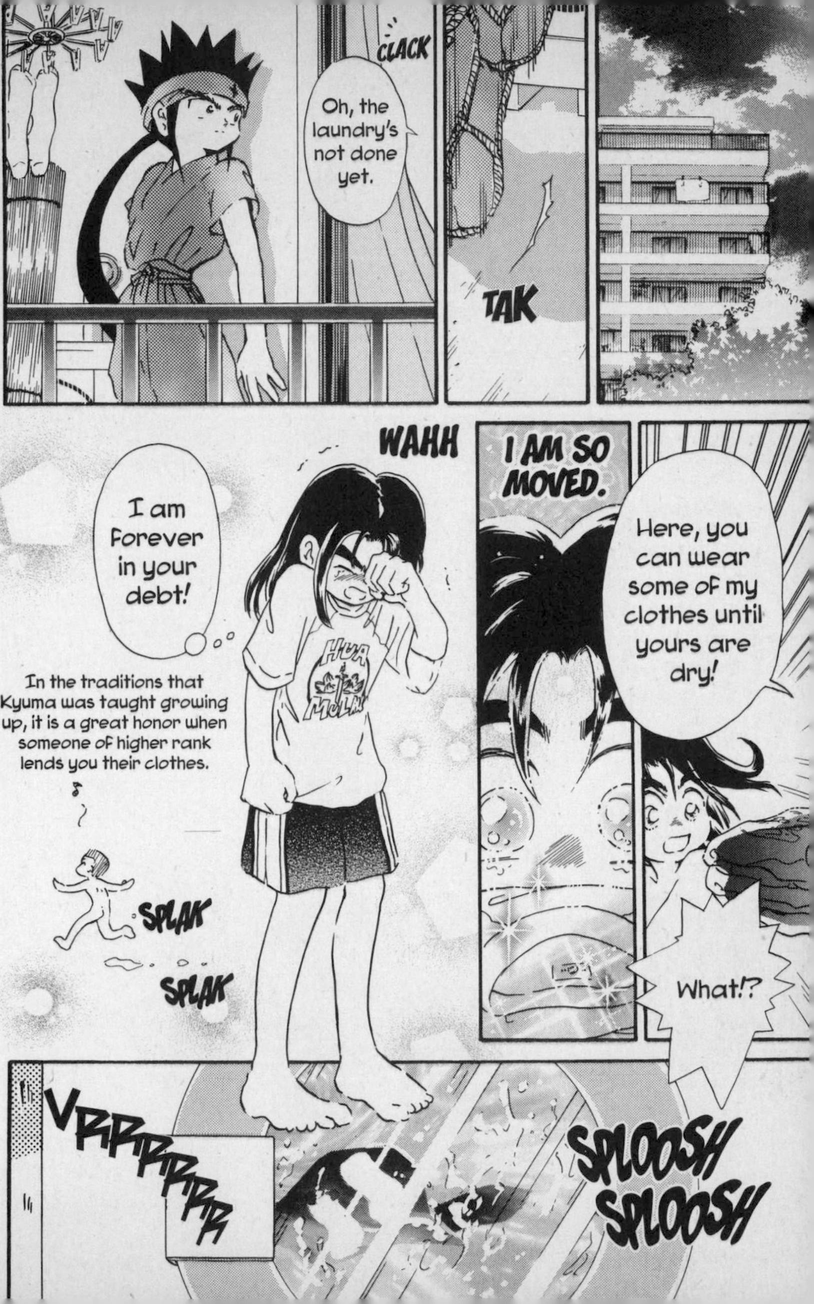

TAK
CLACK
Oh, the laundry's not done yet.
Here, you can wear some of my clothes until yours are dry!
What!?
I AM SO MOVED.
WAHH
I am forever in your debt!
In the traditions that Kyuma was taught growing up, it is a great honor when someone of higher rank lends you their clothes.
SPLAK
SPLAK
SPLOOSH SPLOOSH
VRRRRRRR

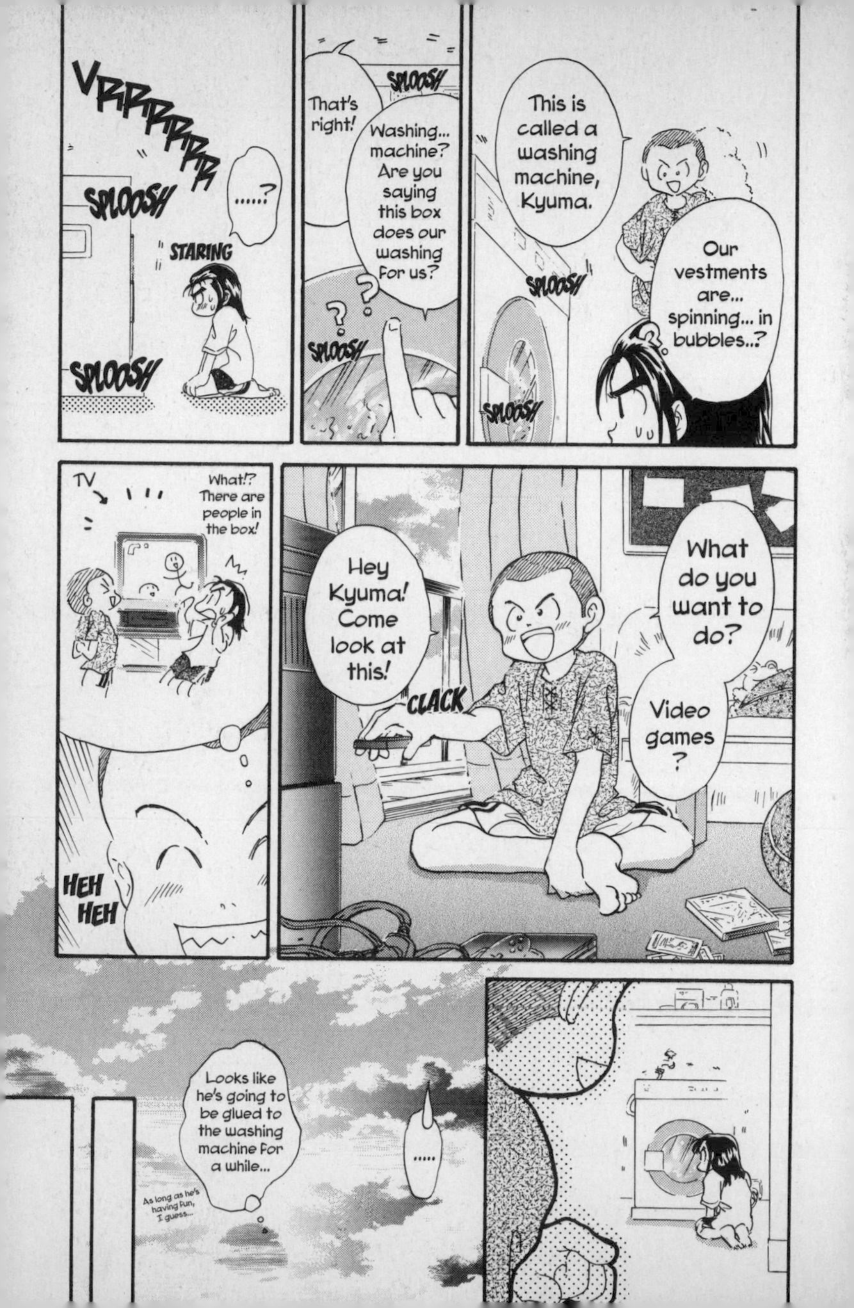
This is called a washing machine, Kyuma.
SPLOOSH
Our vestments are... spinning... in bubbles..?
SPLOOSH
SPLOOSH
Washing... machine? Are you saying this box does our washing for us?
That's right!
SPLOOSH
VRRRRRRR
SPLOOSH
......?
STARING
SPLOOSH
What do you want to do?
Video games?
Hey Kyuma! Come look at this!
CLACK
What!? There are people in the box!
TV
HEH HEH
.....
Looks like he's going to be glued to the washing machine for a while...
As long as he's having fun, I guess...

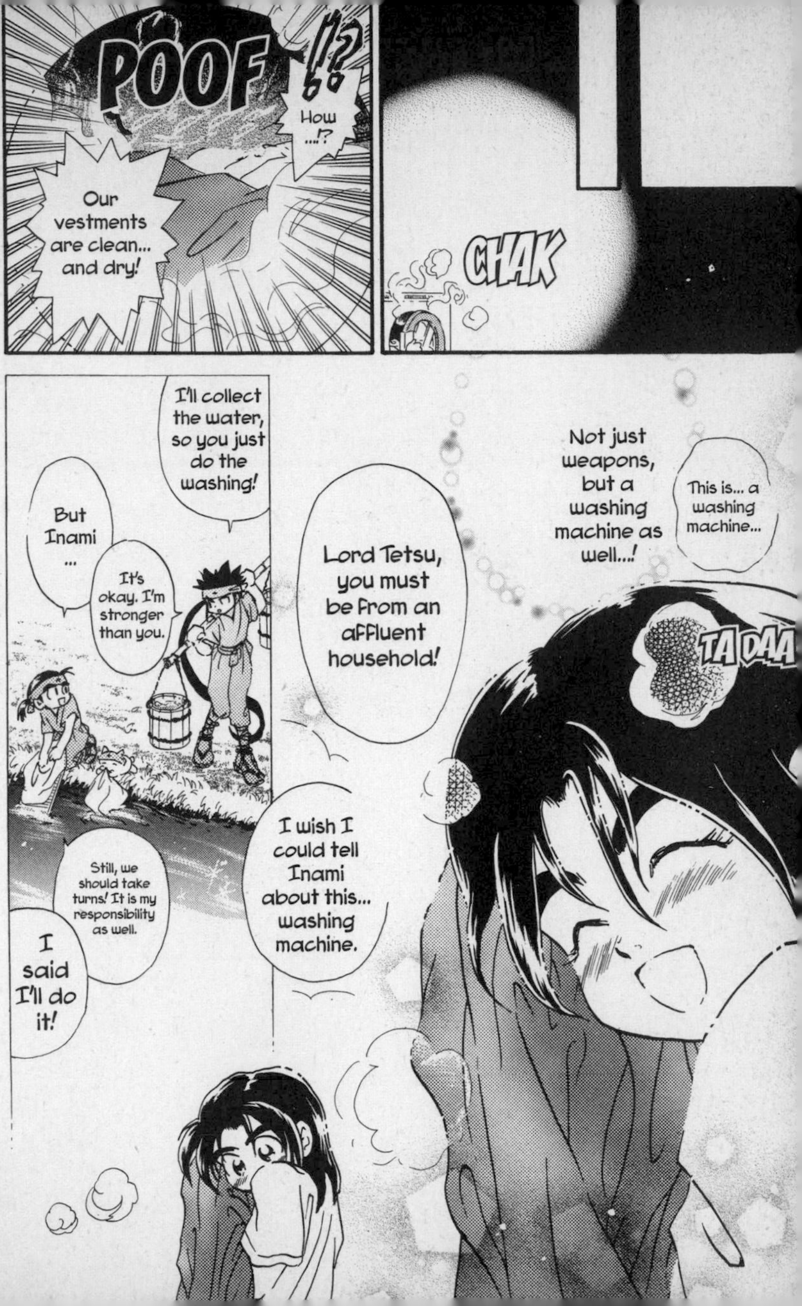
CHAK
POOF
!?
How ...!?
Our vestments are clean... and dry!
This is... a washing machine...
Not just weapons, but a washing machine as well...!
TA DAA
Lord Tetsu, you must be from an affluent household!
I wish I could tell Inami about this... washing machine.
I'll collect the water, so you just do the washing!
But Inami ...
It's okay. I'm stronger than you.
Still, we should take turns! It is my responsibility as well.
I said I'll do it!

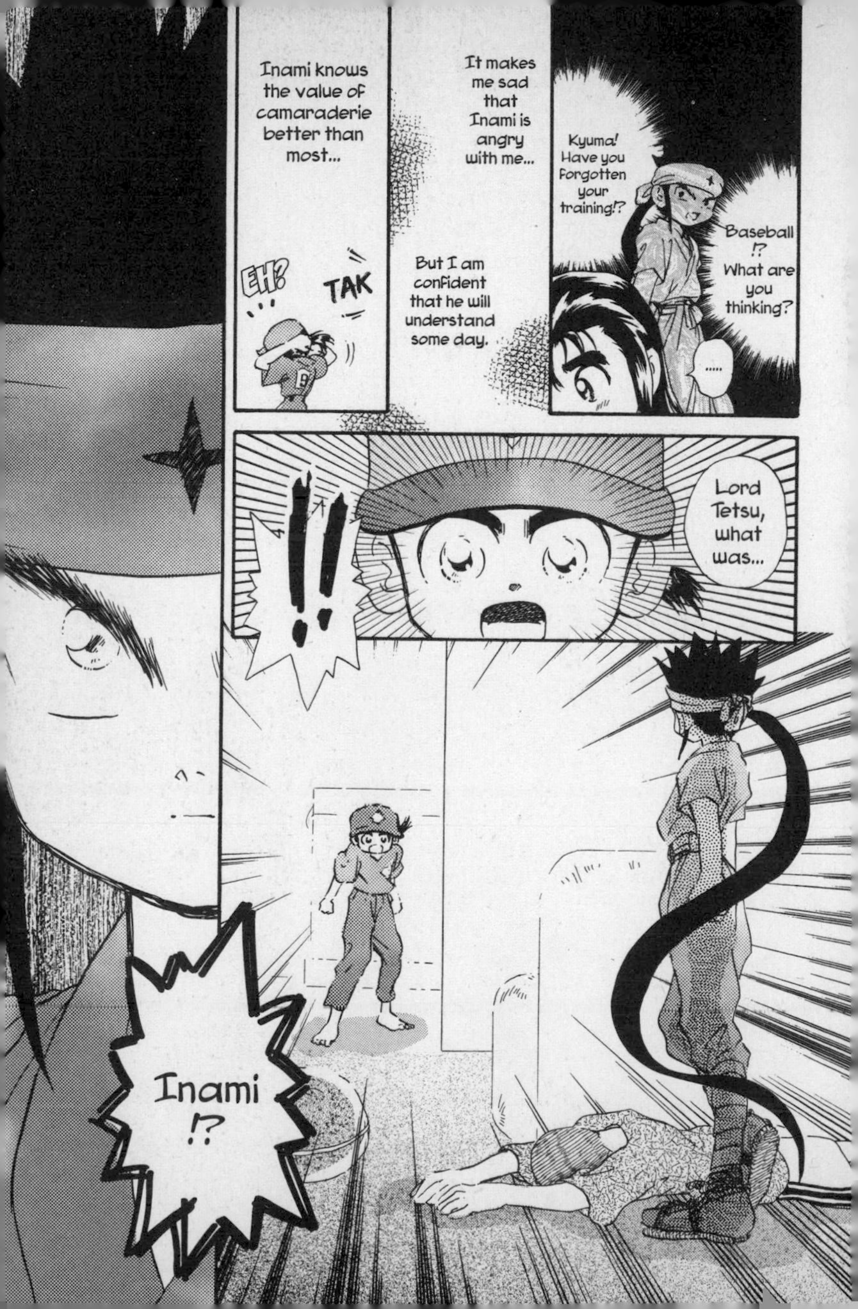
Kyuma! Have you forgotten your training!?
Baseball !? What are you thinking?
.....
It makes me sad that Inami is angry with me...
But I am confident that he will understand some day.
Inami knows the value of camaraderie better than most...
EH?
TAK
Lord Tetsu, what was...
!!
Inami !?

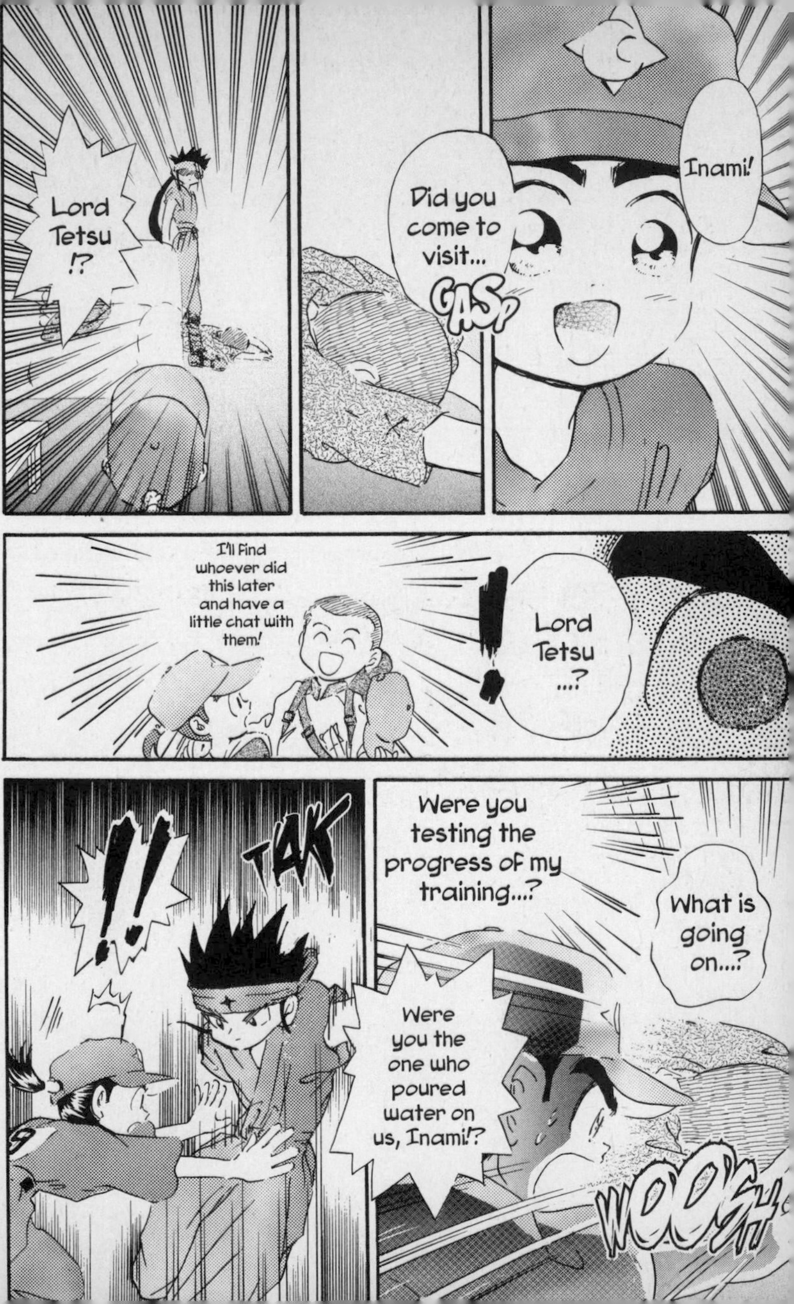
Inami!
Did you come to visit...
GASP
Lord Tetsu!?
Lord Tetsu...?
I'll find whoever did this later and have a little chat with them!
What is going on...?
Were you testing the progress of my training...?
Were you the one who poured water on us, Inami!?
WOOSH
TAK

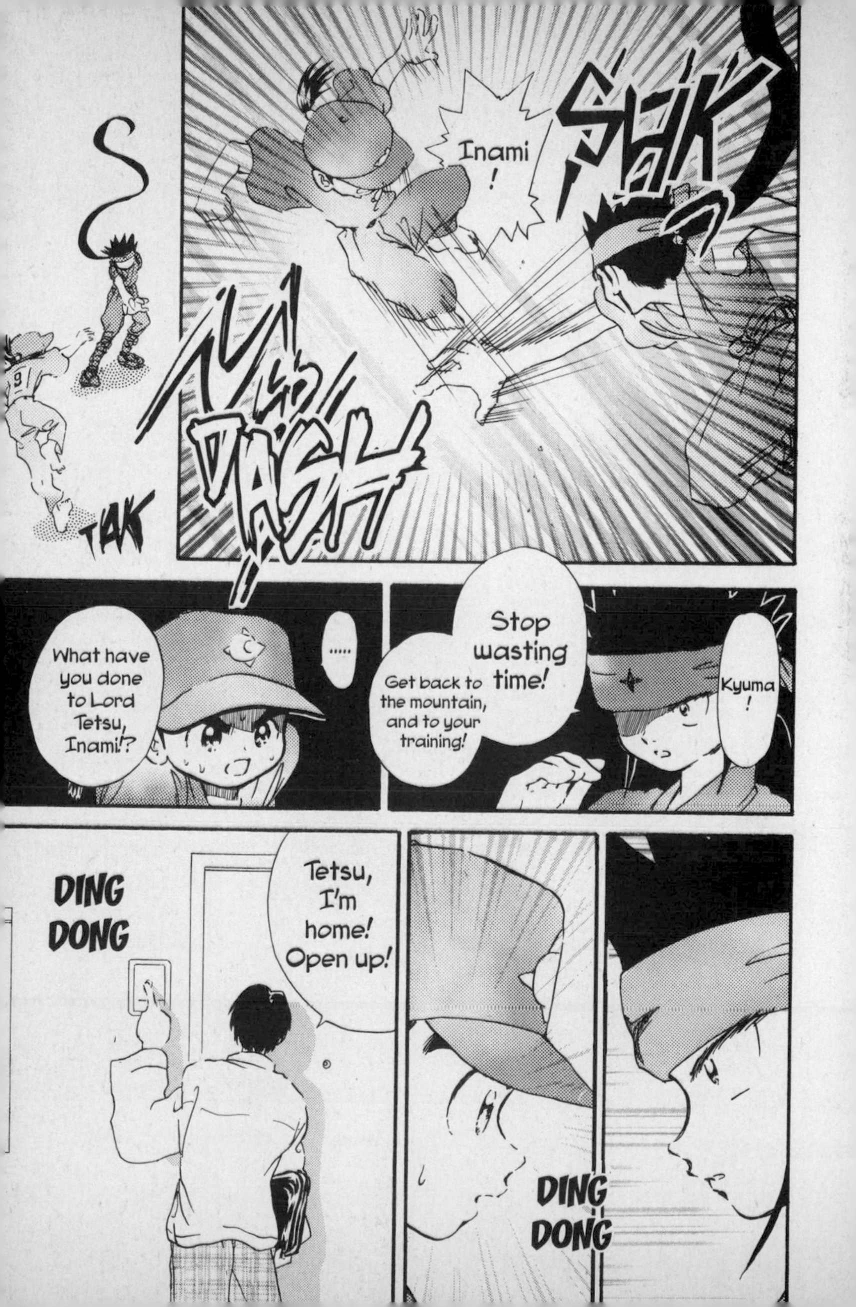
Inami !
DASH
TAK
Kyuma !
Stop wasting time!
Get back to the mountain, and to your training!
.....
What have you done to Lord Tetsu, Inami!?
DING DONG
Tetsu, I'm home! Open up!
DING DONG

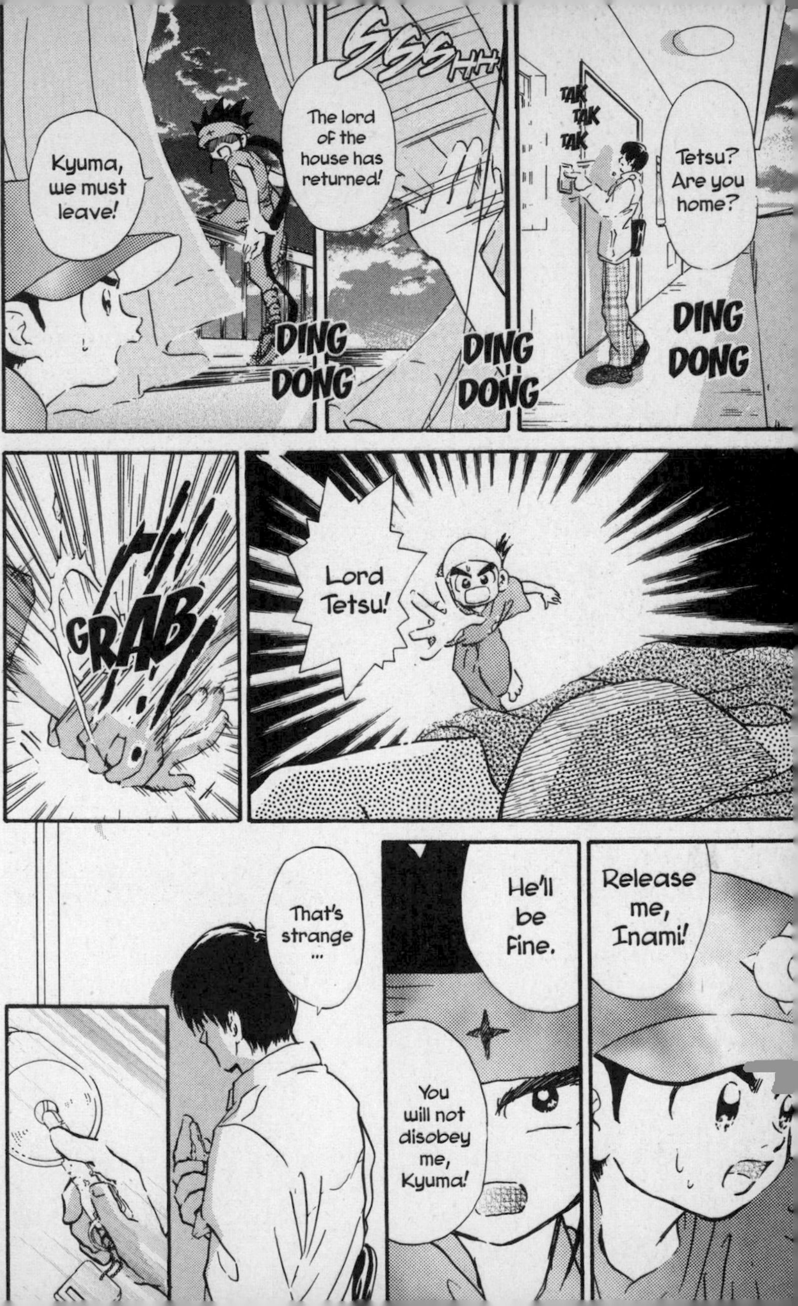
TAK
TAK
TAK
Tetsu? Are you home?
DING DONG
SSSHHH
The lord of the house has returned!
DING DONG
Kyuma, we must leave!
DING DONG
Lord Tetsu!
GRAB
Release me, Inami!
He'll be fine.
You will not disobey me, Kyuma!
That's strange ...

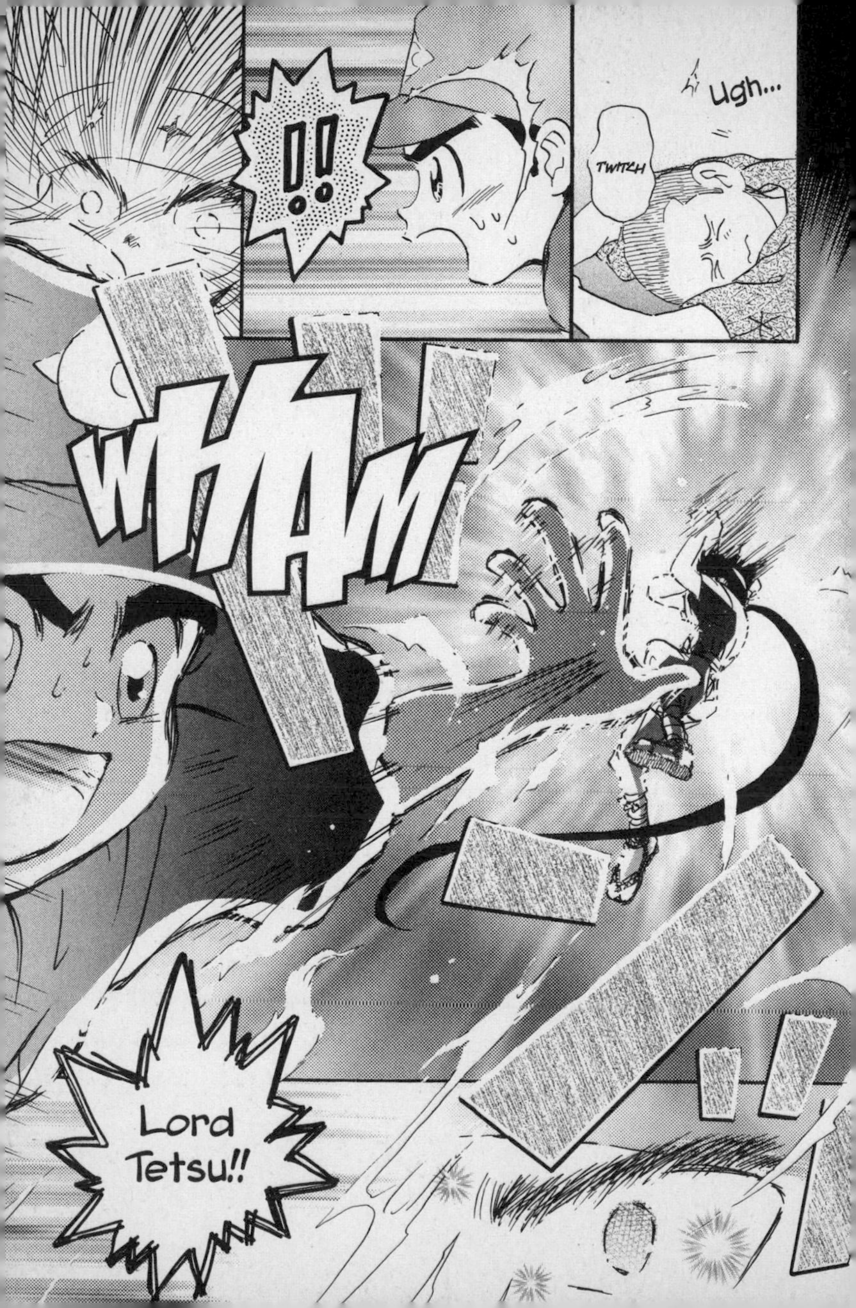
Ugh...
TWITCH
!!
WHAM
!!
Lord Tetsu!!

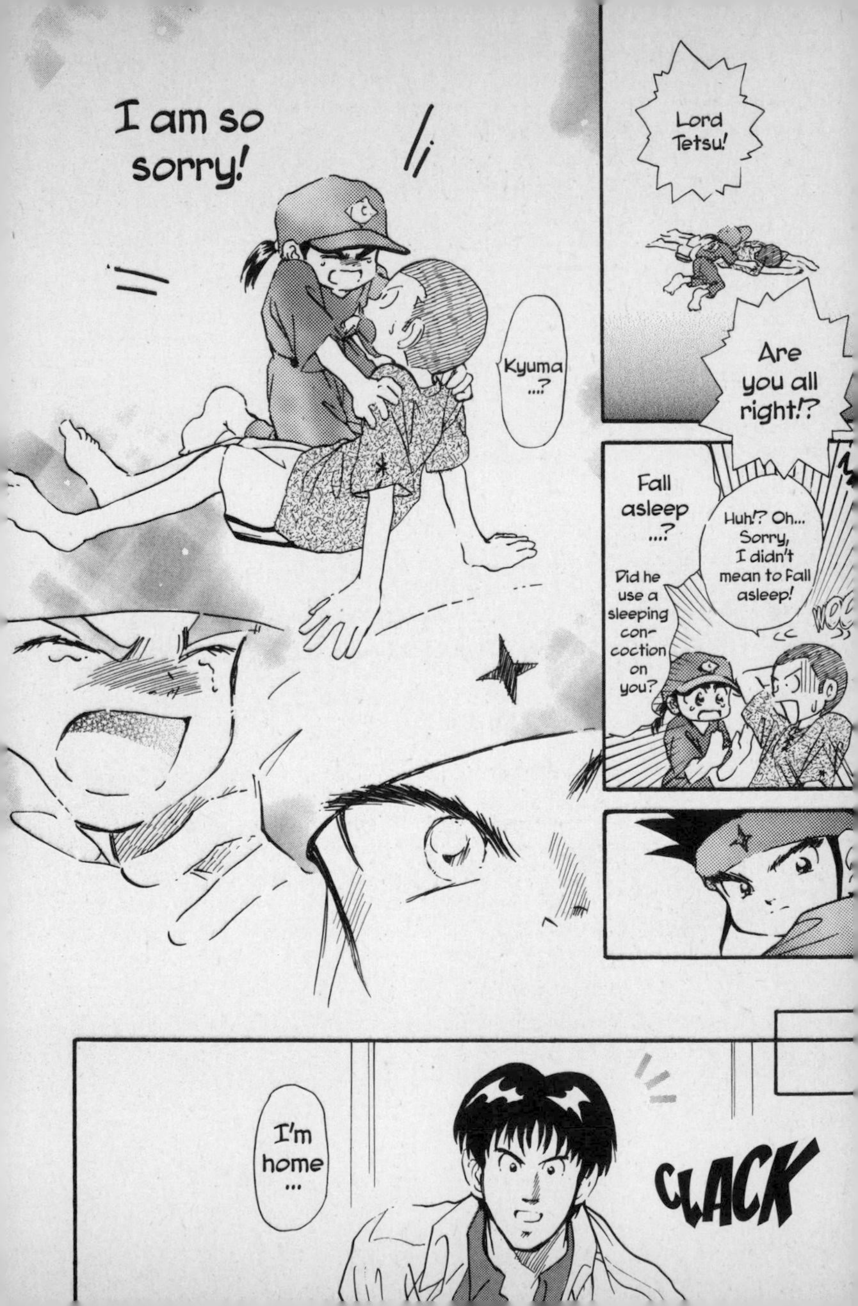
Lord Tetsu!
Are you all right!?
Huh!? Oh... Sorry, I didn't mean to fall asleep!
Fall asleep ...?
Did he use a sleeping con-coction on you?
Kyuma ...?
I am so sorry!
I'm home ...
CLACK

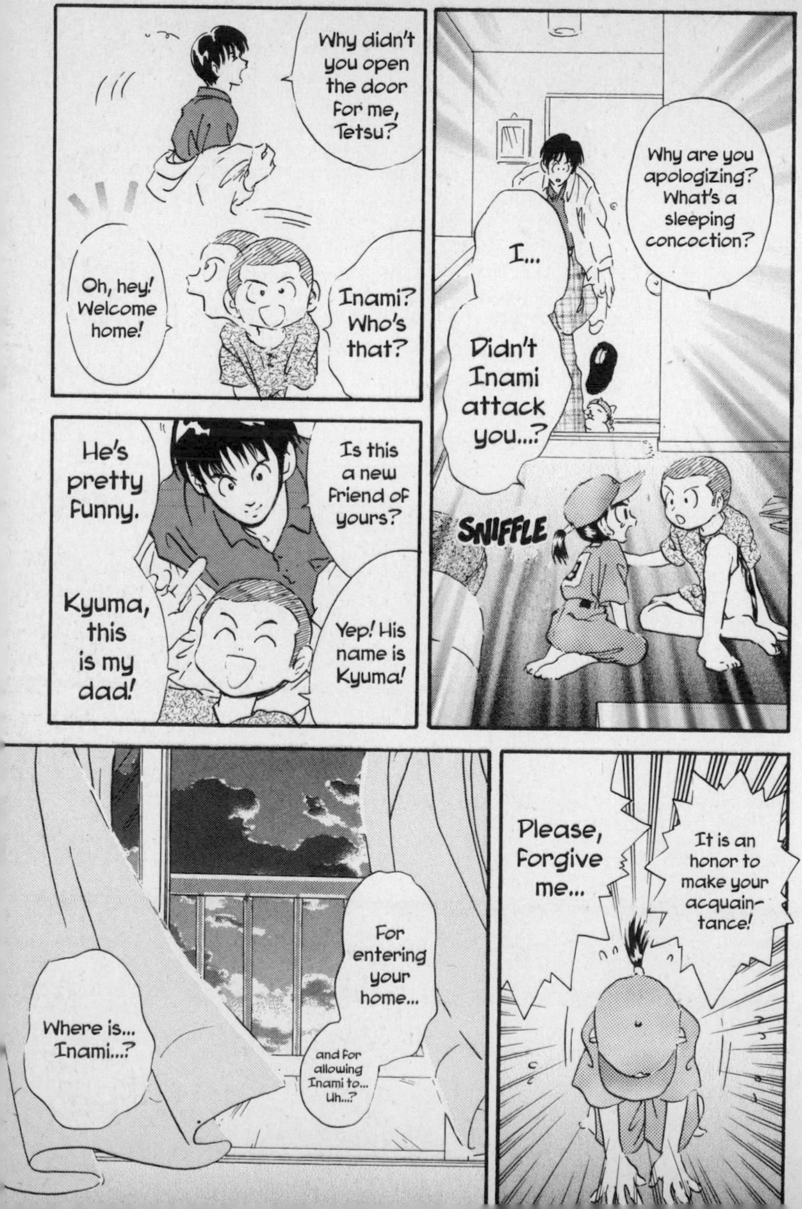
Why are you apologizing? What's a sleeping concoction?
I...
Didn't Inami attack you...?
SNIFFLE
Why didn't you open the door for me, Tetsu?
Inami? Who's that?
Oh, hey! Welcome home!
Is this a new friend of yours?
He's pretty funny.
Yep! His name is Kyuma!
Kyuma, this is my dad!
It is an honor to make your acquaintance!
Please, forgive me...
For entering your home...
and for allowing Inami to... Uh...?
Where is... Inami...?

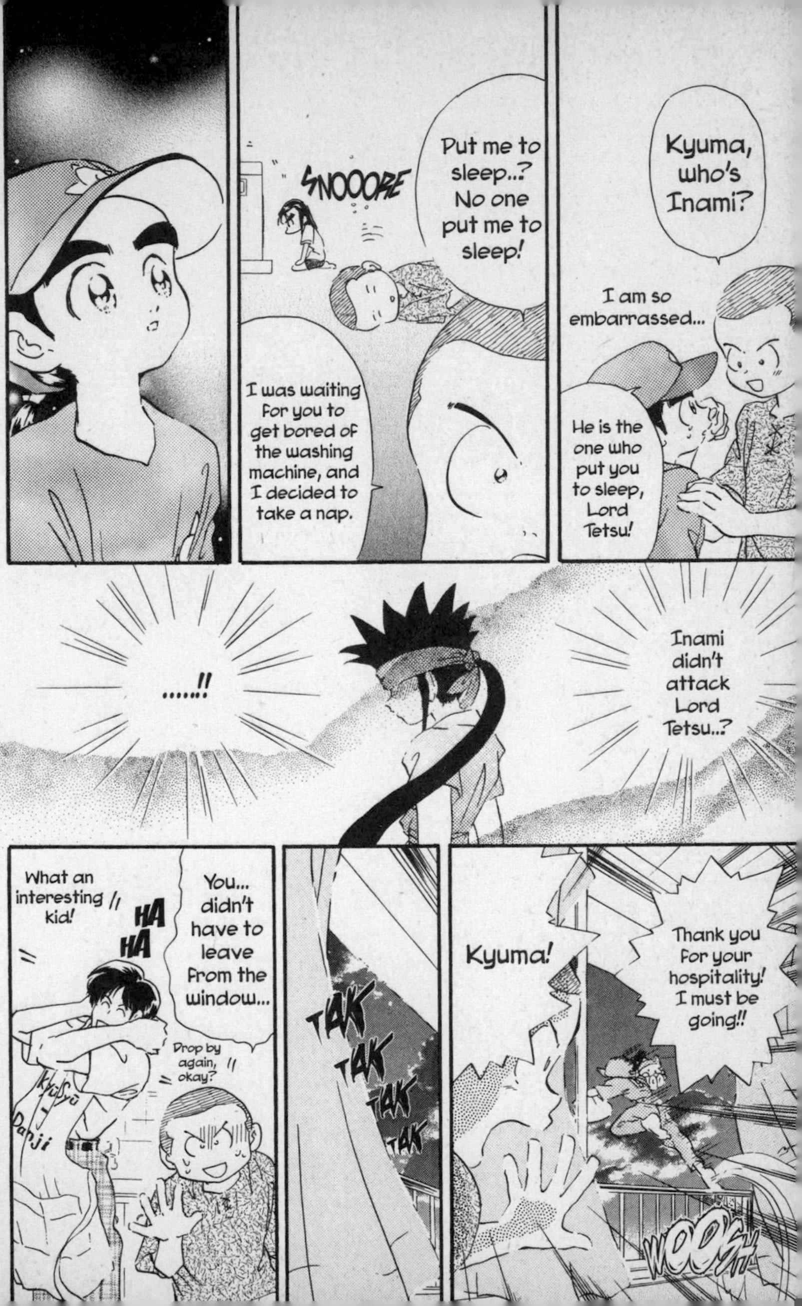

Kyuma, who's Inami?
I am so embarrassed...
He is the one who put you to sleep, Lord Tetsu!
Put me to sleep..? No one put me to sleep!
SNOOORE
I was waiting for you to get bored of the washing machine, and I decided to take a nap.
Inami didn't attack Lord Tetsu..?
......!!
Thank you for your hospitality! I must be going!!
Kyuma!
WOOSH
TAK
TAK
TAK
TAK
You... didn't have to leave from the window...
What an interesting kid!
HA HA
Drop by again, okay?
Kyūsyū Danji

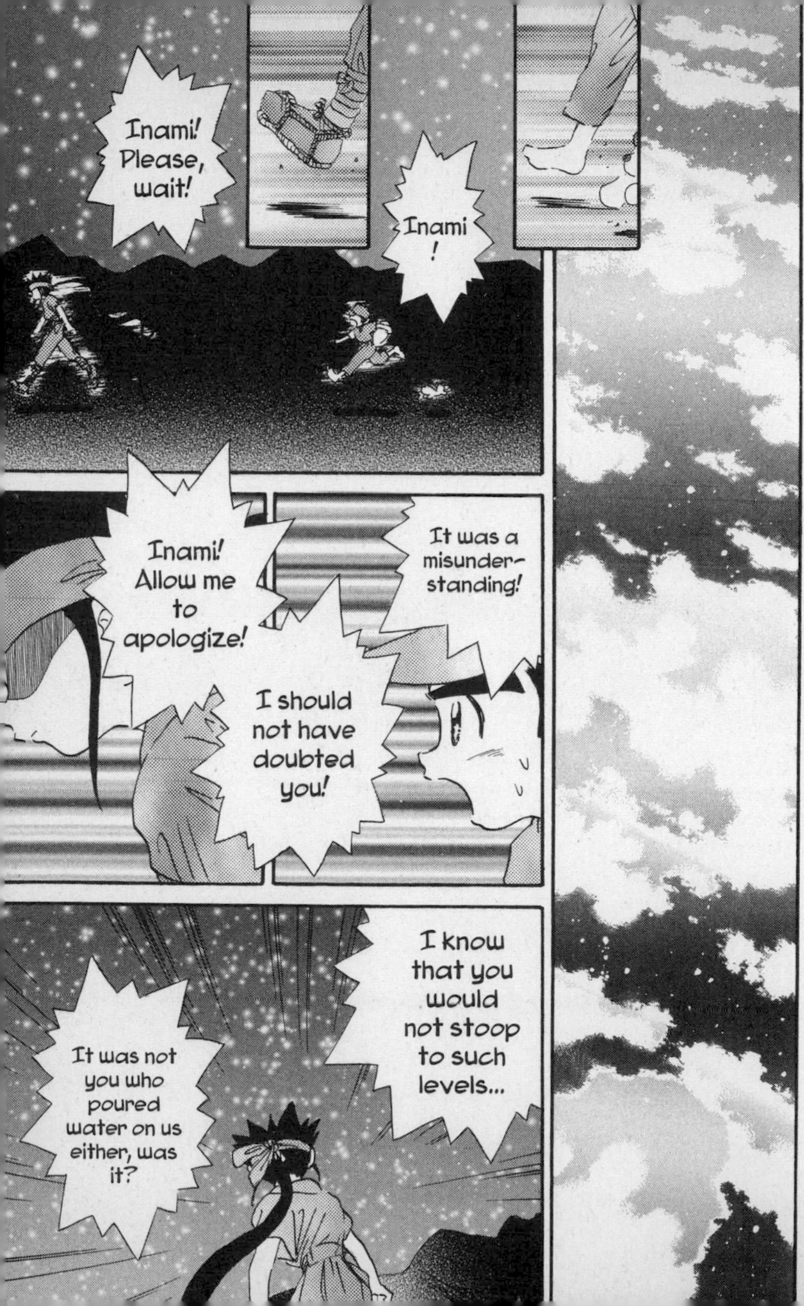
Inami!
Inami! Please, wait!
It was a misunder-standing!
I should not have doubted you!
Inami! Allow me to apologize!
I know that you would not stoop to such levels...
It was not you who poured water on us either, was it?

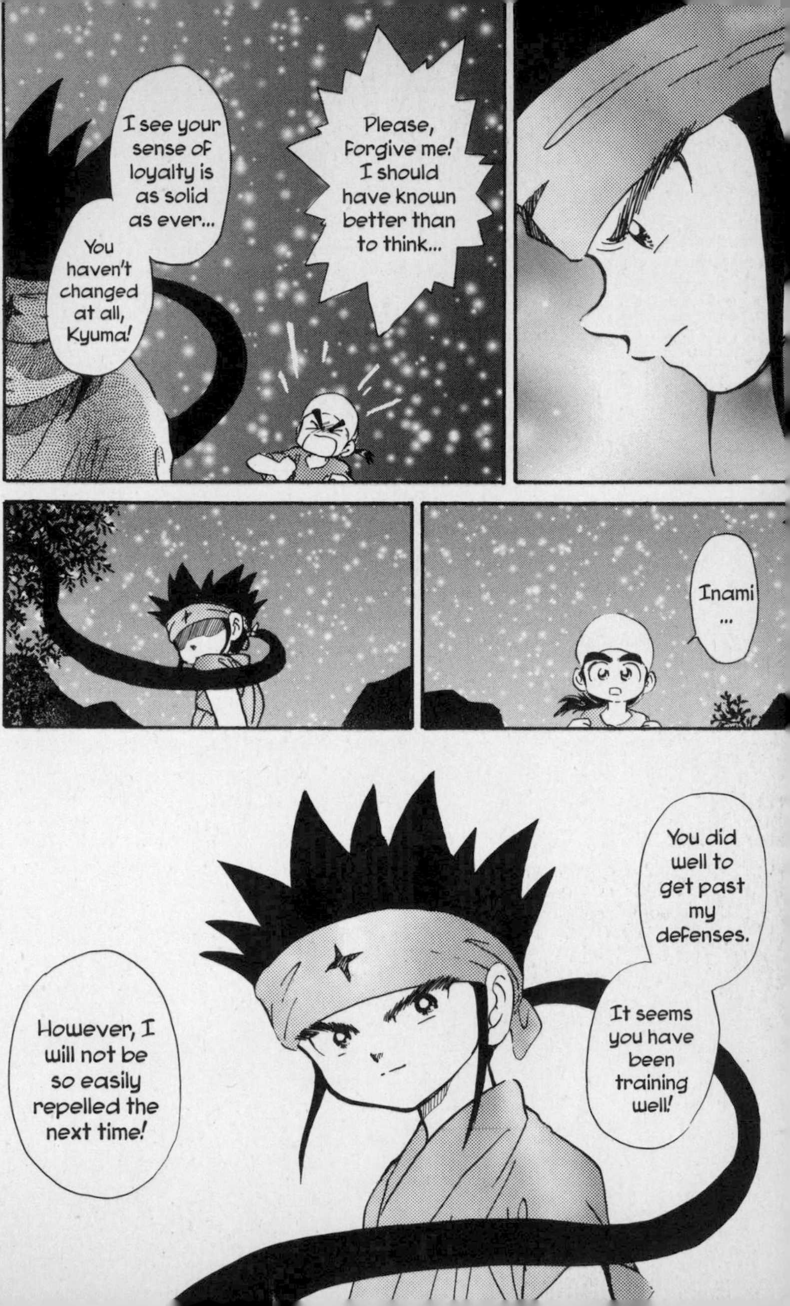
Please, forgive me! I should have known better than to think...
I see your sense of loyalty is as solid as ever...
You haven't changed at all, Kyuma!
Inami ...
You did well to get past my defenses.
It seems you have been training well!
However, I will not be so easily repelled the next time!

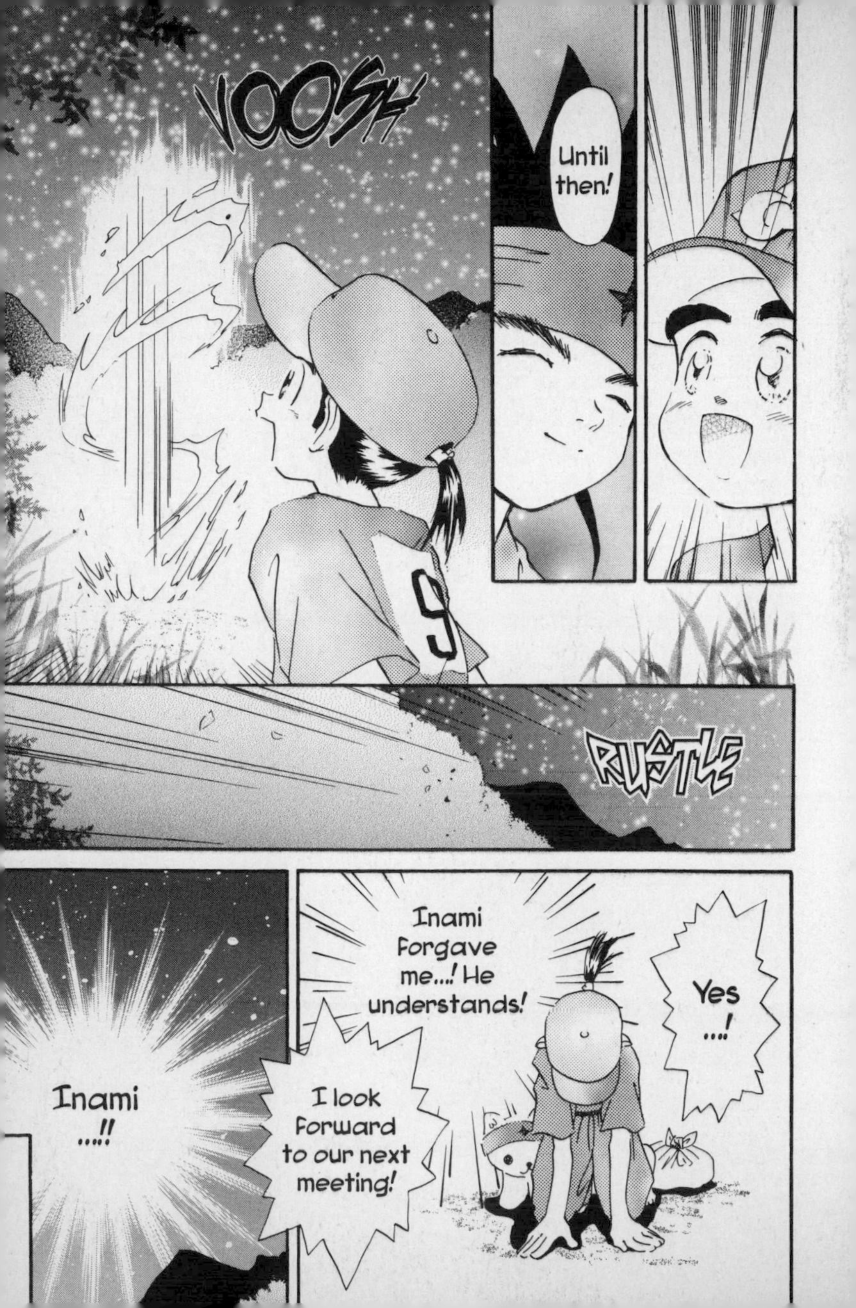
Until then!
VOOSH
RUSTLE
Yes ...!
Inami forgave me...! He understands!
I look forward to our next meeting!
Inami ...!!

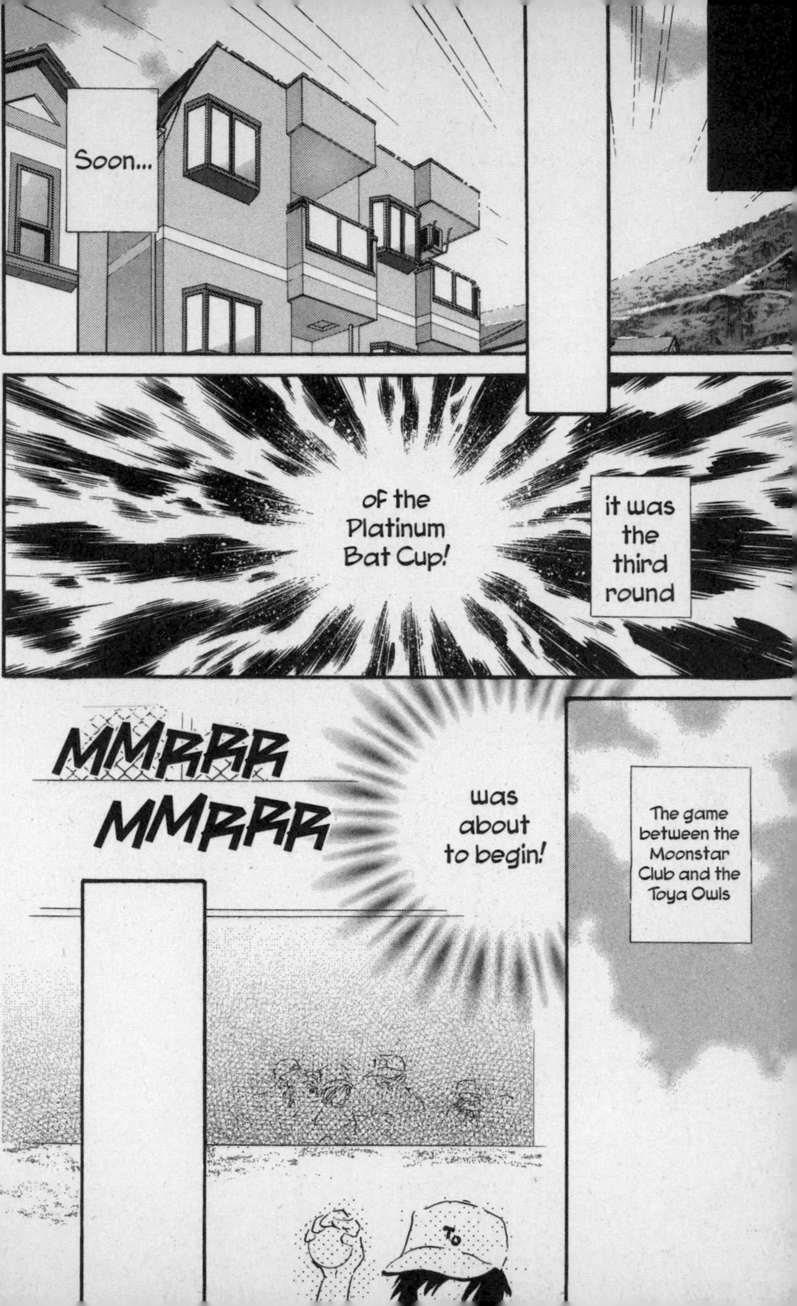
Soon...
it was the third round
of the Platinum Bat Cup!
The game between the Moonstar Club and the Toya Owls
was about to begin!
MMRRR
MMRRR

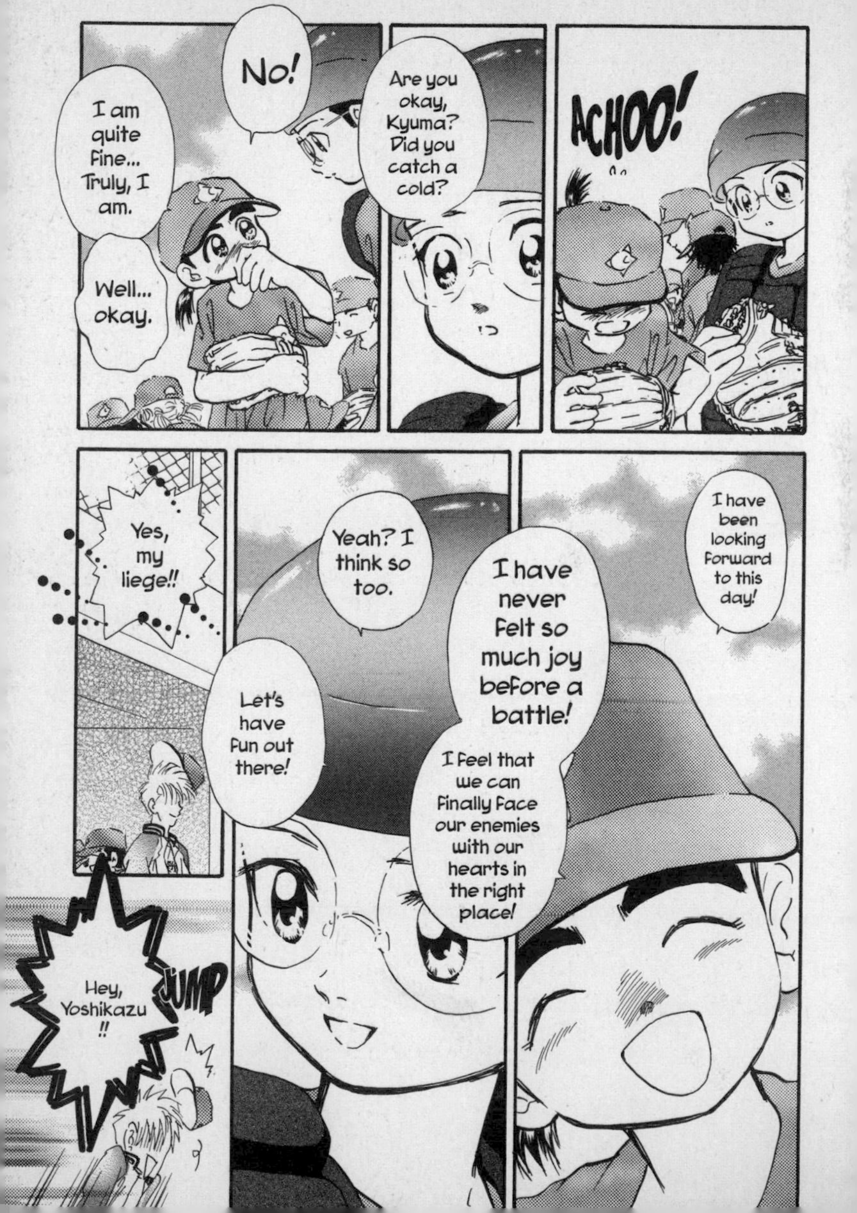
ACHOO!
Are you okay, Kyuma? Did you catch a cold?
No!
I am quite fine... Truly, I am.
Well... okay.
I have been looking forward to this day!
I have never felt so much joy before a battle!
I feel that we can finally face our enemies with our hearts in the right place!
Yeah? I think so too.
Let's have fun out there!
Yes, my liege!!
Hey, Yoshikazu!!
JUMP

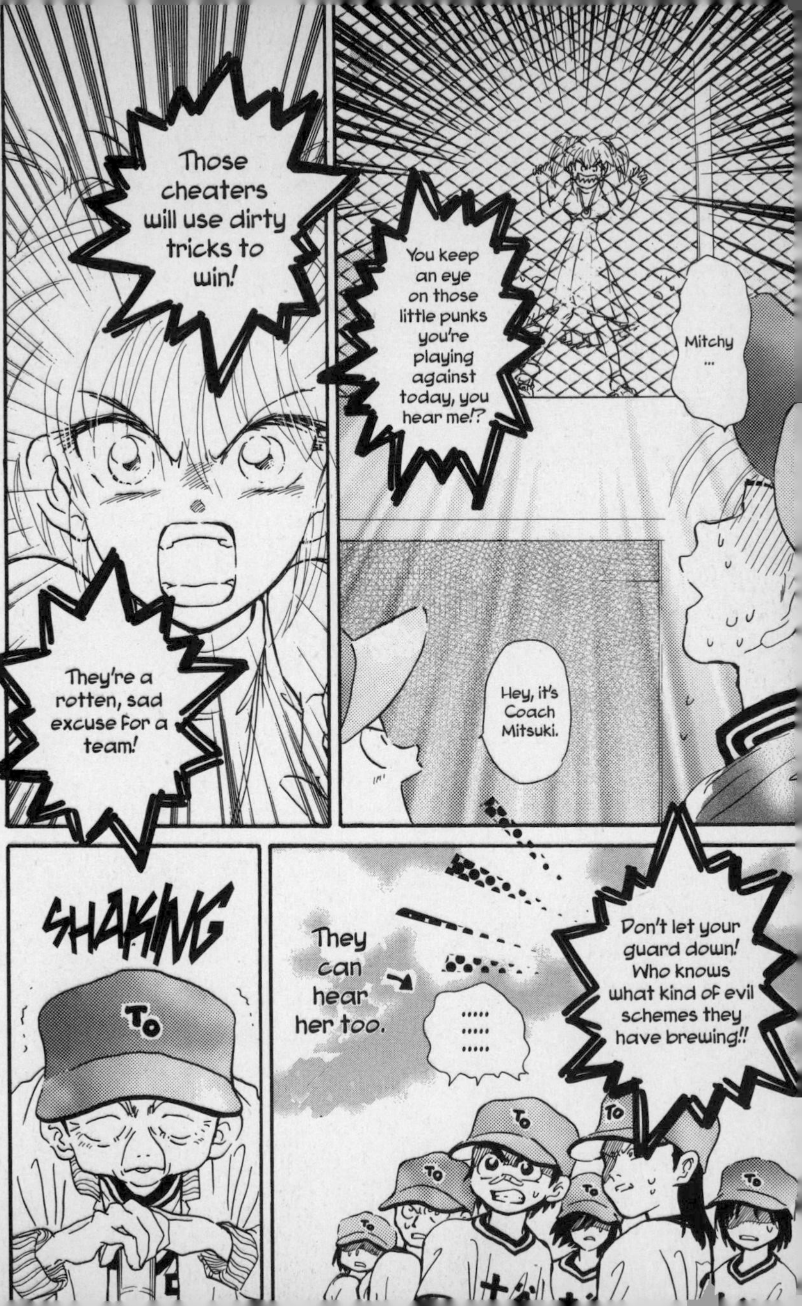

You keep an eye on those little punks you're playing against today, you hear me!?
Mitchy ...
Hey, it's Coach Mitsuki.
Those cheaters will use dirty tricks to win!
They're a rotten, sad excuse for a team!
Don't let your guard down! Who knows what kind of evil schemes they have brewing!!
......
......
......
They can hear her too.
SHAKING
TO

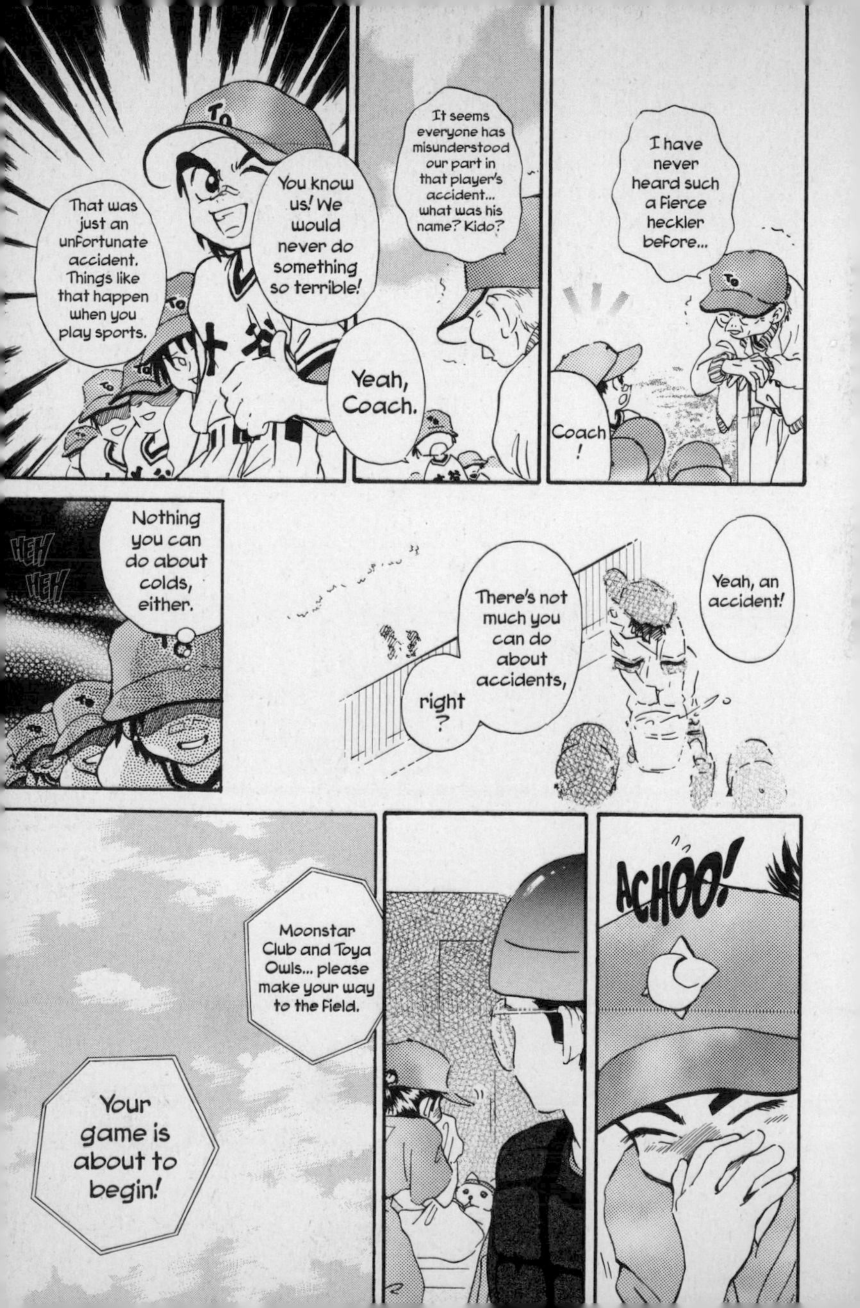
I have never heard such a fierce heckler before...
Coach!
It seems everyone has misunderstood our part in that player's accident... what was his name? Kido?
Yeah, Coach.
You know us! We would never do something so terrible!
That was just an unfortunate accident. Things like that happen when you play sports.
Yeah, an accident!
There's not much you can do about accidents, right?
Nothing you can do about colds, either.
HEH HEH
ACHOO!
Moonstar Club and Toya Owls... please make your way to the field.
Your game is about to begin!

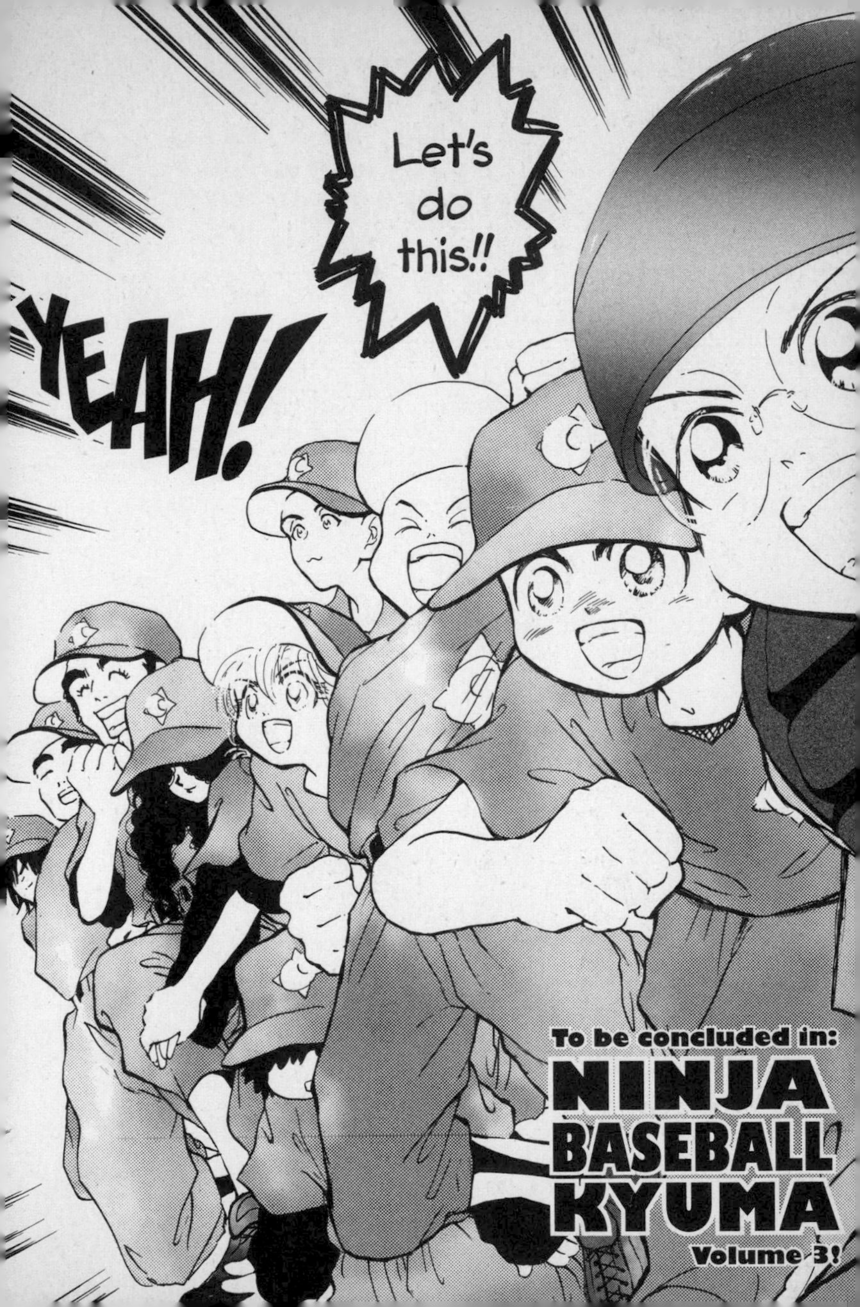
Let's do this!!
YEAH!
To be concluded in:
NINJA BASEBALL KYUMA
Volume 3!

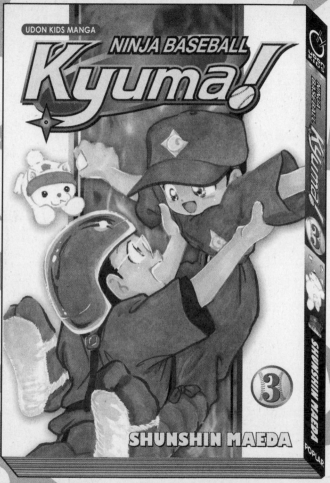

THE BIG ADVENTURES OF MAJOKO

Vol.1 (APR 2009)
ISBN: 978-1-897376-81-2

Vol.2 (JUL 2009)
ISBN: 978-1-897376-82-9

Vol.3 (NOV 2009)
ISBN: 978-1-897376-83-6

NINJA BASEBALL KYUMA

Vol.1 (APR 2009)
ISBN: 978-1-897376-86-7

Vol.2 (SEP 2009)
ISBN: 978-1-897376-87-4

Vol.3 (FEB 2010)
ISBN: 978-1-897376-88-1

FAIRY IDOL KANON

Vol.1 (MAY 2009)
ISBN: 978-1-897376-89-8

Vol.2 (AUG 2009)
ISBN: 978-1-897376-90-4

Vol.3 (JAN 2010)
ISBN: 978-1-897376-91-1

SWANS IN SPACE

Vol.1 (JUN 2009)
ISBN: 978-1-897376-93-5

Vol.2 (OCT 2009)
ISBN: 978-1-897376-94-2

Vol.3 (APR 2010)
ISBN: 978-1-897376-95-9